GOOD ENOUGH

GOOD ENOUGH

SHEILA KIELY

BALLYDEVLIN PUBLISHING

BALLYDEVLIN PUBLISHING

ISBN 978-1-7398916-0-2

About this book

You are invited to enjoy
an interactive experience
while reading this book.

Please check out the following social media platforms

Each Chapter has a Reel on Instagram
Watch & Engage with the Author
Instagram Account: @good_enough_novel

Listen to the Playlist on Spotify
(each chapter has a theme song)
Spotify Playlist: good enough novel

Visit the blog-posts on Wordpress
(each chapter has a blog-post)
Wordpress Blog: www.gimmetherecipe.com

To my children
With love
Johnnie, Ellie, Daire, Eimear, Niall & Denny

Contents

Chapter 1

(SCRAMBLED EGGS ON TOAST)

The writing pad felt crisp and fresh as Eva put pen to paper and began to quickly scribble a grocery list. Her efforts were interrupted by the ringing of her mobile phone. It was an unknown number and she chose to ignore it, she hardly ever answered her phone these days as they were generally scams or sales calls.

Reaching for a mug Eva poured herself a coffee from the filter pot and after a quick sip emptied it into the sink as it had gone bitter and lukewarm. With no time to make a fresh pot she munched on a chocolate hobnob biscuit and brushing away the crumbs resumed writing her list.

With the list completed she pulled a battered looking card from her handbag that had been lounging there for weeks now and the edges of the envelope were beginning to fray. She had meant to send it along with the Christmas cards.

It was a congratulations card to her friend Elaine who had recently bought her new home in Boston after fifteen years of apartment rental.

Eva wrote quickly giving Elaine a snapshot of the recent goings on. She told her briefly about their friend Vivienne's new job at the University and how her own two kids were growing by the minute.

Signing off she hoped that Elaine would be able to decipher the teeny tiny writing and wished that she wasn't always in such a hurry.

It did feel quite the accomplishment to have handwritten a card though. She loved receiving them herself and tried to remember all her friends' birthdays with cards. Handwriting, a slowly dying art-form that she was single-handedly trying to keep alive by getting her Christmas cards out early and sending the odd thank you card when warranted too, so much more personal than a short-handed text stuffed with birthday cake and smiley faced emojis or emails that looked scant on the plain page.

Popping the card and list into her handbag she began rushing around packing up pyjamas and clothes for the kids' weekend away. 'Where the hell is the other trainer?' she huffed as she lay on the floor groaning and reaching in under Luke's bed. She pulled out a mess of dishevelled football magazines, some balled up socks and finally the offending shoe.

Wiping the dust from her hands she threw the trainers into Luke's gear bag and moved onto Hannah's bedroom. Pulling up the cover of the bed and opening the curtains to a bright January afternoon, Eva shook her head wondering yet again why it was that they just wouldn't at least make their beds before heading off to school in the morning. *My fault, bad training,* she mused, a tiger mom she most certainly was not.

With the kids' bags packed and ready Eva quickly checked her makeup in the mirror of her en suite. She brushed her teeth before reapplying a raspberry stained lip-gloss and ran a little argan oil through the tips of her long blonde hair to tame the flyaways.

With skinny jeans tucked into knee high black leather boots she hoped that she didn't look like she had just mucked out the horses at some stables.

With one final assessment of her rear view in the mirror finally she was off. It was five to three by the time Eva started up her silver SUV and began the short journey to the school gates to meet her two children.

Douglas village was always crazy on a Friday afternoon and parking at the school was the usual bedlam.

Eva double-parked and hopping out she grabbed the kids' weekend bags from the back of the jeep.

Their Grandmother was there already and the kids were standing beside her. Hugging her mother-in-law Mary warmly, Eva thanked her for taking the children for the weekend as she handed over their bags.

'Always a pleasure Eva,' Mary replied as she tousled Luke's hair. It was all the eleven year old could do not to pull away as he cringed in mortification outside his school gates.

'I'm delighted to have them to myself for a whole weekend Eva. Now you go on and have a great time and don't be thinking about us. We'll be grand.'

Luke barely allowed Eva to hug him as they said goodbye but Hannah still harnessed the nonchalance and innocence of an eight year old girl and kissed and hugged her Mum tightly before happily heading off to their Gran's.

Returning to her jeep Eva was on the receiving end of some fairly disgruntled looks from the driver she had hemmed in with her careless parking but she didn't really care as she feigned surprise and mouthed an exaggerated 'Sorry' towards the eye-roller.

The weekend was here and it was the first time in months that she and Alan would be away together without the kids. Her next port of call was the hairdressers. She was badly in need of fresh highlights as her roots and a few stray greys were impossible to disguise.

She also hoped to have enough time for a quick browse in 'Elizabeth's Boutique' afterwards to find something new to wear to dinner later that evening. The weekend together was going to be a surprise for Alan and he had no idea what lay ahead. It wasn't quite their anniversary yet but it was close enough and they hadn't had much time together at all lately. They would be thirteen years married in May and he still made her stomach flutter, well occasionally anyway.

Turning her attention from the Beckham's in 'Hello' magazine, back to her reflection in the hair-salon's mirror she smiled. Her blue eyes sparkled as the beige and gold highlights brightened her fair complexion and the chunky long layered style made her look younger than her thirty-six years - okay maybe six months younger but better anyway. *This is the life,* she thought as the manicurist set to work on turning Eva's neglected nails into something a bit more polished and the hairdresser finished drying her hair.

The boutique was within easy walking distance of the hairdresser's premises and as she entered Eva nodded to the shop assistants as if she knew them and got big fake smiles in return. A boutique like this was not somewhere that Eva visited very often and always made her feel a little bit uncomfortable.

She loved clothes shopping though but what was it about pricey boutiques that made her feel like a peasant? She always felt the need to surreptitiously fish down the inside of the garment for the price tags and a quick discreet look before deciding whether to try on or not. Why couldn't they be a little bit more obvious? When you did buy something the bags were a status symbol in themselves, glossy and opulently tied with ribbons they safely guarded your delicate purchases cradled in between sheets of crinkly mauve tissue paper. The assistants could be a bit over the top sometimes though and there was one in particular who was a professional fawner. Fair enough to offer assistance but to give unsolicited opinions when trying on was a no-no for Eva.

Please don't come near me, she silently begged in the dressing room. The black velvet dress was 'made for her' the assistant purred as Eva stood awkwardly on display in front of the full-length wall mirror. You had to come out of the dressing room to really see the outfit you were trying on properly and this was definitely just another marketing ploy.

The assistant was really starting to bug her and instead of feeling pressured she was beginning to feel annoyed although Eva said nothing and just smiled equally falsely back at the assistant. She had only come out of the dressing room to have a look in a longer mirror but now she felt like all eyes in the shop were on her.

As much as Eva despised being told that everything was "stunning" on her, this time she had to agree. It would be perfect. Being tall and yet curvy the dress hung beautifully from her sculpted shoulders. The black velvet dress was pure Audrey Hepburn. It had cap sleeves, a sweetheart neckline and was

4

beautifully fitted to the waist from where it swept out propped with a layer of chiffon underneath, finishing just below the knee. It was a classic little black dress that would sashay with her as she walked and she would get loads of wear out of it, she just couldn't resist.

Next she admired herself in a silk slip skirt and a cashmere short sleeved sweater. The tiny paisley print of the skirt with mauve, silvers and grey was timeless yet girly and fun and the grey kitten heel suede slingback shoes were divine. It wasn't like she really needed more clothes but she felt like splashing out for this weekend. Handing over her credit card gave her quite the power buzz or was it a hot flush of panic at spending so much?

Eva's next stop was at the lingerie shop next door where she picked out a beautiful set of mauve coloured bra and knickers delicately embroidered with tiny pretty pink and lilac flowers, and another more racy black set. *Stockings,* she thought, Alan loves stockings and it had been ages since Eva had even contemplated wearing them. The ones she had at home were well at the back of her underwear drawer strangling each other and probably snagged. Hopefully in some very dim candlelight and with enough vino on board she might get away with actually wearing them if she were brave enough.

Finally her shopping spree culminated in the grocery department of the supermarket where she picked up some orange juice, rashers and eggs for a decadent breakfast in the morning to fortify them ahead of her planned foray to the countryside. Remembering to pop the congratulations card to Elaine into the post-box on her way back to her car she began to feel really buoyant and on top of things.

Once home again Eva took her time bringing in the groceries and shopping bags stepping over the scattering of letters and flyers that lay on the doormat. Usually these things were a rushed ordeal but this weekend she intended to savour every moment. As she put the groceries away her stomach rumbled and she fixed herself a snack of cream cheese on cream crackers topped with red-onion relish and cracked black pepper.

After flicking through the not very exciting mail and recycling the rubbish – what a waste of paper - Eva made two phone calls. One was to her in-law's to check on the kids and the other was to Alan or rather to his voicemail. His mobile was switched off so she left a quick message to get home soon. It was 7pm and he would surely be finishing up soon. He still had no idea of her plans for the weekend ahead though surely he must suspect something by now; after all she had already left him a voicemail that morning to finish up early if he could.

Eva had made reservations for a special dinner in Hayfield Manor and then in the morning they would drive an hour and a half drive down the coast to an exclusive country guesthouse for a romantic Saturday night away together. She'd made their dinner booking for 8.30pm and was glad of her snack now, she would be famished otherwise as they probably wouldn't get a bit past a nut or an olive until at least 9pm.

After her phone calls she kicked off her boots and changed into a soft cotton loose beige sweater and joggers and a pair of fluffy socks. Padding around in her room she carefully laid out her clothes for that evening and began to pack for their trip. She loved the crinkly sound that the tissue paper made as she unfolded the cashmere top she had just bought. She needed all the time she had to get ready.

Topping up the bathwater, Eva lit a few scented candles, carefully tied up her newly coiffed hair and indulged for a little bit longer than her usual 10 minute soak. The phone rang a number of times in the bedroom but she closed her eyes and savoured the silence when it stopped. She wasn't going to risk slipping by jumping out of the bath only to get there on the final ring. *Pure bliss.* It was never like this when the kids were around.

It was almost too quiet, so after wrapping a soft lilac bath sheet around herself she walked into her bedroom and put on a CD. It was a David Gray one that she had bought for herself years ago, she loved the song 'Babylon' and turning up the volume she glanced at herself in the mirror and could see the reflection of the lit up screen on her mobile phone signalling a message. As soon as she heard Alan's voice she knew by his tone that something was up.

'Hi hon. Look, things are running a bit late here, so I'll grab something to eat and work through, talk to you later. Bye.'

Eva quickly tried his mobile number and again it was switched off. Ringing the office number was equally thankless as it rang out and out.

'Fuck it,' she muttered. There was nothing for it at this stage but to cancel the restaurant. *That's what she got for trying to surprise him,* she thought as she rang to cancel. 'Friday evening and I'm on my own,' she fumed. Eva was not of the self-pitying high-maintenance variety though and quickly resolved that she was well able to start off the weekend by herself. This way she would have time to top-up her fake tan and give herself a pedicure. Every cloud has a silver lining and all that.

Flicking through the old romantic movie options she settled on 'French Kiss,' opened a chilled bottle of Chenin Blanc and nestled herself into a cosy corner of the couch. She then ordered a delivery of Chinese food and poured herself a glass of the chilled wine. *Heaven.*

Settling into the soft cream leather sofa and pulling a silvery grey faux fur throw around herself she relaxed admiring her professionally manicured fingernails and the not so bad home pedicure attempt as the fake tan set to work under her loose grey cotton pyjamas.

Meg Ryan was adorable as always and that actor, what was his name, pulled off the French accent really well. *What was his name though? He had been in a 'Fish Called Wanda' too*, that was going to bug her now. Racking her brains for the actor's name she sipped some more wine and soon enough the Chinese delivery arrived.

In the kitchen she put the prawn crackers into a Stephen Pearce pottery serving bowl, the one with the scalloped edges that had been a wedding present and then proceeded to open the foil container of chicken and green peppers with black bean sauce with all those lovely crunchy water chestnuts, bamboo shoots and bean sprouts tumbling together, it smelled just divine. She tipped almost the entire container of Chinese over the chips on a plate, nice big chunky fat chips that would soak up the black bean sauce.

Putting her plate on a tray with the bowl of prawn crackers she refilled her wine glass and returned to her cosy spot on the sofa with her mouth-watering to begin her feast. *Yes, food was comfort indeed,* she thought as she tucked in.

Time melted away as Eva got lost in the movie. France looked absolutely heavenly, the endless vineyards were so romantic and that hotel in the South of France was sheer decadence.

Besides getting glammed up and going out for a fabulous meal for an evening, this was the next best thing she could think of as she cuddled the throw around her and sipped her glass of wine. The movie ended and she watched the credits roll up the screen to see that it had been Kevin Kline who had played the ruffian Frenchman Luc Teyssier.

After glossing through some interior design magazines and flicking back and forth between the end of Friday night chat shows on TV, Eva finally gave up on Alan and made her way to bed. The wine helped her to nod off quickly and she slept soundly until morning.

She hadn't heard Alan coming in and hadn't a clue how late he had worked so when she rose she did her best not to disturb him and decided to treat him to breakfast in bed. He barely stirred as she left the bedroom as quietly as she could. He probably didn't even realise that they had the house to themselves yet.

Eva brewed up a fresh pot of coffee and got engrossed in the property section of the delivered Saturday morning newspaper when she could hear the noise of Alan having a shower upstairs.

Glancing at the clock she saw that it was almost nine-thirty and thought that they had better get a move on if they were ever going to get away for the weekend. Alan was still clueless and the thought of surprising him excited her as she rustled around the kitchen.

Eva whipped up a delicious breakfast of scrambled eggs made with real butter and cream, some diced crispy bacon and fresh chopped chives. Chunky brown bread smothered with butter and steaming hot coffee completed the lot.

'Creamy Scrambled Eggs with Crispy Bacon & Chives'

You will need: (Serves 2)
4 eggs
Splash cream
Knob butter
3 rashers of bacon
Oil to fry
Chives to garnish

Method:
Lightly beat the eggs and a little cream together in a bowl, using a fork or whisk.
Chop the bacon into pieces using kitchen scissors and fry until crispy in a little oil. While the bacon cooks melt the knob of butter in a saucepan over a medium heat, once melted turn up the heat a little and adding in the eggs, keep stirring the eggs as they cook, using a wooden spoon or spatula to stop them from sticking.
Meanwhile fry up the rashers in a little oil until crispy. Once the eggs are cooked, serve garnished with the chopped up crispy rashers and snipped chives.

[RECIPE ENDS]

'Smells wonderful,' Alan enthused as he entered the kitchen. He poured himself a mug of coffee, sat on one of the high stools at the counter and buried his nose in the sports section of the paper.

'Did you notice anything Alan?' Eva inquired.

'Hmm, sorry what did you say?' he replied, speaking directly to the Munster Rugby captain in the paper.

'I said did you notice anything?' she repeated feeling slightly miffed now.

'No,' he said, this time lifting his head. 'Should I? Oh yeah, your hair is it? Did you get it done? Yes, it's lovely.'

9

Eva smiled brightly as she said 'Yes Alan, I did get my hair done, but that wasn't it. Haven't you noticed how quiet it is?'

'What do you mean?' he replied, looking over at her more intently now as he raised a brow.

'The kids, Alan. The kids aren't here.'

'Why, where are they?'

'They're at your mother's for the weekend and I've booked us into SilverBirch House for a night of wining and dining and whatever else you fancy,' she giggled with a coquettish smile.

'Oh...., oh, great,' he replied 'fantastic, yeah,' as he began to tuck in to a plate of the rich creamy scrambled egg speckled with chives and crispy bacon. 'Yum,' he said, 'this is delicious.'

'Glad you like it,' Eva replied as she watched him consume a forkful of the sublime concoction. There was a satisfaction to be had from preparing and cooking good food and then watching it being savoured and enjoyed.

His reaction to the surprise of a weekend away wasn't quite as enthusiastic as Eva had anticipated though, but things had been sprung on him and Alan really wasn't a spontaneous or excitable kind of guy. As he sat there enjoying the food she had prepared she decided not to tell him about the plans she had cancelled for the previous evening. There wasn't any point now anyway and she didn't want him to think that she had been disappointed.

Their drive down to West Cork proved idyllic. The watery winter sunshine bounced off the Atlantic as they made their way through Ballydehob and Schull and along the coast road, until just over an hour and a half from home they pulled up onto the gravelled drive of SilverBirch House.

Eva loved the sound of the crunching gravel under her boots as the sea breeze whipped gently around them. They made their entrance through the large front door and into the foyer of the house where they were greeted firstly by the flickers of a welcoming open fire and then by the lady of the house.

Family-owned SilverBirch House was a charming old Georgian mansion that had been painstakingly restored retaining as much of the original features as possible. They were led to their room which had a magnificent view of the sea lying about two hundred meters away. Centre stage in the bedroom stood a four-poster hardwood bed with an overhanging creamy muslin canopy. The curtains that clothed the tall windows were deep wine coloured velvet trimmed with burnished gold tassels. A huge gold gilded mirror hung over their bedroom fireplace, which was set and ready to be lit. It was sumptuously luxurious in every way imaginable.

Eva was anxious to make the most of their afternoon and suggested a walk on the beach but Alan wasn't a bit keen on exploring the surroundings with her. 'To be honest love, I'm kind of tired after the drive and wouldn't mind a nap,' he replied.

So Eva left him to it and ended up walking to the beach on her own, which she didn't really mind. The sea was calm and the wind was gentle with the air invigoratingly fresh. Hopefully he'll perk up after a nap she thought as her mind turned to the beauty of her environs.

The Alan of fifteen years ago would never have opted for a nap, he would have been quite different. If beamed back she had no doubt that instead of walking on her own she would instead have been ravished in front of a blazing fire in the bedroom and it wouldn't have been the wind that would have brought the colour to her cheeks. He was behaving like an eighty year old going for his nap.

Kicking the pebbles and shells on the beach she stopped and bent to examine them. The little pebbles fascinated her and she began to bend, examine and collect. She selected some shiny polished white ones and filled her pocket. She would use them in glass vases and bowls as a base for candles or at Christmas time she might roughly spray them with silver spray paint and put them in a bowl of floating candles or just scatter them on the mantelpiece. They were really pretty.

The sand changed textures as she walked onwards. Sometimes rough with pebbles or shells and other times so smooth. Eva loved beachcombing and was always on the lookout for that perfect piece of driftwood. Sitting on one of the large stones at the base of the dunes she admired the wild grasses and thistles that grew there.

11

Was it called marram grass or pampas or was that just grass from an African plain? Whatever it was called, it was beautiful. Collectively the sand, the pebbles and the dancing grasses worked with the calming tidal wash of the sea and the gentle breezes to soothe the mind.

Eva loved colour and texture in everything and one of her greatest loves was food. She loved to cook and entertain and would collect recipes and pore over food and wine magazines longingly. Thinking of food made her realise that they hadn't eaten since their late breakfast and she was now ravenous. It had to be at least three o'clock.

When she got back Alan was already ensconced in the lounge where Eva joined him. He was in the middle of a pint and halfway through a club sandwich.

'That looks good,' she said as she helped herself to a big juicy mouthful of crispy bacon and tomato. Tasty and all as the sandwich was Eva wanted to save her appetite for a fabulous dinner later on so she ordered a bowl of soup and some sparkling mineral water. The hearty bowl of tomato and red pepper soup arrived with a thick garnish of double cream accompanied with chunks of brown bread and real Irish butter.

After a quick chat about what was in the paper Alan decided that he was now going to go for a walk and so Eva returned to her room for a long soak in the bath on her own. Bliss she thought as she added some more warm water although having already had a bath the previous evening she would rather have spent some time with Alan than start to prune.

They had dinner at seven and Alan admired her dress and then asked if it was new. Eva knew she looked good in it. It was a bit over the top for dinner in a country house but it flattered her and she looked and felt fantastic. Most of their conversation revolved around the kids with Eva filling Alan in on their recent activities and upcoming parent/teacher meetings. As usual it was Eva who did most of the talking.

Dinner was a sumptuous feast with Alan enthusing over his starter of prawn risotto with peas. Eva went for an aubergine puree served with a sweet pepper sauce to start and then followed with spiced pork roast with apple and thyme cream sauce as a main. Alan decided on the roast lamb with garlic and country herbs for his main course and every mouthful was savoured.

It was so lovely to sit back and be waited on for a change Eva thought as a second bottle of Beaujolais was about to be poured. They opted to share a tasters menu for dessert which was sheer indulgence as mouthfuls of mouth-watering mini lime cheesecake merged with a decadent miniature warm chocolate pudding filled with melting dark chocolate and generously dolloped with jersey cream, the selection of fresh fruit providing a lovely bite and balance.

Over coffee and then brandy Eva tentatively brought up her plans to return to work. This was something that surfaced from time to time but had always been put off because the timing had never been right. However, now that the kids were well settled into school and both finishing at the later time, she felt the time was right to give it a go.

Eva wanted to try something new this time and had taken an online course in interior design. She wanted to start small, maybe offering an interior design consultancy service from home and eventually growing towards opening her own interiors store. She babbled enthusiastically talking about her ideas but Alan's stifled yawn and glazed expression made her realize that it was time to stop nattering and get back to having a relaxing weekend. Eva pushed her ideas to the back of her mind but promised herself that she would pursue this whether Alan showed any encouragement or not this time.

Hardly fit to budge after their meal Eva suggested a stroll on the beach to wake them up a bit. The sea air refreshed and revived them somewhat and soon banished all thoughts of dozing off. It was a beautiful moonlit night but getting cold so Eva snuggled closer to Alan as all she had around her was a woollen wrap. Taking off his jacket as they walked along the shore Alan put it gently around her shoulders and Eva nestled into him as closely as she could.

They sat together on the rocks that had been Eva's resting place that afternoon, now lit by the moonlight they listened to the whoosh of the sea. Eva drew a breath as Alan took her completely by surprise pulling her towards him and kissing her hard and passionately. Closing her eyes Eva responded eagerly and they continued to move symphonically with the cadence of the sea. The energetic rises and falls of the waves crashing onto the shore mimicked their beautiful rhythm. She felt like an irresponsible nineteen year old who had gone too far on a frivolous fling as they strolled back to their guesthouse later. Where had that come from she wondered, from this man beside her who was usually so laid back and reserved?

The following morning they indulged in a late breakfast selected from a range of fresh juices, bowls of muesli and cereals, a choice of omelette or full Irish breakfast and stacks of pancakes. The brown bread and scones were homemade and served with curls of real butter soft enough to spread without sticking in clumps on the bread. Excellent coffee washed everything down and after packing their belongings they made their way slowly back up the coast stopping off for a wander around Schull.

Discovering a quaint little restaurant come crafts-shop, Eva picked out a set of four pottery mugs for her mother-in-law and some books and sweets for the kids while Alan sat drinking coffee with his nose once again in the newspaper.

Driving onwards Eva suggested they take a 'quick' detour to Kinsale. Alan had rolled his eyes but silently acquiesced and hovered at the doorways of the galleries and antique shops that Eva chose to loiter in.

Two hours and a takeaway coffee later they headed off to Alan's Mum's house to pick up the kids. Luke and Hannah were bursting with news of the great weekend that they had spent on the farm.

The kids chatted incessantly about feeding newborn calves as Eva gazed dreamily out the window thinking about her plans for an interior design business as they drove home. The visits to the crafts-shops and galleries had been even more inspiration and

14

reminded Eva how much she cherished beautiful things.

The weekend had been wonderful and that night Eva found dreams and slept alongside Alan easily with a head full of their breathless entanglement blissfully unaware that she would never make love to her husband again.

Chapter 2

(STUFFED PEPPERS)

Waking on Monday morning Eva threw back the curtains to a slowly brightening morning. Alan was probably at his desk at work already and had risen at least an hour earlier. Eva quickly showered without washing her hair and tying it up she put on her gym gear and called the kids for school.

She gathered the laundry on her way downstairs and after putting on the kettle she loaded the washing machine and switched it on.

Eva listened for a minute and besides the whirr of the washing machine and the rattle from the kettle there wasn't a sound to be heard.

Would they ever make a move and get out of their flipping beds, she thought as she shouted up the stairs to them again.

Hannah meandered slowly down the stairs in plush animal slippers wearily rubbing her eyes.

'Do we have to go to school?' she whinged as she climbed up onto the chair tucking the bunnies on her feet underneath her.

'Yes,' replied Eva matter-of-factly, 'now what do you want for your breakfast, Coco pops or Crunchy nut?'

'Mmmm dunno.'

'Hannah,' Eva said, trying to keep her tone calm.

'Alright I'll have Crunchy Nut sssooooo.'

16

You'd have sworn it was a dose of cough syrup she was being offered rather than her breakfast. After calling Luke twice more Eva eventually had to go up and pull the blankets off him thus ensuring that he started the day off with both legs firmly in his grumpy trousers.

Eva buttered bread for sandwiches in between sips of coffee as the pair grudgingly ate their breakfast. They were not morning people. Eva rummaged in the cupboard for the lunchboxes until remembering that the school bags had gone to their Gran's house at the weekend and they were still in the back of Alan's car.

Rooting around in the corner cupboard once more produced two old takeaway cartons and finally the lids too. They would have to do. After thirty minutes of looking for shoes, finding library books and trying to get them to finish their breakfast they finally loaded into the jeep and headed for school.

After dropping them off Eva went to the gym for a forty-minute workout. Her head was spinning and running on the treadmill gave her some time to think uninterrupted. She found herself thinking of nothing but plans for her business venture. *I'm doing it this time*, she said to herself, as if she needed convincing.

She would have to get started without input from Alan though as he had shown as much interest as he did in the fashion section of the Sunday newspaper, unless there was a lingerie feature of course, then he would show a keen but short-lived interest in the fashion world.

Where would she get finance and how much would she need, she wondered? There was always the remainder of her inheritance to fall back on although she wanted to keep the bulk of that for the children's future. She'd already used a chunk of it for their house deposit years ago. Where would she source the stock and where would she locate the business? These were questions that were spinning around and she hadn't a clue where to start.

Maybe she should do one of those 'start your own business' courses. She knew she had a flair for putting looks together and had proven that when she'd worked as a trainee buyer in the main department store in Cork city. Alan hadn't been exactly enthusiastic or overly encouraging about her going it alone now but then again he hadn't objected either.

Eva was sure of one thing though, she knew she needed something to call her own. After twelve years of being a stay at home Mum it was time to get back out there. Too often she waited for Alan to come home to talk to her. She needed her own corner of the world back and to stop being so dependent on him.

Looking around the gym she wondered what these other women did for a living and if any of them ran their own business. Plenty of women did so why shouldn't she?

Back at home she quickly fixed herself a toasted bagel spread with cream cheese and sprinkled with freshly chopped spring onions. The bagel was one of the habits she had picked up from her trips to visit Elaine in Boston many years ago. She had yet to shower and wolfed the bagel down too quickly to really enjoy it but she needed to get a move on if she was going to do anything with her morning.

After showering Eva surveyed her wardrobe as she was going to be meeting Vivienne for lunch. She picked out an Oliva Rubin long sleeve rib knit dress in pink with a cut-out back and needing something to keep her warm pulled out a baby-pink cashmere ballet style wrap cardigan. Alan had given it to her for the previous year's Valentine's Day.

Well to say that he had given it to her was a bit of a stretch. He was always great to take a hint when a week before an event like Valentine's or her birthday Eva would gaze longingly, oohing and aahing and wistfully pointing out items in a magazine or online. How else could he possibly know what she would like and what would be the point in falsely smiling and pretending to like something akin to cutlery dangling dangerously from your ears? Eva already had a fine collection of unwanted and unwearable gifts and was doing her best not to expand the range.

She took her time drying her hair and doing her make-up and being so dressed up she was reluctant to do any housework. Forcing herself to hang the washing to dry on the clothes horse near the radiator she then made a half-hearted day-dreamy attempt to do some ironing. Her efforts at housework were soon distractedly abandoned in the name of doing some research for her business and she justified that she couldn't be exerting herself in a cashmere cardigan anyway now could she?

With a pot of fresh coffee brewed Eva perched herself up at the kitchen counter on a stool with a bundle of old interior design magazines that she had hoarded over the years.

Flicking through the pages she jotted down a list of things that appealed to her. She spotted trendy looking stainless steel kitchen storage jars and some colourful kitchen utensils. She fell in love with textured cushions, old-fashioned clocks and weather-worn picture frames.

By the time she had to leave to meet Viv for lunch she had quite a long list compiled and glancing through it she realised that everything she listed was an accessory. There were no big pieces of furniture and it looked like she might have a starting point or at least had established a focus for her business - home accessories.

Eva arrived at 'Spice' five minutes early and ordered sparkling water and began to peruse the menu. She didn't think she could possibly be hungry again after the bagel but a glance at the menu soon whetted her appetite.

The restaurant was buzzing as usual and full of well-heeled Cork women. This was the kind of place where you just had to dress up. Going to the loo was like a first time stumble onto a catwalk where you could feel eyes on your outfit critiquing every detail as you tried your best to walk tall, suck in the tummy and not trip up.

It was pretentious but it was an excuse to dress up and it was an escape from a sometimes drudging reality. Briefly contemplating that maybe it was a bit early in the season to be wearing baby-pink she took in the splashes of spring pastel colours going on in a number of other outfits on those around her and took solace.

Eva wondered what to have as jazz music played in the background. The stuffed peppers sounded tasty and the beef tomato and mozzarella mille feuille also looked like an interesting choice. Cajun chicken perhaps or maybe the trio of fresh fish.

She was so engrossed that she hardly noticed Vivienne arriving. She looked stunning as usual. Her chestnut brown hair fell sleekly at her shoulders and she had the deep brown eyes of a loveable puppy.

How she was still single and on a permanent quest for 'Mr. Right' was beyond Eva's comprehension. Viv got plenty of envious glances as she slid into her seat opposite Eva.

'You look gorgeous Viv I love your top, is that new?'

Vivienne was wearing smart navy wool trousers with a V-neck mink coloured knitted sweater embellished with a random splattering of tiny faux pearls.

'Oh thanks. No it's not that new, well it's kind of I suppose. I bought it for Christmas and didn't wear it that much, so I must try and get a bit of wear out of it before the weather warms up. Listen, what's the news? Tell us how was the weekend away?'

'Oh it was just fab Viv. An open fire, windswept beach, great food and good lovin'!' Eva giggled.

'Hmmm, go on you vixen. I'm jealous. What I'd give for a weekend away and a bit of passion.'

'As if now you don't have the opportunity, sure you could head off whenever you liked.'

'Chance would be a fine thing Eva. There isn't even a sniff of a man.'

'Yeah right Viv, there's always someone after you.'

'I wish,' Viv sighed.

'So how're things anyway? How's the new job going? Are you mad busy?' Eva inquired.

'Ah not too bad, busy enough like. I love the job but I just find it so hard to drag myself out of the bed these mornings. I can't wait for the summer. For a bit of heat you know? At least then it would be easier to get dressed.'

'I know yeah, roll on the summer. Are you hungry?'

'Starving, I skipped breakfast this morning and my stomach is speaking to me now,' replied Viv.

Turning back to the menu, Eva decided on the stuffed peppers with a side salad.

'Stuffed Peppers'

You will need: (Serves 2)
2 large red peppers
75g cherry tomatoes (4) quartered
2 cloves garlic crushed or finely chopped
1 medium carrot peeled
1 small red onion finely chopped
2 handfuls / 35g breadcrumbs (1 slice bread made into breadcrumbs)
Handful fresh herbs such as parsley
Olive oil
8 mini mozzarella balls (bocconcini or ciliegine)
Small chunk / 35g parmesan grated.

Method:
Preheat the oven to 190°C.

Cut the tops off the peppers to create a cap and then de-seed them. Put pepper bases and tops into the hot oven, drizzle some oil and top and bake for 10 minutes.

While they are cooking use the vegetable peeler to make carrot ribbons in a large bowl. Add in the finely chopped red onion, garlic, mozzarella balls and quartered cherry tomatoes. Season with salt and pepper.

In a separate bowl mix together the breadcrumbs, chopped parsley and grated parmesan.

Remove the semi-cooked peppers from the oven and spill out and discard any juices that may have gathered then fill the bases with the tomato mixture and top generously with the breadcrumbs. Return to the oven with the pepper tops on the side to cook for a further 15 to 20 minutes until the breadcrumbs are golden brown.

Serve with pepper caps on top and with a simple baby leaf salad and dressing.

[RECIPE ENDS]

As they ate lunch Eva brought up her plans to return to work. Vivienne had a marketing degree and a master's on top of that but as she had always worked in academia so she had no real industrial business experience as such. Viv did offer her plenty of sound advice though and pointed her in the right direction with the first stop being to develop a business plan. Eva hadn't a clue what that would involve. Viv advised her that because she would need capital to finance her venture a sound business plan would be absolutely essential. This would involve research, number crunching, legal and financial advice before even approaching a bank.

'You can get a template for a business plan online,' Viv advised, 'just google it.'

Later on as Eva drove to collect the kids from school she was feeling excited after her lunch with Viv. Her head was so full of ideas and it had been lovely to have someone listen to her and take her seriously. She was really dying to get started but she knew that there would be no point in trying to do anything when the kids were around. She would have to wait until the next day.

At home the kids changed out of their uniforms and Eva fixed them a snack before they sat down to do their homework. Hannah was great to do hers and just got on with it but as for Luke, trying to get him to focus and get it over with, that was some form of torture. He had improved as the years went on but the spelling was still a disaster. Invariably he'd lob the copybook up on the countertop usually while Eva was in the middle of preparing the dinner and he'd order 'Test me Mum.' Knowing full well that he hadn't so much as glanced at the spellings Eva would push them back at him and tell him to at least read them out loud first. After a bit of arguing with Luke the homework got done and Eva was sitting in her kitchen having a coffee. She'd bunged a chicken casserole in the oven and as that cooked Eva enjoyed the relative quietness of her home. It was warmish for January and once the kids had done their homework they had literally ran out the door to their friends' houses. The only noise was the hum of the fan oven as the casserole cooked.

She made herself another coffee and knew that this was getting to be a bad habit. She knew that she should try to drink water or green tea instead but it just didn't do it for her. Browsing through another one of her interior design magazines she lusted after a luxurious looking red chenille covered couch. She would love to redo her own living room but if she was serious about a business venture any home improvements would have to be shelved for a while.

Eva shifted herself from her high stool to get on with the dinner before the kids would come in and start swinging out of the fridge. It really bugged her when they insisted on eating so close to dinnertime and Luke had a terrible habit of drinking straight out of the juice jug or a milk carton. At least most of it ended up in his mouth these days and not down his clothes and on the floor as it used to do although it still wasn't the most hygienic practice in the world. Eva would scold him half-heartedly as she really didn't think that his germs were about to pass on anything particularly life threatening if shared.

She thinly sliced some raw potatoes and added them on top of the already simmering chicken casserole. It was a cheat of a dinner with very little preparation at all. All she'd done was browned four breasts of chicken in the base of the casserole in some oil, added a clove of chopped garlic, four chopped carrots and a jar of Spanish chicken sauce from the supermarket. With the potatoes now on top they would absorb some of the sauce as it all cooked together for another half an hour.

Hannah was back in her own garden now playing on the swing with one of the neighbours' kids as happy as could be. She was eight years old and very independent. Luke was probably down the road playing soccer on the green, eleven years of age and already grown up. Looking after them was easy now as they could do so much for themselves, nearly too much sometimes. Bedtime was when Eva felt closest to them, watching their eyes get heavy as she read them a story and they drifted off. Although Luke mostly read his own stories now or he might listen to some music in his room, he still liked to have a chat with her sitting on the edge of his bed before he went to sleep.

Eva set the table for the three of them and didn't bother setting a place for Alan. He was never home in time for dinner these days and would reheat his dinner later. Eva looked at her magazine again and an advert immediately caught her attention. It was advertising a new interior's place opening the following week. She felt a bit queasy as she read it and realized that she was actually feeling a pang of jealousy. She looked at it again and felt that maybe she was too late to open a similar store but then she gave herself an inspiring pep talk.

Eva talked to herself a lot, not aloud, but in her head, talking herself up, reasoning, reassuring. She was definitely spending too much time in her own company. Speaking to Viv earlier had made the prospect of starting her own business very real to her and it was all she had been thinking about since. *There were always going to be other stores and hers would just have to be better.* The opening of this new one could be a research opportunity and she marked the opening date onto the wall-mounted calendar. But for now it was time to get the kids in for dinner.

Alan arrived home just after nine and as usual Hannah and Luke were both already asleep by the time he got in. He didn't touch the dried out offerings in the oven and just had a cup of tea instead as he watched the end of the evening news. Eva was dying to talk to him about Viv's advice but could see that he was exhausted and just sat beside him quietly instead. He hadn't given her any positive feedback when she had tried to discuss it with him on their weekend away together but he didn't dissuade her either. And maybe she should just leave it at that and get on with it. She'd do all the research, finalise the business plan and approach the bank and if they took her seriously then she would involve Alan but until then there really was no need to.

Eva spent the remainder of the week much like she had started it. She managed to get to the gym twice more, stay on top of the housework and compile even more lists of the items that appealed to her in her old magazines. She was beginning to take note of the stockists' names and where she could buy them from.

On Friday she took a break from cooking dinners and went for an easier option of pizza and garlic bread with salad. At least the kids would be sure to eat it and wouldn't be pushing vegetables around the plate protesting that they were disgusting. So stone-baked pizza with a sweet chilli chicken topping accompanied by garlic and herb ciabatta cooked in the oven and the Caesar salad couldn't be simpler to assemble.

The weekend passed in a busy haze of swimming lessons, soccer practice, a birthday party and a basket full of ironing for Eva. It was much the same every weekend now that they were back to school after the Christmas holidays and Eva was already looking forward to the mid-term break when they could sleep-in and stay in pyjamas on a Saturday morning instead of all this rushing around again.

The following Monday morning she dropped the kids off to school and instead of hitting the gym she made her trip to the newly opened interiors place called 'Room & Board.' *Nice name*, she thought, as she entered what resembled a warehouse. From the outside it didn't look too promising but as she stepped inside it was very inviting. The ceilings were high and airy with some glass panels allowing the natural light to beam in. As she went up a couple of steps to the first area there was a display of bedroom furniture. Sleigh beds seemed to be a popular style and the beds were made up with beautiful duvet covers. One that really appealed to her was crisp white with a scattering of pink tulips that seemed to be appliquéd onto the cover giving a feeling of depth and delicate luxury. A large selection of duvet covers were displayed on wooden shelving units that stood against the walls.

Faux fur throws and leopard print cushions were scattered on some of the beds. Some island display units were stocked with cotton waffle slippers and robes and an exclusive brand of hand and body lotion. Eva imagined herself dressed in one of the robes tossing fragrant salts into the bath and relaxing with scented candles glowing softly all around her.

25

Moving into the living section there were a number of sumptuous leather couches and beanbags scattered around. Candles and candle-holders, chunky hardwood coffee tables and again more fur and velvet cushions. There were also some magnificent paintings, vibrant and warm with colours of burnt umber, sepia and gold.

An assistant asked her if she'd like a glass of wine and there were some white, silver and gold balloons hung with long delicate white ribbons at the desk area. *Nice touch,* she thought to herself. Declining the offer of the glass of wine she mentally noted the effort for the opening week. As she paid for a pair of the white cotton waffle slippers she wondered what the mark-up was on them. They were simple and handmade in India.

When she returned home Eva made herself a pot of fresh coffee and pulled out her writing pad which by now was full of pages and pages of lists. She turned to a new page and wrote the name of the store 'Room & Board' at the top. She wrote 'Competitor' underneath and then she drew a line down the middle of the page. On one side she began to write a list of what she had liked and on the other she listed what she didn't like about the store.

Eva was taking list writing to a whole new level. It was something that she had always done. From when she was a student taking more time to do up a study timetable than to actually study, to writing lists for jobs that needed to be done around the house. Having lists for things was a mental start and it meant that something was going to get done sometime. Even if the reality was that the downstairs loo wasn't going to get painted for another six months it was on a list somewhere so at least the intention was there. It may not have been the finest logic in the world but writing things down for Eva was a bit like taking a walk on the beach that would therapeutically clear the mind, at least for a little while.

Over the following weeks Eva began to collect heaps of information. She bought herself a desk and an office chair and set up a study area for researching her business in the box-room of the house. It had previously been used for storage and required a good clear out and trips to the charity shop. What was she keeping all those old books for anyway? And the wedding china dinnerware? If she hadn't liked it thirteen years ago she never would.

She picked up a beautiful study lamp with a worn brass finish and a fresh cream pleated shade that could be angled as needed. Eva organized the stacks of magazines that she had been hoarding for years. There were fashion magazines, food magazines and interior design magazines.

Flicking through the pages, images seemed to jump out at her. New York, Turkey and India all appealed to her tastes and style. New York for clean lines, neat finish, sharp, bright, executive looks. Turkey for an exotic sumptuous harem type atmosphere with voile curtains, rich velvets, plush deep coloured throws and intricately woven rugs. India for hardwood furniture, hand embroidered fabrics and rich bright colours.

Eva loved colour and texture and one of her other great loves was food. She also loved the beach and the seaside feel that a travel feature on Cape Cod gave her with photographs of driftwood, pebbles and sand.

She looked at her list of likes and dislikes from the newly opened home furnishing store that she had just visited and tried to decide what the main focus of her own store should be. She knew her own lists were more about accessorising than anything but would she offer big pieces too? Or should she just stick to the accessories that she loved and forget about the larger pieces of furniture?

Looking at the stack of magazines just added to her confusion. Viv had emailed her a business plan template and a sample business plan for starting a small business and Eva began to try to fill in the blanks. The first thing that needed to be written was the business proposal, so she knew that she really had to get a handle on what her business would be about. She needed to define her business objectives, her target market, the market size, her competitors, her market research and her research findings. She decided to focus on defining her business objectives and on researching her market.

She looked up interior designers in Cork online and it brought back pages of results. Who were these people and why had she never heard of most of them? One even offered 'holistic interiors' whatever that was. Okay, so there was an abundance of interior designers out there but how many home furnishing stores were out there? Searching for competitors wasn't difficult as they were easy to find but how could she define or quantify the potential market and then there was the number crunching. Too much was turning out to be guesswork on her behalf. She had to get her head around forecasting future performance and coming up with cash flow projections, whatever that meant. The template from Viv was a start but she needed some more expert advice to pull this business plan together if things were ever going to be turned from ideas and magazine clippings into something real.

February and the mid-term break came and with the kids off school for a full week Eva's research came to a standstill. There was just no point in trying to work when they were around as they kept interrupting her. She tried to sit at her desk a couple of evenings when they were in bed and do something with the financial aspects of the business plan but she was too tired after a full day with them at home and decided to leave it again until after the school holidays were over. Eva was sorry that they hadn't booked a holiday in the sun like some of her neighbours. *Wouldn't it be lovely to be on holiday,* she thought. *Getting up to sunshine in the morning, lounging by the pool and prancing around in nothing more than a bikini all day long.*

The kids returned to school and Eva resumed her business research. She made an appointment with an accountant and got some more advice on how to determine what her start-up costs would be. Asking Alan for help was a disappointment but she should have known better. He would either pretend not to hear the question, say 'could we talk about it later', or mumble something about being too tired from looking at figures all day at work and the last thing he wanted was to look at them at home. In the end Eva stopped asking.

Chapter 3

(CAPPUCCINO)

It was a fresh day in late February. The kids were at school, Eva had been to the gym and was at home again finally loading the breakfast plates into the dishwasher when the doorbell rang. Wiping her hands on a deep blue and white check tea towel she went to answer it.

'Daniel,' she exclaimed and kissed him on both cheeks. 'What a surprise! It's great to see you, come on in.'

Daniel was her brother David's oldest friend and felt like a sibling to Eva too. They had grown up in the same neighbourhood and he was easy going and great company. He was so funny, finding humour in anything and always making Eva laugh.

Since David had moved abroad Eva had grown even closer to Daniel. It had been ages since he'd been over though. It had been just before Christmas when he had last visited with his traditional gift of chocolate Santas for the kids. Mostly he called a couple of times a year to catch up but it was unusual that he would call midweek.

He wasn't in the door five minutes when Eva had him ensconced at the kitchen table with a cup of coffee in hand and was asking him where he thought would be a good location for her business. She offered him a piece of shop bought carrot cake which he declined.

The perfunctory inquiries had been quickly dispensed with as to how he was keeping and Eva was chattering almost breathlessly about her business plans. Eva had bounced ideas off him in the past and he had always seemed genuinely engaged and enthusiastic. She was delighted with the opportunity to talk to him over coffee and pick his brains as he was in the property business himself and had great business insight. But today he was just listening and nodding and not giving her any feedback at all. Eva was beginning to feel a bit foolish. It was as if he was bored, he was so quiet, but then he interrupted her.

'Look Eva,' he paused before adding, 'I have to tell you something.'

He spoke in a tone that Eva had never heard him use before, he was usually so jovial and now he was sombre.

She felt strange. *What was wrong? He must be sick or something*, she thought to herself. She had never seen him look so grim.

'Daniel, what is it?' she asked softly, wondering *was it his health or something*?

Daniel visibly swallowed hard before replying.

'Eva, I feel sick having to be the one to tell you this but Alan has been seeing someone else.'

Eva froze rigid. She couldn't quite take in what he had said, had she heard him correctly?

'What?' She asked in a half whisper. Her throat was suddenly sandpaper dry and her stomach was clenching involuntarily.

Daniel calmly repeated himself saying 'Alan is seeing someone else.'

'What?' she asked incredulously again, her voice rising a little this time. 'What are you saying Daniel?'

'I'm really sorry Eva,' he said.

'What do you mean Alan's seeing someone else? Are you saying that Alan's having an affair or something?'

Daniel remained solemn and nodded his head slowly.

'I'm sorry Eva,' he said, 'but it's true. Alan is having an affair and I had to tell you. You deserve to know.'

30

'Daniel stop saying that. You're our friend. You're my friend, why would you say such a thing?'

All Daniel could do was quietly say 'I'm sorry Eva, I'm really, really sorry. I couldn't know about it and not tell you.'

'Daniel would you for heaven's sake stop saying I'm sorry, will you?' her voice was angry and raised.

'Eva, look I...'

But Eva cut him off and was standing before he could finish his sentence.

'No, you look,' she commanded as if reprimanding a troublesome teenager. 'I don't know why you are doing this Daniel, but I know it simply isn't true and I think you should just leave.'

'Eva...'

'No,' she said firmly, trying to calm herself, 'just go Daniel.'

Daniel got up and left without another word, softly closing the front door behind him and he was gone.

The house was quiet again. The house was dead still but Eva could hear Daniel's words as if they were ricocheting from wall to wall, 'Alan has been seeing someone else.'

She heard it over and over. This was an old friend saying this to her. It couldn't be true. Alan would never cheat on her. He would never do that to his children.

Eva sat numbly at the kitchen table. At first she was asking herself why Daniel would say such a thing? What was wrong with him? But somewhere along the line her questions took a different turn and changed to questioning if it could be true? Her stomach was heaving and her mouth kept filling with saliva. *Could Alan be seeing someone else?* She tried to dismiss these thoughts and was saying 'No,' out loud slowly shaking her head. 'No,' she said. 'No, no, no.' Despite her voiced denials, her throat burned with each swallow as she tried to steady her breathing and then Eva's tears began to fall onto the table in a steady flow.

A glance at the clock jolted her and realising that she was late for collecting the children from school she went into autopilot as she quickly splashed her face with water and made herself drink

31

some of it too. She felt like throwing up, instead she put on some tinted moisturizer and lip gloss and drove to collect them, hiding her eyes behind a pair of sunglasses. Her stomach was in turmoil.

'Where were you Mum?' Luke complained loudly. 'We were waiting for ages and it was freezing.'

'Yes, well I told you to take a jacket this morning but you wouldn't, would you!' Eva snapped back at him. He flinched a little at her tone, his eyes narrowing as he studied her before asking 'and why are you wearing sunglasses?'

Eva ignored his question as Hannah chimed in and whinged about being hungry. Apparently she didn't like ham sandwiches anymore, hadn't eaten her lunch and was now starving. Eva felt a slow rage beginning to build inside her but somehow gathered herself enough to drive on to the shopping centre. She couldn't take whining and moaning right now and as much as she needed to be on her own she knew she had to placate the kids first.

Seemingly they were no longer on the verge of hypothermia anymore as the pair of them tucked happily into tubs packed with two scoops of chocolate ice-cream smothered in chocolate sauce and covered with sprinkles.

Eva sat quietly and absentmindedly sipped a frothy cappuccino. She felt like she was in the middle of a blurry dream. People were flitting past them in the shopping centre yet she didn't see a single face. There was a continuous flow of movement and she wished it would stop. Was it the cappuccino that was making her feel nauseous or was it the hurry and chatter of the masses?

Eva wanted to scream, she wanted to yell "shut up" at everyone. Anger was building that she was attempting to quell but it was bubbling inside her, she *really really* needed to be on her own. Clamping her hands over her ears to drown out the noise her heartbeat thudded in her eardrums. She breathed deeply and let out a long sigh trying to calm herself.

Luke at eleven years of age had chocolate sauce all around his mouth and dripping down the length of the plastic spoon into a sticky mess in his hand with splodges here and there on his school jumper. Eva rolled her eyes heavenwards and sighed again. There wasn't much point in giving out now anyway. Feeling a little calmer but still nauseous Eva let them finish their ice creams before sending Luke to the washrooms to clean up a bit.

She couldn't face going home yet and distracted herself by buying badly needed new trainers for Luke and a pretty pair of shoes for Hannah.

Eva followed them in a trance-like daze from the shoe shop into the arts and crafts-shop. She felt like she was drunk or something.

There was a demonstration going on in one corner of the arts store where the kids happily watched a young shop assistant paint decorations onto a kite. Eva didn't pause to argue when they begged her to buy them each a customised kite and she handed over her card to pay without hesitation.

As they were leaving the shopping centre it didn't take much to persuade Eva to stop off at McDonald's and they whiled away another hour there. Eva tried to eat a chip but took one bite and could hardly swallow it. She hadn't eaten anything since breakfast.

It was half-past seven by the time they got home. Luke and Hannah went straight out the door again, still in their uniforms, to show off their kites to their friends and attempt to fly them. Eva sat in the quietness of her home at the kitchen table where Daniel had sat that morning.

There were two messages on her mobile phone. Eva sat listening, firstly to Daniel asking her to give him a call, and secondly to Alan stating that he'd be working late and would grab something to eat at the office. Eva tried returning Alan's call but it went straight to his voicemail service and she hung up. She tried the office number and it went to voicemail too.

By nine-thirty the children were in bed and Alan still wasn't home. They had gotten ready for bed and hugged her without even asking where their father was. Eva hadn't noticed this before but they were just so used to not seeing him during the week. It was a Wednesday and it was nearly a pattern in recent times that Alan worked late mid-week. In fact he worked late most days and was rarely home for dinner.

For some reason Eva went to look at the calendar that hung on the kitchen wall. A date in January had been circled for a parent-teacher meeting, a Wednesday, and she remembered how she had to get a babysitter because Alan was working late. Her stomach heaved as she ran to the en suite of her bedroom and threw up. The feeling of nausea had been building all day and now it got the better of her. *Why hadn't she even noticed before? Who works late every Wednesday night?*

She began to cry and sat down propped against the door of her bathroom with her arms wrapped around her knees rocking herself gently back and forth. It had taken ten hours but now she just knew it was true. In her heart she just knew that what Daniel had told her was true. She sobbed to herself and looking at herself in the mirror crying, she kept asking how could he do this to her?

Her face was red and blotchy with cheeks stinging from crying and her nose was getting sore from snivelling and wiping it with toilet tissue soggy from her tears. She cried and stopped and each time she thought she was finished crying she cried some more. Feeling wretched she forced herself to rise from the floor. Her limbs and joints were stiff and her throat was raw. Splashing her face with cold water she emerged and checked the time. It was ten forty-five and there was still no sign of Alan.

She went downstairs to the kitchen and made herself a cup of tea with a slice of buttered toast. She turned on the TV and flicked through the channels to find some noise. The tea and toast sat untouched on the coffee table. By eleven-thirty Eva felt dizzy as she rose from the couch, turned off the TV and headed for the stairs. It felt like she was walking on a moving ship as she dragged her way slowly up to her bedroom.

Crawling on top of the bedcovers with her clothes still on, she turned out the bedside light and tried to close her eyes but they kept popping open. She tried some yoga breathing, tried to clear her mind of everything, but Alan's image wouldn't leave her and Daniel's words kept replaying over and over.

Warm trickles of tears slowly zigzagged down the side of her face, some pooled in her ear and when she turned to the other side

34

she realized that the pillow was almost saturated. Sitting up to turn the pillow over and flicking the light back on she saw that it was now twelve forty-five a.m.

Where the hell was he?

Her mind raced and she felt panicked. A memory flickered into her head. It had been a Sunday afternoon and they were invited for drinks after a birthday party of a neighbourhood friend of Hannah's. Alan had drank a soda, engaged in chitchat and then politely excused himself explaining that he had to drive to Waterford where he was doing a presentation the next day.

All those late nights at work too. Was she a fool or what? What about those weekend business trips to the U.K.? It hadn't occurred to her before now, that it was strange to go for a business trip at the weekend rather than mid-week. She got up, walked zombie-like to the walk-in closet and began to methodically search through his side of the wardrobe. She patted his suit pockets like an airport security guard on speed but she found nothing. Next she rifled through his underwear drawer but there was nothing there either. Eva sat cross-legged on the bed with her face buried in her hands. She felt a wave of panic rush through her. *What the hell was she supposed to do now?*

She turned off the light and tried to sleep again but it just wouldn't come. She tossed and then lay still listening for noises, for car doors. With the light off things were even worse. She felt utterly alone and she thought of the children sleeping in their cosy beds in their cosy rooms. The thought of confronting Alan was making her feel ill. *How the hell was she going to handle this? What was she going to say?*

With a mind in turmoil somehow the wisps of sleep caught her and she drifted for a while until something in the night disturbed her. It was the jangle of Alan's keys and the soft thud of the front door closing. Next she heard his shoes plopping onto the floor.

Lying rigidly still she felt paralysed. Her breathing seemed fast and loud and she tried to slow it down as she heard him, slowly easing his way up the stairs. She felt as if her heart-beat was audible. He stole into the room and made straight for the bathroom and Eva just lay there trying to steady her breathing. When he re-entered the room she sat up, flicked on the light and startled him.

'Jesus Eva, you gave me a fright. I thought you were asleep.' He stood there with tiny droplets of water still glistening on his face.

'Well you woke me Alan,' she said quietly.

'Sorry love,' he replied.

'Alan where were you until three o'clock in the morning?' she asked calmly.

'Oh, at at… at a club with some clients. Pouring wine into them.'

She listened carefully to his reply.

'Really?' She asked coldly, all the while studying his face for a reaction.

'Yes, of course really, where else would I be?' His tone had changed. He was almost cross.

'Alan I wouldn't have a clue or I wouldn't be asking. So why don't you tell me where you were?' Eva's tone was stroppy now.

'Eva I told you already that I was in a club with clients. What's with the inquisition?'

'What *club*?' she asked with a half sneer in her voice.

'This is ridiculous Eva.' Alan was now glaring at her indignantly. 'What the hell are you asking me all these questions for at this hour of the night? I'm tired, it's been a busy day and I just want to go to sleep.'

'I'm asking you Alan because I don't believe you.'

'Eva, what are you on about? What's wrong with you?' he asked, injecting a bit of calmness into his tone.

'What's wrong with *me*? You're the one who is out until three o'clock in the morning and is acting as if that's normal.' Her voice was now loud and she could feel herself shaking with anger.

'Eva take it easy would you. What's wrong with you?'

'Just fucking answer me Alan?'

'I told you already Eva, I was at a….. club with clients,' his voice faltered.

'What club?' she asked calmly this time.

'We were in a bar in town and went back to their hotel for drinks afterwards.'

'What hotel?'

'The Metropolis, Eva you're being ridiculous. I need to get some sleep.'

He grabbed his dressing gown and then closed the bedroom door after himself. Lying breathlessly still Eva heard the creak of the guestroom door.

Panic crept over her and it felt like her skin was actually tingling. She still wasn't breathing properly.

Exhausted and confused she turned out the light, lay down and replayed every word in her head, over and over. Anger was replaced by humiliation and in turn by despair. *What the hell was going on? Was Daniel right?*

Somehow sleep rescued her from her muddled thoughts for a little while. Waking at six a.m. a gloomy morning light seeped through the gap between the curtains. She arose and quickly threw on her gym gear.

Going downstairs as quietly as she could she picked up Alan's abandoned shoes and placed them neatly together. Forcing herself to drink a glass of orange juice her throat felt raw as she swallowed in hard gulps. She then scribbled some instructions for Alan on a piece of paper about kids lunches and school times and went back upstairs to wake him. He sat up in the bed and looked like a complete wreck.

'Get up and get the children to school and please be here when I get back,' she instructed as calmly as she could.

He said nothing as she turned and left and practically ran down the stairs and out the door. Driving in a showery February morning tears were streaming down her face again and she felt like getting sick. When she reached the hotel the last thing that she wanted to do was to go inside. Somehow she forced herself out of the jeep.

Ten minutes was all it took. The night porter was still on duty and adamant that there definitely was no wallet left in the bar the previous night and no they didn't do late night bar service during the week so she must have been mistaken.

The roads were still very quiet as she drove to the gym. Flashing her membership card she blankly made her way to the locker-room. Already dressed in her workout gear Eva stuffed her jacket and keys into a locker and headed for the treadmill. She tried to run but had to change from a running to a walking pace when she almost stumbled. Her thoughts were all over the place. She felt like she was in a dark cave with no way out, there were only walls. *What the hell am I going to do?* But mostly she wondered about what he had actually been doing the previous evening. All those times that she had been at home alone looking after their children and their home, had he really been out somewhere with someone and making a fool out of her?

The treadmill began to slow to a stop and Eva was jolted from her head debate back to the gym. She had walked 6km on the treadmill without knowing it and the machine was trundling to a halt. Eva didn't want to get off. She wanted it to start again, to rotate round and round. She wanted to stay within the stainless steel framed confines of this predictable oasis where she could set the pace, change the pace and be in control.

Feeling at a loss, with tears threatening to spill and it was all she could do to get off the treadmill, grab her jacket and head out the door before they began to flow again. It was only seven-thirty a.m. and too soon to head home so she sat in her car for a while and then began to doubt.

What if he was telling the truth, she thought. *He could have just been out with clients and mixed up the hotel. Maybe he fell out with Daniel or something*. Thinking back to their weekend away in January the doubts really began to settle in. *How could he have been with me like that if he's having an affair? You couldn't. Could you?*

Not knowing what to believe she started the car and absentmindedly drove out in the direction of Monkstown. Work and school traffic was flowing now and she was glad of the busy roads which forced her to focus her thinking on her driving for a bit until eventually she pulled over, got out and walked over to look into the water and breathe in the sea air.

An hour passed and Alan was surely on the way to drop the kids off at school by now and it would be safe to go home.

She wondered how Alan would answer their questions at breakfast as to where she was and why he was bringing them to school? She couldn't have faced them this morning and held it together. She needed answers now. She was going to tell Alan what Daniel had said, she had to.

Sitting back into the jeep she felt sick to her stomach. *What would the kids be thinking in the car on the way to school? What would he say when they asked where she was? No doubt he'd make up some lie and say she'd gone shopping or something. Maybe he was used to lying to them all by now.*

Eva sat there for a while unable to start up the jeep and head for home. *What if it isn't true?* That question kept popping up. *What if it isn't true?* She knew she was in shock but what did she really know? *There was Daniel's word and there was all the circumstantial stuff that could add up to an affair, maybe? What other explanation could there be? Could Daniel just be a jealous friend and Alan a workaholic? Do I even really want to know?*

Eva's cheeks were stinging again and knowing that she couldn't sit there any longer she eventually started the jeep and drove homewards in a blurry daze glad of the condensation on the windows. She still had no idea what she was going to say to Alan.

It was hard to concentrate on the driving again as she hit the now crawling morning traffic. Somehow she found herself pulling into their empty driveway. His car was gone, he either wasn't back from the school run yet or he was gone to work already without talking to her.

Breathing deeply she headed into the kitchen and put on a pot of coffee and then some toast. Turning on the radio to fill the void of the kitchen she sat on a stool at the counter and waited. The toast popped and the front door opened. What happened next seemed to take place in slow motion and Eva was able to replay every word for days afterwards. Alan coolly walked towards her and stood with the counter in between them. She remained sitting on one side while he stood on the other.

'Eva I'm sorry,' he said.

Eva said nothing and stared at him blankly.

A minute must have passed in which he turned off the radio and then he repeated himself.

'Eva, I said I'm sorry.'

Again she said nothing.

'Look Eva, I really am sorry.'

Eva took a deep breath before she spoke.

'For what Alan? What are you sorry for?'

'All of it. I'm sorry. I let you down.'

'Did you cheat on me Alan?'

'I'm sorry,' he said.

Eva sat numbly with her eyes prickling as the tears rolled slowly and Alan just stood there looking at her. Who knew how much time passed before he broke the silence again with yet another 'I'm sorry.'

'Alan, you're only sorry that you were caught,' she replied coldly.

'That's not true Eva, I'm sorry this ever happened.'

'Alan 'this' didn't just happen. You cheated on me and you were caught and now we're finished.'

Her words had come out of nowhere. They had just popped out of her mouth and with them said she immediately regretted it.

'Ah for God's sake Eva, don't be so rash. Let's talk about it.' He couldn't have used a more patronising tone.

'Who the hell do you think you are, telling me that I'm being rash?' Eva exclaimed.

'Sorry. I....'

'You can be sorry all you like Alan, but that doesn't change a thing. I can never trust you again.' She broke down crying, holding her head in her hands, her body convulsing softly.

And it was more than a fling. She just knew that. Whatever he was up to must have been going on for ages. Sure how else would Daniel have known about it if it wasn't? And for Daniel to be the

40

one to tell her meant that a lot of people knew about it, which only added to her humiliation. *Did Viv know too?* she wondered.

Trying to think practically, a jumble of thoughts were going through her head. *There seemed to be three choices. He leaves, she leaves or they try again. There was no way that I'm going anywhere,* she thought. She wasn't going to leave her kids or her home and she'd nowhere to go anyway. So really there were only two options. If he left, where would he go? There was the apartment that they owned in the city but that had tenants. He could go to his parents. But then she thought of the kids and was overwhelmed by what would be their sadness.

Eva's throat felt sore as she went to speak again and her heart and chest were hurting her, they felt knotted and tight and broken.

'Alan I want you to leave,' she whispered.

He stared at her.

He just looked straight at her and said nothing. Neither of them said anything. The clock on the wall ticked steadily and both of them were conscious of the slowly dripping tap. The air felt tight and Eva found it difficult to breathe steadily.

Fifteen minutes must have passed and Alan was just looking at his shoes. Eva felt a tightness welling up in her chest and she wanted to explode. She wanted to shatter the silence with screams and shouts but she managed to hold it in somehow until she repeated slowly 'Alan I want you to leave'.

She felt outside of herself in that moment as if she was playing a part in a play or something. It didn't feel real at all.

'Jesus Eva, when did you get to be so cold?' He said in a half shocked, hard done by response.

Silence again. Eva was feeling angry now. Seeing the empty coffee mug on the worktop, she visualised herself grabbing it, smashing it and going for him. She just wanted to hurt the fucking bastard, who the hell was he to call her cold? Screaming on the inside she steeled herself and replied.

'Alan, you're the one who's been screwing around and I want you to get the fuck out of my house.'

Alan's mouth opened as if he'd been struck.

41

'Eva come on, can't we talk.'

'So talk Alan. What is it that you want to say?'

'I just think you're being a bit drastic. Can't we talk before we make any rash decisions?'

Alan's calmness was really starting to get under her skin and as much as she felt like thumping him she managed to regain some composure.

'Alan this is not a work conference. *We* are not making any rash decisions here, *I* am deciding on how *I* want my life to go on from here, and as for you, you have already made your choice.'

'Eva I haven't made any choices. I love you Eva, I love my kids can't we talk about this?'

'Alan you do not love me or you would not have been fooling around with someone so blatantly that half of Cork knows about it before I do. You have humiliated me and you have hurt me and….,' she paused as the tears came again. Eva couldn't talk anymore as she lowered her head into her hands and cried.

Alan came around beside and tried to put an arm around her but Eva just lunged at him. She hit him and hit him, pounding his chest with her fists until he held her wrists. Through her tears she shouted at him 'Alan, why did you do this to me? Why? Do you know that it was Daniel who told me? Do you have any idea how that feels?'

'I'm sorry Eva,' he replied quietly as he stared down at his feet again. 'I'm sorry. It was a huge mistake. I'm so sorry,' he said, trying to hold her.

Pulling away Eva wiped her face with some paper towel and caught her breath before calmly saying 'just go, Alan, just get out. Get away from me.'

Alan's expression was unfamiliar. Was it defeat or dismay, or was it something else? Could it have been relief? Was that it? Did he actually look relieved? He turned briskly, grabbing his keys from the counter and was gone.

Eva felt sick, she wanted to run after him, to hug him and to make everything better. She still loved him but she knew in her aching heart that he no longer loved her no matter what he said.

He would never have gone so easily if he loved her. *Why wasn't he fighting for her? Why wasn't he on his knees begging for a second chance?* But he wasn't.

So she just sat there and cried and cried. She sobbed like she had when she was a child with a gashed knee, but there was nobody there to comfort her better with a magic kiss now. Her throat was burning hot and raw and her cheeks were on fire again. She got a face cloth and packed it full of ice and held it to her eyes to try and reduce the puffiness.

Why did he do this to me? Why doesn't he love me anymore? He was her life. The kids and him. Everything she did revolved around them. What was she supposed to do now?

Chapter 4

(GUACAMOLE)

For the remainder of the afternoon Eva did her best to get on with things. She made the beds, emptied the dishwasher, vacuumed and washed the floors. She went through the motions and was doing okay until she started the ironing. Her mobile phone lay silently next to the basket of clothes and she looked at it, willing it to ring. All the clothes were jumbled together and as she took a shirt of Alan's out of the basket and shook it free a school sock of Hannah's fell to the floor. Eva crumpled to a heap beside it. That's what he was doing, he was just casting them all aside and ignoring their existence. *Where was he now? Why wasn't he here banging the door down and fighting for her?* She reached up for her phone and instinctively called his mobile but as it began to ring she cut it off and just sat there looking at it again willing it to call back. But it didn't.

She began to call Vivienne's number but changed her mind about that too. She needed to clear her head, to think and get her thoughts straight. Time was slipping by and Eva eventually forced herself up off the floor knowing that she'd have to pull it together enough to go and collect the children from school.

She wiped her face and contemplated wearing sunglasses again but that would look too ridiculous in the rain. She would just have to do her best to hide behind her umbrella and blame the elements for her ruddy complexion.

44

It was unusual for Eva not to speak to someone as she waited by the school railings but today she hung back and kept to herself until the kids spilled out the doors and Hannah skipped obliviously alongside Luke as he walked to the jeep. Gratefully complying with Luke's request to play his favourite CD she drove home without saying a word.

Homework got done and was followed by a snack of crackers with cheese, glasses of milk and then cookies. The noise of two TVs blaring filled the house.

Eva was still wearing her gym gear from that morning and remained un-showered as she busied herself dusting furniture and pointlessly fluffing cushions until it was time to feed the children again. She wanted to cry every time she looked at them but kept biting the inside of her bottom lip or digging her thumbnail into her middle finger to avert the urge.

She had just put the children's tea on the table in front of them when she heard Alan's key turn in the door.

'Daddy,' Hannah squealed as she rushed to hug him and give him a kiss.

Eva swallowed hard and forced herself to say 'hi' trying to sound as normal as possible in front of the children. Her mind was racing.

What the hell was he doing home? What was he going to say? She tried a bit of yoga breathing to calm herself but it wasn't doing any good and she felt like she could explode at any minute. She had to hold it together in front of the kids.

Hannah returned to her plate of pizza and chips while Luke abandoned his now empty plate with a slice of pizza in each hand and ran off to watch 'The Simpsons'.

Alan stole a chip from Hannah's plate then dipped it in ketchup and as he ate it Eva silently wished for a moment that he would begin to choke. He chewed slowly and then announced to Hannah that Daddy had to go away for a few days but that he'd see her the following week. Eva felt her jaw drop and her stomach plummet.

'Why do you have to go Daddy?' Hannah asked.

'Work pet,' he replied and patted her head before joining Luke

45

in the TV room. Eva heard him make the same announcement to Luke who equally unperturbed just said 'okay,' and after a short pause he added 'will you bring us back something nice?'

'I will Luke, I will.'

And that was it. Without so much as a nod to Eva he walked through the kitchen, passed her as if she were the hired help and went up the stairs to pack.

He filled two suitcases and with a hug for each of the children he was gone. She noticed that he had taken the spare set of keys to their city apartment which didn't make sense as it had tenants. It was all too much for Eva to handle. She had stood rooted to the spot in the kitchen the whole time that he was in the house. All he had said to her was 'hi' when he had arrived and on his way out the door he said 'I'll call you tomorrow.'

Eva was numb. It was as if a whirlwind was swirling around her and she was standing still in the middle while everything else was spinning higher and higher up into the air beyond her reach and out of her control.

Instinctively she reached for her mobile and called Vivienne, this time she let it ring through as she walked away from Hannah and out of earshot.

'Hi hon,' Vivienne chirped at the other end, 'how are things?'

'Not good Viv, not good,' Eva replied in a half whisper.

'Why what's wrong? Is it the kids, is someone sick?'

'No Viv, it's me,' Eva replied, trying to hold her composure. 'It's me and Alan. Look I can't talk about it on the phone because of the kids but could you come over?'

'I'll be there in half an hour, pet.'

The tears started trickling again as Eva turned to clear the plates and load them into the dishwasher. With 'The Simpsons' programme now over the kids protested at being sent to their rooms so early but Eva bribed them with a couple of mini chocolate bars and a promise that they could watch a video on their ipads and keep their lights on as late as they wanted to.

Eva made a cup of tea for herself and as she waited for her friend to arrive she forced herself to eat a handful of leftover chips.

The doorbell soon chimed and Eva rushed to answer it. She ushered Viv into the living room before the children would realise that she was in the house. Closing the door quietly she turned to Vivienne and asked 'do you know?'

'Know, know what love?' Viv responded gently. 'What is it? Is there something wrong with Alan?'

'He's been cheating on me Viv,' Eva sobbed. 'He's having an affair.'

'Oh,' Viv replied. She was visibly shocked. 'Oh my God,' she said, holding out her arms, 'come here to me love, come here.' And Eva sat beside her and cried with her friend's arms hugging and comforting her.

After a while she said 'Eva, this is probably a stupid question but are you sure? I mean how do you know?'

As Eva replayed the entire scenario aloud the truth was obvious and there was no doubt. Alan's words and actions of the previous twenty-four hours spoke for themselves. Twenty-four hours. That was all it took to deconstruct a marriage. One day.

Viv stayed until after midnight as Eva relived the day over and over again. Viv left promising to come over after work on the following day and to stay over for the weekend.

Eva stayed up on her own staring blankly at the muted television for another couple of hours before finally dragging herself up to bed in the early hours of the morning. Hannah woke her, shaking her gently and asking 'Mummy do we have school today?'

Eva was a dishevelled mess having slept in the same gym gear that she had worn the day before, 'Sweaty Betty' was living up to the brand name. She tied back her hair and hid herself under a baseball cap before making a mad dash to school. Somehow they managed to arrive with lunches made and dressed in their uniforms only five minutes late.

Returning home to her quiet house she sat in the kitchen with a fresh cup of coffee and tried to think. *What is going to happen now?* Alan had said he would call her so she sat looking at her phone wondering when he would call.

47

Her mind was a jumble of thoughts. How come he was the one who was going to call and why did she feel so powerless, like she was letting things just happen? Why hadn't she started her business years ago when she first started talking about it? Why had she waited so long? What she would give to be completely independent. She wanted to stay in the house. This was so unfair. She had given up her job and her business plans were only plans, so here she was well and truly trapped.

Pouring another coffee she realized it was stone cold so she absentmindedly brewed another pot and then sat just looking at it.

The phone sprang to life ringing loudly and it was Alan. He kept the conversation brief and direct with Eva just listening to him, too shocked to say anything other than a murmured 'yes' when he asked her to meet him on the following afternoon to discuss things. He had coldly said that he knew that there was no going back and he wanted to talk about arrangements for the children.

When the call ended she buried her head in her hands and cried. She still loved him. She didn't want it to be over. How could he suddenly have no feelings for her? This wasn't the Alan she knew.

The coffee pot was cold again and it was lunchtime so Eva tried to force herself to eat a cheese sandwich and struggled to swallow a mouthful. She had eaten practically nothing for the last two days.

She thought of Daniel and what he had told her on Wednesday. Thursday had been a blur of Alan and now it was Friday, a day filled with hours that were dissolving away one cold coffee pot at a time. It would soon be time to collect the kids and she needed to pull herself together.

She forced herself to shower but having cried her way through it she still looked an absolute mess of blotchy skin and swollen puffy eyes. *Thank God for make-up and Yves St Laurent,* she thought as she applied touche-eclat concealer to practically her entire face. She slipped on a pair of black slim fit ankle length Citizens of Humanity denims and a brightly patterned sweater paired with flat black patent French Sole pumps.

Slicking on her lip-gloss she appraised herself in the mirror. To anybody else she looked like a fairly normal thirty-something Mum but as she stared back at herself in the mirror all she could see was the lifeless watery pools that were her eyes. There was no sparkle, she felt hollow and flat inside. Beds were unmade, lights were still on and curtains remained closed in some of the bedrooms. The kitchen still had breakfast bowls and boxes of cereal cluttering the counter. Eva did a hasty tidy up, piling the dishes in the sink and headed off to collect the children.

The school pick-up was the usual craziness of a Friday afternoon but at last the weekend had arrived. The thought of Viv calling over later to stay for the weekend was something to look forward to. At least somebody cared about her.

Vivienne was a great friend and she had known her for years. Viv was a vivacious and compassionate person. She had travelled a bit since college but knew her roots were in Cork and that this was where she wanted to settle down. She had recently moved back from Dublin for a new job at the University and it was going well. When it came to romance though Viv didn't seem to be living in the real world at all as her expectations were so high. Eva had watched as she had dismissed one boyfriend after another sometimes for the daftest of reasons.

Viv called her to say that she'd be over at eight and was bringing a couple of bottles of wine. Eva threw on a pizza and garlic bread for the children's tea. She told them that Viv was coming over to stay and that they could watch a movie and eat some treats but they had to promise that they would go to bed at nine-thirty so Eva could have some time with her friend.

This was going to be the third night in a row of junk food. She felt momentarily guilty about their diet and vowed to make something healthy for the following day's dinner.

They hadn't asked for their father at all and he hadn't called to speak to them or to say goodnight or anything.

Eva opened a large bag of Mexican tortilla chips and a pot of Greek yogurt and then whipped up some guacamole for herself and Viv to snack on.

49

'Guacamole'

You will need:
2 Avocados
1 small red onion finely chopped
1 garlic clove
Juice of 1 Lime
2 tbsp Greek Yogurt
Fresh coriander optional

Method:
Combine the mashed ripe Avocados with finely chopped red onion and mix well.
Add in the crushed garlic, lime juice and Greek yogurt and lime juice.
Season to your liking with salt and pepper and add in some chopped coriander if you like it.

[RECIPE ENDS]

Eva liked to keep the guacamole chunky.

'Mmmm these are addictive,' said Viv as she scooped up some guacamole with a tortilla chip.

'Thanks for coming over hon.'

'Are you kidding me girl, sure where else would I be?'

Viv had given comic books to Luke and Hannah and when bedtime came they headed up to bed without arguing to look at them.

The two friends started to talk about what Eva was going to do now. Well mostly it was Eva who talked and Viv who listened as they tried to decide her approach when she would meet Alan on Saturday. Every so often Eva would crumple and sob. She couldn't believe her life was changing so fast.

Again it was the early hours of the morning before Eva got to bed but at least this time she was so wiped out that she fell asleep quickly. With Viv staying over it made Eva feel like somebody was looking after her.

Saturday began with swimming lessons and soccer practice and Hannah also had a birthday party at a friend's house in the afternoon. Birthday parties were endless and seemed to crop up every other week with each one more lavish than the last. Thankfully both Luke and Hannah's birthdays were a while away yet and would fall in November.

Eva dropped Hannah off and went to meet Alan on the pretence of doing some shopping while Viv stayed at home to look after Luke.

Alan had a lot to say and seemed to have thought of everything. They met at a quiet restaurant and sat well out of the earshot of fellow diners. As others around them lunched happily they ordered coffee and Eva didn't even touch that. She sat and listened and everything he suggested seemed fair. He even told her that she should see their solicitor to formalise the agreement and that he would get a new solicitor. He said that he would cover the kids' costs and the mortgage with a generous allowance for her as well. She wanted to say something about her business plans and her future but whenever she attempted to speak she could feel her chest rise and knew that if she did she would start to cry.

He began to suggest arrangements for the children, stating that it would be in their best interest to stay with Eva full-time and to stay with him every second weekend. Eva struggled to hold back the tears when he started talking about them so matter-of-factly. It all sounded like a carefully thought out plan. She was shell-shocked.

It was only on the drive home that Eva began to realise that Alan's arrangements were so well thought out that this was something he must have been thinking about for a long time. That hurt. Had he been thinking of leaving her when they had been together on the beach two months ago?

Eva picked Hannah up from the birthday party and headed home to where Viv was cooking her speciality of spaghetti Bolognese. Sitting around the table with Luke and Hannah competing to suck up the longest string of spaghetti it was heart-breaking to think of what lay ahead for them. They would have to be told eventually.

In the evening the four of them snuggled up on the couch together and watched a movie. Having Viv in the house was a distraction but Eva's mind continuously wandered as she sipped on wine mentally replaying snippets of Alan's monologue from the restaurant earlier until eventually she started to doze off. Eva had drained most of the bottle herself and when she slid into bed later she waited for the room to stop spinning before drowsily closing her eyes.

On Sunday morning Eva arose late with a head that thumped unforgivingly and no mind for the fry-up that Viv had cooked for brunch. She spent the afternoon quietly in the kitchen attempting to clean up while Viv headed off to do some shopping with the kids.

When they returned Viv had picked up some of her things on the way so that she could stay over again even though Eva told her that she needn't but in the end she was glad when Viv insisted that she would. She needed to talk. When the kids were gone to bed Eva recounted the previous day's discussions with Alan.

'Do you think I rushed things Viv? Be honest. I shouldn't have told him to leave.'

'Eva love, what choice did you have?

'But I never asked him to stay? I could have tried to make a go of it. I still could. Do you think I should?'

'I don't know love. Do you want to?'

'I don't know. Yes. Part of me does.'

'Do you think you could take him back Eva?'

'I don't know, but maybe I should try.'

'Well whatever you do Eva just take some time first and remember that all this has happened because of what Alan did. It's not your fault.'

Chapter 5

(LAMB & AUBERGINE PARMIGIANA)

Standing in her kitchen on the first morning of May, Eva looked around. Everywhere she glanced there were reminders of Alan and how happy their family had been.

There were holiday photographs of all of them with smiling faces beaming out from the frames. There was no evidence of discontent in Alan's face in a photograph that had only been taken the previous summer. Was her marriage in decline then or had it been a more recent descent? Only he could answer that.

His Father's-Day mug hung on the wooden mug-tree unused and the stool where he used to habitually perch and read the paper on a Saturday morning sat empty.

The pain inside Eva burned from her stomach up through her ribcage to the back of her throat where it stung the most.

She tried her best to be cheerful for Hannah when she came down for breakfast but she could see that she was unhappy.

Two months had passed and they were all still hurting.

'I don't want to go to school today Mum. I want to stay at home with you,' she pleaded.

'I know pet, but you have to go,' Eva replied softly.

'Why Mum? I don't feel good.'

'I know love but you'll feel better later,' Eva lied.

Luke came down and said nothing at all. He poured himself a bowl of cereal but barely touched it and returned to his room to change into his uniform without a word.

Persuading Hannah to get dressed was an ordeal but Eva got around her with a bit of bribery and eventually they set off to school together. Luke was silent all the way.

At the gym as she cycled to nowhere on the exercise bike she thought about what Alan had said to the kids when he had tried to explain why he wouldn't be living with them anymore. He had told Luke that he didn't know how long he would be moving out for but she knew in her heart he hadn't a notion of ever coming back, no matter what he said.

Thinking back to their discussions from the very beginning it maddened her to think of how one-sided everything had been. He had an affair, he moved out and he told her what the arrangements would be regarding the children. It wasn't that there was anything wrong with the arrangements he had suggested, it was just that he seemed to be dictating how her life would unfold.

Thinking about it she decided that she would look for more. She would go along with all his suggestions but she would tell him that she wanted to go ahead with her business plan and that she would need to use the house as collateral for a business loan. Eva knew she would have to prepare herself for a rejection and a lot of questions about the feasibility of her business and it was time to start taking herself seriously. He could well afford to support them and had plenty of money invested here and there. She knew that much.

She might even suggest that, all going well, she would take on meeting half of the mortgage payment after her business was up and running for a while. There were only seven more years left on it anyway and it wasn't really that much but Eva wanted to feel that it was her home. It had been her money that had financed the original down-payment after all. She was definitely going to get it signed over to her. But maybe that was her pride talking. 'I'm not going to be made a fool of anymore,' she whispered to herself solemnly.

Eva splashed her face with cold water in the locker-room toilets before grabbing her keys and jacket to leave. At home again she showered and as she picked out her clothes for the day. She pulled on a pair of now loose 7 jeans and teamed them with a navy t-shirt and navy leather and raffia wedge shoes. There were shadows under her eyes and she disguised them with make-up and then tried to distract herself with attempts to complete her business plan.

Sitting at her study desk and surveying the stacks of magazines and the pad full of lists it all felt a bit pointless. It was hard to believe that weeks ago she had been all guns blazing and excited about her project but now it just looked like a mess of muddled magazine clippings and she was tempted to throw the whole lot in the bin.

Sitting there, staring at bits of paper she grabbed her mobile and made an appointment to meet her solicitor. She needed to know where she stood, she needed to know her rights and so she made an appointment for the following week.

Eva was tempted to ask Viv to come over again after work but she didn't. She was leaning on her far too much and she needed to start dealing with things by herself. She badly wanted to talk to someone though and thought about calling Elaine in Boston. Why was it that whenever she contemplated calling her it was never the right time? It was probably early morning there and Elaine would be at work so Eva would have to wait until the weekend to catch her at home.

There was Fiona in Paris but she hadn't been in touch with her for ages.

There didn't seem to be anyone else to talk to besides Viv. Eva's own mother had died when she was nine and her Dad had been the best that Eva could have wished for. She loved him deeply but he was never the same after her Mum's death. He did his best for her and her brother though and gave them everything they ever wanted but he had passed away not long after Eva's twenty-second birthday and now she had nobody. She would have loved to have a sister to share things with but she didn't and her brother David was sporadic at best in terms of communication and it just wasn't a call she wanted to make.

Her wedding day had been an emotional one and without her mother and father there they had kept it very small. Thinking about their wedding set Eva off crying again and she went in search of their wedding album. She hadn't looked at it for years and the cover was dusty.

Wiping it off she slowly opened the cover and knew that she shouldn't. She was torturing herself but she couldn't help it. There she was smiling out of the pictures in their wedding album with Alan. They looked so young and so happy and so in love. It was only thirteen years ago but there was a big difference between being twenty-something and thirty-something and she could see that they both had aged since then. Daniel was there in the photographs as well as Viv, Elaine and Fiona who were Eva's bridesmaids.

She really should call Elaine and Fiona and let them know what was going on. And there were Alan's parents, his Mum Mary looked radiant in the photographs as she always did. Eva knew that she was heartbroken and disappointed in equal measure at the failure of their marriage. Alan had hurt so many people.

Closing the photo album Eva went to the kitchen and looked into the cupboards. Talk about bare. There was half a box of cereal, some stale bread and crackers and the fridge wasn't much better. Eva badly needed to do some grocery shopping and did her best to look presentable before heading off to collect the kids from school

In the supermarket Eva avoided eye contact with anyone she passed and couldn't bear the thought of having to speak to someone. She began to stock up with plenty of easy to prepare food as she didn't want to have to shop again for at least a week. They loaded up the trolley with an assortment of frozen pizzas, potato wedges and a couple of bags of ready washed salads. These were joined by bags of baby potatoes, tubs of coleslaw and boxes of couscous. A selection of salamis joined cooked ham, fresh bread rolls, pickles, tomatoes and boxes of cereal in the now heaving trolley. She wanted to have food in the house and not to have to think about what to eat.

She bought some tortilla chips, bags of ready grated cheese and tins of chopped tomatoes. Finally she tossed in some avocados, aubergines, mozzarella, parmesan, red onion and limes and was ready to head home. If all else failed they could survive on nachos.

Needless to say, the kids had taken full advantage of her unusually blasé attitude towards the grocery shopping and had flung in various bags of fun-size treats and assorted crisps. The checkout lady scanned everything and Eva said nothing as the sea of junk-food sailed past her and the kids eagerly packed it into the shopping bags. Their spirits seemed to have lifted a little.

At bedtime Eva read Hannah a story but she kept asking her when Daddy was coming back. Eva tried her best to brush off the question without giving a definitive answer but Hannah wasn't satisfied. She managed to distract her with another story and then told her that it was time to go to sleep.

When would this all begin to sink in? And was she handling it properly at all? Maybe she should go to a doctor or a counsellor for advice. And what about the school? She should probably tell the teachers what was going on, in case it would make a difference to their behaviour at school. How would you approach that?

When Eva went in to say goodnight to Luke he gave her a bigger hug goodnight than usual but said there was nothing he wanted to talk about when she asked him. She turned out his lamp for him and quietly left his room with tears rolling down her cheeks again. Where was Alan now, she wondered, and what was he doing? Was he out wining and dining his new woman or was he having a cosy night in? The thought of him with someone else made Eva sick to her stomach and she thought she was going to throw up.

The next day Eva made a decided effort to get up on time and forced herself out of bed as soon as the alarm buzzer sounded. No more snooze-button. She showered and took some time to dress and put on make-up vowing that she would not end up at the school gates in gym gear yet again. She wore a pair of fawn leather ankle boots under white denims, with a lightweight beige knit sweater. Her clothes said classy springtime even if her face was less than full of the joys of it. A slick of lip-gloss, some bronzing powder and large sunglasses soon hid her anguish from the rest of the world.

Back at her study desk later she tried to make sense of the mounds of papers and clippings and figures that she had abandoned weeks ago.

The words 'Business Plan' leapt out from one page and that was her starting point. She went back to where she had left off and began to summarise her idea for her business. Coming up with the financial figures for the business plan was going to be the hardest part. Eva hadn't a clue where to start with finding a premises or even how a lease worked. She had plenty of research still to do and found that the hours whizzed past as she scribbled away trying to communicate on paper exactly what her business would offer.

A week passed and Eva forced herself to keep going and to get things back into some sort of normal routine for herself by going to the gym every other day. She also did a big grocery shop, this time without all the extra junk that the kids wanted and she started to cook proper meals again.

Feeding the children properly gave her great pleasure and they loved her home-cooking. Lasagne and salad was a favourite, as was chicken stir-fry with wholegrain rice and lots of fresh vegetables. She had begun to regain her own appetite somewhat and was eating a proper dinner with the kids and forcing herself to eat fruit. She was more conscious now of her own health and the need to stay well for her kids. What if she got sick or something happened to her? It was a morbid thought but one that preoccupied her mind sometimes.

At night-time she would try to make sense of her 'Start your own Business' book. This wasn't her usual type of bedtime reading and with heavy eyes she would reach across to turn out the bedside light on Alan's side of the bed and feel a wave of sadness but it no longer made her cry.

Flicking through one of her magazines one lunchtime she came across a delicious looking recipe for Parmigiana Di Melanzane, an Italian dish with its roots in Naples. Distracted by the picture in the magazine it looked so tempting with the parmesan coated aubergine slices golden brown and covering layers of melted mozzarella and rich tomato sauce underneath. This one had lamb in it too.

She imagined that every mouthful would taste of summertime and decided that she would try it out for their dinner later.

'Lamb & Aubergine Parmigiana'

You will need: (Serves 6)
Olive oil or rapeseed oil (for frying and drizzling)
500g minced lamb
1 medium onion
2 cloves garlic
2 tsp dried oregano
2 x 400g tinned chopped tomatoes
2 aubergines
200g mozzarella
50g parmesan (about half a regular sized wedge)

Method:
Pre-heat the fan oven to 180C / Gas Mark 6
(You will be layering the meat and aubergine in a baking dish once prepared)
Heat a tbsp of oil in a large pan over a medium heat and brown the mince.
Finely chop the onion, peel and crush the garlic.
Push the browned mince to the side of the pan and add the chopped onion to the centre and allow to soften for a few minutes.
Then add the garlic and cook for a further minute before stirring in the oregano and chopped tomatoes.
Leave to simmer for 10 minutes, stirring occasionally.
Heat a tbsp of oil in another large frying pan/ griddle pan over a medium heat.
Cut the aubergines into 1cm thick round slices and slightly

brown the slices on both sides drizzling over extra oil so that they soften nicely.

Once browned, remove to a plate. You may need to do this in a couple of batches.

Layer meat then aubergine slices topped with grated parmesan and some torn mozzarella into a baking dish and repeat finishing with a generous topping of grated parmesan. Bake in the hot oven until the cheese has melted and the meat is bubbling up underneath the aubergines (30 minutes) Enjoy with some crusty bread.

[RECIPE ENDS]

Eva served this with a simple green salad and the kids loved it. After dinner she helped them to finish their homework and then began to pack some things for going to spend the following weekend with their Dad.

Hannah's sleep was disturbed and she woke up calling out for Eva in the middle of the night. Maybe it was all the cheese in their dinner that had given her a nightmare but it probably had more to do with her father's departure and an imminent night away from home for Hannah. Eva went over to her room and cuddled up alongside her and slept beside her in her single bed. They would be staying with their Dad in their two bedroom apartment in the city. Eva had made sure that they would be staying just with him and it was a humiliating subject to have had to broach with Alan but she had no choice but to discuss it.

Hannah and Luke didn't exactly skip off to school on Friday morning at the thought of spending the night with their Dad. But as much as they weren't looking forward to it they would have to get used to it. Eva had spoken to Alan at length about their sleepover arrangements and he assured her that whenever he had the kids with him or staying over he would be giving his attention to them and there wouldn't be anyone else around. Now that he had moved into the apartment he was taking them every second weekend from Friday after school until Sunday evening as they had agreed. Their arrangements were working okay for now but at the back of her mind she knew things would have to be formalized sooner or later through solicitors.

Eva dropped the kids off to school with their weekend bags and said goodbye at the school gate. Viv had suggested that they go out for something to eat later and it was lovely to have that to look forward to. She went to the gym and started off by running five kilometres on the treadmill. She then cycled five more on an exercise bike and by the end of it she was sweating like crazy. Returning to her empty house, she felt a buzz after her morning's exertion that she hadn't felt in a long while and took a well-earned long hot shower. She picked out her clothes for the day at home, a simple white cotton tee-shirt with three quarter length denims. Opening the upstairs windows she let the gentle May air breeze through her home as she tidied up the children's bedrooms before settling down to some more brainstorming in her study.

She worked at the business plan as fastidiously as she could, taking a short break for a light lunch of cream cheese spread thickly on crackers with slices of juicy vine ripened tomatoes and cracked black pepper. She couldn't help but feel guilty when she thought of the kids and how they might be feeling as they ate their lunches at school. Did they get on with it as they usually did and play with their friends unperturbed, or did the dilemma of their parent's separation gnaw at them? Were they dreading going to spend a night at their father's apartment, or did it bother them at all?

Getting back to her desk she once again flicked through an interiors magazine and lost herself absorbed in a section that explored a reader's home. It was a Victorian house somewhere in South London and it was decorated in a chic palette of neutrals. With high ceilings and windows, the walls were tones of grey against white woodwork with the floorboards stripped-back and stained dark mahogany in one large living room and lighter limed oak in the dining room. One of the walls of the living room was adorned with a magnificent huge canvas that added warmth to the room with a mix of terracotta and blues. A luxurious navy velvet sofa with squishy cushions sat nestled between two large lamps that sat on the end tables with their navy silk lampshades on reclaimed stone balustrade bases lending to the air of opulence. This contrasted with another sofa in cream with low dark wooden block legs. The huge airy windows with opened cream wooden shutters had built-in window seats perfect for relaxing with a coffee and a good book. It was the finishing touches of the well placed lamps, the bluebell filled glass vases and collection of glass decanters lining the shelves that most caught Eva's eye. She worked away between figures, wish lists and defining her business objectives until it was time to get ready to go out for the evening.

Eva showered again before dressing for dinner in a cowl neck cream silk top with high-rise flared cream trousers over high heeled gold sandals. Accessorising with a Tiffany link bracelet she wore her blonde hair long and straight and grabbing her black leather Prada clutch-bag was ready when Viv arrived in a taxi to pick her up. Viv's emerald green silk camisole top looked stunning against her sallow skin and dark hair and her wrists jangled with an assortment of gold bangles. She was wearing peep toe wedges under her white skinny jeans which added at least an inch to her already five foot nine height. Arriving to a beautiful balmy warm May evening in Cork City people were sitting outside the pubs and restaurants that dotted the Coal Quay. It felt like being abroad on holidays. Over the course of two hours they chatted and shared the tapas plates of chicken wings, patatas bravas and vegetable croquettes.

Sipping their way through a bottle of Rioja as Spanish guitar music played they were discussing Viv's love life or lack of it. She believed in fate and Eva had tried in the past to encourage her to get out there more and maybe even try online dating but she wouldn't. It was refreshing not to be talking about herself for a change.

The two friends stayed out late and finished the evening off with cocktails on the terrace of a hotel that sat beside the River Lee. Eva slept that night dreaming of the Mediterranean and champagne and her future.

Chapter 6

(FILLET STEAK)

The children returned from Alan's on Sunday evening and even though they'd school the next day Eva allowed them to stay up late and chat about their weekend. They said that Alan's cooking was okay though they had preferred the takeaway and overall they seemed to have enjoyed the weekend.

Eva tried not to question too much and just let them talk and then she told them that she had been doing a lot of thinking about something that she had wanted to do for a really long time. And when she went on to tell them that she was going to open a shop they were ecstatic. She explained that over the next couple of months she would be doing a lot of paperwork and when all that was done she would do her best to get the shop opened as quickly as she could.

With the children in school the next day Eva had plenty of time to sit down and take a long hard look at her options and plan what she was going to do next.

She had delayed her solicitor's appointment to discuss her plans and also to get some idea of what was involved in getting a divorce so she rearranged a new date for that.

She made another appointment too, this one was with her bank manager and she needed to get her business plan finalised for that. So it was head down to the boring paperwork for the rest of the day. The night out with Viv and the weekend on her own really seemed to punctuate things for her. Life before had revolved around Alan and now she was going to change the focus back to herself.

Another week passed and she was still working on figures. She went to see an accountant that Vivienne had recommended. Eva brought with her what she thought was shaping up to be a sound business plan, however he picked loads of holes in it and told her that she needed to have things much more solid before approaching a bank.

She felt like she'd just had her wrist slapped by a disapproving teacher for some sloppy homework but knew that she'd have to take it on the chin and get on with it. With some good direction from him she agreed to focus on thrashing out the finer details of the plan and to return again to review it before approaching the bank.

Stopping off at a café on the way home from the accountant's office she picked up a large cappuccino. The wafting smell of the coffee made her think of Elaine in Boston and she promised herself that she'd telephone her later and fill her in on what had been going on over the past couple of months.

Thinking of Elaine she hoped that things were working out for her now that she had finally decided to call Boston her home and buy an apartment there. Elaine had done a lot of moving for various reasons over the years but it looked like she may actually be going to settle down in one place for long enough to call it home. Elaine was the kind of person who never seemed completely at ease or content with her lot. It was as if she was looking for something but didn't yet know what that was.

Arriving home again Eva threw the empty cappuccino cup into the compost bin and decided to give Daniel a buzz. She was a little embarrassed as she apologized to him for the way she had spoken to them at their last encounter, which had been well over two months ago now. He couldn't have made it easier for her when she spoke to him and he was the perfect gentleman.

'Eva there's no need for apologies, I just thought that you should know,' he stated matter-of-factly. 'I've been thinking about calling you lately but I just thought I should maybe give you some time.'

'Thanks Daniel and thanks for telling me. I don't know if anyone else would have and I could have been clueless still. Look I'd really like to make up for my atrocious reaction and I'd love it if you would come over for dinner,' she offered and Daniel agreed to come to dinner the following evening.

It would be a Friday and the kids were spending the weekend at Alan's again so they would have plenty of uninterrupted space to talk. After making dinner arrangements with Daniel, Eva tried to call Elaine in Boston but only got her voice-mail. Eva had forgotten about the time difference yet again and made a note to call her before going to bed later.

After collecting the children from school she stopped off to do a quick grocery shop. She wanted to cook the kids something substantial and picked up the ingredients for a home-made cottage pie and also picked out two fillet steaks and a bottle of cabernet sauvignon for entertaining Daniel on Friday. Home again and Hannah brightened up when Eva asked her to help her to cook the dinner. It wouldn't have taken so long to make if Hannah hadn't insisted on being the one to prepare the carrots. Eva bulked up the minced lamb mixture with tomato puree, plum tomatoes and about four grated carrots which was her sneaky way of getting extra veggies into the kids but it worked.

After dinner Eva did some more paperwork at her desk before attempting to call Elaine again. This time she answered, she was just in the door from work. Elaine was a systems analyst with an I.T. consultancy company based in Cambridge and she now lived in a gorgeous brownstone apartment on 'St. Germaine' street just off Mass. Ave in the BackBay area of Boston. Her apartment was walking distance from her workplace which was just across the Charles River and past the M.I.T. campus. She was also living within walking distance of Newbury Street which was probably the most exclusive shopping street in Boston. With branches of Georgio Armani, Versace and Gucci, Eva was in heaven whenever she visited and could happily spend hours on Newbury Street. The restaurants there were superb and Elaine knew all the good ones. Elaine had plenty of cash to indulge herself with and was also a member of the gym and health club at the nearby Hotel where she could go and lounge on the rooftop garden in the good weather whenever she wanted to. A beautiful oasis in the heart of the city.

Elaine's voice sounded bright and cheery at the other side of the Atlantic. When she heard Eva's news though she was shocked and saddened for her friend. She couldn't believe that Alan had cheated on her and had always thought that if any couple would last it would have been them. Eva tried not to get too upset as her eyes welled up with tears. Elaine made her promise to come for a visit soon and said that she would have some holidays coming in July and that they could head down to Cape Cod for a weekend.

Eventually Eva realised that all she had been doing was talking about herself and genuinely wanting to catch up with Elaine's news too she asked what was up in her part of the world. Elaine seemed to be in great form. Apparently there was a new man on the scene, Gary, and she described him as a cross between Ryan Gosling and Chris Hemsworth. Eva tried to visualise Elaine on the arm of this thespian cross-breed and could picture her willowy figure dressed to the nines with her mane of wavy auburn hair flowing behind her as she sashayed down the red-carpet of some movie premiere. But he wasn't an actor though and he worked in the accounts department of the I.T. company and it was doubtful that he'd be up for an Oscar anytime soon.

Elaine said she had received Eva's card in the post and joked about her not moving with the times and still using 'snailmail'. She teased her that she should get herself online with an email account and that she could do all her own holiday bookings on a laptop. 'Well actually I do have email and we do have a PC and I've been using it quite a lot to develop a business plan for something I'm hoping to work on soon,' she retorted. Elaine was intrigued and started to quiz her all about it. She also recommended that Eva should get herself a laptop to bring with her when going to her meetings and this was something that Eva had been seriously thinking about herself. She would need it to cope with all the information and figures she was gathering for her business and to keep it separate from all the children's stuff on their p.c. Elaine gave her some pointers as to what to buy and Eva scribbled everything down and made a mental resolution to go shopping for a laptop the next morning.

Realising that yet again she was talking about herself she tried to get Elaine to talk some more about what was going on in her life but Elaine rarely did talk in any detail about herself anyway. She would invariably brush questions off and turn things back on whomever she was talking to. She had always been the quiet one in their group in college and preferred to take a back seat rather than position herself centre-stage. Attention was not something that she gloried in, if anything it was the opposite. Slow to take compliments, for some reason she never felt herself good enough. If they hadn't been sharing a house together Eva was quite sure they would never have become friends. It wasn't easy to get to know Elaine but when you did you knew you could trust her with absolutely anything. She was no saint and was well able to bitch along with the best of them but she was utterly genuine too. If someone irked her she found it very difficult not to show it and subtlety was never one of her strong points but Eva loved her for it. It was always refreshing to talk to Elaine because whatever she said was forthright and sincere.

After hearing about Elaine's latest shopping spree at Kate Spade New York in the Prudential Center and some more laptop tips on what software packages she recommended Eva promised that her next correspondence would be in an email.

Eva went to bed feeling happy after her contact with her friend and contemplated a potential buying trip to Boston. Why not? There was so much that she had loved about America whenever she had visited before. There must be homeware there that she would love too. She would need to do a lot of research first and make sure it would be worthwhile. The thought of a trip to Boston was very tempting.

Friday morning started with a trip to the gym after dropping the children to school. It felt strange stepping out of the shower at home later realizing that it was going to be this quiet for the entire weekend again. Eva always preferred to dash home after her gym work-out to shower in the comfort of her own bathroom.

Dressing comfortably in Levi's jeans and a baby blue cotton t-shirt and trainers Eva lost herself in tidying up the house and doing the laundry for the remainder of the morning. With Daniel coming over for dinner later she decided to leave her trip to buy the laptop until Saturday and to just concentrate on the business figures for the afternoon. Scraps of paper were everywhere on her desk. Newspaper cuttings, lists, dog-eared magazines and more lists cluttered her workspace. She badly needed some sort of filing system.

Alan was collecting the children straight from school and taking them for the weekend and a part of her ached with the upheaval of it all. She tried to concentrate on her planning and not to think too much about her now disjointed family. Continuing to immerse herself in bits of paper and speculative figures the day flew by and soon she was in the kitchen setting the table for dinner with Daniel. A navy blue linen tablecloth contrasted sharply with the whiteness of the porcelain dinner plates. Eva polished the silver Newbridge cutlery that she saved for special occasions and placed a silver candelabra in the centre of the table. Next she put on some background music to fill the silence.

Herby butter was prepared to go with the potatoes. Made with softened butter, chopped scallions, chives and parsley, crushed garlic and a dash of lemon juice it was a perfect accompaniment to serve on baby potatoes with a juicy steak. The butter was wrapped in clingfilm and placed in the fridge.

Time was moving on and Eva had a quick shower before picking out her clothes for the evening. She chose to wear the silk slip skirt that she had bought for her surprise weekend away with Alan, with the cashmere top and the kitten heel slingbacks. *I may as well get some wear out of them,* she thought sadly.

The doorbell chimed as she was finishing off her make-up, nothing too dramatic just tinted moisturiser, subtle eyeshadow, mascara, black eyeliner and lip-gloss.

Daniel was armed with a bottle of red and a bottle of white wine.

'Didn't know which to go for, so I got both,' he said as she kissed his cheek and guided him into the living room.

He sank into one of the cream leather armchairs and Eva brought the wine to the kitchen where she poured them both a chilled Tio Pepe. On returning she handed him his drink and asked him to toast to her new beginning.

'To your new beginning Eva,' he replied a little awkwardly as he sipped his chilled sherry.

'Daniel about the last time, I am so sorry about how I treated you,' Eva's cheeks coloured slightly as she spoke.

'Shhh Eva, look nobody would react well to that kind of news and I am only sorry that it had to come from me.'

'Thank you Daniel, thank you for telling me.' She said as she did her best to quell the imminent tears and he gave her a reassuring hug.

They talked for a while about how the last two months had brought so many changes to her life and how things were affecting the kids. Eventually she paused and then said 'let's forget all that because it's depressing and I have you here under false pretences.'

'Really, what is it?'

'I need to pick your brains about something.'

'Intriguing,' he replied, 'pick my brains about what exactly?'

'Ah let me get the dinner going and we'll talk about it then. How about you opening that Merlot you brought and letting it breathe for a while.'

Daniel was a wealthy farmer who had inherited land from an Uncle and also ran the family farm. Being a well-established dairy and beef farmer with a pedigree milking herd he was very well off. With the land located near Kinsale he had also developed some of it with a cluster of holiday homes proving to be a goldmine. He also had some other property interests in the city and seemed to be a shrewd investor. Still a bachelor Eva knew that he longed to settle down and have a family of his own. He was an extremely good looking guy, tall with dark curly hair, sallow skin and beautiful brown eyes though Eva always saw him as her brother's friend.

Daniel did his best to help out as Eva got the cooking under way with his most useful skill being topping up their glasses. They moved on from the Tio Pepe to the wine and Eva took her time with the cooking as Daniel munched on some pistachios.

'Fillet Steak with a Whiskey Jus'

You will need: (Serves 2)
2 Irish beef fillet steaks (room temperature)
1 tbsp oil
Knob of salted butter
Sea salt and freshly ground black pepper to season
2 tbsp Irish whiskey & half tsp of ground black pepper for sauce

Method:
Heat a non-stick griddle pan or frying pan without any oil over a high heat. Place the steaks on a plate, drizzle them with a tablespoon of oil and season with ground sea salt and freshly ground black pepper.

Cook them for 3 minutes on each side for medium-rare, adding a knob of butter on top once turned onto the second side.

Once the steaks are cooked, transfer them to a wooden board to rest.

Deglaze the steak pan by turning the heat to high and splashing in the Whiskey and ½ teaspoon of ground black pepper. Turn the heat off but leave the pan on the hob until you're ready to serve.

Serve with baby potatoes topped with herby butter, the steaks with a little of the jus on top and a simple side salad.

[RECIPE ENDS]

Both she and Daniel preferred their steaks on the rare side of medium so three minutes a side was plenty. Eva was absolutely ravenous and their meal was scrumptious.

Having the adult company to share a bottle of wine with made the meal all the more enjoyable though Daniel was stretching his one glass by drinking water too as he had to drive home later.

'So what are you scheming anyway?' Daniel asked as he tucked into his steak.

'Well do you remember me waffling on about an Interior Design business?' she asked.

'Hmmm,' he replied

'I've decided that I'm going to give it a go.'

'Well are you now?'

'I am.'

'Good on you girl, I always knew you'd do it sometime.'

'Did you really?'

'Of course I did. Sure you've been going on about it for ages and I know you well enough to know that you're the kind of person who doesn't say something unless they mean it.'

Eva was delighted with Daniel's positive attitude. He didn't ask one doubtful question and gave her lots of sound business advice. But best of all he thought he might know of a property that would be an ideal location and said he would make some calls about it. When he left he told her not to raise her hopes but promised that he'd make a few calls and talk to her about the property he had in mind after the weekend.

Besides talking about her business venture it was inevitable that conversation came around once more to her marriage break-up. Daniel kept apologising for telling her but at the same time said himself that he had to. He thought too much of her to sit back and say nothing.

As Daniel only drank the one glass of wine with dinner Eva was quite weepy by the time she had gotten to the end of the bottle of Merlot. He hugged her warmly as he left and Eva was glad of the head haze from the wine as she made her way upstairs to her solitary bed in her empty house.

Waking with the dull thump of a vague hangover Eva did her best to rehydrate by downing two glasses of water before heading out to the shops. She spent most of Saturday going around computer shops and by the end of the day she had a new laptop and a printer in the back of the jeep with 'Intel Inside' and actually knew what that meant. Like anything, once you started to use the jargon you got more confident and by nine o'clock she was set up in her home office and making attempts to get her laptop online. The box room of the house was starting to look more like a real office now. She would have to go shopping for some sort of bookshelf for all of the magazines and clippings of paper that now found a home on the floor.

Sitting on her swivel chair she slowly read and meticulously followed the instructions until the computer connected to their broadband service. She couldn't believe that it had worked. She tested the set-up with a google search for 'Interior Design'. There were over two billion results to view! She searched for cushions, homeware and then candles, scrolling through pages of results. She went on refining her searches and searched for home furnishing in Cork. The results were being scaled back somewhat but still there were loads.

She started to play around with the spreadsheet package that Elaine had recommended and began to enter some figures. She dreamed up some imagined figures for the costs it would take to get her business up and running. Using the help facility she found a way to input a formula to add up her column of numbers and was mesmerized as she sat back and realized that as she changed a figure the formula automatically recalculated and the total was always updated and correct. She checked it a few times on her calculator before finally putting it in the drawer and trusting the machine. Eva had been working for hours since she had turned on her new laptop and her eyes were beginning to hurt from the glare. It was two o'clock in the morning before she dragged herself off to bed and she slept soundly until twelve noon.

Resisting the temptation to start up the laptop again Eva made herself a brunch of scrambled egg with crispy bacon and bagels and then went out for a walk and to buy the Sunday newspaper. The sun was shining and Eva sat out in her back garden to read the paper for a while. She could hear the sound of other children playing happily and was lonely for her own. But there was washing and ironing to be done and she busied herself with that until their return. Alan dropped the kids back at five o'clock and it was great to have their noises filling the house again. Luke squealed with excitement when he discovered the laptop in Eva's study and spent an hour exploring it. He was impressed that she had picked it out herself and how much faster than their pc it was – she didn't bother to tell him about being advised by Elaine, impressing Luke was not easy and she was going to hang onto this nugget of praise for herself. The evening passed too quickly and soon Eva was reading a bedtime story to Hannah who gave her a big hug before going to sleep.

Monday morning began with the usual chaos of chasing mislaid school bags, lunch boxes and missing shoes but eventually Eva found herself on the treadmill at the gym thinking about her business again. She had done a night class on Interior Design the winter that she had fallen pregnant with Luke and was trying to remember where she had put the notes that she had taken during the course. They had to be at home somewhere. Most people had been there for the fun of it or to get out in the evening but Eva had been there to learn. Working as a trainee furnishings buyer during the day she had been doing the course to advance her career but then Luke had arrived and she'd taken what she'd always thought of as a temporary career break. She had soaked it all up and learned all about colour wheels and how to go about accessorising a room. Different types of window dressing could change the entire feel of a room with sumptuous rich velvet curtains lending themselves to a room for relaxation whereas stark white window blinds would probably be more suited to a study. Of course a lot of it was a matter of personal taste and what appealed to one person might not appeal to another but you had to be true to your own tastes. There was no point in going with a look just because it was in if you didn't really like it and Eva realised that she would probably only stock what would appeal to her own tastes in her store. She knew that she couldn't be enthusiastic about something that she wouldn't like herself and hoped that her tastes would be appealing.

Eva had loved putting together the storyboards which had been their homework every week and she had kept them all, if only she could remember where they were. Maybe they were in the large chest with the children's school drawings and artwork or could they be lurking on top of a wardrobe. The storyboards were like pieces of art themselves. They were collages of paint samples, magazine cuttings, wallpaper and fabric samples and some included something from nature like a pebble or a seashell. Eva knew that she had made one that was inspired by the beach with pictures of driftwood, some smooth white pebbles and a scattering of sand. If you could create a room which conjured up the feel of fine warm beige sand, weather-worn timber decking, marram grass and the sounds of the sea that would have been Eva's idea of perfection, an oasis of calm. It was a scheme that would probably be more suited to a luxurious bathroom in a mansion or a health spa than in a regular semi-d but if you could realise it wouldn't it be bliss? A place to indulge, relax and escape.

Eva returned home and was showered and ready to work by eleven-thirty. The time at the gym had really eaten into her morning but it wasn't something that she could see herself giving up. Besides, she always felt more energised afterwards and believed there was a lot of truth in the suggestion that exercise releases happy hormones or pheromones or something positive anyway. She spent the bones of an hour ferreting around for the storyboards and when she found them she blue tacked them up onto her study wall. She also found a colour wheel and her office was beginning to look like the workplace of a real interior designer.

Sitting down at her new laptop she began to transfer her business plan from paper into a document. Her two finger typing started off slowly but picked up after a while and it did look a lot more impressive in print than handwritten. It was really starting to come together now and she called the accountant to arrange to go over the plan again the next day. Glancing at her watch she realised she was going to be late for the school pickup if she didn't hurry and ignored her mobile phone as it started to ring just as she was rushing out the door to pick up Luke and Hannah.

Bare cupboards once more necessitated a stop off for groceries on the way home. Shopping could be an awful drag sometimes. With the groceries hauled in and put away she tested Hannah's spellings before making a coffee and finally getting a chance to check her voicemail. There was one message and it was from Daniel saying to call her back as soon as she could. Eva was so excited as she hit callback that she could hardly breathe.

'Hi Daniel, how's it going? I just got your message and I'm dying to know what this news is.'

'Eva hi, well I think I may have a location for your business venture if you're interested?'

'Daniel, are you serious, where?' she replied eagerly.

'Do you know the new South Village development in Douglas?'

'You mean up towards the carpet shop?'

'Yes, just opposite that. Well basically there's an old Mill House that's been restored and turned into a complex of exclusive apartments with retail units on the ground level and I've just had confirmation that one is still available.'

'Wow that sounds amazing, how did you find out about all this?'

'Let's just say that I keep my ears open. Anyway the rent is as reasonable as you'll get for the area and it's bound to get snapped up soon so I'd advise you to have a look as soon as you can if you're interested.'

'Absolutely. When could I see it?'

'Would you be free for lunch tomorrow to look at the plans.'

'Of course, where will I meet you?'

'Say 'Barry's' for lunch oneish. I'll try and arrange to get access to the premises if I can. It's still very much a building site but it's in the final stages so you'll be able to get a good idea of the potential.'

Eva said goodbye, ended the call and stared at her phone. In her gut she felt a mixture of excitement, anguish and self-doubt.

What was she doing? A phone-call to Viv had her back on track again. Sure there was no harm in looking at the place and her plan wouldn't get the go ahead unless the bank thought it was sound so she should definitely give it a chance was Viv's reasoning.

With the children playing outside she went to her office again for a while. She pulled out a diary and looked at the dates. The month of May was almost over and with June about to start Eva would seriously have to sort out some child-minding options for the summer if the business was going to get the attention that it would need.

Chapter 7

(COTTAGE PIE)

Arriving early to meet Daniel at 'Barry's' bar and restaurant Eva felt nervous. It was buzzing as it was 'the' place in Douglas for a working lunch and there was plenty of schmoozing going on all around her. She ordered a coffee and people watched while waiting for Daniel.

Eva was agitated and kept watching the door for him. She sipped her coffee and fidgeted with her phone sending a text message to Viv to tell her what she was up to. She wished that Daniel would hurry up and come as she seemed to be the only person in the pub sitting alone and was beginning to feel a bit out of place. When Daniel finally arrived Eva couldn't contain her excitement as she pored over the building plans. It was a large open plan space except for two small rooms and a loo at the back. One room could maybe be a small storeroom and the other could be an office, but she'd need a lot more storage than that for bigger pieces.

'What about renting some warehouse space? I'm sure that's what a lot of furniture places do,' Daniel suggested.

'I hadn't even thought about storage until now Daniel, who am I kidding? I haven't a clue.'

'Eva, come on, don't talk negatively before you get started, you're just nervous. Look there's plenty of places where you can rent storage for your stock so just focus on the premises for now.'

'Okay, you're right. This place looks perfect on paper Daniel. The location is unbelievable. I just can't wait to see it.'

Eva couldn't eat a bite and waited impatiently for Daniel to finish his sandwich before heading for a tour of her potential future. The building was a renovated Mill-house that stood five proud red-bricked storeys in height. Apartments occupied the top four floors with the penthouse on the top floor having a private patio and garden space. The ground floor was divided into four large retail outlets and a restaurant. Three of them were ear-marked for an upmarket boutique, an exclusive beauty salon and a specialist wine outlet. Eva toured the last remaining unit with trepidation. It felt really spacious with one internal wall of beautiful exposed brickwork and the remainder roughly plastered. Eva visualized finishing it off with an off-white paint that would give a rustic whitewashed effect and of course leaving the natural brick wall exposed. Perfect. With plenty of connections for lighting in the ceiling there was a high electrical spec. throughout. Terms all sounded very reasonable. All she had to do was make the business work.

'Well Eva?' Daniel inquired. 'No pressure but the developer will need a decision on it as soon as possible.'

'How soon is soon?'

'Well I've asked him to reserve it for you for as long as possible but he will need to have your decision by the end of the week.'

'The end of the week, that is soon.'

'It's your decision Eva but I will say that a location like this won't come up every week.'

'I know yeah. It's perfect. When will it be ready?'

'There's still a lot of work to be done but you can take occupancy in September but can't do anything internally before then.'

'September,' Eva squealed, 'that would be brilliant.'

'Sleep on it tonight Eva and give me a call tomorrow.'

'No,' she said. 'My mind's made up. I really, really, want it.'

'Great. Well let me know how you get on with your bank manager and I'll arrange a meeting with the developer by the end of the week. You'll probably need to get an engineer's report sorted for the bank too but I can organize that for you if you want.'

The afternoon flew by and it was six o'clock by the time Eva got home. Alan had agreed to collect the kids after school and would be dropping them off at around eight after giving them dinner. This gave her a little bit of breathing space to gather her thoughts and calm down a bit. Realising that she was famished with hunger having skipped lunch she began to rummage in the fridge. She needed something quick and easy. Poking around she rooted out some cold cooked potatoes, a red pepper, mushrooms and onions. These were quickly chopped and sautéed in olive oil with a crushed clove of garlic and a big dash of paprika and ten minutes later she was enjoying the lot with a large dollop of sour cream and a chilled glass of Semillon-Chardonnay. Delicious. The colours of the food were warmth on a plate, the fiery paprika, the golden potato wedges and the sweet red peppers. Food was definitely a source of comfort and she savoured each tangy mouthful.

When the children were home and settled in bed she started up her laptop and opened a new spreadsheet giving it the name 'Wish List'. In this she listed all the products that she could think of that she would like to stock.

Tableware, glassware,

Knick-knacks and gadgets for kitchen and cooking,

Leather cushions and sumptuous velvet covered bean-bags

Dark wooden framed mirrors and picture frames.'

She wanted her stock to be unique and knew that she'd have to travel further afield than Ireland to get it. She decided to start her search with a trip to both Cape Cod and France. They were places that she was relatively familiar with and having travelled to both before she knew she would find things there that she liked. The antique markets in Paris were a treasure trove and would be a good starting point. Maybe she could stay with her friend Fiona there.

The thought of France had her fantasising. Raids of the cluttered Clignancourt markets could be followed by a trip to the south stopping off at Perpignan and then on to Collioure. Perhaps a visit to the open markets of Marseille would prove fruitful. They often featured on British programs as a hunting ground for antiques dealers. Perhaps some red wine from a Chateau could be a runner in her new store and she added it to her list. She quickly deleted the wine when licensing laws and customs and excise complications crossed her mind. Sure the supermarkets were already importing plenty of it and besides if one of the other outlets in the Mill was going to be a wine specialist store then they would be less than impressed with her if she was trying to compete with them.

Pottery and paintings from the sunny southernmost regions of France with influences of Picasso and Dali adding wild splashes of distorted still-life and vibrant colour were also added to her 'Wish List'. As for Cape Cod she wanted a section in her store with that white washed and sky-blue cotton look, everything with fresh clean lines. Something very all-American, perhaps with a nautical influence.

Tiredness eventually got the better of her and with a 'Wish List' that was now pages long she went to bed in the early hours of the morning.

A few days of intense preparation passed in a blur of paperwork, phone-calls and meetings and somehow Eva emerged at the end of it with an agreement with Alan. The alarm went off at seven on Thursday morning and she showered and dressed carefully for a meeting first at the accountants and then at the bank. Little had she thought the previous week when she had made the appointment with the bank that she would be under very real pressure to secure funding so that she could go ahead and lease an actual business premises.

Hannah admired Eva's suit at breakfast and told her that she looked very smart. Eva tried to eat a slice of toast but could hardly swallow the first bite as she felt so nervous so she abandoned it and sipped a coffee instead.

Eva loved the coffee making ritual that started her mornings and she loved trying out different types. Maybe coffee beans, grinders and cafetieres should be something she should sell and she made a mental note.

Giving herself a final appraisal as she reapplied her lip-gloss she knew she looked the part. Her black Max Mara trouser suit was an old staple. Time to go at last she thought as she started up her jeep with three copies of the business plan on the passenger seat beside her. With the kids in school she had a brief meeting with the accountant who raised an impressed eyebrow when he gave her plan the once-over, so far so good. With half an hour to kill before her meeting at the bank she attempted to distract herself by wandering around some of the boutiques in the old village quarter shopping centre.

Sitting waiting for her turn at the bank Eva felt a little like a disruptive teenager sitting outside the principal's office. It was very open with customers coming and going and queuing to do their business at various machines. When eventually she was summoned to a small office she steeled herself and went into presentation mode. An hour later she walked out euphoric. The manager had liked her plan and was very impressed that she had found such a prime location for the business. When asked how she had located it she had spoofed and replied that it had taken a lot of research and of course contacts to find the right place.

She had gone into the bank as a stay-at-home Mum and had left as a businesswoman. Meeting up with Daniel for lunch with an appetite that was well and truly intact she devoured a ciabatta steak sandwich along with a strong coffee.

Daniel was delighted for her. He made a call there and then to the business manager of the new development and arranged that the next day she would sign the lease. Saying goodbye to Daniel she thanked him again and headed into her new life. She was a businesswoman now and things would need to start happening very quickly. Her head was spinning with plans. She needed to get online and check out flights and dates for some buying trips. She needed to plan the layout of the store. She needed to find out about hiring staff. There was so much to do that her first priority would have to be to make yet another list. So after collecting the kids, while they did their homework she wrote a list of all the things that she needed to do and then tried to number them to prioritise where she should start. She called Viv to let her know the good news and invited her over after work for a bite to eat and a glass of wine.

Abandoning her list she set about making their dinner and decided on a comforting homely cottage pie. Once again she got Hannah to help her out.

'Cottage Pie'

You will need: (Serves 6)
10 to 12 medium-sized potatoes
1 tbsp olive oil
500g round steak mince
3 medium carrots
1 tsp mixed herbs
2 tbsp tomato puree
Butter for mashing and topping potatoes
500ml hot vegetable stock (from cube is fine)
300g frozen peas

Method:
Preheat the oven to 190°C/Gas Mark 6.
Peel the potatoes, cut to an even size and boil in a saucepan of boiling water until tender.
Heat the olive oil in a large frying or saucepan and brown the mince over a medium heat.
Meanwhile, peel and grate the carrots and set aside.
Add the mixed herbs to the browned mince and mix through.
Add the tomato puree to the meat and cook for 1 minute, then add the grated carrots.
When the potatoes are cooked, mash them with butter.
Make up the 500ml of vegetable stock in a jug of boiling water, add the frozen peas and leave to stand for 1 minute.

Pour the peas and stock into the bottom of a casserole dish. Top with the meat and carrot mix and then the mashed potatoes. Put a few dots of butter here and there on top of the potatoes. Cook in the oven for 30 minutes.

Serve hot with a garnish of chopped parsley.

[RECIPE ENDS]

The kids loved this tasty dinner and as much as they hated vegetables the disguised grated carrots were eaten without protest. Viv thoroughly enjoyed the home-cooked meal and had brought a Black Forest gateau for a celebratory dessert along with a bottle of Bollinger Champagne. Clinking glasses Eva savoured the moment and with her children smiling proudly at her she wanted to succeed more than ever.

Friday arrived and the week had flown by with so much happening that Eva could hardly take it in. After getting the kids to school she brewed up a fresh pot of coffee and took a piping hot mug of it with her to her study to phone Fiona. Eva felt a bit presumptuous ringing her out of the blue and asking if she would put her up when she came over to Paris however Fiona put her at ease straight away and was genuinely delighted to have her stay as she was always inviting her over to visit anyway. They had last met up the previous Christmas and had promised to keep in touch more often but the months had flown by yet again. Fiona was married to a gorgeous French guy called Philippe and they had one son Jacques who was almost four.

Eva couldn't fathom how Fiona managed to rear a child in a two-bedroom third storey apartment in central Paris. Okay so you have lots of parks and green space and interesting places to go for walks not to mention cafes but what about at three o'clock in the morning when your teething cranky baby has to be hushed so as not to upset the neighbours. There was no such thing as a lift either, so shopping, baby and buggy had to be hauled up three flights of stairs. Not easy, and with no family support nearby they got very few breaks in the early years. He had his mother's blue,

blue eyes and his father's chestnut brown hair and sallow skin. Eva could never figure out how French people and their kids had such shiny, healthy looking hair. And they always managed to look pristine and immaculately turned out. Healthy diet and sunshine, she thought. Abundant markets overflowed with fresh fruit and vegetables and sunshine every summer. They always looked so polished and no matter how glammed up Eva was she always felt just a little bit shabby when she was in Paris.

After exchanging email addresses and discussing dates Eva set about searching online for flights.

It was early June already and Eva needed to get all her travel arrangements made as soon as possible. She could order a lot of things through catalogues if she desired but she wanted to source some truly unique items personally.

As well as making plans for herself she also needed to think about the children's summer. Alan hadn't mentioned the summer holidays yet and Eva knew it would be up to her to see that they had a good one. They would be finishing up school in three weeks' time and Eva wanted to check out some summer camps for them. She knew that she would need most of her time this summer to make arrangements for her store but she also wanted to make it a memorable summer for them. Luke could go to soccer camp for a week in July and August and Hannah could go to a sports activities camp on those weeks.

Eva eventually decided on eight nights in total for the trip to France and telephoned Alan to figure things out before booking her flights. He said that he would take some time off in July for holidays so she could work around those dates. As for a later trip to Boston and Cape Cod, Alan suggested that the kids could maybe stay with his parents for that week. This was going to be easier than she had anticipated as Alan was being surprisingly accommodating. With the premises located all she had to do now was find the right stock and fit out the store and she had the entire summer to do it. The kids would love the prospect of going down to the farm and doing their jobs and that was where they always stayed when she and Alan went away for breaks so they were well used to it. The thought of their last break together made her catch her breath. *I wonder does his girlfriend know that he was still sleeping with me then?* 'Stop it' Eva she told herself softly, 'stop looking back.'

After talking to Alan she went online again and booked her flights to France. She was going to go to Paris for four full days to scour the markets there and then on south to Perpignan for three more days where she hoped to source some things with a Spanish or Mediterranean influence.

She knew that she would have to telephone her mother-in-law Mary to talk to her about the dates in August. They hadn't spoken properly since the split. The children had seen her on some of the Sundays that Alan had minded them and they had visited her on the farm. Thinking about it, Eva decided that it would be better to talk to her in person and put it off for a few more days.

After booking her French flights and emailing the details to Fiona she started browsing online again. This time she was looking for a holiday for herself and the kids. She didn't want to go abroad and came up with a lovely renovated cottage in a village called Goleen on the coastline of West Cork and booked it for the last week in July hoping that the weather would be good.

It was almost lunchtime and Eva had to get the papers for the lease signed before collecting the kids from school. What a morning. The Paris trip was planned, the Cape Cod trip was on the cards, holidays with the kids were sorted and summer camps were booked. She took her time doing her make-up and gave herself a subtle smokey looking eye accentuated with a gel eyeliner. A spritz of Chanel perfume and 'on y va' she said to herself.

Chapter 8

(QUICHE LORRAINE)

The kids were buzzing with excitement when she picked them up from school. It was Friday after all, which meant no homework and the sun was shining.

Eva surprised them on the drive home when she announced that they would go to Fota Wildlife Park on Saturday after swimming lessons. 'Yay,' they chorused.

'Can Mark come too?' Luke asked about his best friend.

'Why not?' Eva replied ' as long as his Mum and Dad say it's okay'.

'You mean his Mum *or* his Dad' Luke corrected 'they don't live together anymore either.'

'Oh.'

They were momentarily quiet until Hannah piped up with 'what about Susie?'

'Of course. Susie can come too.'

Eva knew that it would be easier with the pals than without them anyway so the more the merrier. Having their friends around would distract Luke and Hannah from their usual annoying squabbles over petty little things like where to sit in the jeep and how far to put down the window.

Saturday afternoon saw them heading for the wildlife park on Fota Island just outside the city. It was really well laid out with lots of different animals but the new baby giraffes were definitely

Hannah's favourite. Eva strolled as the children sped excitedly ahead from one enclosure to another. Most of the animals weren't enclosed at all though as it was more like a safari park than a zoo there was so much freedom there.

They spent a happy three hours exploring the park stopping off at the café for some pizza and ice-cream and of course a coffee for Eva. As they ate, three kangaroos causally hopped past them and went down to the water's edge. The place was teeming with peacocks and all kinds of birds and they wandered about completely relaxed in their surroundings.

The kids were exhausted after several attempts to outdo each other on climbing frames and monkey bars and were ready for a quiet evening when they got home. They watched a silly game-show together and shared some Häagen-Dazs chocolate ice-cream straight out of the tub until it was scraped clean.

On Sunday Eva took them to the leisure club for a swim and then to a hotel for a carvery lunch afterwards. A swim always meant they were hungry afterwards and they all polished off their Sunday roasts.

Eva casually told them about how her business would mean that she would need to take some trips away in the summertime. Hannah was still excited about the prospect of owning a shop but Luke was a bit more sedate and with a long face asked 'what about us?'

Eva explained that their Dad would look after them and that they would also have a holiday on their grandparent's farm and that cheered him up. Hannah began babbling about her upcoming school tour and Luke chimed in until each one of them was talking over the other and not quite making sense but Eva let them talk away, happy with the normality of it all.

Monday started another week of school and lots of free time for Eva to work. She sat at her desk a lot of the time writing lists and drinking way too much coffee. With all the benefits that her laptop gave her, deleting on a keyboard would never give the same satisfaction as crossing an item off by hand. By the time she stopped for lunch she had several new lists. She had 'Fitting out

Shop,' 'Buying Trip to France,' and 'Buying Trip to U.S.' Her favourite list was called 'Product Range – Wish List,' and then there was the boring but necessary list called 'Legal and Business Admin Stuff,' and finally 'Groceries.'

She would have to do yet another big grocery shop after picking the kids up from school. Her own lunch consisted of a crust of toasted bread topped with melted cheddar, chopped red onion and black pepper. While it was scrumptiously tasty it was more or less the last of the food in the house. As she was out of both teabags and coffee she had washed it down with diluted orange cordial, not the greatest combination in the world and she felt parched for a cup of tea. Time to stock-up.

Checking the cupboards she added 'butter and flour' to her list of groceries. She was in the mood for baking something with pastry. This mood didn't often descend, maybe once every six months but when it did she thoroughly enjoyed it.

There was nothing like the smell of home-baking wafting through the kitchen.

Remembering some scented candles that she had seen in a magazine recently that were supposed to give off the aroma of home-baking she wondered should she try and source some for her store. There were others that smelled like coffee and vanilla too. She added scented candles to her 'Product Wish List'.

A couple of hours later she was home again with the shopping put away.

She pulled out aprons for both herself and Hannah to get messy with flour. They made enough pastry for three quiches, a dozen sausage rolls and two apple pies.

A quiche and apple pie were for their own tea and the sausage rolls were for school lunches. She would freeze a quiche and take the remaining quiche and apple pie down to her mother-in-law's on Tuesday.

Eva had mastered pastry making by sticking to a fool proof no nonsense recipe for short-crust pastry; it dated back to an old secondary school cookery book for a home economics class.

Eva liked to add leek to her Quiche Lorraine instead of onion.

'Bacon and Leek Quiche Lorraine' Part I

First make short-crust pastry which will need to rest in the fridge for at least 30 minutes.

Shortcrust pastry
You will need:
250g plain flour
125g butter (cold)
½ tsp salt
1 egg yolk
3 tbsp water
Flour for dusting and kneading, etc.

Method:
Sift the flour into a bowl, chop the butter into cubes and rub it in with your fingertips until the mixture resembles fine breadcrumbs.

Stir in the salt and then use a fork to begin to bring the dough together with the egg yolk and the cold water.

Use your hands to gather the pastry dough into a ball and then knead it lightly on a floured board.

Shape into a ball, wrap in cling film and press out into a disc shape and leave to rest in the fridge for at least 30 minutes before use.

'Bacon and Leek Quiche Lorraine' Part II

You will need:
1 quantity shortcrust pastry (above)
1 leek
40g unsalted butter
8 bacon rashers
8 eggs
3 tbsp Dijon mustard
200ml cream

250g Gruyere or any hard cheese (a combination of cheddar and Parmesan works well)
Sea salt and ground pepper
Flour for dusting
Butter to grease tin

Method:
Divide the pastry in two and roll each half out on a floured board, and use to line a 20cm loose-bottomed greased cake tin
Chill the pastry in the fridge for 15 minutes, then prick the base of the pastry with a fork, line it with parchment paper and fill with pie weights or dry beans.
While the pastry lined tins are chilling, preheat the oven to 160°C/Gas Mark 4.
Bake blind in the preheated oven for 15 minutes. Remove the beans and parchment paper and return the pastry case to the oven for 5–10 minutes, until very lightly coloured.
While the pastry is baking blind, prepare the filling.
Slice the leek in half lengthways and rinse under a cold tap. Finely slice the leek and rinse again in a colander (as the leek grows in layers dirt can get trapped in between).
Chop the rashers with kitchen scissors.
Melt the butter in a frying pan and gently fry the leeks and rashers over a low to medium heat for 10 minutes until the leeks soften.
Whisk the eggs, Dijon mustard and cream together in a bowl.
Grate the cheese and add to the egg mixture, season with salt and black pepper and add the leek and bacon and pour into the part-baked pastry cases.
Bake at 180°C/Gas Mark 6 for 25–30 minutes or until set and golden.

[RECIPE ENDS]

The next morning, after the school run, Eva set off to visit her mother-in-law who lived about fifteen miles outside the city.

Armed with her apple-pie and quiche she felt apprehensive as she approached the door.

Mary however, was delighted to see her and she greeted her like a long lost friend.

Wiping away a tear Mary brewed up a pot of tea and cut them both a thick slice of apple pie.

'Eva I'm thrilled that you came,' she said. 'I was worried that you wouldn't want to see me anymore.'

'Oh Mary of course I'll always want to see you,' Eva replied.

'I don't want to pry Eva and I don't want to upset you but is there any hope for you and Alan?'

Eva shook her head slowly. 'I'm afraid not Mary,' she replied sadly with tears in her eyes, 'our marriage is over and he has finished it off completely by moving in with his girlfriend.'

'I'm sorry love. I'm so sorry. And I'm so cross with him. He tells me nothing you know and I'd be afraid he'd get odd if I ask too much. He brought the kids out for dinner the Sunday before last and it was just so lovely to see them.'

'I know, they told me all about it. They love visiting here. Actually Mary, the main reason I'm here is to ask you for a big favour. I'm hoping to go over to Boston and stay with my friend Elaine in August. It'll be a bit of a business trip actually and I was wondering could you take the kids for a week or ten days?'

'I'd be delighted to Eva, delighted,' she beamed. 'Anytime at all, you know I love to see those kids.'

'And they love to see you. Hannah says her favourite chore is collecting the eggs on Gran's farm and wants to know why we can't have a hen shed.'

'A hen shed in the city,' Mary chuckled. 'I'm sure your neighbours would love you for the noise and the smell.'

'I'm sure they would.'

'Eva there's something you said and I know I shouldn't pry but...'

'Go ahead Mary, what is it?'

'Well it's just, are you sure that Alan has moved in with someone else? I just can't imagine it.'

'Am I sure? Well to be honest I haven't asked but I presume that's where he went when he moved out as there were still tenants in the apartment back then.'

'But he didn't Eva.'

'He didn't what?'

'He didn't move in with someone else after he left home. No Eva love, he came here. He just turned up and said he couldn't talk about it but needed to stay for a while.'

'Oh.' Eva was truly baffled.

'Yes love, he stayed here for two weeks and then he moved into the apartment and he hasn't said anything about a girlfriend or anyone else.'

'Really? I just presumed that that was where he went.'

'But are you sure there is a girlfriend?'

'Of course there is. Sure Daniel was the one who told me?'

'I see. I'm sorry for asking Eva, I just don't want it to be true.'

'I know.'

After finishing another cup of tea it was time for Eva to leave and Mary hugged her warmly before she left. Eva felt happier inside knowing that there were no bad feelings between her and her mother-in-law. If anything it was the opposite and it was good to know that they could still stay close. Mary was always going to have a special place in Eva's heart and was like the mother that she had never really known. Mary had helped them out so much in the first couple of months when Luke was a baby and again when Hannah arrived. She had come over and cooked their dinners and baked her renowned brown bread. She was like a mother to Eva and it meant the world to her that they could stay close. It would be through Eva's children rather than Mary's son now but they would have that bond forever no matter what happened between her and Alan.

She could see how disappointed she was in Alan and how desperate she was for them not to break up. It was a surprise alright though, to learn that Alan hadn't been shacking up with the mistress though. *What was the story there?* Eva wondered, *was she living with him now as she suspected and if she was, where did she go when the kids were over for the weekend? Maybe they weren't living together at all.*

Not that that should make any difference. But it kind of did.

Eva collected both Luke and Hannah from school and told them about her visit to Mary's. Hannah was particularly delighted to hear about staying on the farm in August.

'Did Gran say I could help with the eggs and the baking?' she queried.

'Of course she did sweetheart. She loves to have you to help out.'

The following weekend the Saturday came out gloriously warm and there was nothing for it but to have a barbecue. Eva had never done one on her own before but decided what the hell, it would just be a few friends, neighbours and mostly kids who wouldn't care if all they got was pan-fried cocktail sausages. How hard could it be to light a few coals?

Viv came over early and stayed with Hannah and Luke while Eva went shopping. She was a little nervous about it and overloaded her shopping trolley with twice as much as she actually needed. Just in case, just in case, it would never do to run out

She had to push the trolley at an angle as the wheels were refusing to go in the right direction as she struggled awkwardly to the car.

Eva squashed the shopping bags into the boot and others onto seats and tried to secure the drinks on the floor of the front passenger seat with some rolls of kitchen paper to wedge it still, however a bottle of wine still managed to roll around threateningly but made it home intact.

Viv helped her to bring everything in and Hannah over-zealous in her unpacking sent a tub of garlic stuffed olives onto the floor.

'Oh shit,' said Hannah.

'Hannah!' Eva said sternly, 'I've told you not to use that language.'

Eva glanced at Viv who was biting her lower lip and trying to keep a straight face.

'Sorry Mum.'

'Okay but don't let me hear it again,' Eva scolded as she began to mop up the mess with paper towel.

'Look Hannah, can you empty that other tub of olives into one of the small black bowls and cut the feta cheese into cubes and stick in a few cocktail sticks and I'll finish the unpacking.'

'Anything for me to do?' asked Viv and Eva gave her instructions on prepping some veggie skewers for the barbecue, stringing together cherry tomatoes, mushroom slices and chunks of red onion and mixed peppers.

Eva tossed together the Caesar salad ingredients that came ready to mix from a bag. She opened some dips and chips and all that remained was to light up the coals.

Luke was dying to be the chef so an hour later as he turned burgers Eva sipped a viognier and began to relax. Daniel arrived with a couple of bottles of wine and began to help Luke outside. He was very sociable and mixed easily with the small gathering of friends and neighbours.

'He's great with kids Eva isn't he,' Viv said to Eva as they were clearing up in the kitchen afterwards. They could see Daniel out in the garden organizing five-aside football and making sure to include Hannah.

'He is. He's been great Viv. He's really given me support with my business plans too.'

'Smart and good-looking,' Viv teased as she went back out to the garden to refill some glasses.

Eva looked out at Daniel and probably for the first time in a long time saw him as a man rather than as a friend and quite a good looking man at that. He kept in shape and was lucky enough not to have inherited a receding hairline. Abandoning the washing up she joined Viv in the garden and enjoyed the rest of the evening with her friends.

The sun continued to shine faithfully for the remainder of June and Eva and the kids dined al fresco most weekends that they were with her. They'd cook inside and bring their dishes out onto the patio and eat at the garden table during the week. The school holidays were looming and Eva still had a mountain of arrangements to make. She was determined to give the kids a good time as well as looking after her business venture. As long as she could get three or four hours of work done during the day and maybe a further two when they were gone to bed she hoped this would be enough to keep on top of everything.

Eva booked her flight to Boston for August and emailed the details to Elaine. Every few days she would visit the business premises to keep an eye on progress and it was all going according to schedule.

The kids got their holidays on the last Friday in June and finishing on a half-day Eva whisked them straight from school to Inchydoney Island beach for the remainder of the afternoon. Lots of other Mums obviously had the same idea as the place was thronged. It was warm enough to tog off and paddle around and for those brave enough to take a dip it was chilly going down but once you got used to it was worth the initial icy Atlantic plunge.

Eva got engrossed in her favourite seaside activity of beach-combing while the kids paddled and ran to join her periodically. She loved strolling slowly scrutinising the sand for the perfect pebble or shell, driftwood would be a real find. She knew you weren't really supposed to take these things from the beach but it wasn't as if she drove off with half a ton of sand in the boot of her car, just the odd handful of pebbles and seashells. Hannah loved to help out while Luke made friends with anyone who had a ball or showed an interest in his.

They finished off the day with pub-grub in the nearby hotel. As the kids tucked into their curly fries a wave of sadness came over Eva. She thought of Alan and tears came into her eyes. They had spent a weekend at the same hotel for Valentine's a few years ago. It had been fantastic. Sipping pints as they watched international rugby in a pub in nearby Clonakilty, romantic walks on the beach in the late afternoon, pampering treatments in the spa, savouring aperitifs while perusing the dinner menu.

Her throat suddenly felt sore and raw and she swallowed hard to stop herself from blubbering. Had he gone on romantic breaks with the mistress she wondered and what were they doing now? Would she ever be over him? Would she ever stop caring?

The kids soon distracted her with pleas for ice-cream so they paid up and left the hotel and picked up some 99s from an ice-cream van on the way home.

Later that evening when the kids were in bed, worn out from the sea-air, Eva went online and started seriously planning her trip to Paris.

Antiques markets were going to be her main focus in Paris. She had visited some years ago but that was just for fun. She planned to see what was available and hopefully buy enough for her French section to keep going until the Spring. She also toyed with the idea of asking Fiona to do some buying for her. The thought of heading southwards to Perpignan on her own really excited her. The weather would be glorious in July and she pictured herself dining at exquisite restaurants in between hunting for unusual pottery and hand painted silk wall hangings. Clignancourt looked like the best bet for antiques hunting in Paris. It was located a little bit out from the center of Paris but she hoped that public transport would make it easy to access.

Eva emailed Fiona and told her that she hoped to visit the antiques market each day and wondered if she would be able to go with her any day. She would stay in Paris for four days and then fly down to Perpignan by herself.

The next day, Saturday, was spent catching up on the laundry as Eva wanted to be completely on top of the housework before she headed off to Paris.

Daniel popped in for lunch and as it was a surprise 'just passing' visit Eva wasn't at all prepared. She rooted around the fridge and came up with a very passable salad and defrosted the remaining quiche that she had made with Hannah.

Daniel tucked in heartily and quizzed her about her trip to Paris. Hannah and Luke were in and out so their conversation was very broken but he did assure her that he would check progress on her premises at least once while she was away and she could phone him from France to check if there were any problems.

'You're only going for a week, Eva' he jibed.

'Yeah I know, I know,' she replied, 'but time is flying by and I just want to keep on top of things.'

Daniel had plenty going on too it seemed, he had just recently hired a farm manager and had freed his own time up to pursue his other interests.

'Sounds like you're mad busy too' Eva probed.

'I'm in the middle of something alright but you know yourself there's always something to be doing.'

'Hmmm…you're a bit of a cagey fish aren't you Daniel?' mused Eva.

'Sure you know what they say about holding your cards close to your chest?'

'Ah I'm only slagging you Daniel.'

'I know. I just don't like talking things up until I know where I stand.'

'I know what you mean. I'm like a super sleuth myself and haven't said anything to the neighbours about opening the store. I'd say half of them are convinced I'm having an affair of my own, I'm so evasive about my comings and goings these days.'

Daniel hung around and played soccer with the kids in the back garden for a little while before he headed away. Just minutes after he left the doorbell chimed and Eva thought he must have forgotten something but was surprised to see Viv standing there instead.

'Viv, how are you? I thought you were Daniel, he just left.'

'Yeah I just literally bumped into him as he was coming out. So you're Miss Popular today aren't you?' she teased.

'Ha, ha,' Eva replied dryly, 'you know full well he's just a friend.'

Viv had a carrier bag full of summer clothes with her.

'I thought you might like to borrow these for France,' she offered, handing over the bag.

'Wow,' Eva was chuffed when she pulled out a couple of cotton summer dresses.

One was pale pink with a tiny daisy printed pattern and the other was primrose yellow with a halter neck and very low back.

97

Viv stayed for tea and they nattered away about everything and anything until it was bedtime for the kids. Viv had dumped her latest short-lived fling and had some new guy in mind, apparently she had been interested in him for a few months but he had yet to show any real interest.

When the kids were in bed and Viv was gone home Eva had a long soak in the bath. She gave herself a good scrubbing with a sea-salt based exfoliating scrub before getting out. She planned to put on fake tan in the morning so she slathered body lotion all over herself and took her time rubbing it in. She read some magazines for a little while until she drowsily drifted off into dreamland. A light tapping sound on the bedroom door woke her. The door opened very slowly and there was Hannah and Luke struggling with a breakfast tray between them.

'Happy Birthday,' they chorused.

'What a lovely surprise, thank you soooo much,' Eva injected as much enthusiasm as she could muster at seven o'clock in the morning.

The kids were chuffed with themselves, and piled into the bed beside her and they all munched happily on very crispy toast with marmalade washed down with orange juice. She silently toasted her thirty-seven year old self.

'Do you have to go away to Paris Mummy?' Hannah asked solemnly.

'Oh sweetheart, it's only for a week pet, and Daddy will mind you and you'll have Luke as well.'

'But I want you Mum,' her voice was faltering and her eyes were beginning to water.

'And I want you sweetie, so I will only be gone for eight sleeps and then I'll be back. And I'll bring you something nice. Sure I won't be going until next week so I'll tell you what, we'll do whatever you want to do today.'

'Can we go to the toyshop?' asked Luke.

'And can we go to McDonalds?' Hannah implored.

'Alright, here's the deal, you get dressed and go downstairs and watch TV while I get ready and then we'll go into town and maybe buy something to bring to Daddy's and then go to McDonalds, okay?'

'Deal,' said Luke.

'Deal,' echoed Hannah as they bolted out the door to get ready. Eva swept the crumbs off the duvet and onto the floor easing herself slowly out of bed. Today will be their day she promised herself, no work talk, no distractions, just them.

After a quick shower she stood in front of the full-length mirror and carefully applied her tan. *Here's hoping for no streaks,* she thought to herself. After five minutes of lolling around the bedroom in the nip and then struggling to get a suitcase down from the top shelf of her walk-in wardrobe, she put on an old navy dressing gown and went downstairs.

'Mum why aren't you dressed yet?' Hannah asked aghast at the state of her mother.

'I just need one cup of coffee first,' Eva pleaded, 'and another five minutes for this tan to dry a bit,' she added in a whisper. You could dress straight away if you believed what it said on the bottle but Eva didn't trust that notion and liked giving the tan a bit of time to settle. Taking her coffee up to her room she almost tripped over the suitcase and pushed it under the bed anticipating packing for her Paris trip. Sitting at her dressing table she filed her nails giving the tan just a bit more time to soak in. She opened her birthday cards and a present that Viv had left for her, a simple gold bracelet. Scrolling through birthday messages on her phone there was nothing from Alan.

Twenty minutes later she was dressed. She wore faded denims and a blue Sweaty Betty sweatshirt with trainers. She didn't want to wear anything too clingy as her tan developed.

'So we're off then,' she called to the kids as she stood jangling her keys in the hallway.

After a fairly clear run they had the jeep parked in the city multi-storey car park by half-past one. Eva was tempted to call into the homeware section of the department store but reminded herself that despite it being her birthday today was a day for the kids and headed out through the automatic doors and down Maylor Street

99

to Smyth's Toys. An hour passed easily and they both got what they wanted.

They then strolled across Patrick's Bridge and down MacCurtain Street to an entertainment centre. Eva picked up the Sunday paper in a newsagent's on the way and happily read while Luke and Hannah went into the play zone. Luke was back after fifteen minutes complaining that it was boring so they decided to do some bowling instead. Eva played with them and was sure that the Dad in the next lane was giving her the eye, perhaps it was her imagination but she was sure that he had smiled at her and it felt strange.

By the time they crossed back over the river they were all ravenous and Eva convinced them to go for a freshly baked pizza and homemade ice cream at a nice restaurant rather than a 'happy meal'. Dipping a spoon into Hannah's 'Death by Chocolate', Eva people-watched from the café window looking onto Oliver Plunkett Street, admiring some of the style. Eva dug down to the bottom of Hannah's dessert to scrape out a spoonful of warm chocolatey syrup mingled with chocolate ice cream.

They finished up and drove home via Douglas village stopping off at the park on the way. Luke was getting too old for it and preferred to kick his ball around but Hannah still loved the climbing frames, slides and rope bridges. Sitting on a bench Eva looked around and wondered for the second time that day whether it was her imagination or was she on the receiving end of an admiring eye. Nope, she caught him again. This guy was definitely looking at her. She didn't reciprocate but it did feel nice to be noticed. She had long forgotten what that felt like. It felt nice.

The first weekend of the school holidays came to an end and Eva had just one more week to go before heading off to Paris. As she tucked the kids into bed that night and looked at their content wiped out faces she had serious misgivings about going to Paris. There had been so much upheaval in their short lives over the past few months that it didn't seem fair to take off and leave them for a week. And what if something happened to her? She wrote a note to herself to look into updating her will and with some morbid thoughts filling her head she tried to get to sleep.

Despite a fitful night things did not seem as dubious in the morning and she reminded herself that she needed to stop thinking about everybody else. She made arrangements with Alan to come and collect the kids and take them over to his place that Thursday evening because she would be flying out early on Friday morning.

Eva had yet to see Alan's house. He had recently decided to move from the city centre apartment to the suburbs as he didn't think it was suitable for the children. He was now living in a four bedroom detached house in a new development in Ballincollig. With the link road to the city there was a vast amount of development being undertaken in the area, it was set to become the 'new Douglas' apparently. She didn't know what the story was with his girlfriend and whether she had moved in with him or not but Eva had made it quite clear that under no circumstances would she tolerate the kids staying over with Alan and him having another woman there. She never came straight out and asked the kids if she was ever there and would just ask them if it was just them and their Dad in the house at the weekend or did anybody call. So far Alan seemed to be abiding by her wishes and surely he knew himself that it wouldn't be right for them to see another woman in their father's life so soon.

Eva had avoided any chances of meeting the new girlfriend as well, curious and all as she was to see her in the flesh. Daniel had described her as a brunette and said she worked with Alan and was young and Eva didn't want to know any more than that for now. What would it be like to meet this other woman? Would she be able to stop herself from lashing out at her? She had visions of grabbing her by the hair, dragging her to the ground and banging her head off the pavement; she could almost hear the hollow thud of skull on concrete. Or a slap. A really sharp satisfyingly stinging slap that connected perfectly with her cheek.

That kind of thinking did her no good at all and so she just tried to accept it. Maybe this girl had seduced Alan but whatever way things were played out he was the married one and he was the betrayer. Saying goodbye to the kids as they drove off with their

101

father on Thursday evening was really, really hard. It had taken the bones of an hour to pack up for Hannah and Luke. She had packed their clothes while they decided what games and gadgets to bring and seemed to be quite excited by the whole escapade. But Eva wasn't excited with her head full of second thoughts, and as she had folded little vests for Hannah and put in her 'blankie' she began to cry.

The kids didn't notice her red watery eyes as she forced smiles and hugged them at the door as they left with Alan. 'Yes I'll bring you back something nice,' she answered as they waved goodbye to her from the car.

Chapter 9

(SALMON WITH CORIANDER & LIME)

Packing for the trip to France was a joy. She threw in the pretty summer dresses that Viv had loaned her plus some of her own and a classy black dress for evening wear. Next she carefully packed a cropped white palazzo trousers, an assortment of silk tops and high heeled sandals. Denim shorts and a selection of tees followed next along with comfortable trainers for all the walking and lastly flip-flops and two bikinis just-in case.

Packing her make-up and jewellery took longer than the clothes. She had some travel size bottles of cleanser and moisturizer but everything else was full size and took up a lot of room. She gave up trying to eliminate stuff and ended up with one big bag and one medium size bag and of course her handbag.

One restless night's sleep later and Eva was on her way. She left her jeep at Cork airport and soon checked in, ridding herself of the bigger piece of luggage. The airport was buzzing with holidaymakers. Eva always enjoyed flying as the whole experience made her feel very cosmopolitan for a little while. You were taking part in a bit of a fantasy as nobody knew who you were and in your own head you could be someone famous just jetting off to Paris on a whim. She browsed in the newsagents and picked up a romance novel and a couple of magazines. In duty-free she bought a Clinique travel pack and Lancome's Miracle eau de Toilette for Fiona and an Yves St Laurent Touche Eclat concealer pen for herself. She swore by Touche Eclat, it gave a bit of radiance and covered up at the same time and was a saviour the morning after a late night out. One of the magazines she had bought was of course on interior design in Ireland and she sat browsing and coveting many items before her flight was called. Looking at what was available gave her cold feet about her imminent venture but just momentarily.

I will be a success, she reassured herself as she tried to visualise an advertisement for her shop in the magazine. *It will have something for everyone and every price bracket,* she promised herself as she glossed through the pages. She wanted people to feel comfortable shopping in her store. No pushy sales people and plenty of space to browse. Most of all she wanted her place to be welcoming, not somewhere where once you were in you felt a bit trapped and obliged to buy. She decided to make a list of the stores that made her feel like that and work out why and see if she could avoid that somehow.

Arriving into Charles de Gaulle airport alone was intimidating. Crowds of people all busily going in various directions and Eva felt like she was standing out like a whimpering lost puppy as she went to collect her baggage. She was to meet up with Fiona at an Irish bar, The James Joyce. It mightn't be the chosen Parisian rendezvous of a seasoned traveller but for Eva it gave her comfort that the next part of her journey would see her arriving at something familiar.

She hesitantly followed Fiona's directions and located the 'Air France' bus stop just outside Terminal 1. She was to get the bus to Porte Maillot and noticed the name was painted on the ground.

After a ten minute wait the bus arrived but it was already quite full, chaos reigned as people pushed to get on and Eva held her ground and was one of the last allowed to board. There was only one seat available at the back so she struggled down to it only to be greeted, or rather not greeted, by an ignoramus with his bag plonked on the last unoccupied seat on the bus.

It took just a little bit too long for him to move the bag so that by the time Eva sat down she was feeling a little bit peeved.

Breathing deeply she distracted herself from her ignorant companion by looking out the window of the bus as it made its way into the Paris bound traffic and an 'IKEA' sailed by. Fiona had instructed her that there was an underground shopping mall that she could browse through at Porte Maillot if she arrived early and 'The James Joyce' pub was close by.

Eva disembarked at the bus stop, reclaimed her bags and glancing across the street she identified the pub. With an hour to kill before meeting Fiona she decided to go and browse the mall, which was deceptively large and sprawled in all directions underground. Having lugged her baggage over to the entrance to the mall she discovered that as it was Friday most of the shops were really busy. She couldn't face battling through people with luggage and turned around again to go back and cross the road to the pub. It was dark inside and smelled of spilled stale beer but her eyes quickly adjusted and she ordered a coffee. Choosing to perch herself on a high stool in view of the door she ordered from the friendly Irish barman and began to flick through her magazine again. She felt really excited about the prospect of visiting the markets. She had been to Clignancourt once before and had spent half a day browsing around and had loved it.

Eva sipped her coffee slowly and browsed through her magazine glancing towards the door every time it opened until at last Fiona arrived and greeted her warmly with kisses on each cheek. She looked tanned, healthy, and of course groomed. They left without delay as Fiona was badly parked outside the pub and drove to her apartment block.

Parking was accessed underground through automated garage doors with a keypad for security code entry to open the door. Each apartment had its own separate lock-up. Again there was a door to this that was automated but Eva had to get out of the car and take her luggage out of the boot before Fiona backed in. The space was extremely tight. 'That's the French for you,' Fiona said 'they waste nothing'.

Going from the parking area through another heavy door that required another code Eva followed Fiona up some stairs to the

105

ground floor. There was a concierge office where any maintenance issues were dealt with and the front wall of the building that exited onto the street was completely made of glass. Another glass wall at the back exited to a small garden area nicely laid out with mature shrubs, some seating, a bird table and a sand-pit for kids. All the glass flooded light into the lobby area of the building and the impression was that it was airy and very well looked after.

While the ground floor had been bright, Fiona's third-floor apartment seemed dark at first but there were net curtains in place that were obscuring much of the light. The apartment looked onto the street below and had a sizeable veranda with a table and chairs, but it also faced another apartment block directly opposite and Eva could see the need for the curtains. Fiona's furnishings were mostly old French antique pieces. There was a beautiful writing bureau and the light fittings were crystal chandeliers. She also had two rather funky orange leather couches and a black 'Le Corbusier' chaise longue. While it was an eclectic mix of furnishings it all worked really well together. 'Wow,' Eva said, looking around and admiring the room, 'this is absolutely gorgeous'.

'Thanks Eva, do you really like it?'

'Of course, it's divine. I love your couches.'

'Well have a seat and I'll get us a drink.'

'Sounds good,' said Eva as she sat down and took in the details of her surroundings.

The kitchen area was just inside the front door of the apartment and extremely compact, functional, but definitely compact. There was a shelving unit between the living area and kitchen with a glass back that allowed you to see into the kitchen and let some natural light in too. On the other side of the apartment were three doors. Two were bedrooms and the other the bathroom. There were only two windows in the entire apartment, they were very large though. One was in the living room and had access to the outside veranda looking onto the street and the other was in the main bedroom again facing the street.

Fiona emerged from the kitchen with two glasses of Rosé wine.

'I recognize these glasses do I?' asked Eva.

'Yes! They were your wedding present. John Rocha for 'Waterford Glass' I believe?

'Indeed!'

The glasses were lovely and solid to hold and featured an indented design.

Fiona returned to the kitchen and after a couple of minutes she emerged with a wooden board heaped with crusty bread, pâte, thinly sliced Parma ham, some cheese and a bunch of large juicy grapes still glistening with beads of water.

'Cheers,' said Eva, raising her glass, 'and let's not leave it so long until next time.'

'It's kids that do it to us you know,' Fiona replied. 'They take over our lives, determine our schedules and put us in a completely different realm from the friends who aren't yet settled down. Isn't that an awful word – settled, as if we couldn't be bothered anymore and resigned ourselves to our lot.'

'Well I'm far from settled now,' Eva replied 'but yes you're right about the kids' part, they change everything. It's the responsibility that's the biggest change I think, you have them and then every issue that surrounds them is yours. It's amazing to see them grow and go through the stages although I'm not looking forward to the teenage years.'

'Well you've a bit to go until that anyway.'

The old friends chatted away and after several top ups had just drained the bottle of rosé when Philippe and Jacques arrived. Eva rose to greet them and welcomed kisses on both cheeks from father and son.

Philippe was charming, attentive and strikingly handsome to boot. Sallow skin, chestnut brown hair worn slightly long and the deepest melting pot of chocolate brown eyes that Eva had ever seen. She felt herself staring at him and smiling like a teenager to the point where she was becoming self-conscious about not being able to take her eyes off him. Tall, strong and impeccably dressed it was impossible not to admire him just a teensy bit. He quickly got to work in the kitchen and emerged in no time with a delicious fettuccine pasta immersed in a sublime cream based sauce coating

107

chunks of tender succulent chicken mildly flavoured with garlic and sprinkled with freshly chopped parsley.

'And he cooks too!' Eva exclaimed, a little too flirtatiously perhaps after all that wine, as she began to tuck into her bowl of pasta.

Fiona just smiled and said 'ah, yes Philippe likes to show off in the kitchen,' with a teasing laugh.

The pasta was served with a baguette that Philippe had picked up at the local bakery on his way home.

'You will see the queues outside the bakery in the morning,' Fiona explained. 'Everyone buys their bread fresh in the morning and in the evening.'

'The French do appreciate their food alright,' Eva agreed.

The rosè had been finished off so Philippe opened up a nice crisp Alsace white wine full of flavour without being too heavy for their meal.

Eva refused a second glass of the white wine when it was offered, switching to a glass of water instead.

'That's not like you to refuse alcohol,' Fiona giggled.

'I know, it's just that I want to get up early in the morning and get a good start on these markets.'

'Well I suppose I'd better call it a night too then, seeing as I'm driving you.'

'Thanks Fiona, are you sure it suits you to come with me?'

'Eva I have been looking forward to this for weeks. You'll think I'm a right saddo but this is the most exciting thing I've done in ages. Sorry Philippe,' she chuckled. 'Seriously, I love the markets so let's get you off to bed and I'll give you a shout in the morning, if we're there by ten o'clock it'll be soon enough as we'll have all day.'

'Sounds like a plan,' Eva replied.

'However we are going out on the town tomorrow night, agreed?'

'Cool, where are we going?'

'Well it's you, me and a friend from work who has relocated from the U.S. and we're going to have a 'Sex and The City' night out.'

'Tell me more,' Eva smiled intrigued.

'Well myself and my friend Emily have been getting together to watch the old 'Sex and The City' series on Netflix and every so often we've been visiting the locations used when Carrie did her stint in Paris, restaurants, cafes etc.'

'So where are we going tomorrow night?'

'It's a restaurant called Kong. Did you watch Sex And The City?'

'Absolutely, I don't think I missed an episode.'

'Well do you remember when Carrie met the Russian boyfriend's ex-wife and she was really dissing the décor, even though it was tres cool?'

'Oh yes, the tres chic lady with the shiny hair?'

'Yes, well we're checking out that restaurant tomorrow night, so be prepared for a late night out.'

'Great, that sounds like fun but I think I'll hit the bed now, I'm wiped out.'

Eva soon snuggled up in the freshly made guest bed and pulled the white cotton covered duvet up around her. The wine had gone straight to her head and with visions of armoire's and Chantilly lace swirling in her head she dozed off easily.

Fortified by toasted baguette and hot chocolate their first stop the next morning was the Marché aux Puces at the Porte de Clignancourt in the 18th arrondissement of Paris. Literally translated it meant Market of the Fleas and supposedly the largest marketplace in the world. Fiona was lucky to get parking just near the metro station stop and they emerged to a bustling crowd of eager Saturday morning bargain hunters.

Eva had visited Clignancourt years before as a tourist though it made this visit less daunting to be somewhat familiar with it. The vastness of the area could be overwhelming and Eva was glad that she had read up on the Internet before the trip and the names had some familiarity to her. Eva skimmed her notes and listed off the names of the five large markets, all located off the Rue des Rosiers.

'Dauphine, Biron, Marché Vernaison, Malassis, and Paul Bert/Serpette.'

'Is that supposed to mean something to me?' giggled Fiona 'I'm supposed to know more French than you, you know.'

'They are the names of the five main markets apparently, so on y va!'

'Let's go indeed!'

Marché Vernaison was the first one that they came across on the Rue des Rosiers. They spent over an hour wandering from one dealer to the next until Eva gave a big beaming smile as she held up an old wash jug to Fiona.

'This is it,' she whispered excitedly, 'this is the kind of thing I'm after.'

After a bit of negotiating the jug was Eva's for twenty euros.

They wandered on and after a further two hours had accumulated so many bits and pieces that they had to make several trips back to the car.

Most of the items were pottery vessels of some description in varying sizes and materials from delicate china to rustic terracotta. She'd picked up some beautiful large platters and knew her mark-up could be 50% on those at least and bought twenty.

For lunch they located a small bistro where they fortified themselves with 'croque monsieur' and 'pommes frites'. Steering away from the wine menu they stuck to Evian and began to mull over the problems that were emerging.

'How are we going to protect this stuff from getting broken Eva? That's my main concern, not to mind how we are going to transport it all?' Fiona was perplexed.

'Hmmm,' Eva mused as she flicked through her notes again. 'I've thought of that and I have some notes on making transportation arrangements here somewhere.'

Eva continued rustling through her notes and eventually exclaimed

'yes, here it is,' and read for a few minutes until she came to a list of website addresses and telephone numbers that she had researched.

Fiona made some queries by mobile phone and tried to sound like she knew precisely what she was talking about.

Eventually they located a courier service that would take care of the packing and shipment and would even provide a porter for collecting boxes of items directly from the dealers.

By mid-afternoon they had unloaded the car and dropped off all their morning's work to the transporter - aptly named "Transportation Internationale" - and moved on to the next market. Across the street from Vernaison was Marché Malassis. It was on two levels and offered plenty of interesting dealers.

They continued to pick up pieces of pottery and their negotiating skills improved with every deal. They were becoming more adept at reading the dealer's body language and held back as much of their own enthusiasm for the pieces as they could. Each purchase was like a mini triumph. As well as pottery they also bought some interesting wall fixtures that could be used for holding utensils in the kitchen and some old shop signs. Bronze 'boules' were easily obtained and Eva thought they would make nice displays in wooden bowls or simply scattered on a mantelpiece or even as a paperweight on a desk. Also some hand-made hammered metal salad servers along with delicate pastry forks and cake cutters would make practical gifts. They made two further trips to the transporters office and by the end of trade had three crates full. Each crate was a neat four foot by four foot wooden box with the same depth and each piece was being bubble wrapped and further protected with wood shavings. By the end of one day she had bought over 200 items. There were multiple porcelain teapots, pairs of gilded vases, assorted sized earthenware urns, serving platters and silverware and all in she had spent 4,000 euro. She also took lots of photographs on her phone and on their way back to Fiona's apartment in her car Eva put a proposal to her.

'Fiona,' she said tentatively 'I'm going to ask you something and I want you to think about it before you answer me but would you consider being my French buyer?'

'Buyer?' quizzed Fiona, 'what do you mean?'

'Well I'm going to need six more crates of similar items to make the shipment viable and I'd like you to do the picking for me. You

111

know what I'm after now. I'd be paying you a decent daily rate of course.'

'I'd love to!'

'Really. Oh wow, wow, wow Fiona. Do you need to talk to Philippe about it?'

'Well of course but I know he'll be happy as long as I'm happy and I'd love to do it. Spending someone else's money is quite invigorating.'

Returning to Fiona's house by 7p.m. they were exhausted. Philippe and Jacques were home before them and had already eaten. Fiona had thoroughly enjoyed her day out and enthused to Philippe about some of their finds. Eva could see Philippe's eyes glazing over as Fiona went into way too much detail about haggling techniques so Eva swiftly diverted attention over to Jacques and his trip to the park. It was lovely to listen to his chatter in French with a smattering of English words here and there. He was a handsome child and full of life, his eyes lighting up as he talked about feeding "les canards."

The thought of a night out wasn't overly enticing for Eva but after a quick shower she was revitalised and ready to make the most of a Saturday night of freedom in Paris. She attempted a classic French look with her little black sleeveless dress with black slingback heels.

'Wow,' exclaimed Fiona, who was a little more conservatively dressed. She was wearing simple tailored black trousers and a silk blouse in a deep burgundy colour with a loose bow at the neck. She looked impeccably chic and sexy to boot with her short blonde choppy bobbed hair and gold stud earrings.

They hailed a taxi and then whizzed alongside the Seine until they were neatly deposited by the taxi driver at Pont Neuf. Eva couldn't help but think of Princess Diana and her last journey on these roadways, such a sad loss, such an iconic lady. Looking around there were no obvious signs of the restaurant and after a few detours they discovered that it was located on the top floor of a very cool looking building. The view was amazing, as for the décor it was on the funky side too but not that plush. The

112

transparent plastic chairs were not the most comfortable but one suffered for style. They were however pleasantly surprised by how reasonable the prices were on the menu.

Fiona's friend Emily arrived and Eva played along with the double cheek kissing business although it felt strange to greet a complete stranger in that way. Emily was from Chicago and in her late twenties, she had been moved to Paris to work in social media for the same marketing firm as Fiona. She wore a yellow and black print Ganni camisole and skirt with black strappy sandals and her long brown hair hung in loose curls.

They chatted away with ease and the first hour of conversation focused on a debate as to who was which character in Sex and The City. They all wanted to be Carrie of course, mainly for her wardrobe and sassiness. By main course they were on their second bottle of wine and discussing the seriousness of grooming in France. Being waxed in France was like washing your hair or brushing your teeth, it was considered necessary and something that had to be done.

Not yet ready to go home after their meal they headed for a nearby pub. It was more of a club than a bar with a DJ playing and unlike most French bars that Eva had visited before people were standing around and mingling rather than sitting around their tables in little closed groups.

Music was loud and conversation was difficult and she noticed Emily was giving a huge flirty smile to a handsome recipient that she had spotted at the bar. He flashed back a confident grin and looked from Emily to Fiona to Eva and he continued to look right into her eyes. Eva's heart was racing.

'What are you doing?' she half-whispered to Emily.

'What?'

'You're flirting with the guy at the bar and now he keeps staring at us.'

'Flirting, that's not flirting, looking at someone isn't flirting Eva! That's just being friendly,' Emily giggled. 'Just relax and have fun!'

Eva wasn't sure if she was giddy or dizzy or both but she was now half afraid to look in the direction of the bar.

Turning to ask Fiona's opinion, she found her raising a glass of Moët to her lips with the just opened bottle in an ice-bucket on the table beside her. She pointed at a sharply dressed guy two tables over and then began to fill two glasses for them.

'Did he buy that for you?' Eva asked, sort of concerned.

'Yes, well for us all probably, go on have some.'

'What? No. I don't know, I mean isn't that a bit much?'

'Not at all Eva, this is Paris, there are guys around here with more money than sense and this is what they do.'

'Seriously?'

'That guy expects nothing more than a smile and will be complimented if you drink his champagne.'

'No way?'

'Honestly Eva this is what they do.'

'Sure go on so and pour me a glass.'

With the bubbles tingling her palette Eva closed her eyes to take a sip and when she opened them she looked up into the eyes of the handsome Frenchman from the bar hovering beside her.

'Bonsoir,' he said with a smile, 'may I join you?'

'Hello,' she half-giggled back. She had never felt more out of her comfort zone and didn't know what else to say.

'Michel,' he said smoothly, extending a hand, 'may I sit?'

'Eva,' she replied, trying to regain composure and quell the giggles inside her as she shook his manicured hand.

'You are too beautiful for this place Eva, you should be instead in the finest hotel with the finest view of Paris with me.'

Eva nearly fell off her stool.

'Thank you,' she replied, feeling a warm glow creeping up from the base of her neck until her cheeks blushed. She was mortified and didn't know what else to say. Maintaining his gaze she continued to sip on her champagne. He had magnificent eyes she surveyed, dark brown and with a complexion to match.

Eva attempted to counter his charm with a balance of cool aloofness and humour but knew she was failing. Something must have been keeping him interested as he continued to up the level of compliments until she felt like the most beautiful woman in

114

Paris. She wasn't buying a word of it but it was flattering all the same.

Meanwhile both Emily and Fiona were chatting to the businessman who had gifted the 'Moët'.

Eva's head began to spin lightly and she knew it was definitely time to go. Michel was handsome and had made her feel great but she knew if she stayed any longer she was in danger of embarrassing herself. The alcohol was beginning to take its toll. She excused herself and whispered to Fiona that she needed to go, and now.

The three girls emerged onto the street entwined in a giggly ensemble of girliness and hailed a cab.

'Why did you leave so quickly? Did he say something to upset you?' Emily asked in the cab.

'Emily, I couldn't stay a moment longer. I didn't know what to do with myself or what to say. He was the most charming man I have ever met. His face was so close to mine, I could feel his hot breath and he kept gently brushing my hair back from my face, I didn't know what to do!'

'I know what I would have done,' Emily giggled 'Eva he was gorgeous, you should have gone for it. You are in Paris after all.'

'What! I couldn't, I wouldn't know what to do, I was dying a death in there.'

'Ah Eva, times have changed since you were last dating I'd say. If you want something now you go for it.' Fiona piped up.

'Fiona!!! Cop on. I'm only here five minutes and you're telling me I should be pouncing on a Frenchman.

Soon the taxi pulled over and two of them got out swapping double kisses goodnight with Emily who stayed in the cab.

'Will she be alright on her own?' Eva asked as they turned away.

'Absolutely, there is no problem with taxi drivers here. There is much more respect for women in general than you'll find at home.'

'I'm beginning to see that, no wonder the women are all full of themselves,' she laughed.

The two friends giggled their way up to the apartment and tried to quietly drink some water before going to bed. It was 3a.m. Eva

115

couldn't believe it. There would be no point in trying to get up for an early start with hung-over heads so they decided to sleep until they woke up and take it from there.

The following morning they decided to go by metro instead of taking the car and battling the traffic. They took metro line #4, to Porte de Clignancourt. Exiting up the steps to the street they continued straight until they crossed under the peripherique and took a left turn onto the Rue des Rosiers. It felt familiar by now and their second day at the markets resumed down the Rue des Rosiers at Marché Dauphine, another 'new' designed space that had opened in 1992. There were two floors with over three hundred dealers and thankfully cafes and benches for rest stops.

By mid-afternoon they had crossed over to Marché Biron, which housed higher quality goods. Eva couldn't count the number of places she had entered and promptly departed after looking at a price-tag. Who could afford to buy in those price ranges she wondered. Most of the offerings at Marché Biron were well beyond her price bracket.

They ended the day with a scouring of Marché Serpette and Marche Paul Bert. Located under a large red sign saying 'Serpette' it was a little highbrow with Marché Paul Bert, an exterior market alongside it, being less expensive. There, Eva came across item after item to add to her collection and by end of trade four more crates had been filled.

Considering that they had only gotten up at 10a.m. they had done champion work. On return to Fiona's apartment Eva collapsed on the sofa while Fiona brewed up some coffee. Weary after the day's work but high on excitement, Eva began to make lists of all her purchases, prices paid and details of the shipment costs for the crates. Everything had gone better than planned and she could fill the whole store with Parisian fare if she chose to. The hard part was going to be to stop herself from buying too much there.

Slowly opening her eyes the next morning after what felt like only a couple of hours sleep, the early morning Parisian light was squinting through the gap in the curtains.

116

She could hear Fiona in the shower already.

Eventually Eva traipsed wearily from the bedroom to the kitchen still in her pyjamas. Taking the coffee Fiona offered, she inquired where the others were.

'Philippe is gone to work and Jacques is gone with him to the crèche.'

'What about you Fiona, don't you have work today?'

'No. Sure I told you that. I'm job-sharing so I'm off Monday and Tuesday.'

'Oh right yeah and yes to more coffee please.'

'Are you still up to hitting the markets again today?' Fiona asked.

'Yes, first shower, then markets.'

By noon they had filled the final crate and were finalizing shipment arrangements. With eight containers now filled with assorted pieces Eva was completely satisfied. With plenty of stock to keep her 'Parisian' section going they spent some time revisiting dealers she had bought from and taking details and notes on the type of stock they carried and the price ranges.

She looked at some larger pieces of furniture in hardwoods but to buy any nice big antique pieces would be outside her budget and well outside that of the market she was aiming for. Fiona was a complete star and enjoyed the whole experience so much she said she would be delighted to do some buying for Eva if she was sure that was what she wanted.

That evening they dined locally, just the four of them. Going to a restaurant in Paris was no huge excursion. It was not saved for special or rare occasions, eating out was a part of life and restaurants dotted most of the streets. Fiona's and Philippe's local restaurant was typical, with red and white checked tablecloths on tables and the obligatory flippant French waiter.

Eva's fourth and last day in Paris was spent as a tourist, they had shopped enough. She wandered along the Champs-Élysées and back down towards the Eiffel Tower where she had lunch with Fiona overlooking the Seine. They took a walk through the Champ de Mars and strolled back towards the river along the

117

various quays until they crossed at Pont Royal to Musée du Louvre.

Visiting a food market, Eva came across a stall specializing in all sorts of products derived from olives. There were vacuum packed olives, olives in jars, various strengths of olive oils and even some cosmetics. She couldn't resist buying a jar of olive oil based body moisturizer for herself and a wonderful little olive oil dispenser for her kitchen which was like a miniature oiling can in stainless steel. She made enquiries about the suppliers of some of the items and the store-owner was more than helpful giving her a catalogue and contact information.

Eva had decided that she was going to cook up a sumptuous feast as a further thank you for Fiona and Philippe's hospitality. Knowing that she could not match Philippe's culinary skills in the kitchen she decided not to be too adventurous with the menu. Stopping at the fish stall she spotted fresh darnes of salmon which would be perfect. At the vegetable market she filled a paper bag with handfuls of green beans.

'Salmon with Coriander and Lime'

You will need: (Serves 4)
4 salmon darnes
Green beans
Oil for frying
Butter
1 lime
50g unsalted butter
1 tbsp flour
1 tsp ground coriander
250ml cream

Method:
Pan fry the salmon darnes in a little oil over a medium to high heat
Cook the green beans in a pan of salted water

118

Meanwhile, zest and then juice the lime.

Melt the 50g butter in a saucepan over a low heat, add the flour and use a wooden spoon to mix into a paste (roux).

Add the ground coriander and lime zest and mix well.

Turn up the heat to medium high and add the lime juice.

Keep stirring and then slowly add in the cream.

Bring to a gentle simmer for a minute or so.

Serve the salmon with a little of the sauce on top with buttered and seasoned green beans on the side.

[RECIPE ENDS]

And that was it. One last sleep in Fiona's apartment and it was time to say goodbye to Paris. With her credit card nicely dented she flew early on Friday morning south to Perpignan confident that Fiona would be a fabulous buyer for her and could easily do another shipment whenever she needed it.

'Au revoir Paris,' she said quietly as the Eiffel Tower disappeared in the distance and her plane rose into the air.

Chapter 10

(COGNAC)

Arriving into Perpignan airport was far less intimidating than Charles de Gaulle had been. It was quite small and the hire-car office was easily located. Standing in line to pick up the car keys Eva noticed that the vast majority of travellers were either elderly or young children. Looking again she realized that a lot of these were grandparents either collecting, accompanying or sending home their grandchildren. The children varied in age but some were very young and looked so vulnerable with their boarding cards in a see-through plastic wallet that was hung around their necks. Eva thought how awful to pack your kid off like that, but looking again she realized that the children were quite happy with their lot.

Eva was soon getting to grips with the zippy little Peugeot and located the Motorway relatively easily with the help of sat nav. She had keyed in directions to Le Boulou and her hotel was situated outside the small town in the foothills of the Pyrenees. She drove south and left the motorway at Le Boulou. Eva wasn't feeling too confident on the small quiet country however it wasn't long until she rounded yet another bend and there it was tucked in off the road, Hôtel du Repos. Parking her car she noticed there were only three others parked alongside, all with French registrations. Following the small stone path upwards she spied the swimming pool at a lower level, looking invitingly cool. Through the evergreens she came to the terrace. The double doors stood open with their net curtains billowing an invitation in a gentle breeze.

'Ah, Madame, vous avez arrivés! Welcome.'

The greeting was warm and genuine and came from the proprietor's daughter Renée who spoke impeccable English. She showed her to her room and inquired if she would dine with them later. Explaining that their tradition was to dine casually at a big table with any of the guests who chose to join them. There would be a choice of two main courses and it sounded too wonderful to pass up.

Her room was enchantingly furnished with a four poster double bed and beautifully upholstered chairs with ornate legs and armrests. The bathroom was simple in plain white and chrome and fitted with an American style rainforest pressurized shower.

As it was afternoon already Eva decided on a quick change into lighter clothes before setting off to visit Collioure. It was much hotter than in Paris and was into the low thirties so Eva quickly showered and changed into one of the pretty flower printed cotton dresses that Viv had loaned to her. Driving with the windows open she passed fields of heaving vines as the warm breeze streamed in on top of her.

Collioure reminded her in many ways of the seaside town of Kinsale outside Cork city but on a much grander scale. With huge fortress walls and towers, a magnificent harbour and intimate little cobbled streets there was a fabulous buzz of summer about the place. Young families walked around stopping to buy 'glace au chocolat' or whatever flavour they fancied at the various ice-cream vendors that dotted the street corners. Outside dining was ongoing and crafts-shops were plentiful. It was the latter that Eva had come to see but she really had to get something to eat first. A freshly baked flatbread with some spicy hummus from a food-stall soon sustained her as she began to explore the tiny roadways. She admired hand-painted silk wall hangings and pretty seascape water-colours and oils on canvas but they were all far too pricey to even consider. Pottery was colourful and tempting but already marked up in price so she wouldn't be able to charge much more than she

121

would pay for it making it not worthwhile either. After wandering the streets for over two hours with no luck Eva finally decided that Collioure was too geared for the tourist and she wasn't going to find anything suitable there. Feeling hot and sticky she decided to head back to the hotel for a leisurely swim before dinner.

As she swam she found it hard to believe that this would already be her sixth night in France, maybe she hadn't allowed enough time for the South she worried. Only two more full days and nights and then she would be leaving again. The pool area was deserted and Eva relaxed on a lounger for a little while and wondered where all the other guests were. As she rested with the rays of the sun drying out her bikini and her eyes closed her thoughts soon became clouded with a shadowy visit from guilt. She'd been calling the children twice a day, usually first thing in the morning and then again in the evening and they always sounded cheerful enough but how selfish was she being just to abandon them like this and go off to invest in herself so heavily? She should be at home, she should be cooking for them, talking to them, minding them. Feeling a little deflated she gathered her towel and belongings and meandered back to her room.

Showering again she decided to wear her hair up for a change and coiled it into a sophisticated chignon á la Hepburn. Looking at her reflection in the mirror she forced herself to smile. This trip was for her and she needed it and deserved it. She shouldn't have to continuously pep-talk herself into believing such a thing, mais voilá, the joy of being a mother is always accompanied by guilt. Going without a bra under a silk halter-neck top felt risqué, not something she had ever done before, this was France though, being braless was allowed! The white three quarter length trousers were comfortable and cool and required nude coloured underwear as they were practically see-through. Simple flat bandeau style flip-flops in cream finished her outfit. She dusted her shoulders with some Bobbi-Brown bronzing powder, slicked on some lip gloss and a couple of coats of mascara and she was ready. Catching her breath she softly whispered 'here it goes,' to herself and made her way to the lounge area. She had never done anything like this before. It was surreal. It was a warm evening and she was feeling unusually confident, her Parisian flirtation had given her that. Dining on her own made her feel like the central heroine in a novel. *A mystery novel or a romantic novel? Romantic,* she decided, *with a touch of mystery!* The two steps down to the sunken sofas gave the lounge a seventies vibe. Eva was the only one there and felt a bit uneasy until Renée appeared and offered her an aperitif serving a fresh deliciously sweet Rivesaltes. A middle-aged couple soon joined her. They had also travelled from Paris but had stopped off in Bordeaux for a few days en route and they were now nearing the end of a week in this area. Speaking in broken French and English conversation flowed freely enough if a little hesitant at times. Yet another couple joined them and rather than feeling uncomfortable Eva was made to feel more and more relaxed as they made sure to include her in conversation. A bell chimed and Renée beckoned them to join her family and staff on the 'Terrasse' where the breakfast tables had been pushed together and now seated a bustling party of twelve. Renée introduced everyone and Eva found herself surrounded by men. On either side were the men from the couples she had just met and across the table was Renée's brother Sébastien. With melting brown eyes, sallow skin and a disarming smile he seemed to immediately focus his attention entirely on Eva. *What was going on?,* she thought, *she couldn't possibly be attracting yet another French man!* Nobody raised an eyebrow when Sébastien suggested to her across the table that they take a stroll later so that he could show her the gardens. Eva accepted and slipped away with him after coffee was finished. They wandered through the grounds together in the moonlight and on their return sat on loungers next to the pool.

Whether it was that accent again or his eyes or the amount of attention and compliments he paid her or maybe the wine they'd had earlier, Eva eagerly welcomed his advances. He sat beside her and gently leaned in to kiss her before going in search of a nightcap for them both. Eva sat and waited, listening to the night-time crickets in the warm south of France air and contemplated her second encounter with a French man over the past number of

123

days. He returned with Cognacs and each sip coated the inside of her mouth with flavour before gliding back to warm her throat. Sébastien wasted no time in kissing her again and she savoured the taste of his lips moistened with Cognac. She felt like she was either floating or dreaming. Somewhere nearby a car door closed and jolted Eva back to the present.

Standing up to leave she excused herself and strolled back to her room leaving Sébastien gazing after her. The room was warm so she threw open the window, a faint breeze vaguely relieving the heat of the night as she undressed. Sleep came easily.

Awakening early with the sun beaming through the still opened curtains a faint smile crossed her face as she rose naked to close them and returned to her cosy spot in the bed to doze for a little longer. Sleep eluded her however as snatches of her poolside encounter were remembered. Giving up on a return to slumber she headed for the shower and hummed to herself as the power of the water massaged her body leaving her invigorated and ready to start the day.

Just two more days and with nothing bought yet in the South the hunt was on. Eva needed to get serious. She decided to skip breakfast and try and catch whatever was left of early morning markets. This time she headed inland on a short but beautiful drive to Céret. The town could have been the setting of a romantic drama; it was that enchanting. There was a strong sense of history and culture about the place and Eva parked her car and wandered around stopping to admire 'La Fountaine des Neuf Jets' dating back as far as the 1300s, however Eva didn't have time for culture today.

The open air market was already bustling with activity. Fruit and vegetable stalls displayed a luscious array of every fruit and vegetable imaginable as well as baskets of olives, pâtés, cheeses, jams and to one side there was a line of temporary tables erected by sellers of various curios and antiques. Eva browsed for a while deftly examining pieces of pottery and lamps but it wasn't what she was looking for. The pieces were too similar to what she had already picked up in Paris so instead she tried to locate some local crafts-shops.

Wandering around she passed the charming 'Eglise Saint Pierre' church and the imposing 'La Porte de France' which was the old entrance to the town with its beautiful façade. Eventually she came across a souvenir and gift shop which stocked some modern brightly glazed dinner-ware. Huge platters and pasta dishes, bowls for olives and pâtés, this was more like it, they definitely had a more southerly influence. Explaining that she was interested in importing to Ireland she enquired as to the supplier and learned that the workshop was located just a few miles further inland.

The drive was beautiful with olive trees and vines filling the neatly laid out fields which gently sloped in all directions. The pottery workshop and kiln was located in a converted outhouse of a farm. Eva introduced herself and the owner was very welcoming. She showed her around the works area and then into the stores where wooden shelves were literally heaving under the weight of some of the larger pots. Eva quickly identified exactly what she wanted and chose two different ranges. They were perfect. One was terracotta with a real earthy natural feel and the other was very brightly glazed in blues, yellows, reds and greens. Eva ordered four complete dinner sets of each and then supplemented the order with an additional twenty serving dishes and platters of varying sizes and then twenty storage jars some of which were labelled in French for 'sucre' etc. and others that were plain. Packing and shipping would all be looked after and all Eva had to do was pay. It was a relief to finalise the arrangements and collect all the contact information she would need for any future shipments. Having struck it lucky and blown the remains of her France budget Eva realised that the rest of her stay was her own and she could now truly relax and enjoy it.

She drove back towards the hotel planning to change her clothes and maybe have a swim before returning to Collioure to soak up the holiday atmosphere. Listening to French pop music with the car window open as she drove she began to think again about the previous evening. The al fresco terrace dining, the enchanting French man, *had it really happened?*

Eva felt strangely excited as she pulled her car into her parking space and wandered slowly up the steps towards her room. There wasn't a sign of Sébastien or anyone else for that matter. All was quiet, was it 'siesta' time maybe? In her room she discovered that a handwritten note had been passed under her door. Her tummy fluttered as she read and reread the brief note.

'Cher Eva, tonight you may come and dine with me, non? Si you do not half plans I will see you at 7.30p.m. À bientôt, Sébastien.'

'Aaaagh,' Eva muffled a giggly scream and rolled onto the bed. Instinctively she reached for her mobile to call Viv and then thought better of it and hung up. Feeling like a schoolgirl she took a long shower and changed into a daisy print cotton summer dress. She didn't bother to go for a swim and returned to Collioure instead. It was late afternoon and Eva had eaten nothing yet. Within minutes of parking in Collioure she wandered down into the town and chose one of the many restaurants where she enjoyed a coffee and half a pastry, she would save her appetite for later she decided.

Eating outside in the heat was wonderful. Happy people; couples, families, young and old alike were milling around slowly, adding to the already relaxed ambience of the town. Even the waiters failed to show the remotest sign of stress, they were efficient without being hurried and always polite which was so unlike Paris. Eva took her time finishing off a second strong coffee and felt fortified as she began to wander the streets once more. Browsing at her leisure she picked out a new pair of earrings that were gold and just the right amount of dangly. Feeling excited about her date with Sébastien she wanted to jazz up her 'little black dress' and soon found some magnificent gold strappy high heeled sandals that would really set it off.

126

Browsing some more she came across a boutique full of pretty girls' dresses which made her think of Hannah. She really missed both her and Luke and was glad that this trip was nearly at an end. As well as calling the kids everyday she had also made a call to Daniel. He had no major news for her, the development was making progress maybe just a bit slowly but nothing to worry about yet. He said that he'd let the Irish warehouse know about the French shipments that should be arriving in a couple of weeks. He seemed to have a contact for everything.

With enough browsing done Eva returned to the hotel for a cool dip in the pool. She lounged in the sunshine for a while before returning to her bedroom and showering yet again. Hoping that high heels wouldn't be over the top for Sébastien's dinner plans Eva carefully applied her make-up. Sébastien was ready and waiting for her when she strolled out to the reception area and when she saw how smartly dressed he was she was glad that she had dressed up and splashed out on the new shoes. One of the couples she had met at dinner was there too and they nodded their greeting without a hint of inquiry as to her liaison.

Sébastien took her to dinner at a restaurant near Château de Castelnou. What an evening it was. Pure decadence and luxury the like of which Eva had never before experienced. The drive was deep into the countryside with the roads winding and rising going higher into the mountains. When they parked at the Castle they had to walk up towards this magnificent medieval fortress. It was floodlit on all sides and had undergone a number of restorations over time. With the restaurant specializing in the Catalan cuisine of the region, the setting was out of a fairy-tale and felt both romantic and lavish at the same time.

Eva was spellbound as Sébastien went into great detail on the history of the castle. It was surprisingly interesting. Eva was not normally interested in history, being bombarded with dates and names usually overwhelmed her, but Sébastien told it like an enchanting story, his voice was hypnotic in its melodic huskiness. She loved listening to him punctuate his sentences with uhhhhs and ahhs struggling for some words and sending her into fits of giggles when he chose some that were totally inappropriate. He told her how at the height of the Middle Ages the Castelnou family had been the most powerful family in the country and in recent times the estate had been run as a business.

The castle now attracted a growing number of tourists to see not only the castle but also the gardens which were quite famous too. There was an extensive Mediterranean garden where flowers bloomed all year round and the estate also produced its own wines. This was probably the most impressive place that Eva had ever been taken on a date and certainly one that would stay in her memory for a long time. It felt like time was standing still.

Later they enjoyed nightcaps sitting on the sunken couches back at the hotel and Sébastien was making clear his interest to do more than kiss Eva but again no, she wasn't planning on taking things any further. For now a kiss would have to be good enough.

Eva woke once again to streams of daylight and a gentle breeze coming through her opened bedroom window.

Sébastien joined her as she was having breakfast on the Terrasse and by now she felt sure the others must be thinking that they were lovers. But it didn't matter. She was in France and she was free to do as she pleased. Sébastien wanted to show her some more of this beautiful country and as they drove Eva sat back and watched the coast roll by as they passed Port Vendres, Paulilles, Banyuls-sur-Mer and finally stopped in Cerbere. Each town was full of tourists and stopping in Cerbere for lunch Sébastien pointed out that they were practically in Spain. Tempted to drive on they decided against it and went for a tour of a winery instead. Eva loved to drink wine and to see where the processing took place was amazing, huge stainless steel temperature controlled vats either busy maturing for bottling or awaiting the upcoming harvest.

They drove back up to Collioure where they stopped to indulge in a home-made ice-cream and strolled down to see the boats by the water. It was glorious and so picturesque with the lookout towers majestically guarding the port. Returning back to Le Bolou they enjoyed another evening among fellow guests and Sébastien's family again. This time Sébastien sat beside her and kept a protective arm around her chair for most of the evening, often reaching to touch her hair or stroke her hand. Despite her previous intentions to not take things further what followed was a night that was romantic, slow and considered like nothing Eva had ever experienced before.

Rising early the following morning Sébastien gave her a warm hug and whispered French words softly into her ear before kissing her gently and saying goodbye. It was time for Eva to leave and she soon departed, driving alone in the direction of Perpignan airport to catch her flight to Charles de Gaulle. A few yards up the road she was crying soft tears overcome by just how special Sébastien had made her feel. Wiping her cheeks she turned on the radio. It had just been a fling and now she was back to being on her own again. Well not on her own, she had her kids and who could ask for more? Thinking about seeing them cheered her up enormously and she couldn't wait to hug them again. The flight from Perpignan landed back in Paris on schedule followed by a bit of a wait for the connecting flight from Charles de Gaulle. The travel was tiring but as the plane approached Cork airport she felt a rush of happiness as she caught site of her city coming into view.

Chapter 11

(CHOCOLATE CAKE)

Eva couldn't wait to see the shop the next day even though it was a Sunday she was there with the kids by 9.30a.m. She took them on the pretence of buying some fresh croissants and as she didn't have keys yet she could only peer through the windows. Outside was looking much more impressive now that some more had been done. The scaffolding had been taken away and the pavements swept and cleared of all the building debris. There was a space above the window for the store's name which was something that she had yet to decide. When they returned home Eva made hot chocolate to go with the croissants and sipped it while absently browsing the Sunday newspaper and thinking about her week in France. Little did she think she would be returning home after a romantic encounter and she couldn't wait to meet up with Viv so she could relive all the details. Viv however had a date so they managed a phone call instead with Eva hiding in the utility room and whispering as much as she dared about her escapades with Sébastien without being overheard by the children. The rest of the day at home was spent doing laundry, day-dreaming and catching up with the kids.

On Monday morning she brought Hannah and Luke down to the store again but this time they were able to get in for a look around and it was beginning to shape up nicely. Returning home Eva sipped some coffee and pulled out one of her many lists. This one was for the shop interior and she began to make additions and amendments. Flooring was the next priority, some black slate for the first few yards inside the door and then some wide reclaimed oak boards for the remainder. There was no way that Hannah and Luke would stand for being dragged around suppliers for the day though so that would have to wait.

Light-fittings were going to be another big purchase. She would need some advice and probably to look around some of her competitors to see what their set-up was like to get some ideas. She was only just back and wanted to be off again but the kids would have to come first. Instead of dragging them around shops she promised them a trip to the cinema in the afternoon if they could occupy themselves until lunchtime while she made some phone calls.

The shipment from Paris was due within two weeks and storage had to be secured so she set about requesting quotes over the phone for warehousing companies. The costs for this varied enormously with security and insurance adding to it. Picking out three of the most competitive and geographically suitable she made appointments to view them the following day. She telephoned Mary and apologising for the late notice asked if there was any way she could come and mind the kids for the following afternoon. Mary was delighted to oblige as Eva knew she would be, but she also knew she couldn't be calling on her every time and would have to come up with alternative arrangements. The following week would be fine as the kids were both enrolled for soccer and activity camps and the last week in July they would all be going on holidays in West Cork but for now she was at a bit of a loss.

After the cinema as she cooked supper for the children she got a brainwave to telephone the babysitter Helen that she and Alan used to use. At seventeen she was carefree for the summer and responded enthusiastically to the prospect of looking after the two kids whenever Eva would need her. Eva asked her to come for the remaining afternoons of that week and then she would need her again in August for another two weeks.

When she looked at the calendar she realised that with the week in West Cork and the sports camps she wasn't going to need the babysitter too much and the kids should have a fairly good summer really. On paper September appeared to be looming all too closely even though the summer holidays had just begun. Chiding herself to stop the negative thinking she returned to her lists after eating pizza with the kids and began to prioritise her tasks and cross off the ones that had been completed.

With the Boston flight booked for August, Eva opened her notebook and began yet another product wish list this time for Boston / Cape Cod.

She had arranged ten nights in all for her trip to America and now with the experience of the Paris and Perpignan trips behind her she knew that good planning would be essential. Boston city itself would not be the place to shop and she planned to head for some of the towns just outside it and then down the coast to Hyannis Port and maybe even across to Nantucket Island or Martha's Vineyard. After browsing online for what seemed like minutes but was actually a couple of hours Hannah interrupted to inform her that she was 'starving'.

'Be there in 5 minutes,' Eva replied with just a tiny hint of exasperation.

She sent off a short email to Elaine to let her know what she was planning for her Boston visit. As soon as she hit send/receive Eva was just about to shut down her laptop when she noticed a new email arriving in. Clicking to open it up she could see the sender's name was Sébastien. She held her breath as she opened it feeling like a love-struck teenager. It was brief and showed his hesitancy to use English, he enquired about her business and children, and signed off 'miss you, Sébastien.'

Hannah's shouts up the stairs jolted her back to reality. She had to log off and didn't have time to reply.

How could they possibly be hungry again? Eva asked herself as she made the kids a snack of toasted sandwiches. They were after a load of popcorn and fizzy drinks at the cinema and had pizza for tea and were still 'starving'. Eventually all were satisfied and another day had flown by with what felt like very little achieved.

Mary babysat the following afternoon while Eva visited the warehouses and some flooring specialists. With Helen then doing the child-minding for the remaining afternoons of that week Eva was finally able to dedicate herself to the store.

The shop layout needed to be thoroughly planned and this involved visiting competitors and researching shop fitters. Accounts for power supply for lighting and heating had to be sorted out as did the whole financial aspect of running the business. There was so much to learn. When she wasn't out visiting the accountant to discuss employment logistics or at the bank figuring out lodgements, how to handle cash, credit card and laser machines etc. she was to be found with her nose stuck in the latest 'How to Start a Business' handbook.

In between the business goings on she was making packed lunches and picking up the kids from sports camps. Both of her French shipments had arrived safely from France and were held in secure warehouse storage awaiting a place on a shelf in her store.

Eva had got through what felt like a vast amount of work over the recent weeks and felt deserving of her break in West Cork with the kids.

She still hadn't made time to reply to Sébastien's email and wasn't sure if she should. It felt a little bit wrong.

The three of them set off bright and early on a Saturday morning in the last week in July. From Douglas they got onto the link road and headed west, exiting at the Bishopstown roundabout where they took the road towards Bandon. Towns and villages whizzed by until they reached Skibbereen where the roads got busier and more winding as they drove towards Ballydehob. Rounding the corner on the road into Schull the breath-taking view of the harbour came into sight with boats bobbing happily on the glistening water. The town itself was buzzing with holidaymakers and locals trying to stay on the pavement but inevitably spilled onto the street as they encountered al fresco diners and smokers filling the chairs and tables outside the pubs and restaurants. The last stretch of their journey finally ended as they pulled to a stop in the much quieter village of Goleen.

The key was to be picked up in the local shop and having done that they followed directions through the village and located the cottage very easily. Gravel crunched under the jeep wheels as they parked and the kids quickly bailed out to explore. Within minutes Hannah was squealing delightedly – 'Mum, Mum, come quick – look at the stream and the bridge', in truth it wasn't much of a stream but the owner had cleverly made a feature of it with a small wooden bridge and a gate, adding to the quaintness of the cottage. Inside the cottage was very roomy and every comfort was available, including a welcome basket.

After a hasty lunch of bread rolls and cheese they set off again in the jeep to explore the beaches. The first one they came across 'White Strand' was also known as 'cockleshell beach' which was just that, it looked beautiful but it was so bestrewn with seashells that it was hardly pleasant to walk on, not to mind run about on. They drove onwards passing the caravan park on their right and the 'pitch and putt' course on the left. The next beach they came to 'Lackenakea Bay Beach' or 'stoney beach' looked gorgeous. The pathway from the road down to the beach was picked out through smooth boulders which lined the whole length of the beach. The sun was bouncing off the water and the beach was thronged. Again they decided to drive on until after turning yet another bend on the road they could see below them the vastness that was golden 'Barleycove beach'. It was canopied by sand-dunes with coarse grass behind it and a hotel with pretty holiday chalets overlooking it on the far side. On the nearside lay a meandering tidal river that could be crossed by means of a floating pontoon bridge with access to the carpark picked out by a long boardwalk. It was breath-taking. The tide was out and had left an assortment of pools ideal for the toddlers and little children that were splashing about in the shallow water being warmed by the afternoon sun.

They drove on until they were parked in the car-park and then carried their beach bags along the boardwalk. Walking barefoot on the wind sanded boards with the soft dust from the beach coating

134

your toes was the next best thing to a pedicure. Rough skin made smooth, polished by the sand and then the lap of the water at the edge of the ocean back and forth beckoning a gentle foot-spa. On the beach Luke soon announced that he had found the perfect spot. Throwing down their bags Hannah and Luke togged off as quickly as they could and shrieked as they fled down to the water. Eva took her time laying out the towels and then stripped down to her white halter-neck bikini and sauntered down to join the kids at the water's edge.

'This is the life,' she said to herself as she returned to her towel and lay back, briefly closing her eyes and feeling the heat of the sun on her face. Opening her eyes again and propping herself up on her elbows she kept an eye on Hannah and Luke as they played, splashing in the sea. Being on holidays alone with them for the first time was a strange experience. There was no-one to share the responsibility of looking after them and no-one to share the task of applying sun-screen or helping to dry the sand from between the toes.

On Sunday morning they took a trip into Schull and followed the signs for the Country Market. It was a food lover's paradise. Selections of salamis made from pork and venison, assorted pâtes, salsas, olives, smoked almonds and the variety of local cheeses. Pickled onions, sun blushed tomatoes, smoked peppers in garlic oil and loaves of fresh crusty bread ready for ripping open. Leaving with a basket full of assorted tubs and wax paper wrapped parcels they were well stocked for at least a couple of day's picnics at the beach.

Every day they headed to the beach with the sun in their faces as they drove along the coast road. The sea accompanied them on their left with what resembled thousands of glistening diamonds bouncing on frothy waves shimmering under a baby blue sky. Crookhaven village beckoned from across the water as sailing boats bobbed up and down and various colourful yachts and larger boats decorated the inlet.

The days were spent on the beach, with the kids in and out of the water and exploring the rocks. Eva was trepidatious about

135

taking a dip beyond knee-deep but when she finally did she emerged with a euphoric glow. On the hot still days she floated in the mineral rich waters and on the fresher days she rock-climbed and hunted for treasures hidden in the rock pools with the kids. Among the scattered jewels strewn on the beach they discovered mother of pearl sea combs or razor clam shells, seahorses, starfish and scallop shells. After the beach there was no better way to finish the day than to stop off in Crookhaven to sit outside O'Sullivan's pub with cold drinks enjoyed either on the benches or on the pier walls with legs dangling over the edge. Back at the cottage they relaxed in the evening and Eva cooked easy meals like barbecued steak or burgers with salad and crusty bread eaten outside and it was heavenly. Sometimes they would walk into the village to the playground or down to the village pier. The week passed blissfully and like all good things their stay in Goleen was over much too quickly. On the last day they packed up and reluctantly handed the keys back into the shop by noon. After one last visit to the beach they stopped off in Crookhaven for their last holiday lunch where Eva ordered an open crab sandwich which fortified her for the return journey home.

Although sad that their break had ended, it felt good to turn the key in her own front door once again at home. Flicking on the kettle was habitually the first thing she did when she entered the kitchen. It was almost six o'clock and the kids were hungry again, so after shoving a pizza in the oven Eva unpacked the jeep. Emptying their bags she tipped everything out onto the floor of the utility room for washing and then swept up the sand. Hannah and Luke had run straight onto the green to reunite with their pals who were busily playing soccer.

Eva gave Alan a quick call to let him know that they were back. He seemed to take more interest in the children now than he ever had before they split up and asked lots of questions. She also rang Viv and arranged to meet for lunch on the following Monday. They hadn't met up since Eva's trip to France and they both had lots of news for each other that they wanted to share in-person. After bundling a load of towels and swimming togs into the washing machine she called Hannah and Luke in for their tea. Feeling a bit tired now after her driving she wanted to have a bath and get an early night.

Two hours later she was enjoying her soak. *Nothing like your own bathroom with all the accoutrements* she thought as she lay back and raised her right leg to shave it. Topping up the bath-water she sank into the bubbles and closed her eyes enjoying the scent of a lavender candle she'd brought back from France. Eva still hadn't replied to Sébastien's email and wanted to discuss it with Viv before she did. Thinking of Sébastien and his husky voice made her tummy flutter.

Eva slept soundly after her bath and woke up early on Sunday morning. Alan arrived to take the kids for the day and Eva spent much of it browsing online. There was so much information out there it was just amazing. She decided to try out shopping online for her groceries. Signing up was straightforward and while it took her the most part of an hour to do her first shop she was thrilled when after selecting her time she got confirmation that her shopping would be delivered the next afternoon between 4-6pm. How cool was that? This was going to save her at least an hour, between locating a parking spot, manoeuvring a trolley, loading and unloading, it would save all the hassle as well.

After lunch she began to plan her trip to Cape Cod. She googled for crafts-shops and pottery makers and by the end of the day had a route planned from Boston to Cape Cod that culminated in a trip to Nantucket Island. She sent an email to Elaine with the details of their route to see what she thought and then turned her attention to a list of things to do the following day. Feeling satisfied with her work the kids arrived home wiped out and all were ready for another early night.

Helen, the babysitter, arrived bright and early at 8.30a.m on Monday morning and was going to do likewise every day for the following two weeks. Eva was relishing the flexibility that this gave her. She worked in the office until noon and then went to meet Viv for lunch in the village. Viv was radiant and wearing a

Reformation floral camisole top and matching skirt that enhanced her curves.

'It's the bra,' Viv confided, 'great support.'

'Well you look gorgeous. So tell us girl, what have you been up to for the past few weeks?' Eva enquired.

'Well...' she replied coyly.

'What, oh it's a man isn't it? I know you Viv, come on, tell me?' Eva implored.

'Well yes, there is someone, but to be honest I don't know what to make of him Eva.'

'Go on you vixen, spill, I want all the details.'

'Well I don't really know him that well yet but he seems really nice actually it's still very much in the stand-off stage yet.'

'What do you mean stand-off stage, do you like him?'

'Definitely, but I'm playing it cool.'

'Viv for heaven's sake if you like the guy why are you playing it cool?'

'Well you know... I don't want to seem too eager. He texted on Saturday and asked me out for Saturday night but I said I was busy.'

'And you weren't, I suppose?'

'No. Definitely not busy. I was sorry as soon as I sent the text but sure what could I do then, it was too late, it was a bit late notice anyway don't you think?'

'Viv the guy wanted to go out with you!'

'I know, I know and now I don't know whether to call him or what. I mean I thought he'd call again on Sunday but no word yet.'

'Seriously, you think he's going to call you again? Why would he, sure you're after blowing him off, do you think he's going to come crawling for another slap in the face?'

'Do you think? Maybe, yeah I'll text him, I will. Anyway, how was your week on the Irish Med?'

'Fabulous. It was exactly what I needed Viv. Time spent with the children, no rushing around and lots of late morning lie-ins. I didn't get a chance to tell you before I went away but guess what?'

she paused and lowering her voice to a whisper said 'I have heard from Sébastien!'

'Oh you mean the 'roi d'amour Sébastien,' Viv exaggerated in her best effort at imitating a husky French accent.

'He emailed me a couple of weeks ago and said that he missed me, actually that's making too much of it.'

'Well, did he say he missed you?'

'He signed it 'missing you.' '

'Same thing.'

'Is it?'

'Of course, and what did you say?'

'Nothing.'

'WHAT!'

'Nothing.'

'Ah stop, Eva, you think I'm bad!. The poor fellow is probably logged on day and night waiting to hear from you.'

'Yeah right – dream on, I, I just don't know if I should reply or if I do what to say.'

'We're as bad as each other. Eva you need to email him straight away and say that you've been away for a few days and that you miss him too.'

'I can't say that Viv!'

'You can. You say "Dear Sébastien, great to hear from you, things are going well, very busy. Miss you too, x Eva"'

'I can't.'

'You can. You tell me that I have to be straight but what about yourself?'

'It's too forward.'

'What do you mean forward?'

'Well then he'd know that I like him.'

'Eva you're worse than me,' Viv laughed. 'But listen to me if you're even in the slightest bit interested, throw him some bit of a line so that he knows that you haven't fallen off the face of the earth or into a hole or something.'

'I know, I will, yes, I will. OH, look who just came in,' Eva motioned with her eyes towards the right.

139

'Look what she's wearing! State!' Viv tried to stop herself laughing, 'we shouldn't be so mean, but that is brutal.'

After catching up on some more news they went their separate ways and Eva popped over to visit the shop.

Wow, she thought to herself as she admired the outside. It was beginning to really look like something now and the thought that this was hers made her swallow hard with a mixed feeling of fear and excitement. There was so much still to do to get the place ready.

Returning home it was time to let Helen off. 8.30am to 3pm was enough child-minding for any teenager. Eva could see that she was great with them and it was obvious that they liked her too, particularly Hannah.

An unexpected ring of the doorbell signalled the first delivery of her Internet purchased groceries. The delivery man was friendly and courteous as he brought in crates of shopping to be unloaded and Luke and Hannah eagerly assisted, no doubt in search of any goodies that may have been bought. *This is the way to do it alright,* Eva thought to herself, no more struggling with wonky-wheeled shopping trollies.

With the cupboards well-stocked Eva prepared a quick meal of pasta with grated parmesan, crispy bacon and pesto. Later on she sat flicking through the pages of her business plan. All the figures were there including those for staff and all the various overheads like heating and lighting etc. Costs for shop fittings were there as well but now she needed to get even more practical. How long in advance should she start recruiting staff? Let's say that she did take occupancy of the store in September as scheduled when would she need to have staff? The fittings would need to go in first so that was the most pressing issue. Designing the store layout, now that called for the experts but Eva wanted to have a lot of personal input too. What would be the point in paying a professional to design something that she would probably end up changing anyway? She decided that the thing to do was to figure out exactly what she wanted herself first and the best way to do that was to visit more stores and take notes and start sketching herself. So

140

every day of the first two weeks of August was spent visiting a store or two in the morning and then having lunch in a quiet café and writing down her immediate impressions of them. What colours were used? Did she like them? What kind of lighting was used? How many checkout tills were there? Where was the check-out situated? Was shelving high or low or both, modern or classical? Did the staff have a uniform? How many staff members were there and were they busy?

At the end of the two weeks her head was frazzled but she had come up with a final sketch of exactly what she wanted from the shop-fitters. The next stage would be to get a quote from a number of them with the stipulation that whoever she would appoint would be available to start on the first of September. Knowing that this was very short notice she tried to quell rising feelings of panic.

Design issues had been her obsession over the previous couple of weeks but it had been an essential part of the process. If the store layout wasn't inviting or appealing then it wouldn't matter what was on display if shoppers weren't enticed in.

Eva had another mini-panic attack when the first bank statement for the business account arrived and it took a sensible talking to from Vivienne to remind her that yes, this was what she should be expecting and that she had it all factored into her business plan which had been approved. Although reassured, she couldn't help feeling that taking off to Boston in a couple of days to do another hefty bit of debt digging did seem a little reckless.

Two weeks had passed since her last lunch out with Vivienne and while they called and messaged each other frequently it wasn't the same as getting together for a good old natter. Being so preoccupied with the progress of the business Eva felt like she was neglecting her friendship and although Viv reassured her when Eva had to cancel yet another lunch, she got the feeling there was something that Viv wanted to talk to her about.

With the trip to the States being even longer than the trip to France Eva was going through the same pre-departure guilt phase over leaving the kids. As much as she liked the buzz of the airport and travelling to another country it wasn't the same travelling alone. On her last day at home with the kids Eva involved Hannah in a bit of a baking spree. They threw together a batch of sausage rolls, two quiches and two apple pies to take to their Grandmother's house. Eva knew full well that Mary would be well stocked up in anticipation of her grandchildren's arrival but she wanted to send some food with them all the same. As well as the baking to take to their Gran's house they also baked a chocolate cake to have for their tea.

'Chocolate & Raspberry Birthday Cake'

You will need:
2 tbsp cocoa powder, heaped
5 tbsp warm water
200g unsalted butter
200g caster sugar
200g self-raising flour
2 tsp baking powder
4 eggs
12 raspberries for cake mix
Butter to grease tin
Rich Chocolate Butter Icing to decorate (see recipe below)
Chocolate button sweets & extra raspberries to decorate

Method:
Preheat the oven to 170°C/Gas Mark 5.
Grease and line two round cake tins (20cm or 8") with a little butter and parchment paper.
Make up the cocoa with the warm water in a cup and set aside to cool a little until needed.
Use an electric mixer to cream the butter and sugar together.
Sift the flour and baking powder together in a separate bowl and set aside.
Beat the eggs in a bowl and add about a third of the beaten eggs to the butter and sugar mix, followed by about a third

of the flour. Continue adding the next third of egg and then flour, alternating until all are added.

Mix in 12 roughly chopped raspberries, then add the cooled cocoa and mix well.

Divide the mixture between the two cake tins.

Bake the cakes for 30–35 minutes, testing with a skewer to see if it is baked – if any wet mixture clings to the skewer return to the oven for a further 5 minutes and test again.

Remove the cakes from the tins and cool on wire rack tray before icing.

Fill the centre with chocolate icing and sliced berries and smooth more chocolate icing all over the top and sides before decorating with more berries and chocolate buttons.

Tip: If you do not have time to make icing just sandwich the cake together with some jam and dust over the top with icing sugar.

'Rich Chocolate Butter Icing'

You will need:
For a less sugary, and richer, more chocolatey icing.
100g dark chocolate (70% cocoa content)
250g icing sugar
25g unsalted butter (approximately 1 heaped tbsp)
3 tbsp hot water

Method:
Break up the chocolate into a bowl and microwave it on low power for 1 to 2 minutes until melted.

Sift the icing sugar into a bowl and stir in the melted chocolate.

Add the butter and hot water and beat well with a wooden spoon until smooth.

[RECIPE ENDS]

Hannah happily licked the spoon clean of any remaining icing and later helped Eva packing for the children's holiday on the farm. She remembered to pack her wellies, her favourite cuddly rabbit and a book. Luke insisted on packing his PlayStation and a handful of games. The kids stayed up late and snacked on huge slices of the chocolate cake with a glass of milk before brushing off the crumbs and going to bed. Hannah was tearful going to sleep that night and Eva loathed leaving them in the morning. She stayed up late packing for herself and then turned on her laptop to print off her planned itinerary for the trip.

The last thing she did before shutting down her laptop was to finally write a carefully worded email to Sébastien. It read :

'Sébastien. I received your email a few weeks ago and I must apologise for not replying sooner. Things have been very busy here working on my business plans and with the children on holidays. I'm off to Boston for ten days to look into some more stock ideas for my store. Hope you are keeping well. Will be in touch. Á bientôt, Eva.'

And with a click of the mouse it was gone. She must have read it back to herself ten times. Did it say the right thing? Was it too formal? Á bientôt seemed to be the right thing to say. She hadn't looked it up or checked the spelling but if memory served her she felt that it should mean soon or until later or something that could be interpreted as being interested. Well it was gone now so what more could she do?

Chapter 12

(SURF & TURF)

Eva's plane took off from Shannon airport at lunchtime on Monday and touched down in Logan International Airport almost seven hours later. Stepping outside and joining the queue for a taxi, the warmth of the August afternoon heat hit her like a hairdryer on slow speed. She breathed it in and relaxed as her luggage was placed in the boot of a yellow cab for her and then gazed out the window as they headed for Elaine's downtown apartment.

The street where Elaine lived in the Boston BackBay area was off the main thoroughfare of Massachusetts Avenue and was tree-lined and cobble-stoned. Elaine's apartment was on the second floor and Eva stood in the heat looking up at the bay windows as she pressed on the buzzer for Ms Sheridan's apartment. Elaine came down to help her with her luggage and the two friends hugged each other warmly. There was no elevator here so between them they hauled Eva's suitcases up the narrow stairs. Once inside the first thing that Eva noticed was the wall of exposed brownstone brickwork and fireplace. The second thing she noticed was the large windows and the cool air being blasted from the air-conditioner.

Elaine looked amazing. With wavy auburn hair combined with the glow of golden brown skin shimmering with tiny freckles, she was the picture of health. She was over the moon to see her friend and insisting that Eva must be starving ushered her out the door almost as soon as she had dropped her bags. Elaine was a self-confessed disaster in the kitchen. She could make coffee, tea and just about stretched to beans and toast in an emergency but other than that nothing. Her small freezer was jammed with ready-made meals for one and her fridge was full of fruit, cheese, yoghurt, left-over Chinese food and water. Supplemented by at least three meals out a week Elaine knew the best local restaurants.

Self-conscious but undeniably pretty, attention from men had always been lauded on Elaine. In her teens she had been painfully shy and hadn't recognised the attention that she used to get from boys for what it was. Elaine now realised that if she had shown the slightest bit of interest she could have had plenty of boyfriends but she had always sent out the wrong messages. She tried to project an image of cool aloofness to cover her shyness and it worked far too well and she arrived into college life utterly inexperienced and trying to pretend she was worldly. However this icy front was interpreted as something else completely by the college boys and she was seldom without a boyfriend in those years. While good for her confidence it still didn't make it any easier to open up to other people and she could come across as a bit closed and cold. Life after college had been hard as her career took her away from her circle of friends and into a world where she had to interact with professionals often in a wining and dining environment based in London and these were situations that she avoided whenever she could. Travelling and staying in hotels was not at all glamorous and left very little time for a personal life. For Elaine, because she was not a natural mixer, it became a very lonely life and eventually depressing in every sense of the word.

She hadn't realised that she was heading down the path to depression until she was at the dead-end. She literally woke up one morning and could not get out of bed. She felt nauseous at the thought of going to work and meeting people. She couldn't face another day, the thought of showering, dressing and driving felt pointless. She asked herself what for? What's the point? So she turned over, pulled the covers over her head and was in and out of sleep for the remainder of the day. In the afternoon she watched crap day-time television still in her pyjamas, ate cereal and toast with cups of tea and went back to bed at three o'clock in the morning, beginning to perpetuate a cycle that would continue to rotate for the entire week. She ignored the phone calls until eventually someone from work had got in touch with her family and her brother turned up at her door.

That was ten years ago now and she still attended the odd counselling session, but living in the U.S. that was considered normal anyway which made it easier for her to feel like she belonged. Looking back she couldn't have imagined herself developing her career successfully and moving on with her life but she had taken a career break and got herself back on track. She took time out and travelled on her own for a while to take a break from the business world to work out how she would fit back in. One of the things that had stuck in her head from the counselling was to keep reminding herself that she had to get out there doing things and living every day. On days that she would feel low she would try and get out there and do something that she enjoyed. It could be browsing in a bookstore, flicking through a fashion magazine, sipping a cappuccino in a café, or just getting her nails done. Anything at all, once it made her feel good, gave her a buzz and put her out in the world participating. The psychiatrist also made her realize that she wasn't alone. Up until then she hadn't contemplated the possibility that other people suffered inner tortures too, having miniature panic attacks when trying to partake in a run of the mill conversation. She learned that self-esteem was a huge issue for plenty of people and kept a vast number of psychiatrists in green fees and private members clubs.

She had gone on a course of antidepressants in the early days and gradually came off them after a year and a half. While she still experienced periods of glumness she no longer felt completely locked into a pit of nothingness. Like an athlete needed motivation to get out there and train with the reward coming in the euphoric and triumphant feelings that came afterwards, Elaine often had to force herself to get out there and go to that Pilates class or have that massage. The counsellor would say to her at the end of a

147

session, 'Keep doing things Elaine, no matter how small, get out there and keep doing things.' He used the same words at the end of every session and they stuck with her.

Eva followed her friend admiring her style as they made their way to Newbury Street. Elaine was wearing a short-sleeved green and white abstract-print knee length dress and Eva was feeling a little bit on the scruffy side as she walked beside her friend still wearing her travelling outfit of denims, trainers and a white cotton shirt.

Newbury Street bustled with tourists and professionals alike. Eventually they ended up in a restaurant called 'Planet' or something to that effect. It was filled with urns of exotic plants and had huge hand painted pictures of jungle animals covering the walls. It was a bit like being in the middle of a safari. The food was organic vegetarian and Eva tucked into a Mediterranean lasagne laden with aubergines, peppers, courgettes and red onions. It was really tasty and satisfying without being heavy. Elaine had a pizza and they shared a bottle of Californian oaked Chardonnay.

Strolling around after their meal there was only one pace to go at and that was slow. It was a warm and balmy afternoon so they treated themselves to some frozen yogurt at a juice-bar to cool down and sat on a bench at Copley Square beside Trinity Church to enjoy them. They people watched as patrons came and went from the church, a beautiful building dressed in pink granite and trimmed with Longmeadow sandstone it reached up into the vivid azure sky. Everything was reflected in the towering glass windows of the Hancock building standing guard close by.

'I bet you that guy is after confessing to embezzlement from a bank,' Elaine nodded towards a well-dressed businessman as he emerged from the church.

'Nah,' Eva countered, 'definitely adultery. They're all at it apparently.' She laughed half-heartedly.

'Bit of a sore-spot, huh?'

'No I'm just joking.' Eva shook her head as she philosophised. 'It's easy for me to say that they're all bastards and they're all the same but they're not. Just my bastard.'

'I hope you're right Eva. It has often crossed my mind that they're ultimately all the same with the dating luck that I've had over the years but I still live in hope of finding *the* one.'

'Ah he's out there all right Elaine. Sure what about your latest guy, Gary isn't it?' Eva reassured but in her own mind she only half believed her own words.

'Yeah, so far so good with him anyway. I'm sorry that you won't get to meet him this time as he's away on a business trip.'

'I know. You'll have to show me a photo of him. Is he really a cross between Ryan Gosling and Chris Hemsworth? You always get the good looking ones!'

'He's a bit on the scrumptious side alright,' Elaine giggled.

'Anyway, enough about men. Remind me Eva, where are we off to tomorrow?' Elaine was excited at the prospect of setting off on an adventure.

'Well our first stop will be Gloucester, then Ipswich and I've us booked into a B&B in Newburyport for two nights.'

'Sounds good, then what?'

'Then south-west to Northampton for three nights. After that we travel eastwards to Plymouth and Hyannis Port for one night and finally Nantucket. We're spending two nights there and then a day trip back should take us back to Boston for a last night out on the town, all going well.'

'And what are we looking for exactly?' quizzed Elaine.

'Living and dining stuff.'

'You couldn't narrow that down a small bit could you?' Elaine teased.

'Well you know, homey stuff.'

'Like?'

'Like mirrors and cushions, picture-frames, vases, bowls, dinner-ware, breakfast mugs, table-cloths, napkins, quirky pictures but it has to be American.

It needs to be clean, cool and fresh. Think surfing waves, marram grass, sun-bleached timber.' Eva was getting quite animated as she spoke, making sweeping gestures with her arms as if to draw pictures on an imaginary design board.

'Ahh, you had me worried there for a minute with your 'Living & Dining stuff' description. Sounds like you know what you're after alright and I hope I'll be of some help to you. Tell me how's Viv getting on, do you see much of her?'

'Great altogether. Looks stunning as always, loving her job and has some new mystery man on the scene.'

'Mystery man, sounds intriguing,' mused Elaine.

'Well when I say mystery man, it's just that there is someone that she really likes but she's trying to take things slow so I haven't actually met him yet. Now that I think of it I don't even know his name.'

'Sounds like she's being very cagey.'

'Careful I suppose. To be fair, it's been me not asking rather than her not spilling the details. I haven't really seen her that much over the summer and when we do meet up it's for a quick bite in town with me blabbing on about my business. She did want to meet up recently and I had to cancel and I'm sure she wanted to talk to me about the romance but I just couldn't make it.'

'Sure you know she'll understand. With the pressure of this new venture of yours and everything.'

'She will yeah I know. She's been a great help to me with it all. And the closer it gets the scarier it feels.'

'No wonder Eva. Of course you're going to be nervous. Who wouldn't be. I think you're brilliant taking the plunge like that, headlong into the business world. You're dead right, life's too short not to follow your dreams.'

'Thanks Elaine. I've had plenty of doubts and still do but I'll be damned if I'm going to chicken out at this stage. I just want to give it one good try.'

'You'll do more than try Eva so you will. Actually I will guarantee that you will be a raging success story. We're going to find the coolest 'Living & Dining stuff' and everyone is going to want to have it!'

'I hope you're right. Sometimes I get really excited about it and I'm confident that it'll be fine but other times then…'

'You'll be grand Eva. Come on, let's head back.'

Finishing their frozen yogurts they strolled back to Elaine's apartment in the wonderful balmy heat of midsummer in Boston. Coming in from the warmth the air-conditioning was almost too cold and Elaine turned it off for a while. Pouring them both a glass of wine she threw open one of the large windows and let the heat in while they sat chatting and catching up. They snacked on nacho chips that Elaine sprinkled with cheddar and whizzed under the grill to melt. Dipping them into tubs of salsa they worked their way through a bottle of wine until darkness descended on Boston city.

Eva's flight was beginning to catch up with her and after stifling a few yawns they decided to call it a day. She got ready for bed in the large en suite that had a huge mirror over the sink. It was more like a hotel bathroom than an apartment en suite. As Eva removed her make-up and applied an anti-wrinkle night cream she thought of Elaine living in this apartment on her own all the time. She could see that she was perfectly content even though she had mentioned that she was still attending counselling. No doubt there were plenty of advantages to living on your own but it had to get pretty lonely at times.

Eva had gotten to know Elaine when they had shared a house together with Vivienne in college in Cork. Eva had done an Arts degree, Elaine I.T. and Vivienne had done Business Studies. Elaine's good looks made her very popular with the boys in college and she wouldn't have believed it for a minute but both Eva and Viv had often been jealous of her and the ease with which she pulled the men. Her gorgeous full auburn wavy hair that fell past her shoulders and sparkling green eyes were a mesmerising combination and coupled with killer curves she was a stunner.

After finishing her I.T. Degree in Cork, Elaine had spent some time working for an international company in London but with a lot of travelling it was there that she had suffered her breakdown. After a year she decided that the States was for her and headed for New York, then L.A. and finally ended up back on the east coast again in Boston. She had moved around a bit in Boston from one apartment to another but now that she had bought her own place it was here that she felt most at home.

151

Sleep came quickly for Eva in Elaine's comfortable guest bed and it was a solid eight hours before she awoke to the sunshine melting through the cracks in the white painted wooden shutters on the window.

Breakfast was fresh croissants and freshly squeezed orange juice that Elaine picked up from a bakery just across the street. Eva was anxious to get moving and to make the most of her day so after an invigorating power-shower they hit the road. The sky was bright blue and cloudless and by ten-thirty they were on the road and heading north-east of out Boston. They drove with the radio tuned to 'KISS 108' belting out a lively Beyonce tune.

First stop was Gloucester and they arrived there in just over an hour. Reputedly one of the premier art colonies of the United States, Eva held out high hopes of coming across some items of interest there. Gloucester was famous as America's oldest fishing port and had been harvesting seafood since the early 1600s. The harbour was breathtakingly beautiful and the town which had first been named "Le Beauport" did indeed deserve that title. Eva had their itinerary well planned and was able to fill Elaine in on interesting historical facts that she had read about the town and was feeling like a bit of a tour guide.

They spent a good hour and a half strolling around various galleries and crafts-shops however nothing really appealed to Eva and they decided to drive onwards to nearby Ipswich instead.

Ipswich proved to be a real find. Eva was like a history teacher informing Elaine that the picturesque town had a rich history of craftsmanship with lace and stocking-making having been a huge industry there from the late 1800s. While the stocking factories had long gone a diverse cultural heritage remained and Eva hoped to find the crafts that would reflect this.

The town was quaint with a strong English influence on the architecture. Eva had done lots of Internet assisted research and had an address of a crafts-shop come gallery that they successfully sought out. It was like an Aladdin's cave to Eva and offered everything she had hoped for and more. Walls were lined with white painted shelving full of fine crafts in blown glass, forged

152

metal and pottery. Pine wooden dressers were laden with lamps, dishes, soaps and candles while small furniture items filled up any available space on the shop floor.

Eva could hardly contain her excitement about one particular range of pottery and an assortment of coloured glass salad bowls which were quirky yet cool. Like nothing she had ever seen before.

When she asked to speak with the owner she couldn't have been more helpful and Eva arranged to meet with her again the following morning to further discuss the possibility of a business arrangement.

Laden with brochures and catalogues of the various lines Eva and Elaine returned to the car.

It was almost three o'clock and they were both hungry. Not in the mood to wait patiently for an order in a restaurant they picked up some takeout 'subs' and coffee and drove out of Ipswich to nearby 'Crane beach' to enjoy them. The generously filled salad rolls were munched with great relish as they savoured the views on the four mile stretch of white beach.

After taking a break for an hour they hit the road northwards again and soon arrived in Newburyport. Having spent twenty minutes following directions up and down various streets they eventually checked into 'The New Inn Guesthouse'.

Eva had reserved a twin room with en suite and they were both jaded by the time they entered it.

The room had a Quaker feel to it. It was sparsely filled with two simple white beds, a couple of chairs and a big old jug and dish on the dressing table. Bed covers were quaint patchwork quilts and the curtains a pretty blue and white gingham check with a cotton lace trim. It was simple but it was quaint and warm at the same time.

Elaine literally launched herself onto the quilted bed and stretched out.

'I'm exhausted,' she declared.

'Me too,' Eva replied.

'How about an ol' siesta before dinner?'

'Yeah I wouldn't mind a bath myself,' replied Eva.

'Go for it girl. I'm going to get forty winks,' and with that Elaine turned on her side and closed her eyes.

Eva smiled at her pal sprawled out on the bed. *She hasn't changed a bit,* she thought to herself, *not one iota whatever that was or a single jot, she hadn't changed a jot either.*

Giving up on the word games in her head Eva turned her attention to her luggage, unpacking carefully and anticipating a nice long soak. The water gushed forcefully from the tap as Eva emptied in a large dollop of bubble bath and began to swirl it around with her hand creating a whirlpool of spiralling bubbles getting frothier and frothier. Gingerly easing her naked body into the hot water she lay back and rested the back of her head on a folded up towel. The water level rose around her and her two knees protruded like bobbing life buoys in a foaming ocean. Letting out a deep sigh she closed her eyes, sank deeper into the bath and listened to the peculiar crinkly rustling sounds that bubbles made as they clashed with each other.

Eva eventually emerged from the bath with fingers and toes resembling crepe paper. She had stayed in for far too long and her hand-cream wasn't doing much to plump up the crinkled skin of her hands. Taking her time she slowly moisturised her entire body. She put on a white fluffy cotton robe and then polished her toenails with a deep vampish maroon coloured nail polish before returning to the bedroom where she found Elaine exactly as she had left her. It took a few gentle shakes to rouse her but soon enough Elaine was showered and deciding what to wear. This was their first proper night out together and they put plenty of effort into getting ready. Elaine shone in a chic black knee-length dress teamed simply with gold strappy sandals. Eva wore her cream top with matching palazzo trousers. For added height Eva wore a pair of cream wedge heeled leather sandals. She accessorised simply with the gold earrings that she had bought in Collioure and as they dangled they glistened reflecting their radiance onto her glowing skin.

Soon they were venturing out onto the streets of Newburyport in search of some fine dining. After having had only a sandwich for lunch they both felt like they were deserving of a really extravagant meal out. The landlady of the guesthouse had made a few suggestions and they decided to seek out the nearest restaurant on her list of recommendations.

The restaurant was combined with a wine bar for casual dining and suited them perfectly. Elaine started her meal with mussels steamed in pernod with fresh tarragon and shallots served with a herb crusted crostini. Eva's starter was described as Sushi Tuna rolled in Sesame Seeds, Seared Rare and served with Crispy Wonton, Soy Sauce, Ginger and Wasabi. The flavours were just something else but while it sounded like a lot on the menu the portions were not too big and left plenty of room for the main course. Elaine stayed with the Seafood menu and chose baked scallops with bacon, thyme and white wine topped with breadcrumbs and parmesan cheese served with grilled asparagus. She described it as sublime and savoured each one of her perfectly cooked scallops. Eva went with a mains choice from the By Land and By Sea menu. She chose an 8oz fillet mignon and lobster tail with mushroom bordelaise reduction, sautéed spinach and jasmine rice. 'Surf and turf' at its finest. Cooked exactly to her liking she struggled to finish and there was definitely no way that she had any room for dessert after that extravagance. It was heavenly and washed down with a strongly flavoured Napa Valley Chardonnay.

Not fit to budge they moved the short distance from their table back to the wine bar where they slowly sipped another glass of the Californian Chardonnay. They spent the next couple of hours getting progressively giddier, chatting up the barman while the jukebox belted out some country music. They were in flying form and anything even vaguely humorous had them both in fits of laughter and feeling like carefree youngsters again.

Melting out of the restaurant onto the street they ambled unevenly in the direction of the guesthouse along the wide pavement until they came across a small park with an empty bandstand that looked really pretty under the street lamps and moonlight. Elaine was the first to climb the steps and launched into a performance of Abba's 'Dancing Queen'. Now Elaine was a

155

passable singer but Eva didn't have a note in her head, undeterred however, she joined Elaine to belt out their own version of 'Rocketman.' Eva was warbling her way through it when Elaine pulled her sharply by the elbow and out of the bandstand setting a peppy pace in the direction of the guesthouse.

'Cop car,' she hissed 'c'mon quick,' Elaine said in a tone that sparked more of excited glee than trepidation.

'Just as well,' replied Eva giggling, 'I'm bursting for a pee.'

That set the two of them off giggling again as they stumbled their way back towards the lodgings with Eva trying to walk and do her kegel exercises at the same time.

Night-time beauty regimes went out the window as they both collapsed onto their beds. Mascara, lipstick and blusher all took their turns to slide onto the pillow-cases as the two friends slipped off into Lalaland.

There wasn't a budge from either of them until just after 9a.m.

'Oh Joseph my head,' Eva half whispered with her two hands clamping her temples as she attempted to raise her head off the pillow.

'What time is it?' groaned Elaine.

'Mmmm just after nine,' Eva replied.

'Do we have to get up?'

'Afraid so, I've to meet that lady in Ipswich at 12.30 remember? To talk about shipping and things.'

'Oh yeah, we'd better get a move on so,' Elaine replied

'Sure look it. Can't you stay there Elaine if you want and I could drive down myself?'

'No no, not at all, I'll be up in a minute.'

Forty minutes, two bottles of water and a few layers of concealer later and they were presentable and en route back to Ipswich again. Elaine drove as Eva flicked through catalogues and brochures trying to be ruthless in her selection of products. Eventually she settled on one range of locally made pottery in a very distinctive blue and creamy white that had a feel of nautical freshness and was chunky in size. She also picked out some two toned candles and some quirky comical looking seagulls made

156

from porcelain, pebbles and seashells. She only picked the things that she would definitely buy for herself.

Eva left Elaine to stroll and browse around the town while she discussed costs and shipping arrangements with the gallery owner Mrs Crompton. Eva was delighted to learn that everything could be done online, all her ordering and payment details could be transferred electronically. She wouldn't have to be worried about time differences and could just place an order whenever she needed to.

'Sure you'll have to get your own website up and running too Eva. It wouldn't take much to do it you know,' Elaine suggested on the way back to Newburyport.

'Viv had suggested the same thing but I don't know won't it be very complicated?' Eva inquired.

'Absolutely not Eva, they are so easy to set-up. I could get someone to design something over here for you and I could guarantee you that it would cost a lot less than it would in Ireland. Seriously you could get a really decent site professionally designed for less than half the cost of back home.'

'Yeah, that sounds great, I'll probably leave it until the shop is up and running though.'

'If you like, but you should register a site name so that you can print it on your stationery and business cards etc. I'll send something on to you about it. Online is where it's at these days Eva and opens up the whole world to you.'

'Bags,' Eva replied with a half worried look on her face.

'Yes, put the website address on the bags too.'

'No I mean I completely forgot about bags, and wrapping paper and all that kind of paraphernalia.'

'Don't worry Eva, that'll be easily sorted.'

''But what else have I forgotten?'

'It'll all be sorted in time.'

'You're right, I'm going to stop fretting,' and taking a deep breath she looked out the car window and started mentally writing lists of yet more things she still needed to do and tried not to hyperventilate.

Back in Newburyport they were just about ready to face some proper food again. They had fortified themselves all day with water, orange juice and some crackers and feeling semi-detoxed they enjoyed a late lunch in a quaint café. It was late afternoon before they had a proper look around Newburyport.

Once again Eva assumed the role of tour guide and read from her research. She told Elaine how the town of Newburyport had been famous for its whaling and shipbuilding industry in the nineteenth century and was a seaport rich in history and beauty. Having undergone major renovations in the downtown area in the 1960s and 70s the beautiful brick and granite architecture had been restored to its original quality and charm.

They walked along winding brick pavements and later a waterfront boardwalk. They discovered the heart of the city at Market Square alongside State Street, Pleasant Street and Merrimac Landing. Eva loved reading the names they sounded like poetry. With numerous side streets featuring a variety of boutiques, bookstores, crafts-shops and cafes it had a lovely holiday feel to it and they browsed happily for the next couple of hours. Art galleries were numerous and varied but mainly too upmarket and pricey for what Eva was after.

They were booked into the B&B for a second night and it was lovely to feel completely relaxed and just wander around. They picked out a restaurant for dinner later on and made reservations. That evening they didn't dine until nine and it was a much more subdued affair than the previous evening with them both sticking to sparkling water and skipping both starter and dessert. After another meander along the boardwalk indulgently taking in the sea air they headed for bed and were sound asleep by midnight.

Chapter 13

(NANTUCKET BAY SCALLOPS)

After a breakfast of freshly baked blueberry muffins, freshly squeezed orange juice and strong coffee they hit the road and headed south west in the direction of Northampton which lay about a hundred and forty miles away. Elaine was doing all the driving.

They passed signs for the towns of Lawrence, Lowell, Worcester and made a lunch stop in Springfield. Eva couldn't resist picking up some Simpson's memorabilia for Luke and picked up a Springfield replica number plate for his bedroom wall.

En route again to Northampton Eva pulled out some information she had downloaded and browsing through it she read aloud:

"this small city offers more restaurants and shops, certainly more galleries, theatres and performance venues than most urban centers dozens of times its size. Add two rivers, mountain views, landscaped parks and meadow walks, and you begin to see why people call it paradise."

'Says who?' enquired a sceptical Elaine.

'The Boston Globe,' Eva replied firmly.

As they drove slowly into the city there was something bustling and atmospheric about it and then Eva noticed the posters

159

welcoming tourists that read 'The Northampton's Food Festival, opens for a 3-day feast of the cuisine Northampton is famous for.'

'Looks like we've struck it lucky here then,' Elaine enthused as they followed directions to their lodgings.

It was late afternoon and again they were staying in a B&B. This time it was an old colonial mansion. The house itself was breathtaking with timber decking wrapped right around the first floor and imposing columns and architraving. They had quick showers and changed for the evening and set off to investigate the food festival.

The city was buzzing with diners grazing from one restaurant stall to another indulging themselves in selections from every cuisine imaginable from Indian to Chinese, Mexican, and Japanese. Eva and Elaine bought their 'Food Festival Tickets' and discovered that over thirty restaurants were participating and that there were more than eighty culinary specialities to be sampled.

Between the two of them they spent the following hour tasting from a selection of Barbecued Chicken Sticks, Maki Roll, Chicken and Shrimp Jambalaya, Philly Steak & Cheese, Blackened Filet Tips served over rice with Gorgonzola Beurre Blanc and Pan Blackened Sea Scallops with Mango Ketchup.

It seemed ludicrous to have sampled as much as they did but everything was in really small portions making it possible to savour at most two or three bites and then move on. They had both tried different things and between them has still probably only tasted less than half of what was on offer. When eventually they couldn't face another morsel they sipped on cold beer and listened as Latin, Rhythm and Blues and Rock and Roll bands took turns on the music stage.

The following morning Eva had a list of stores and galleries that she was anxious to investigate and Elaine dutifully accompanied her for the first couple of hours but it was all too business-like an approach to shopping for her and so she skived off to a cooking demonstration in the Chefs Tent at the Taste Festival in the afternoon.

Meeting up back at the B&B at five o'clock they readied themselves for another evening at the food festival. As they explored more new tastes Elaine raved about her day. She had seen two chefs in action, a flame-thrower, a unicyclist and comedian performing and had also discovered a lovely old bookshop which provided a welcome escape when she had had enough of the food fair and she had bought herself a new book.

Likewise Eva also had a successful day. Northampton proved to be a mecca in terms of sourcing items for her new store. The downtown area was made for exploring on foot and very easy to get around. Every block that she strolled unveiled side streets with stores whose doors she found were impossible to pass by. Museums and antique stores offered glimpses into Northampton's rich history and art galleries were everywhere. There were amazing displays of hand-crafted pottery and sculpture and Eva was being spoiled for choice. Her big find was truly unique, something she had never seen in any shop on her travels, she had found Yak fibre rugs. And not only yak, llamas and camels too were being reared in Northampton for fibre which was then dyed and transformed into rugs and sweaters.

She had also picked out some beautiful prints that she was having shipped back, in rich earthy tones they represented maps and journeys. There was some sculpting work in bronze and other metals that she was interested in as well as another range of pottery. But the rugs in the various mixes of yak, lama and camel fibres were amazing. Eva was really excited about them and had arranged a visit to the manufacturer the following day and was thinking about commissioning some wall hangings as well as rugs in various sizes.

Eva knew from her research that hundreds of artists from potters to painters had chosen to call the area home but hadn't anticipated that Northampton would be the highlight of her trip.

On their last day in Northampton Eva set about finalising her orders for some unique yak wall hangings and rugs, bronze sculptures, map inspired prints and made the shipping arrangements while Elaine had booked herself into a spa for the afternoon and indulged in a full body massage, manicure, pedicure and facial. Their time in Northampton had passed far too quickly and Eva would have loved to have stayed for another couple of days but she was more than satisfied with her finds there. Their third and last night exploring Northampton was a lot less indulgent than the previous two with both of them having simple salad for dinner and turning in for an early night.

The next day was a Sunday and they rose early to drive 140 miles eastward to Plymouth arriving there by noon. Eva had chosen to visit Plymouth purely because the name had leapt out at her when she had been studying the map of Massachusetts. Antiques and gift shops were plentiful and there was lots of unique stoneware and porcelain on offer. They browsed through some art galleries and had a late brunch before Eva spent the afternoon checking out some more crafts-shops. Elaine made no secret of the fact that by now she had seen enough pottery to do her for the rest of the year if not forever and happily spent a couple of hours reading her new book on the beach. Eva was beginning to think that by now her pottery range was probably expansive enough anyway with two ranges from the South of France, one from Ipswich, one from Northampton and an assortment of other pieces. What she found in Plymouth was spoons of all things. Beautifully shaped wooden serving spoons made from cherry wood that would be perfect with salad and pasta serving bowls.

Meeting up with Elaine again at five o'clock they had a relatively short drive to Hyannis where they were booked into a motel. The accommodation was fresh, clean and basic with none of the homely touches that they had gotten used to in the B&Bs. A light sea breeze struggled to refresh them as they strolled in search of a restaurant on a warm balmy evening.

They passed the JFK museum and found a bar that served pizza slices that they enjoyed with refreshing cold beers. Elaine was tired from all the sea air and embraced the suggestion of another early night, conking out as soon as her head hit the pillow. But Eva couldn't sleep. She kept thinking about the kids and worrying. Once she started, her worries began to snowball until what had begun as a niggling guilt pang for being away from them evolved into something akin to a panic attack. She felt caught for breath, her chest felt tight and she got up to open the window for some air. Lying back into bed she twisted and turned but couldn't relax enough to find sleep. She thought about the children as babies and how she used to listen for their breathing in the cot by her bedside at night-time. Every raised temperature or sign of a rash had her at the doctor's surgery fearing the worst. When they were sick Alan used to calm her down. He'd hold her strongly in his arms in bed at night and stroke her hair and tell her that the kids were fine and everything would be alright. And she believed him, she always believed him. And now he was gone. Tears flowed steadily down Eva's cheeks thinking about how good things had been. She had been perfectly happy with her life, she loved her complete family and now it was broken. *Why did he stop loving me,* she asked herself, *why?* Why wasn't she good enough? Eva felt alone and miserable, she just wanted to be at home. Silently sobbing into her pillow she focused on steadying her breathing until eventually sleep cradled her.

Woken early by an alarm call Eva felt shattered. Catching sight of her puffy eyes in the mirror she remembered why. Eva splashed her face with ice-cold water after she showered and then spent time on her make-up dabbing on some highlighter in an attempt to look brighter before waking Elaine who had happily slept through the alarm.

Eva left her to get ready and went to pick up some coffees and to make a call home. They were five hours ahead and it was lunch-time in Ireland. Hannah confidently answered her Grandmother's phone and sounded like the right little grown-up. A ten minute phone call later and Eva was right as rain again. The kids were fine and having a ball. While they did ask how many days before she'd be home she knew they weren't pining after her and that all was well.

Returning with coffee and croissants she could hear Elaine singing in the shower and shouted at her to get a move on. They really needed to push on if they were going to make the early ferry.

Leaving the car in Hyannis Port they travelled as foot passengers on the ferry from the shores of Cape Cod thirty miles to Nantucket. On arrival they took a short but very bumpy taxi ride through the main cobbled street of Nantucket and up some narrow streets until they arrived at their lodgings in a very quaint guesthouse called the 'Bluebell Inn'. The landlady gave them a warm welcome and showed them to their rooms. This time they had separate rooms, both beautifully decorated. Four poster beds with mattresses high off the ground were simply covered with patchwork quilts and the bathroom was well equipped with complimentary fizzing bath bombs, body lotion and sumptuously thick white cotton towels ensuring a feeling of being well pampered.

They dropped their bags and set off on foot again. With only two days to spend in Nantucket they set off to explore some of the boutiques off the main street and quickly discovered that shopping in Nantucket was not for the fainthearted. Prices were exorbitant in comparison to the mainland. Accommodation was expensive as was eating out and shopping. Despite that Eva fell in love with the Nantucket friendship basket, a traditional hand woven shopping basket in various styles and sizes and she was eager to source some. They could possibly make upmarket gift-baskets filled with candles and soaps etc.

Elaine had just about had her fill of boutiques and galleries by now and when they passed a bike shop and saw an elderly couple gearing up with helmets she persuaded Eva to do the same. They hired their bikes, bought a pre-packed lunch and strolled the bikes back to their lodgings where they changed into shorts and trainers and packed their swimsuits and towels into a backpack.

Like unsteady pre-schoolers for the first mile or so they gradually got the hang of it again. It must have been at least two decades since either of them had cycled anywhere. But once they got used to it, it was heavenly. Cycling along the dedicated bike paths with a breeze in their faces they could only feel happy, alive and carefree. Stopping at 'Surfside' beach about two miles out of town, they parked the bikes and chose a spot on the beach for lunch. Two delicious hours were passed balmed out on the expansive sandy beach, eyes closed, shades on and slathered in sun cream. *Balmed out*, Eva mused to herself, *a peculiarly Cork expression.*

'This is the life, isn't it Elaine?'

'You're telling me Eva. It's been wonderful.'

'Nearly time to head back to the real world though. It's been fabulous but the guilt is beginning to hit me and I'm really starting to miss the kids. What kind of mother takes off and leaves her kids for ten days in the summer?'

'Ah Eva, don't be so hard on yourself. You know fine well those two are having a ball at their Grandmother's and besides you're building their future. Would you be a better mother wallowing on the couch all day and watching talk-shows do you think?'

'I know Elaine, I just feel a bit guilty.'

'I don't know any more useless emotion than guilt'

'Ah but us Catholics thrive on it don't we though?'

'Reared on it we were, girl.'

'Do you remember breaking lent and feeling like the world's worst for having scoffed a chocolate biscuit?' Eva asked.

'Or feeling all good and pure after confession and trying your hardest not to say a bad word and put a black spot on your soul.' Elaine laughed.

'Bananas isn't it?'

'Nuts.'

'Well shall we mosey before we fry ourselves completely? I think I've gained enough wrinkles for one afternoon.' Eva began to gather up her belongings and stood to shake the sand off her towel. Her eyes locked onto the horizon and she gazed for a few seconds thinking of her beautiful children on the other side of the water.

Elaine led the way as they cycled back to the guest-house. The showers in America were fantastic, *no need for exfoliation,* thought Eva as she turned up the pressure and power-hosed her body with a refreshing blast of water. It was so strong that it almost hurt. The afternoon's sunbathing had brought out Eva's tan and she felt

165

really good as she moisturised her skin with a 'Pure Body Nantucket - Nourishing Body Oil.' Simply packaged, Eva made a mental note to inquire about the supplier.

They had decided to treat themselves to dinner in a nice restaurant and to glam up for the night. Time for a little black dress again Eva decided as she rummaged through her clothes that she had hung in the wardrobe. She pulled out the knee length halterneck dress with a very low scooping back that needed to be worn braless. Needless to say the dress hadn't gotten very many outings in Ireland but now that her tan gave her an extra glow she decided to brave it again and grabbed a wrap that was actually meant to be a sarong in case she felt the need to cover up. Unfortunately because her three inch high heels would have looked a bit ridiculous manoeuvring the cobbled streets she had to stick with the safer height of her kitten heels and even that was tricky.

Elaine had gone all out and looked sensational in a dusky pink calf length silk dress with shoestring straps and plunging neck-line accessorised with a simple pair of diamond stud earrings. Her footwear was also more sensible than she would have liked but rather than risk a twisted ankle she opted for flat but pretty leather flip flops which were embellished with beading and sequins in pinks and gold.

With an hour to pass before dinner they strolled down to the dockyard to admire the yachts that were moored there. The boats came in all shapes and sizes, with some of them being virtually floating houses.

Originally a booming whaling port the facilities on offer were first-class. The place reeked of money. Middle aged couples in pristine white cotton shorts and pastel coloured polo shirts and sweaters manned the decks with many of the women draped in chunky gold necklaces and bracelets.

'Gosh, she'd want to put the crown jewels in the galley wouldn't she?' Elaine remarked of one particularly heavily jewellery-laden shipmate. 'That lot would pull her under in a second,' she giggled.

'You're only jealous Elaine.' Eva was chuckling as she imagined

166

the anchor on the woman's faith, hope and charity necklace becoming larger than life and dragging her overboard.

'Not funny really,' Eva said, trying to be serious and recover decorum as they strolled onwards. Nantucket Island really was one of the prettiest places that Eva had ever visited. A little bit like Kinsale but without the traffic. Nobody was rushing around, it was so relaxing. Again they wandered in and out of the boutiques that stocked some beautiful crafts, unusual handmade jewellery and lots of artwork.

They had made dinner reservations at a seafood restaurant and because they had booked early managed to get one of the more popular tables outside on the terrace.

Their dining experience was an indulgent laid back affair with Eva doing justice to succulent Nantucket bay scallops in a white wine sauce and Elaine polishing off a platter of garlic scented mussels. Lingering over the last of the wine before returning to their guesthouse they were very glad of their choice of footwear as they cautiously picked their way across the cobbled street. You couldn't possibly beat this Island for old worldliness and charm.

Eva gave her final day on Nantucket one last go to supplement the stock for her shop. She came across a range of salt and pepper mills in strikingly modern blue, red and white. Useful and attractive and made on the island Eva made arrangements to ship an order and got email information for subsequent orders.

The friendship baskets however proved much too costly an item for her to order though she compromised by buying one of the baskets for herself.

Beach chairs were another Nantucket find. A classic range of deck chairs in red oak, with heavyweight canvas in sand, navy, red and forest green Eva decided to order forty of them, ten of each in each colour. It would also be possible to customise them with a logo and she thought that this would make for unusual corporate merchandising and imagined herself pitching ideas to the local stout company about emblazoning a picture of a pint on the chair with their slogan or whatever. It would be worth giving it a shot and could bring another dimension to her business.

167

Elaine by now was well and truly sated with visits to crafts-shops and was making no secret of it, groaning audibly every time Eva paused outside yet another one. She eventually decided to abandon Eva for the afternoon and set off for another one of the many beaches on a rented bike with her book for company. It was almost the end of Eva's trip to the States and it had been more successful than she could have imagined. By mid-afternoon Eva decided that enough was enough, she had plenty to stock her Cape Cod inspired section and it was time to relax and enjoy what was left of her stay and cycled out to Madaket beach to join her friend.

Arriving back to their lodgings later neither of them had either the energy or inclination to dress up for a second night of gourmet dining in Nantucket and without bothering to change they went in search of casual dining. What they found suited them perfectly. It was a little restaurant and bar with an artsy cinema at the back. Ravenous from the sea-air and cycling they dined on buffalo wings, crab cakes with a cranberry relish and potato skins topped with dollops of sour-cream and chives and of course a side-salad just to keep it healthy! The only deserving accompaniment could be a well-chilled beer and nothing could have tasted so refreshing in the heat of the evening.

Sleep was slow to come to Eva yet again not because of longing for her children but because her mind was working overtime with ideas. The cranberry relish that had been served with the crab cakes had been absolutely delicious. The only time that Eva had ever tasted cranberries had been in a sauce on Christmas day and it never occurred to her to open a jar at any other time of the year to dress something other than turkey. Besides the relish there were all sorts of other cranberry products available like jams, jellies, syrups and glazes. They were extremely versatile and could be used as hors d'oeuvres, spilled over cream cheese, heated as a sauce for chicken or pork, or as a glaze baked on a roasted chicken. *Would a food section work in the store?* she wondered. *Keep it a select offering,* she thought, *with unusual but high quality products, but was this diversifying too much, should she just stick to the interiors* ? she pondered as she dozed off to sleep and began dreaming of cranberries.

168

Setting sail early next morning on the ferry they both were a little sad to wave goodbye to Nantucket island as they passed the Brant Lighthouse standing majestically proud of its guard duties.

Picking up the car in Hyannis Port they started their journey back to Boston and the drive passed quietly with both of them solitary in their thoughts. Elaine felt sad that her week off with her friend was coming to an end and that by Monday she would be facing back into work again and Eva savoured the last few glimpses of the Cape Cod coastline equally sad to leave but so looking forward to heading home to Ireland again to see her beautiful children.

Elaine negotiated the tricky task of driving Boston's complex network of roads with ease and they were parked at her apartment building by lunch-time. They unloaded the car and by now Eva had accumulated quite a few bits and pieces. She had samples of pottery and candles from Ipswich, a rug made of yak fibres from Northampton, a modern bronze sculpted piece that she couldn't resist buying for herself, some samples of cherry wood salad serving spoons from Plymouth, her friendship basket from Nantucket and a vast array of catalogues. She could have had these things shipped back with her various orders from their origin but wanted to have them to look at while waiting for the shipments to arrive at home.

With her flight the next day Eva set off on some last minute shopping in search of gifts for Hannah and Luke. Elaine was less than subtle when she declined to join her with a firm response of 'No!' so Eva headed from Newbury Street towards Boylston Street in search of a toy-store.

Walking in the warm Boston air she passed the people's park and noticed red and yellow line markings on the pavement marking various trails that you could follow easily exploring Boston's history and landmarks. Taking her time she strolled in the direction of Faneuil Hall & Quincy Market.

Throbbing with tourists, street performers provided free entertainment while there were over a hundred shops and restaurants to browse and eat in. The indoor food court provided a

169

vast choice of cuisine that could be eaten in the various self-seating areas provided. For a refined dining experience seafood was on offer in the more upmarket exterior restaurants with 'Cape Cod Lobster' featuring on most menu boards. Eva opted for a slice of pizza from an Italian food stall accompanied with a can of Coke.

After eating she explored the marketplace shops and found gifts for Luke and Hannah. Feeling like her trip to Boston had just slipped away she returned to Elaine's where she gratefully accepted a glass of chilled Californian Zinfandel and sank into a sumptuously padded cream leather armchair.

'I can see the attraction of Boston, Elaine.'

'So you don't think I'm mad to settle down here then.'

'Not at all girl, sure this is the life,' Eva replied, sipping her wine and resting her weary feet up on the glass coffee table.

'Well I do hate to try and move you but do you realise it's almost seven and I've made us reservations for eight o'clock at my favourite steakhouse.'

Eva groaned as she tried to ease herself out of the armchair.

'I'll just finish this glass first Elaine and I'll be ready in a jiffy,' she pleaded as she sank back into the chair again.

'You wouldn't know a jiffy if it hit you over the head Eva,' Elaine teased as she headed off to grab a quick shower.

The heat of the sun was still strong as it beamed through the window of Elaine's apartment and Eva savoured the last few mouthfuls of her glass of wine before forcing herself out of the chair and picking out something to wear for the evening. She had bought herself a delicate pistachio green silk sleeveless top in one of the shops on Newbury Street and decided to give it an outing. Teamed with a pair of designer denims she hoped she looked more 'Sex and the City' than 'Desperate housewives'.

The meal was heavenly with both of them having steaks and truffle tries. Dessert was a shared 'Loaded Brownie Sundae' which was a celebration of all things chocolate, the brownie, the chocolate chips with sticky chocolate sauce, ice-cream and cream was heavenly.

As they walked home Eva said that all her guilt had made her

170

want to do something really special with the kids and she put a suggestion to Elaine.

'You might not be interested,' she began, 'but I was thinking it might be nice to bring the kids on a shopping trip to New York before Christmas and you could join us if you wanted to. What do you think?'

'Oh Eva I'd love that!'

'Really? It's just I want to do something really special to celebrate their birthdays and there's no way I can face hosting a party for them this year.'

'Absolutely, New York would be magical for the kids coming up to Christmas,' enthused Elaine, 'and there's the ice-skating in Central Park at that time of year too.'

'Brilliant! I'll look into it when I get back.'

The evening drew to a close with the two friends polishing off the remnants of the bottle of wine from earlier, sitting out on Elaine's deck at the back of her apartment. It was still warm enough to sit outside even though the moonlight had by now long replaced the sunshine. Being light headed from the alcohol they both spoke more freely than they might have done in daylight sobriety with Eva expressing her anxieties at going back to try and both establish a business and divorce her husband at the same time. Elaine encouraged her in both endeavours and told her she would support her in any way she could.

'At least you're going back with a plan. You know what you need to do and it will all come together,' Elaine encouraged.

'It's more of a confidence thing than anything. Sure what do I know about running a business?' Eva replied.

'About as much as anybody else does when starting any business from scratch, next to nothing. But it's a learning curve. You'll ask questions, you'll gather information and before you know it you'll be in full control.'

'Do you think? Yeah, I suppose you're right. There's no turning back now anyway.'

'Eva all you need is the nerve to try it and you have that.'

'It's daunting all the same.'

171

'Of course it is. But you're back out there. You're doing stuff and you're living Eva. It has taken me a long time to realise that it's only you that can make things happen not anybody else. I mean the good stuff. Whatever you achieve in life is down to one person. Yourself. That's the one message that all the counselling sessions have finally driven home to me. In the beginning it sounded too simple, too clichéd but experience has proven it to be true. They kept telling me to do the things that make me feel good. I used to think that you either felt good or you didn't. I mean what would you say are the things that make you feel good Eva?'

'Lots of things I suppose.'

'Like…?'

'Like my kids, good food, nice clothes, good wine, friendship…..'

'But it's not just them as entities is it Eva? I mean it's not just the kids, the food, the clothes, it's your experiences of them. It's you enjoying good food. It's you trying a new recipe. It's you playing with your kids. It's living Eva not just existing. It's living life and partaking in the things that make you feel good as much as you can, this wine is making me very philosophical isn't it?'

'In a way, but what you're saying isn't what you'd call deep though, it's simple but it's true' Eva replied.

'Yes, simple. We over-complicate things. We worry too much. Kids for the most part are happy aren't they? They have short-term goals and do the things they want to do without worry.'

'Do you worry a lot Elaine?'

'I sit back too much and doing that can let things slide.'

'Like what?'

'Just like my form I suppose. That's why I keep going to counselling. It's only once a month but it usually gives me a kick-start and reinforces all those positive messages. It's one thing telling myself and telling you to just get out there and do stuff and not to worry but I need to hear it from a professional from time to time as well. Sounds stupid doesn't it?'

'Gosh Elaine, not at all. There are some things that I have to force myself to do as well, like going to the gym for instance but you feel glad that you went and especially afterwards for having done it.'

'Sometimes even buying food gets me down,' Elaine replied. Can you imagine going into a supermarket jammed full of food, all that choice and just standing there in the aisles feeling like a fool with a basket in your hand and not knowing what to do, turning what should be a simple task into a mammoth issue. I have on occasion left with nothing, which only makes me feel worse. How stupid is that?'

'Elaine it's not stupid. Come on. Don't be so hard on yourself.'

'No, I'm not. I'm fine. I know how to deal with these situations now. I have learned these little pull yourself together skills that I do. There's yoga breathing and writing notes to myself. One therapist actually encouraged me to write how I felt with one hand and then write something to talk away that issue with the other hand. Writing with your left hand isn't easy you know. I think it's nearly more the effort that goes into the task rather than the task itself that sets you on the right track again.'

'Yoga's great for lots of things isn't it? I did it when I was pregnant with Hannah and used to nearly float out after the classes,' Eva enthused.

'Yeah. Although apart from the odd bit of relaxation breathing that I practise myself I haven't been to a class in ages. It's 'Pilates' that's all the rage here now.'

'Have you been? I've seen notices up at my gym and was wondering about going myself,' Eva enquired.

'Yeah. It's super for toning up, especially the tummy area. I went to a six week course and will probably sign up for one again soon.

'Well we'd better hit the sack if you're to be in any fit state for travelling tomorrow,' Elaine suggested as she yawned and looked at her watch.

It was almost 2a.m. and even though Eva's flight wasn't until evening time the following day they were both feeling jaded after their travels over the past week and agreed to sleep in until they woke.

173

Chapter 14

(ROAST CHICKEN & GRAVY)

Eva arrived in to Shannon airport on a damp Irish August Friday morning. Although it was wet and slightly misty it held some promise of a good day ahead as the sun was making watery efforts to burn its way through. Signs of welcome to Bunratty, Limerick, Charleville and Mallow town all whizzed by until finally she parked outside her home in Douglas.

It felt strange to turn the key in her door and enter into quietness. It was still early and she had a few hours before the children would come home from their Gran's house at noon.

She busied herself by doing some laundry then had a coffee and began to look through the post half-heartedly. She was dying to see the kids but not wanting to put pressure on Mary to bring them over sooner than agreed she resisted the temptation to call them. Time seemed to move even more slowly when all you wanted it to do was hurry up. Being alone in the house made her feel sad. This was it. This was her life now. No partner delighted to see her and welcome her home with a big hug.

Well when they did arrive the buzz of the children soon dissipated any negative feelings. Overwhelmed with love she wrapped her arms around them tightly and bear-hugged them both. She had missed them so much and they her. Luke was delighted with his new gadget and as always it wasn't long before he was running out the door to call to his friend and play on the green. Hannah stayed around for a while chattering about all the things she had done on the farm with her Gran. It sounded like she'd had a lovely time. She asked loads of questions too and it was lovely that she was interested to hear about the places that Eva had visited and to see the things that she had bought and was hoping to sell in her shop.

Hannah of course praised everything which was truly sweet of her. *As if an eight year old would have any interest in a bit of pottery,* Eva thought but it just showed how eager Hannah was to make her Mum happy. Mary stayed long enough to brew up a pot of tea and Eva tucked into a slice of her freshly baked brown bread smothered in butter and home-made blackberry jam. Hannah had helped to pick the berries and to make the jam too.

It wasn't long before it was time for tea and Eva rooted around in the freezer and pulled out pizza, oven chips and garlic bread. The healthy eating would have to wait one more day as she just couldn't face the thought of going to the supermarket.

After tea the kids headed out to play with their friends again and Eva decided to give online shopping another go. Feeling very satisfied with her second grocery shop ordered, Eva had yet another mug of coffee and a chocolate hobnob. There was nothing quite like the melted chocolate after a quick dunk in the coffee and the lovely crunch of the oatmeal base of the biscuit.

With the early morning journey beginning to catch up on her she called the kids in for a bath before hitting the sack. She slept well and even better knowing that in the morning groceries would be delivered and that it would be once less thing to do for the week ahead.

Saturday morning was spent trying to muster some enthusiasm to do a bit more housework. The house was badly in need of dusting and vacuuming and while Hannah did help out eagerly enough at the start it wasn't long before her enthusiasm waned and she ran off outside to play with her friends.

Eva soon tired of the housework herself and by lunch-time she was eager to go down to the store for a peek at how the last couple

175

of weeks had changed things. On the pretext of a visit to the park that's what they did. There was nobody on site as it was a Saturday afternoon so Eva peered through the windows alongside the children who were up on their tippy-toes straining for a look. It didn't look to her like much had changed at all.

Feeling a little dismayed she headed to the park with the kids and while they played she called Vivienne to invite her over later. Viv however couldn't make it as she had a date but she promised to come over the next day for tea. Eva had detected a bit of hesitancy in Viv's voice and couldn't make out what could be up with her.

They returned home and Eva made a home-made lasagne for dinner with a green salad. Later she opened a bottle of white wine and threw herself down on the couch in front of a movie for the evening.

Thinking about Viv and her date made her thoughts wander to Sébastien. *Had he replied to her email yet?*, she wondered but she still hadn't set her email up on her phone and was too comfortable to extricate herself into going to check her laptop. That could wait until morning she decided as Hannah joined her on the couch and the pair of them cuddled up as Eva poured herself another glass of wine.

Sunday was a lie-in morning and Eva found it nigh on impossible to get out of the bed. Eventually dragging herself downstairs still in pyjamas and dressing gown where she sat on the couch with a mug of coffee flicking through interior design magazines while the kids happily munched cereal in front of cartoon TV. Alan called over to take the kids out at lunch-time and Eva finally got dressed and started to seriously look through her mail and emails.

There was an email notification from the warehouse that her shipment from Paris had arrived but nothing from Sébastien. The thought of her crates sitting safely in a warehouse in Cork gave her a warm excited feeling.

Quotes had arrived for fitting out the shop and they were fairly competitive with each of them being in and around the same price

176

which didn't make it any easier to pick one out of all of them. Eventually she decided to have a closer look at the one with the nicest name, *well how else would you choose?* she thought. She should probably ask for references she decided but if they did furnish her with details of some satisfied clients then the job would probably be theirs.

This thought led her on to thinking again about the name for her own shop. What the hell was she going to call it? It was important. She wanted it to be cool and modern but at the same time speak for itself. 'Habitat' would of course have been perfect but she couldn't really rip that off. She could always be cheeky and call it 'Habitat2' or something. 'Casa' was already taken and then there were the cool surname pairings that somehow managed to become synonymous with household furnishings. Her married surname 'White & Co.' sounded more like a solicitor's office than home furnishings and with her maiden name Murphy being more suited to a bar she decided to leave surnames out of the equation.

Her search for a store name was interrupted by a phone call from Viv to cancel the arrangement to come over for tea. She wasn't feeling the best after a heavy night out and was spending the day recovering. Eva wasn't too put out as she was so engrossed in the task of finding a name for her shop. 'House-stuff,' 'Homeware,' and 'Decorate It,' were a few of Viv's suggestions. Writing these on a sheet of paper and drawing a blank Eva realised that she would need some proper help for this decision too as it was really important and needed to be decided soon.

There were only a few more days left in August so in reality she needed the name by the end of the week if she was going to have a sign up and stationery and bags and business cards all printed up in time for opening. She thought about asking the children to come up with ten possible names and also Elaine and Fiona but then if she didn't pick one of them she could end up upsetting them, well the children anyway. She didn't really want the expense of enlisting a marketing company but maybe she should. That got her thinking about other things like P.R. tasks like advertising, media announcements and an official launch, who would organise all that

177

and how? Maybe she should hire a professional after all. She often had flyers coming through her own letterbox and that was probably another effective way of making her new business known but it would have to look right and have some kind of logo.

She went to bed tossing and turning about it all and by morning had made up her mind to hire a P.R. company or image designer or whatever they were called to come up with a name, image, and marketing or launch strategy, no messing this was going to be done properly.

Eva was up and dressed and the kids were still in bed when Helen arrived to babysit at eight-thirty on Monday morning. With Helen in charge of the house Eva headed for her study and prioritised her tasks for the day on a sheet of a notebook and as an afterthought added school shoes to the list of things to do. Helen would be finishing up at three o'clock and if Eva didn't get the shoes sorted out pronto they wouldn't have any for going back to school on Thursday. As usual she had put off the school shopping until the last minute. She remembered when cluelessly getting ready to send Luke to big school for the first time how she had gone into town in search of school shirts for him with a week to go only to be informed at one particular chain store that they were sold out of his size, wouldn't be ordering more and didn't she know that people had been shopping for school since June! So here she was once again with days to go and all to organise.

Who were these people who shopped for school stuff in June? she wondered, surmising that *they probably did their Christmas shopping in September.*

The summer had absolutely flown by for the kids. They were after a week in West Cork with her and a week with their Dad while she was in Paris. They'd had ten days on the farm at their Gran's, and sports camp so they hadn't done badly at all but it had whizzed by all the same.

Eva would have loved to book a week in the sun for them in October as they used to do every year but that wasn't going to be practical this year, unless Alan was going to take them. Hardly with his new girlfriend in tow she thought cynically and she wouldn't allow that for the kids anyway. Thinking about her own suggestion of a break with Elaine, she decided to look into a shopping trip to New York at the end of November. If they went for just a few days or a long weekend that would have to do if they could manage it. But for now it was back to her lists.

By ten o'clock Eva emerged from her office eager for a coffee and in a hurry to make a ten-thirty appointment at the shop fitters. She had reluctantly inquired about work references on the phone and was pleasantly reassured with the positive reply and the impression that they were readily available. On arrival she was made to feel very important as she was led into a very comfortable office to go through her plans. The meeting took ages but she was extremely impressed. They were able to input the shop dimensions from her blueprints onto a computer and within minutes were able to give her a virtual tour of what could be the layout of her new store. At the click and drag of a mouse shelves were repositioned, desks were relocated and light fittings were changed. She dictated what she wanted until finally the plans were just right. She had gone for white shelving in various arrangements with some displays being rows of shelves fitted to the wall and others being more boxy type dividing units and also decided on brass and glass light-fittings. Two and a half hours later she finished the meeting and left extremely satisfied after her morning's work. With the printouts of the shop fittings and blueprints crammed into her maroon leather satchel she felt quite the important businesswoman.

Lunch was a hastily bought cappuccino from a sandwich bar and a chicken and stuffing sandwich on brown bread to takeaway. Tucking into it she swore under her breath when a chunk of chicken fell onto her lap as she attempted to eat while driving home. Her trousers were dry-clean only and were now decorated with a nice greasy mayonnaise stain. At home again she quickly changed into a pair of white skinny jeans with a white cotton sleeveless top and a pair of raffia wedges. Her tan had developed since her trips to France and Cape Cod and she was now golden brown and the picture of health.

Flicking through pages of search results on her laptop she took note of some numbers for P.R. companies and Image Consultants but time was getting away from her and for now priorities had to change from the business to a school bag and shoe finding expedition. With the children under instruction to get ready for a dash into town she quickly checked out some of the references for the shop fitters and any hesitation to do business with them was rapidly wiped away after a couple of positive telephone calls.

School shoes were located in town without too much difficulty and after picking out some new school shirts and school bags they went to 'Milano' for pizza for their tea.

On Tuesday she made a return visit to the shop fitters where she went over the final adjustments to the shop layout and the dimensions for the storage units. It was amazing to get such a clear idea of what the store would look like from the computer images. While she had always emphasised that they would have to be ready to start in the first week of September, the last minute planning changes necessitated a few days more for materials to be organised but they promised her faithfully that they would be ready to commence work on the following Monday. A couple of days more wasn't going to make that much difference and now that she had a good idea of what the end result would be she was happy enough to wait for them to start work the following week.

On Wednesday she spent the afternoon browsing the web for ideas about P.R. and image consultancy and looked at some of the websites of the more well-known Irish interior's stores. Returning to the google searches again she narrowed down her choice to three. A recommendation would have been better but she didn't know who to ask for one and didn't have time either. It was going to be a bit of potluck what company she would end up with and she picked three companies whose ads were simple but with names that she liked. Her logic was that if the ads weren't too flashy then they wouldn't be the most expensive. Yet again she found herself choosing something by the name and it brought home to her how important it would be to get her own business name right. Having made appointments with the P.R. companies, she was delighted to receive a call from her own solicitor informing her that the developers had been in contact with instructions that she could take occupancy of the store at the end of the week. She hadn't gone near the place since peering through the window the previous Saturday and would wait one more day until she got the key so that the next time she went for a look she could open the door herself.

With no grocery shopping done since her delivery on the previous Friday the cupboards were looking decidedly raided and they were badly in need of a re-stock. With the need for back to school lunch supplies for the following day Luke and Hannah reluctantly joined her on a grocery run. They helped to overfill a trolley and to do all the necessary loading and unloading. Frustrated at the sheer waste of time Eva vowed to get into a habit of doing a regular online shop every week before the cupboards were bare.

Exhausted after putting everything away she opened a bottle of Shiraz as a stone-baked ciabatta based chilli-chicken pizza heated up in the oven. Viv called over unexpectedly and joined her in drinking a large glass of the peppery wine as Eva decided to abandon her diet until the next day.

'Well what's new with you Viv? How're things?' Eva asked.

'Good, yeah not too bad.'

'Just good?' Eva teased.

'Well no actually they're great,' Viv couldn't stop herself beaming.

'Is it the new man? Come on spill.'

'Oh Eva. I feel a bit weird about this and I wanted to tell you before you went to the States but I didn't because I didn't know how things would pan out and anyway…'

'What are you on about?'

'Well like I said I wasn't sure how things would go and because you were so busy I couldn't find the right way to tell you but I have to tell you now…'

'Tell me what?' Eva was completely clueless.

'Well it's the guy. You see you know him. You know who it is,' Viv said using a serious tone.

181

Eva froze and a flash of Alan came into her mind. It couldn't be. She was silent for a moment as the colour drained from her body.

'What? Who is it?'

'It's Daniel,' Viv replied a little hesitantly.

'Daniel!' Eva gasped and then half laughed, 'you're joking me?'

'No seriously Eva. We swapped numbers after the barbecue you had earlier in the summer and then I bumped into him another time coming over here and he just asked me out. So we've had a few dates since then and he's really, really nice.'

Eva had just about steadied herself.

'Yes he is Viv. Really nice. I never thought....I mean I never would have guessed... so you and Daniel hmm?'

'Yep, well sure we'll see how it goes. I hope you don't mind Eva.'

'Of course I don't mind,' she lied impeccably.

'Actually we're heading off to Westport this weekend together and I just can't wait.'

'Isn't it a bit soon?' Eva's words flew out of her mouth before she could stop them and she even surprised herself with the acidity of her tone.

'Soon? Eva you sound like a nun! I mean talk about pot and kettle, after your shenanigans in France after a couple of days aren't you getting very pious all of a sudden!' Vivienne just laughed off Eva's query and hadn't picked up on the undertones.

Swiftly changing the topic of conversation to her business and back-to-school stuff it wasn't until Viv was long gone that Eva realised that she was a little bit jealous of Viv being with Daniel. *What is wrong with me? Why am I feeling jealous? It's not like I've any interest in him myself.* A little confused by how she did actually feel it took her a while to decide firmly that he was just a friend and she would always see him like that. *Could she not have fallen for someone else though?*

Thursday was the first day back at school for the kids and the day disappeared between school runs and boring paperwork. With the kids back at school Eva felt the need to feed them properly and to lay off on the all too frequent pizzas for a while. For dinner she cooked up a roast chicken with thyme and parsley bread stuffing, roast potatoes and gravy.

'Roast Chicken and Roast Potatoes with Herb Stuffing and Gravy'

You will need: (Serves 6)
1 large chicken – 2kg approximately
Olive oil to drizzle
1 lemon
12 medium potatoes (at least)
Sea salt

For the stuffing:
1 large onion
100g unsalted butter
400g breadcrumbs
1 tbsp dried parsley
1 tbsp dried thyme

For the gravy:
2 tbsp flour
500ml chicken stock

Method:
The stuffing
Make up the stuffing and leave it to cool before you put the chicken on to cook.
Peel and finely chop the onion.
Melt the butter in a saucepan over a low heat and soften the onion in the pan with a lid on for 5–10 minutes.
Turn off the heat and stir in the breadcrumbs, parsley and thyme.
Transfer the mixture to a baking dish and leave to cool.

183

The chicken
Preheat the oven to 190°C/Gas Mark 6.
Cut the lemon in half and place both pieces in the cavity of the chicken.
Place the chicken in a roasting tray, drizzle olive oil over the chicken and season with some crumbled sea salt flakes and put it in the oven.
Work out the cooking time of your chicken, *which* will vary by weight (20 minutes per 450g + 20 mins extra).

Cooking the Roast Potatoes
Peel and parboil the potatoes (cut to same size as each other) for 10 minutes.
Drain the potatoes and rattle them in the saucepan to bash the outside for a crunchier roastie.
Roast the parboiled potatoes* for 1 hour around the side of the chicken coated with the chicken juices or in a separate tin drizzled with some oil.

Cooking the Stuffing
Cover the cooled stuffing with tinfoil and cook for 45 minutes towards the end of the cooking time for the chicken. Toss the stuffing with a fork halfway through the cooking time so that it cooks evenly.

Making the Gravy
Remove the chicken and potatoes from the roasting tin and place the tin on the hob over a low heat.
*[If you want your potatoes crispier, return them to the oven, drizzle with oil and blast up the heat while you make the gravy]
Scrape up all the juices and mix with the flour to make a paste and cook for 2 minutes.
Gradually add in the chicken stock, stirring continuously, bringing it to the boil then reduce to simmer for five minutes.

184

Note: If you think there is an excessive amount of fat and juices, pour some off. Generally, 1 tablespoon of flour to 2 tablespoons of fat and juices to 400/500ml stock, and double this for a larger meal, e.g. Christmas dinner. For a thicker gravy, use more flour.

Serve the chicken, stuffing, potatoes and gravy with some roasted carrots and parsnips.

[RECIPE ENDS]

With the first day of school over and no homework to do they all put their feet up after dinner and watched a back to back double repeat episode of 'Modern Family'. Eva kept thinking about Viv and Daniel though and after a while she began to get more used to the idea. She was feeling a little foolish about her earlier reaction and wasn't sure if Viv had picked up on how she really felt. When the kids were in bed later Eva decided to give her a call. She told her how happy she was for her and that she hoped things would go well with Daniel. After wishing her all the best for a great weekend away together she explained that her less than supportive first reaction earlier on had been because she had been taken completely by surprise and she hoped she didn't sound too pathetic. When she sat down and thought about it later Eva knew that Viv couldn't have picked a more decent bloke and she genuinely hoped that it would work out for them. It did leave her feeling a little bit lonely though at the thought that her best friend and Daniel would be heading off for a romantic weekend together and that she had nobody.

The empty feeling stayed with her when she woke the following morning and it had nothing to do with Viv and Daniel having a romance. It was more the reality of being alone without someone to truly share her own life with that was dragging her down. A year ago, even six months ago she had been as happy as Larry, whoever Larry was, and now she was feeling blue.

185

After dropping the children to school on Friday, Eva picked up the keys for the store from the developer and let herself in. She was familiar with every inch of it now and could visualise what the final layout would be like. There was still so much to do to complete it and just for a minute she felt overwhelmed at facing it on her own. Working from her study at home she decided to go ahead and start advertising for staff. Feeling ravenous by lunchtime she heated up pitta bread in the toaster and then stuffed it full of grated cheddar cheese, sliced tomato and chopped spring onion and scoffed the lot with a cup of tea.

Looking through her lists later on and with an hour to go before picking up the children from school a sudden pang of panic gripped her.

'Fuck it,' she moaned loudly.

'Shit no,' she sighed as she sank her face into her hands and shook her head with her eyes firmly closed for the next minute. She had forgotten about the bloody flooring. *Why the hell hadn't she copped it first thing this morning?*

After spending weeks in July visiting suppliers she had decided on exactly what she wanted but she'd forgotten to order it. She had been so busy visiting warehouses, trying to decide on light fittings and planning the layout and they had all taken precedence and she'd completely forgotten about the floor. It was such a basic thing that she couldn't understand how she could have forgotten but there was no point in crying about it now. She even had pricing details and all she had needed to do was to get the place measured up but she had disappeared off to West Cork and forgotten all about it. Another rummage through her lists found the suppliers details and with a begging phone call and a bribe of payment up front she managed to persuade them to squeeze her in to measure up the floor later on that evening.

There would however be a knock-on effect and it meant that the shop-fitters would have to be put back for at least a week. She dreaded messing them around having put them under pressure to start as soon as they could but they were great and didn't give her any hassle about it. She picked the kids up from school and brought them for ice cream and then over to the store to meet the floor guy. Luke and Hannah were delighted to get a peek at the store but the novelty of it soon wore off as it was just an empty shell.

After waiting almost an hour for the measuring guy to show up they were well and truly bored and getting on each other's nerves. Usually when their whinging got to her she would try to placate them but today she just told them firmly to 'shut-up!' With the measuring done, the price was agreed and a fitter arranged for the following Monday morning. Eva would be able to enjoy her weekend now knowing that everything was under control again.

All going well she should still be on schedule if the shop-fitters came as they'd rearranged to do so for the following week. Hannah and Luke were somewhat disgruntled after being told to 'shut-up' by their mother and were hassling her for a trip to McDonald's as they were 'starving'. Instead she let them 'starve' all the way home and amazingly enough they didn't keel over until she rustled up some scrambled eggs on toast.

After their tea the kids hadn't much time to pack their bags for the weekend before Alan called to pick them up. They were throwing their last few bits together when he arrived and Eva invited him into the kitchen to wait for them. It was so weird to have him now as a visitor in his own home.

'How're things?' Eva inquired politely.

'Not too bad Eva and yourself?'

'Alright. Would you like a coffee or something?'

'No, you're grand.'

'Right so I'll just go and hurry them up.'

And that was the extent of their conversation. *Did he feel as awkward as he looked?* she wondered as she went upstairs to escape. Eva knew that they had nothing to say to each other that could be said when the kids were around and making small talk was torturous. Returning back downstairs again to hunt for Luke's trainers, Alan was still standing where she had left him in the kitchen looking even more uncomfortable. He seemed to be agitated and was sort of wringing his hands.

187

'Eva. Look I I..I wanted to say that I'm sorry about what happened and I wondered if we could talk some time?' he asked quietly.

'Oh?' Eva was completely taken aback and didn't know what to say.

'Yeah there's some stuff that I want to tell you and.....'

'Ready!' Luke shouted as he came bounding down the stairs.

'Right so,' Eva replied, going out to say goodbye and to give him a hug. Hannah was making her way slowly down the stairs after him and was a bit teary eyed to leave. Alan didn't say anything more and headed off with the two of them leaving Eva a little perplexed. *What,* she wondered, *had he wanted to say?* She cleared up the dishes in the kitchen and then sat on the couch to relax in front of the TV with a cup of coffee. Dunking a fun-size aero chocolate bar into the coffee she savoured the melting chocolate as it warmly coated the inside of her mouth.

Chapter 15

(TOASTIES)

Eva began Saturday morning with a stint at the gym determined to at least burn off the amount of calories that were in the three mini chocolate bars she'd ended up eating the previous evening. Hitting the treadmill for the first time in weeks she noticed a huge decline in her fitness and she was struggling to keep going after 3kms where previously she would have sailed through 5 no problem. Returning home she took her time to shower and moisturise before heading to the hairdressers. She had managed to get a hair appointment to brighten up her highlights and while she was there she got her nails done as well. There was nothing like an afternoon of pampering to lift the spirits.

Leaving the hairdressers she would have loved to have been heading off somewhere special for the evening but Viv was away for her weekend with Daniel. There wasn't anyone else that she was in the habit of going out with as she'd never really had the need to socialise with anyone other than Alan and couples that they knew through his work. Not one of them had called her since their split. A night in with Netflix beckoned. Much as she enjoyed the movie and the peace and quiet to paint her toenails to match her manicure with nobody complaining about the smell of nail varnish she couldn't help but feel a little lonely again.

She began to think about Alan and wondered what it was that he had wanted to talk about. *What if he wanted to come back and try again?* She tried to push the thoughts out of her mind but they kept creeping back in. He had been everything that she'd ever wanted and with their two beautiful children her life had been complete. Thinking about the children's future really tipped her over the edge. She pictured herself at Hannah's wedding on her own and Alan being there with another woman.

With all the opportunity in the world to avail of a good night's beauty sleep Eva didn't get very much of it and awoke with puffy eyes. A glance at her freshly done hair cheered her up somewhat and she decided to go to the gym again. If she was going to end up at the top of the aisle on her own at Hannah's wedding someday, well then she'd be there feeling her best.

The gym was like a morgue and Eva had the place to herself. She improved her performance on the treadmill and did a hundred stomach crunches at home before she showered. Keeping things healthy she'd a breakfast of a boiled egg and whole-wheat toast and decided to head out for the day in the name of doing a bit of research.

She drove to the shopping complex at Mahon and began to browse through the new autumn arrivals in the household store. There was some beautiful cookware, designer throws, ceramic vases and luxurious towels. Carefully checking the prices of some bedding, lamps, platters and rugs she made a mental note of them. In the end it became more of a torture than a pleasure as she began to question the choices she had made in selecting her own homeware. 'Ah cop on to yourself Eva,' she quietly scolded herself hoping that she didn't look like some crazy person as she stood there muttering with a worried look on her face. The ball was well and truly rolling now towards the opening of her store and it was gathering momentum each day as the 1st of October loomed closer.

Time had flown by and famished by four o'clock she picked up a cappuccino to fortify herself as she drove home. Drinking out of the takeaway cup as she drove made her feel glamorous for some reason. It wasn't something that she had grown up with and had probably only ever seen done by some American film-star so maybe that was why. The kids arrived home at seven and Eva made them all toasted cheese sandwiches. The sandwich-maker was rarely pulled out because it lived at the back of a cupboard hidden behind serving bowls, a cake mixer and lunchboxes. It did make delicious sandwiches though and was worth the rummage. Eva tucked into hers and nearly scalded the roof of her mouth on a slice of tomato as the melted cheese and chopped onion oozed out the sides of the toasted bread.

Monday morning saw Eva leaping out of the bed at cock-crow. She showered and pulled on a pair of denims and a light blue sweatshirt. She shook Luke awake gently to tell him to get ready for school and that she had to go out to do a job but would be back soon. She drove down to her still nameless store to hand over a spare key to the carpenter who was going to fit the floorboards. On her return she found Luke and Hannah sitting in the kitchen eating bowls of breakfast cereal. They weren't impressed at being left in the house on their own for the thirty minutes it had taken Eva to do her errand and listening to them she knew that she shouldn't have. It hadn't felt like that big a deal, she had just popped out to the shop and what choice did she have? She couldn't be arranging babysitters every five minutes of the day and likewise they didn't want to be dragged along unnecessarily either but in future she would have to. Something could have happened. *It was Alan's fault,* she silently justified to herself, *if Alan was here I wouldn't have to be running around like a headless chicken all the time.* Managing to feel a little less guilty for having left them on their own she pushed it to the back of her mind and got them sorted for school. Mom guilt achieves nothing.

Viv was glowing when they met for lunch later. After her two nights away with Daniel she was proclaiming Westport as the most beautiful town she had ever visited. They had stayed in some romantic hotel that had apparently been frequented by Liz Hurley and Hugh Grant at the height of their passion or at least sometime before shenanigans with Divine Brown called a halt to it all.

'Well I hope that you won't catch Daniel in an uncompromising position in his car!' Eva teased, referring to Grant's historic slip-up.

191

Afterwards they parted company with Viv promising to keep Saturday night free so that the two pals could glam it up and go out on the town together.

Eva was busy making arrangements for the store over the next few days. She'd have breakfast with the kids in the morning and lunch was usually a hastily grabbed coffee and sandwich. Last thing at night she would make a list of things to do the following day and cross off the ones of the day just passed.

She was loving the frenetic pace of whizzing out to appointments and calling into the store to see how everything was coming along but what she didn't love was the paperwork. With CVs and quotes coming in, electricity agreements and stock orders going out there was quite a flurry of it. Her filing system was non-existent and with her penchant for writing lists she knew she'd have to get a handle on things before she started losing stuff.

Soon, she promised herself soon, but for now she kept on just shuffling the paper around her desk and rummaging in her handbag.

Having skimmed through the CVs a number of times Eva didn't really know what she was looking for. She didn't have time to interview all of them so in the end she picked out ten promising looking prospects that looked like they had some relevant experience, at least on paper anyway. She telephoned the ten of them and scheduled interviews in a local hotel for the following week.

Her biggest task of the week had involved three meetings at P.R. companies. In all her dealings so far she had yet to come across someone quite as obnoxious as the hag from the first one. Although 'hag' wasn't really a fair description of the platinum blonde creature that Eva had encountered. Groomed to within an inch of her life she had greeted Eva with smiling red and freshly plumped glossy lips framing veneered teeth but the smile had not been matched by her tone. She was so obviously not keen at the thought of launching yet another start-up on an obligatorily tight budget. The start-up date was weeks away and she had practically sneered at the apparently ludicrous suggestion that it was even possible to be ready by then. Eva had politely enquired as to how long it would normally take.

'Oh *months*,' she stressed, 'it would take *months* to do a project like this *properly*.' The stress she was putting on some of the words sounded really condescending.

She went on and on ad nauseam and Eva tuned out for a bit just looking at her lips moving, they never really seemed to touch as she spoke and she wondered if she was even able to close her mouth fully with the size of them. When she did finally take a pause Eva stood up and quickly interjected saying :

'look it really was *lovely* to meet you, however I will have to give it some more thought. Again, so *lovely* to meet you and goodbye now.'

She politely offered her hand which was limply shaken before turning on her heel and leaving.

Eva approached her next P.R. firm with trepidation at the possibility of another frosty encounter. However she needn't have been daunted as she encountered an enthusiastically helpful young gentleman with impeccable manners. It wasn't any harm either that he looked like something straight out of a magazine dressed in a wool-blend steel grey Hugo Boss suit. The third P.R. company was equally welcoming of the business opportunity and both had emailed her proposed project outlines and budgets by Friday morning. There wasn't much between them and in the end Eva opted for the Boss suit. Choosing on the better looking was hardly meritable but ultimately it was all about the image she would project so why not?

With the contract agreed by Friday afternoon PR Guy scheduled a meeting with Eva for the following week to finalise a name for the business. With a hectic week behind her Eva took it easy at home with the children for the evening. They ordered in pizza and watched an old 'Harry Potter' movie together.

Alan took the kids to swimming lessons on Saturday morning and to stay over for the night and Eva took herself off to the gym. She ran on the treadmill and when home did her now habitual ab sit-ups before having a well-earned long hot shower. Smoothing on some self-tanning lotion afterwards she dressed in loose joggers and a grey sweatshirt and pottered around the house for the rest of the afternoon.

Sitting on the couch later Eva contemplated the emptiness of her home. Five and a half months had passed since her marriage had broken up and it just baffled her how quickly things had changed. Her husband, partner and lover of more than a decade was now with someone else. He was once her future and now he was her past. As much as she was sick of crying over it she had no defence against the sharp claws of hurt that still lingered and ripped at her inside causing stinging tears to fall again. She attempted to distract herself with tackling the ever present mound of ironing but after smoothing the wrinkles out of a pair of designer jeans for her night out she turned her back on the rest of it.

Meeting up with Vivienne that evening was an excuse to dress up and go out on the town and forget all about the business and her domestic life. With the next few weeks destined to be busy Eva wanted to really unwind and make the most of it.

She wore a mink coloured strappy silk top with tight fitting jeans and high black sandals. Viv was as glamorous as always and was commanding at least fifty percent of the male clientele's attention and probably ninety nine percent of the females. Starting the night with Bellini cocktails the friends caught up on what was going on over the past week. By their second cocktail they were giddily perusing the. The peach juice and champagne concoction was sinfully easy to drink. They toasted French men, Irish men and the hopeful Romeos who attempted to chat them up at the bar. A little bit of flirtation and flattery did wonders for the ego and Eva's form got better and better as the night wore on.

Waking up on Sunday morning with a pounding head and dull recollections of events from the previous evenings it took Eva a while to get her bearings. The room was unfamiliar at first but then she remembered hailing a taxi back to Viv's and staying over for the night. She had vague memories of a bit of hassle from an over eager admirer who had followed them from the pub to their taxi and had done his best to get an invite home for the night but without success.

Vivienne was up before her and downing a couple of paracetamol with a glass of water in the kitchen. Eva refused the offer of breakfast and instead called a taxi and headed home. With a thumping head and a heaving stomach it was all she could do to lie on the couch and half-heartedly browse through the Sunday newspaper until the kids were dropped home that evening. Alan had hung around for a while when he brought them home and was enthusiastically admiring Hannah's new school bag. Eva had left him to it and shakily returned to the couch as he oohed and ahhed in the kitchen until eventually he left. It felt odd, like there had been a stranger in the house. *What had he stayed so long for?* She wondered. *Was he waiting for the offer of a coffee or something? Maybe he still wanted to tell her something.* He'd always been a bit like that which used to annoy her. Instead of coming straight out and asking her something he'd pussy foot around until she'd end up asking him what was up. *Maybe he wants to take his new woman away for a weekend or something.* Well she'd no intention of making it easy for him if he did. Thankfully Hannah interrupted the mini-drama in her head with a demand for a bedtime story. Eva peeled herself off the couch and up the stairs with the energy of a pensioner to cuddle up beside her daughter in bed and slowly read the storybook. Leaving her daughter to sleep Eva tucked Luke in for the night. He was growing up fast and would be twelve in November and Eva wondered if he would mind not having a party and celebrating in New York instead. He was still awake but she didn't bring it up. Tousling his hair she hugged him goodnight and turned in for an early night herself.

The remnants of her weekend hangover still lingered on Monday morning but there was no return to slumber with a busy day ahead. She had to get the kids out on time and open up the store for the shop-fitters. The reclaimed oak floorboards had turned out beautifully and she was glad now too of the slated area inside the door, on a wet day this would intercept dripping coats and shoes somewhat to save the floorboards. *Hmmm, an umbrella stand needs to be added to the list,* she pondered. The shop fitters arrived an hour later than arranged but were soon making the place feel very busy. Eva left them and headed back home to her office to discover an email from PR Guy confirming a meeting for Thursday to discuss the shop name options and outlining the strategy in detail for the coming weeks. Eva was somewhat dismayed to see that he had scheduled the official launch for early December! *Had he got the dates wrong,* she wondered but when she called him to check he started talking about a soft-launch and explained that while they would advertise and get the name around for the business opening in October an official launch normally took place when a business was somewhat established and the clientele had built up a little. Having talked it through she was re-assured once more that this guy really knew what he was talking about and it did make sense to have the business up and running to some degree before having an official launch. He also told her to think about hiring a suitable celebrity for the launch. All they would do would cut the ribbon but if you had a celebrity name like a D.J. or TV presenter that would often draw in a crowd and some media coverage. Eva wasn't too sure about that though, it seemed a little tacky but agreed to think about it some more before shooting it down and naturally there would be an additional cost element to consider as well. It was long past lunchtime when Eva turned her attention to checking out stationery providers. She would need business cards, headed paper, carrier bags, bubble wrap and tissue paper. All these little extra things were popping up that she hadn't thought about at the business plan stage but she wanted everything to be right.

Time was flying by and Eva was feeling under serious pressure. With staff interviews scheduled all day Tuesday and Wednesday and then PR Guy meeting on Thursday she only had the remainder of Monday and then Friday to get other jobs done for the week. Rustling through her handwritten lists again she ticked off 'arrange interviews' and added 'research couriers' and 'umbrellas stand.' It would be essential to have a reliable courier on hand to make deliveries of bigger items to clients and to deliver stock from the

196

warehouse down to the store. A chime went off on her laptop signalling a new email in the inbox. It was from Sébastien! *Well he seemed to be playing it equally as cool as me,* she thought as she clicked on the envelope symbol with the mouse to open it up.

Four weeks had passed since she had emailed him last and her stomach now fluttered with excitement as she read the brief words:

'Cher Eva,
I visited Collioure today and thought of you. Would like if you had been with me so that I could have taken you to a quiet café that I know, shared a bottle of wine with you and looked into your beautiful eyes. You are busy, non? The tourist season is ending here and things are getting quiet at the guesthouse. I will soon go to a ski-resort at Camurac for work for the winter months. Stay in touch.
Avec amour.
Sébastien.'

Wow. Eva read it over and over. Then taking her time and replying carefully she wrote:

'Dear Sébastien,
I would have loved to have been in Collioure with you today. It would be nice to escape from all the craziness that starting this new business entails but this is what I have chosen so I had better make it work! You are making quite a change swapping the sun for the ski-slopes for the winter. If I was you I would stay with the sun! I have never skied before!
Keep in touch.
x Eva.'

And with a click it was gone. She then read her own words again. *Was it okay? Did it show she was interested?*

Well it was too late to change and it was out there waiting for him to read so all she could do was wait and see.

197

Where was Camurac anyway? She'd certainly never heard of it. Taking a few minutes to search for it on the internet she discovered that it lay inland close to the border of Andorra and was easy to get to from both Carcassonne and Perpignan airports.

Their exchange of emails had brought a new dimension to her life. She felt like she'd just been asked out on a date and for a while it wasn't all just about work. She somehow felt a little mellower about it all. No matter how things went she knew that there was someone thinking about her from time to time and that made her feel special and cheered her up.

The week passed busily and by Friday afternoon Eva was well and truly wiped out. She sat at her desk looking through two pages of possible business names and as hard as she tried to make one fit they just didn't do. PR Guy had told her that the sign would have to go up soon with a name that suggested the nature of the business. He told her that the sooner it went up the better because it would arouse curiosity and interest. He also advised her to put a sign in the window announcing the opening date as soon as possible. Without the name yet decided she went ahead and booked a sign-writer for Monday morning. That gave her the weekend ahead to come up with a name and the push was on to make her mind up. It was proving easier to pick out staff than it was to pick out a name and that afternoon she telephoned her new assistant manager who had been really impressive in the interview plus one full time floor staff member and arranged for both of them to start work in the last week of September. She also made offers to four part time staff to start in November and hoped that she would be busy enough to require them in the lead up to Christmas.

As she sat feeling buried by paperwork her phone rang and it was Alan. She was just about to go to collect the children from school and didn't have much time to talk but he said that he needed to talk to her about their child-minding arrangements. Eva left to pick the kids up from school with the remnants of their conversation in her mind. She had already asked him to pick them up early on Saturday morning and take them to their swimming

198

lessons so Eva agreed to go with them and 'talk about things' as Alan had put it, while the children had their lesson.

Eva didn't sleep at all well that night and waking late had to quickly search for togs, swim hats and goggles the next morning while Alan waited for them in his car outside. It must have been weird for the kids to have her sitting into the car to go with them and their Dad like they used to do.

Sitting opposite Alan in the coffee bar of the leisure centre she felt sure that her jaw had actually dropped when she heard what he had to say. Alan felt that he was seeing too much of the kids at the weekends and that he had no time to himself! Eva was flabbergasted.

'Alan, are you for real?' she questioned calmly, aware that the coffee bar of a leisure centre was no place for an argument.

'Well Eva, we agreed through our solicitors that I could see them when I wanted and would have them with me every other weekend. But it seems like they're with me practically every weekend lately and to be perfectly honest I have no life because of it. I mean you just called me up on Thursday and asked me to take them to swimming lessons presuming I'd no plans or anything.'

Eva was disgusted with him.

'Your kids are cramping your style are they?' she sneered.

'Eva there's no need to be nasty. I want to be reasonable about this but my solicitor says....'

'Alan I couldn't give two fucks what your solicitor says. If you never wanted to see your kids again that would suit me even better as I wouldn't have to clap eyes on you again.'

'Eva, be reasonable. Come on now, be fair.'

'Fair is it? Is that what you want? How bloody fair is it that I am on my own doing all the parenting while I try to start up a business and here you are complaining that you are asked to take them to their swimming lessons. You're fucking unreal, you are Alan.'

'Eva calm down will you, there's no need to be so....'

'So what Alan? What exactly is the word you're looking for – crude is it?'

'No....I..'

199

Eva was fuming but managed to calm as she interrupted him to say ;

'Alan if you want to stick rigidly to what was agreed, then fine by me. I won't ask you for any favours or allow the presence of your children to impinge on your social life any more. And in future you needn't bother coming directly to me with your petty whinging you can contact me through your solicitor. And now would you mind just fucking off?'

Alan was speechless. Eva could see he was infuriated but he just half snorted and left her in the café and went to watch the kids from the viewing gallery.

They met up again in the foyer when the kids were showered and changed.

Feigning civility again in front of the children they agreed that this weekend was not one of Dad's weekends after all and that he would drop them home.

'Thanks a fucking million you prick,' Eva muttered under her breath as she walked ahead of them to Alan's car. Nobody had heard her. Eva wouldn't dream of bad-mouthing their father within earshot of the children but it did give her a certain satisfaction to verbalise her anger.

The kids didn't seem to care either way about the change of plans and didn't appear to have picked up on the enhanced bad feeling between their parents. Arriving home Eva was more determined than ever to get her business up and running and be in the position to give Alan the two fingers. At home Eva pulled out the frying pans and treated them to a brunch of fried rashers and poached eggs on toasted bagels and tucked in heartily herself. Savouring a cup of tea afterwards she flicked through the property supplement of the paper. There were pages now filled with holiday homes abroad. Most of them were in Spain but there was a new leaseback development being released in France and it was on Sébastien's doorstep in the south east. Thinking of him cheered her up and she wondered what kind of father he would be. *What kind of father didn't want to spend all the time they could with their children? What kind of an asshole had she married at all?*

Eva loved her children more than anything and if Alan wasn't going to be accommodating with any extra child-minding she might need then there were plenty of other alternatives. She had needed the extra weekends because of her business trips and doing research but that was all in hand now. If his mother knew that he was turning down opportunities to be with them she'd be absolutely disgusted. Eva knew that Mary would mind them with a heart and a half anytime she needed her to even if her son wouldn't. After brunch Eva dropped Luke to soccer practice and watched from the car with Hannah while he played. Surveying the other parents who looked on from the side-lines or from their cars she could see that the majority were Dads but that there was a fair smattering of Mums as well. Giving them all a once-over, she then tried to guess if they were married, separated or single. Well whatever they were they all had one thing in common and unlike her husband they were obviously big into their kids. Especially those on the side-line, looking on eagerly and giving the odd encouraging shout and in their own heads they were probably kicking the ball themselves too.

So instead of being with their father, the three of them went on an outing to the cinema for the evening. The kids munched into popcorn and drank coke while Eva sipped her bottled water and afterwards they all had ice cream at a café in the shopping centre. They had a lovely time but in the back of her mind Eva couldn't help but obsess over Alan. *What a creep. What kind of father could think he was seeing too much of his kids?* Although now she came to think of it even though he only saw them at weekends they had probably spent more time with him over the past few months than they had in the previous year. Being around them was hardly an ordeal and it must be that his new girlfriend wanted more time alone with him or something. Eva was more angry than hurt and wondered had she ever really known him.

Elaine telephoned from Boston on Sunday afternoon to catch up on the news and latest gossip. They reminisced about their recent travels through Massachusetts and Elaine said that she had spotted some unusual bowls and vases and promised to forward website details for the crafts-shop. Elaine was eager to go ahead with the shopping trip to New York and Eva promised to get back to her with dates as soon as possible. With Alan being such an asshole she was determined to give the kids as good a time as possible for their birthdays. They talked about the upcoming deadline for the signwriting on Monday and how stumped Eva was when it came to deciding on the name.

'You still haven't got a name!' Elaine half teased.

'No and I've got to sort it out soon.'

'But I thought you were going to call it Living and Dining stuff,' Elaine joked.

'Yeah right. No, that's what's going in there but as for the name I haven't got a clue.'

'Well I'll rack my brains and I'll email you on some suggestions if I come up with anything good,' Elaine promised before hanging up.

And for the rest of the evening the list of names in front of Eva merged on the page with nothing at all standing out. It was the only thing that she really had to do for the entire weekend and here she was on Sunday evening with it still hanging over her. It felt like having homework or an essay to do for school with Monday morning looming all too closely. She'd add a name to her list of possibilities and then cross two others out so she was rapidly getting nowhere. She added "Living & Dining stuff" for the hell of it, "Stellar Homeware", "Cranberries & Rosewood" and "Pestle & Mortar" to the end of the list. At least half of them were completely daft. After perusing some more unsuitable suggestions from Elaine she shut down her laptop and went to bed racking her tired brains. Sleep was not going to come easily.

Chapter 16

(SPAGHETTI BOLOGNESE)

Waking early on Monday morning Eva faced into the second last week before her shop would open for business. Breakfast was a hurried bowl of bran cereal scattered with a handful of raisins and a splash of milk.

After dropping the children to school she called into the shop and met with the sign-writer before heading off to the printer to look at sample business cards and packing materials. Lunch was a takeaway cappuccino and sandwich followed by a two hour meeting with the accountant. She did her best to focus as he attempted to guide her through all the administration required in managing staff. It seemed complicated and would bring with it additional paperwork though he was recommending some kind of computer package that would make it all very easy apparently. Bamboozled by the mention of Payroll, PPS numbers and Health & Safety training Eva didn't find it too difficult to tear herself away and go to collect the children from school. She told them that she'd a surprise for them and soon pulled the jeep in just outside the shop.

'Well...what do you think?' Eva asked, pointing up to the sign.

'*Living & Dining etc.,*' Luke read the beautifully scripted gold words slowly.

'It's beautiful Mum, it's so pretty,' Hannah enthused.

'Yeah. It's nice,' Luke agreed.

Eva knew that it was a lot more than nice and looked up in admiration. The sign-writer had done a great job and the large decorative calligraphy filled in gold looked opulent against the deep plum background.

'Living & Dining etc.' Eva read aloud and parked for a while proudly watching as people noticed her sign. Elaine had been right on the mark with the name but Eva had dropped 'stuff' and swapped in 'etc.' and was delighted with the suggestiveness of it. It could suggest anything and she hoped that curiosity would draw people in.

Just then her mobile pinged with a text message from the warehouse informing her that a shipment had arrived from the U.S. She would have loved to have gone straight over but instead had to do a quick grocery shop and go home to cook the kids supper. While they did their homework Eva went online and did a grocery shop which she booked to arrive the following day. She also booked one for the week after that as well and was beginning to feel very much in control. A soft beep from her laptop signalled an email and when she saw Sébastien's name in the Inbox she felt a flutter of excitement.

'Cher Eva,
I can't believe that you have never skied! You are really missing something good. I leave for Camurac next week and it will be a busy Christmas. I know you will be busy then too but perhaps if you take a break you would like to come with your children to ski?
Miss you,
x Sébastien.'

Eva was loving this emailing lark. It was a bit like having a pen-pal in primary school but without the endless wait between letters in the post. The thought of a skiing holiday holed up in a cosy ski lodge with snow outside, cosy fires and Sébastien had her off in fantasy-land until Hannah began to call her to come and check her

204

math's homework. She hastily replied to Sébastien before shutting down her laptop :

'Dear Sébastien,
I would certainly love to ski sometime but I have already made arrangements to go to New York with the kids and my friend Elaine before Christmas. Maybe some other time. Have to go now,
x Eva.'

As soon as she had clicked send she regretted it. Hannah called her again so she headed downstairs and looked over her efforts at problem solving on her workbook. Eva's mind was elsewhere as she thought about her email reply. It had been too blunt and it wasn't one that encouraged a response. She could at least have said 'miss you too' or something. With homework finished Eva made a cup of coffee for herself and started browning the mince for the spaghetti bolognaise.

'Bolognese Sauce'

You will need: (Serves 6)
2 medium onions
3 medium carrots
3 tbsp olive oil
4 garlic cloves
500g minced beef
4 tbsp tomato puree
1 tsp mixed herbs (mix of marjoram, basil, oregano and thyme)
2 x 400g cans plum tomatoes
300ml red wine
1 tsp ground black pepper
2 tsp salt
1 bay leaf

Method:
Peel and finely chop the onions and peel and dice the carrots.

Heat the olive oil in a large saucepan over a medium heat and cook the onions and carrots for 10 minutes until softened.

Crush the garlic and add to the saucepan to cook for 1 minute.

Push the carrots and onions to the side of the pan, turn up the heat and add the mince. Cook for 10 minutes, breaking it up with a spatula as it cooks.

Add the tomato puree and the mixed herbs and mix well.

Add the plum tomatoes, red wine, black pepper, salt and bay leaf.

Bring to the boil and then reduce the heat to simmer for 2 hours until the sauce is well reduced and thickened. Stir occasionally as it cooks and use the back of a wooden spoon to squash and break down the plum tomatoes.

Delicious served with any type of pasta and some crusty garlic bread to mop up the juices. Discard the bay leaf before serving.

Tip: For a quicker version leave out the carrots and bay leaf and simmer for 30 minutes instead of 2 hours.

[RECIPE ENDS]

Eva dished out their dinner into white ceramic pasta bowls that she'd bought ages ago. They were larger than cereal bowls and had the names of different types of pasta scripted in black around the edges.

Thinking of the beautiful gold lettering of her scripted sign 'Living & Dining etc.,' lifted her spirits and there was huge satisfaction in having that job out of the way. She felt sure that people would be looking at it and wondering about it and what the shop would be like.

That night when she tried to sleep she kept thinking about her sign and envisaged herself wrapping some delicate Christmas decorations in plum coloured tissue paper and tying it with gold ribbon.

The first thing she thought of upon waking was her email to Sébastien. She considered writing him another one but she didn't have time and put it off until later on. After the school run Eva went to the warehouse to check on the latest arrivals. The crates from France had been in storage for over a month now and were as yet un-opened and Eva was full of excitement as the storeman carefully prised open one of the lids with a crowbar. The packaging company had done an excellent job. Everything was carefully bubble wrapped and then protected with heaps of shredded paper. Eva carefully unwrapped one of the terracotta earthenware storage pots and admired it.

Turning her attention to the newly arrived U.S. shipment it turned out to be the order from Ipswich. She had almost forgotten what she had chosen as the freshness of the blue and white range of pottery was unwrapped. There were three big boxes of two-toned candles in various shapes and sizes with variations in colours with pinks blending with creams and beiges with caramels. Would she really be able to sell so many she wondered? Next emerged the seagulls made from porcelain, pebbles and seashells, which brought back memories of the trip with Elaine. Thankfully she had only ordered thirty of those and now wondered what she'd been thinking when she had selected them. They wouldn't appeal to everyone's taste but might add a humorous or quirky touch to a corner of a bathroom. Everything was in from Paris and the South of France but the orders from Newburyport, Plymouth and Nantucket in the U.S. had all yet to arrive. These were all separate orders but surely they couldn't be much longer now that the Ipswich order had arrived.

Time seemed to be slipping away and with staff due to begin work stocking shelves the following Monday Eva had just a few more days left to be ready for them. The shop-fitters were well on top of things though and as well as fitting out the units in the shop they had supplied a business p.c. broadband ready with an efficient back-up system, two computerised cash tills with connections for cards payments and had installed both a water-cooler and coffee maker.

Eva spent Wednesday morning with PR guy viewing the flyers he was planning to distribute over the following week and making some alterations to the ads to be placed in the newspaper and online.

PR guy hadn't really commented one way or the other on the name she had chosen and she was a bit disappointed by that. Maybe his nose was out of joint that she hadn't gone with one of their suggestions or was it that he thought it was a crap name? He was happy however that with the outlay for the adverts agreed on they would be submitted for printing and publishing in plenty of time. He had warned her that positioning on the page was paramount as they could easily be shoved into some obscure corner if it wasn't in on time.

Image was everything he kept reminding her. As if she didn't know. Although it did give her food for thought after she left their meeting and started to think about whether or not the staff should wear uniforms. Maybe a black T-shirt or a shirt with a logo would look good. Uniforms were not in the budget but with her staff numbers being so small how expensive could it be? She returned home and added uniforms to a list and then spent an hour scrolling websites and making phone-calls and appointments to view samples.

Thursday saw another shipment arrive from the U.S., this time from Newburyport. The yak fibre wall hangings and rugs were even more stunning than she had remembered. Eva pulled out one of the wall hangings and ran her fingers over it. Yak fibre she had learned was almost as soft and luxurious as cashmere. They blended it with silk to give it sheen and elasticity and once it was dyed it could be used to make almost anything.

Eva didn't pull anything else out of the crates, she just didn't have time but everything was there. The map prints and the bronze sculptures that she had carefully chosen were all nestled together waiting to be put on display. This shipment was extremely valuable and would probably be the most expensive merchandise that she would carry. It would need to sell. Eva spent the remainder of the afternoon being trained in on the till system with the card payment facility being the most pernickety part of it.

Flopping into bed on Friday evening after spending most of the day with her accountant she was absolutely exhausted. This was one of Alan's actual agreed weekends with the children so it would be a relatively quiet one for Eva as he had picked them up straight from school. Her head was spinning though and tired as she was she found it impossible to sleep. She thought about the final week that lay ahead before the opening. Her new staff would be due to start on Monday morning and Eva had arranged training on the tills for them for first thing but after that she would need all hands on deck to be ready for opening the following Saturday. She tried a bit of yoga breathing to calm herself down.

Lying in the dark she began to think about Alan and her replacement, it made her feel nauseous. As much as she was disgusted with him not wanting to spend all the time he could with their kids she resented his new life and still missed him. It hurt her now more than ever thinking that he had cheated on her. The fact that other people knew about it while she had been happily oblivious made her feel really foolish and humiliated. More than that though it hurt that he was now with someone he found more attractive and more interesting. She had been discarded without a second thought.

She pictured her children now in a strange house and tears streamed down her face. *They should be here in our house now, with us.* She'd always thought of her marriage as forever and Alan as the love of her life. He was the one she had fallen in love with and now he didn't love her back. Not anymore. *When did that die*, she wondered? *When did he stop loving me?*

Thinking of the two of them physically hurt her heart and that familiar prickling feeling came from behind her eyes again as warm tears traced a path across her cheeks and down onto her neck. Once again she was a hot snivelling mess. It was almost six months now since Alan had left and Eva had yet to meet her replacement. Eva had never gone to collect the kids at Alan's new house and he had never brought her over when collecting or dropping off the kids. So she had to paint a picture from the titbits of descriptions she got from Daniel but his description didn't yield much. She knew she had brown hair, and was tall and sallow. And she was younger of course. Daniel had once said he could show her a picture on his phone but Eva said no, she just couldn't look at it.

Tossing and turning as she tried to find sleep, Eva's feelings changed from feeling sad to feeling humiliated and then to being angry.

She tried yoga breathing again. No joy. *So much for an early night,* she thought as she padded downstairs to the kitchen in fleece pyjamas and fluffy slippers and made herself a hot chocolate. The house was eerily quiet. Eva sat down and listened as she dunked a chocolate hobnob biscuit into her cup of hot chocolate.

The large black wooden framed clock ticked melodically on the kitchen wall. Eva looked around. All the finishing touches were hers and she loved to just sit there and admire her things. The carefully chosen pair of oil on canvas paintings had taken ages to find and she had come across them for sale on the walls of a small restaurant.

She loved her home and could never see herself leaving it. The ticking of the clock started to annoy her so she put on a CD and sat back to listen for a while. Songs seemed to mean more to her now that she was on her own. Humming along, she got lost in the lyrics for a while until eventually getting tired of feeling heartbroken and alone she changed the music to something more cheerful.

At three o'clock in the morning Eva was sitting in her living room still awake. She turned off the music, switched on the TV instead and dimmed the lamps. Curling up on one of the armchairs she pulled a faux fur throw over herself. Warm and cosy, slumber found her eventually as she struggled to keep her eyes open to watch an old James Stewart movie.

Heading to the gym as soon as she woke on Saturday morning

210

Eva gathered her thoughts as she ran on the treadmill. The anticipation of seeing the ad for her shop in the newspaper was so exciting. Yes, the online campaign was going to start off too but Eva was more of a hard-copy girl. Of all the newspapers that were struggling with circulation numbers 'The Examiner,' especially the one with the weekend supplements, was one that still did well. She planned the day ahead and promised herself not to do too much. Picking up the paper on the way home she must have stared at the ad for her shop for at least half an hour. Vivienne called her to say she had seen it and how good it looked, so did her mother-in-law and Daniel but Alan didn't call at all.

Inevitably Eva ended up at the shop in the afternoon, she just couldn't stay away. It was completely kitted out now with wall mounted shelves and free standing floor units all painted white and waiting to be filled. The tills too stood empty but full of promise. What was it going to feel like to see the first notes being exchanged and the first parcels being wrapped? One of the small rooms at the back of the store housed a compact desk for the computer and printer with cupboards to hold packaging materials and stationery. There was also a coffee maker sitting neatly on a shelf above a little table with a comfortable bench seat for lunch and coffee breaks. Space was tight for staff facilities with a small loo right at the back but with walls painted white it all looked fresh and bright. The other little room was completely fitted out with shelves and would be used to store some back-up stock. Locking up and setting the alarm Eva left her empty shop glancing back to admire the rich gleam of the floorboards contrasted against the matt slate slabs just inside the door. It looked really well and Eva couldn't wait to start filling it.

On Sunday Eva set about doing the housework first thing after breakfast. She threw on a wash and then started to clean. With the kids out of the way she got through it without interruption. She vacuumed from top to bottom, dusted, cleaned bathrooms, changed beds and washed the kitchen floor. After cleaning the house she showered and dressed comfortably in a sage green Lucy Nagle cashmere lounge suit and browsed through the papers for a

211

while before tackling some ironing and getting the laundry sorted for the week ahead.

With an hour to go before the kids would return home and with the house well under control she browsed the Internet for a while and checked out some websites for Interior Design Stores. Targeted ads for her shop had been placed and were due to begin popping up on Facebook and Instagram. Checking on her email there was nothing of significance in the Inbox. She wished Sébastien would write or message her or something. *No wonder,* she thought to herself as she read the last email she had sent, it had hardly been encouraging. She abandoned email to start looking into the New York trip. She looked up flights and shopping packages. She could book everything directly herself or there were some reasonably priced shopping weekends available with a new company running packages direct from Shannon to New York. That would suit her perfectly. She picked out some suitable dates and emailed Elaine to see if any would work for her. She also sent the details to Vivienne in case she was interested in joining them. Sorely tempted to email Sébastien again but deciding against it she switched off the laptop and went to make a coffee before the kids returned home. Sitting in her kitchen her thoughts turned once again to Sébastien. He liked her, she knew that much, but how could there be anything more to it than that, it was just too complicated. Even if she did go to visit him or he came to see her, where could it go from there? Maybe she should just try to forget about him.

Monday began as usual with making the school lunches before calling the kids for breakfast and while they ate she showered and carefully picked out what she would wear for the day. She chose a crisp white cotton shirt and wore it with dark denim boot-cut jeans with high heeled black leather ankle boots. She wanted to look elegant and professional when she met her staff but she didn't want to look stiff or unfriendly either and her clothes had to be practical for the whizzing around that she'd be doing for the day. She arrived at the store after the school run to see her two new staff members waiting outside.

212

Must get keys sorted, was added to a mental list of things to do.

The staff training on the tills was straightforward as both girls had used similar machines before and 11a.m. saw them all having their first staff meeting as Eva brewed up coffee and gave them some options about the uniform. She listened to their preferences before they settled on a short sleeved polo shirt in a deep plum colour with 'Living & Dining etc.' to be embroidered in gold thread. They all agreed that they would team it with either a plain black skirt and tights or black trousers or black denim jeans but they had to look smart, nothing baggy or scruffy looking.

Maggie was the older of the two and Eva assigned her the title of assistant manager with Michelle reporting to her. Maggie was in her early forties with two teenage children and plenty of time on her hands now. She had worked over the years in a department store in the city and prior to that she had held a part-time position in an Interior's store so she knew the ropes already. With a sleek black bob she had the look of a practical woman who knew what she was about. Michelle on the other hand was in her early twenties, perma-tanned with blonde hair worn in a high pony-tail, she epitomised all that was youthful and optimistic.

At noon the courier arrived from the warehouse with the first large crate and manoeuvred it through the double doors of the shop. Maggie and Michelle set about carefully emptying it, unwrapping each item and placing them in one corner of the store. Eva left them to it while she went off to order the plum coloured polo shirts. When she returned at half past three Maggie the new assistant manager was working on her own. Eva panicked as she asked where Michelle was gone and was relieved when Maggie informed her she was on a late lunch. Maggie had taken lunch herself from half-past one until half-past two and now Michelle was gone and due back in another half an hour.

Eva was delighted to see that Maggie was taking charge and showing initiative but she couldn't help secretly asking herself what did they need a full hour for when they could just grab a sandwich and a take-out cappuccino like she did? That she reminded herself was the difference between being the employer and the employee.

213

They had rights and entitlements and they would have to be respected. Five-thirty arrived and the girls said their goodbyes. They had managed to get through opening all of the French shipment and as Eva looked at it all she realised that there was far too much there. The shop would be full if all of it was put on display leaving no room for anything else. At least half of it would have to be re-wrapped and put back into storage. She needed to get some advice on how to store items more efficiently in the warehouse so it would be easy to select what was needed in future.

All of Tuesday morning had to be spent carefully re-wrapping and packing half of the French merchandise back into smaller boxes and carefully itemising the contents and quantities in each box before they were sent back into storage. In the meantime another shipment had arrived from the States. This time it was from Nantucket. Eva locked up the shop and brought the two girls up with her to visit the warehouse and to get a feel for where stock was being stored and how it was being controlled. Maggie in particular would need to build a relationship with the warehouse manager and the couriers as she would be the one dealing with the stock issues and deliveries from time to time. Eva opened the first box to reveal salt and pepper cellar sets. Twenty -five pairs each in blue, red and white. They should sell Eva hoped. They were practical yet smart looking and could make a useful gift. As she opened a large crate she wondered what she had been thinking when she had ordered forty beach chairs as they were now in the middle of Autumn.

Instead of bringing entire crates down to the store they decided to go through stock as it arrived into the warehouse and break it down into smaller boxes there. They would need to carefully maintain an inventory of what was in each box and what was on display in the store. This was proving to be a lot more tedious than Eva had envisaged. Maggie suggested putting everything onto a computerised database and Eva looked at her like she was speaking in riddles. Eva had to admit that she was a newcomer to the computer world and hadn't a clue how you would go about setting up a database or what it would do for you. She also wasn't about to take on the cost of hiring a computer consultant to do so. Maggie quickly assured her it would be straightforward enough and that she could manage it as she used to take care of stock control in her last job using a simple spreadsheet package that was already on the shop's system. The women got to work and remained in the warehouse unpacking, sorting, repacking and writing lists. As they added an item to a list they then labelled boxes appropriately for ease of identification later. Eva left them to it and headed off to collect stationery supplies and packaging materials.

The samples were beautiful. Sheets of plum coloured tissue paper and wrapping paper contrasted beautifully with rolls of gold ribbon. There were rolls of gold stickers with the name and address of the store for closing parcels and big plum coloured carrier bags were embellished with 'Living & Dining etc.' in gold scripted lettering. They were nearly too beautiful to be used. Eva hadn't a clue how many to order but the bigger the order the higher the discount so she took her chances and ordered what she hoped would last for six months.

On return Eva picked up Michelle and Maggie from the warehouse and brought them back down to the shop. Neither of them had cars which meant Eva would have to ferry them to and fro or pay for taxis every time they needed to visit the warehouse.

Eva was now also finding herself in a bit of a pickle with the child-minding arrangements too. Basically she had none. Helen, the local teenage babysitter, was gone back to school which meant that this was the second day in a row that Eva had to pick the kids up and bring them with her to the store. They didn't seem to mind and kept busy doing their homework in the back-office and then messing around on the computer. It was only for a couple of hours but it couldn't continue like that. She couldn't really be in the shop working while the kids were in the back office and she was sure the novelty would soon wear off for them too.

Again Maggie and Michelle vanished on the dot of five-thirty and at the end of their second day of work Eva looked around at the slowly filling shelves. Reluctantly she locked up and headed home with the children, she would have loved to have stayed on and put in some more hours of unwrapping but that wasn't an option.

At home an overwhelming tiredness hit her and she made the mistake of sitting on the couch from where she subsequently could not move. Her period must have been due or something because she felt completely wiped out. And the kids were driving her nuts. Hannah had scribbled on a drawing of Luke's for his homework and there was murder. He thumped her, she pulled his hair and Hannah ended up bawling crying. Trying to get on top of the situation Eva called them both into the kitchen where Hannah reported that Luke had called her an 'F'n B'word'. The Judas of the family received a swift kick to the ankle from her older sibling and you'd have sworn that one of her legs was dangling off such was the wailing high pitched cry. Eva felt her own temper rising and sent them off to their rooms to cool down before she lost it. She contemplated serving them up a jam sandwich and sending them to bed but instead she turned around to cook a stir-fry and tried to drown out their bickering with the sizzling of the pan. There was no let up between the two of them and she could hear them still at each other upstairs. Their humour didn't improve when she called them for their tea and the squabbling elevated until Eva turned around to them and shouted 'would ye ever fucking shut up!' putting all her venom into the 'F' word.

Silence descended for a full minute. Luke just stared at her and eventually Hannah piped up, 'that's a bad word Mummy.'

'Yes I know it is. I shouldn't have said it but ye are just wrecking my head.' In reality she was glad she had said it. A bit of shocked peace and quiet was all she wanted and for them to just be quiet for a while. The three of them ate their stir-fry in relative silence, each of them a bit sore with at least one of their dining companions. Deciding on an early night for all of them met with protest but Eva reminded them that Hannah had wrecked Luke's homework and Luke had used bad language.

'You did too Mum,' Hannah reminded her like a stinging conscience.

'Yes I know I did and I'm sorry, so I'm going to go to bed now too,' Eva sighed with fake regret.

Chapter 17

(BEEF BOURGUIGNON)

The last few days of September were about to slip away and Eva spent Wednesday continuing to stock the shelves. She began with some of the French shipment as the shop staff worked in the warehouse. Her day revolved around dropping the children to school, ferrying the two women up to the warehouse, picking them up for their lunch-breaks, bringing them back up, collecting the kids from school and collecting the staff again. By the end of the day Eva felt like a Hackney Cab driver without the payment.

The stock was almost sorted in the warehouse though so at least on Thursday they all would be working with her in the shop. Hannah had managed to knock over a beautiful earthenware French urn with Eva trying to hide her bitter disappointment. The urn had cracked in two and could be glued back together but she couldn't put it on sale but perhaps she could sell it as seconds at sale time or use it for holding umbrellas or something.

She fretted that she needed to get a child-minder sorted and fast. That evening the kids were bickering at home again and it took all Eva's willpower not to lose her cool. Her own long day wasn't helping her patience either and she struggled to stay calm with them and try to get them to sort their differences amicably until bedtime. Sometimes she felt like she was living in a zoo and she couldn't hear herself think with the raised voices, screeching and squabbling. With so much going on it was just too much for

218

Eva to be handling them by herself and trying to get on with work as well. They needed someone with them after school who could give them undivided attention and she needed to sort something out fast.

The courier arrived down to the store on Thursday with a selection of the American pottery, some wall hangings, a few rugs, prints and sculptures and the staff set to work on finding suitable places on the shelves and the walls.

In the afternoon Maggie started working on computerising the inventory and by the end of the day Eva was very impressed to see that she had set up one spreadsheet for Warehouse Stock and another for Shop Floor Stock. Maggie showed her how to add items to the warehouse database and then move them to the store database and eventually mark them as sold. She had left a column with provision for pricing so the stock value could easily be calculated. Eva studied it and congratulated Maggie. She played around with it for a while and then asked Maggie to show her how to insert another column. She then had a column for stock cost next to stock price and began to fill in what some of the pieces had actually cost her. There were no prices to enter yet though. She went back to her business plan to see what she had put in for mark up and saw that it was very vague. So armed with a print-off of the database Eva headed home and spent the evening with a calculator baffled by percentages as she tried to work out an appropriate mark-up, taking all the costs into consideration.

Yet again the children were acting up. Tension was building amongst them all as Eva's concentration was persistently interrupted by Hannah complaining about Luke. Sending them to their beds early for the second night that week only meant that instead of being angry towards each other the kids were now angry with Eva.

Friday morning saw her having another meeting with her accountant who looked over her calculations and did a bit of rejigging so that by lunch-time she had her pricing worked out. Rushing around in the afternoon collecting staff uniforms, organising a float for the till, rotas for the staff breaks and lunches and collecting the kids meant that it was after three o'clock before she had any lunch herself. Helen was going to be looking after the kids when she got home from school so Eva got them changed and gave them a snack and waited at home with them until she arrived. She had asked Helen to cover on Saturday as well but she knew that this could only be a temporary arrangement because Helen was now in her final year at school and would soon need to be studying for exams.

When Eva arrived back at the store she discovered that her last U.S. shipment had arrived into the warehouse from Plymouth. There was no time to break it down in the warehouse as they would be closing at five so she had no choice but to get the courier to bring it as it was to the store.

Maggie and Michelle set about unpacking with Maggie taking the inventory and adding it to the shop floor database while Michelle tried to find appropriate places for all these spoons on the shelves. That's all that was in the shipment, five hundred beautifully shaped wooden serving spoons made from cherry wood. Michelle placed several pairs of them in serving bowls but there were still so many left that in the end Eva just got her to shove the remainder back in the box and squeeze it into the storeroom at the back of the shop.

When five-thirty arrived Michelle bolted for the door with her social life coming well before loyalty to her new job, there was simply no enticing her to stay on longer even with Eva trying to tempt her with double-time pay. Eva was thoroughly disappointed with Michelle's attitude just ahead of the shop opening but at least she could rely on Maggie.

The pair of them worked away together until Maggie had to leave at eight and then Eva found herself alone in the shop almost ready for opening for business the next morning. Her notice on the window read 'Opening 9am 1st October' and she wasn't quite ready yet. The mixture of fear and excitement was paralyzing.

She stayed on for another hour herself and it was almost nine o'clock when Eva heard a knock at the door. It was Viv and Daniel. This was the first time that Eva had met them together as a

220

couple and it looked so strange to see Daniel's arm comfortably slung around Viv's shoulder. Viv gushed her enthusiasm as Eva showed her around and Daniel was equally complimentary and was most impressed with the wall hangings even saying that he might buy one himself. They left after half an hour and Eva moved a few more things, having one last look around before locking up for the night.

Helen had the kids in bed so Eva walked her home and stopped to chat with her Mum Nora for a few minutes. They lived a couple of doors down but didn't each know each other very well as there was such an age gap between their children.

It was in desperation that she asked her if she knew of anybody locally who might be interested in child-minding after school for a few hours and on school holidays. Eva couldn't believe her luck when Nora said that she'd love to do it herself as she now had greater freedom with her own kids practically reared. She said that she could do with the extra money with college looming for Helen the following year. They agreed that in future Nora would collect the kids from school and mind them until Eva finished work and she would do some Saturdays too if Helen wasn't available. Knowing that child-minding after school was sorted was a tremendous relief.

Returning home Eva opened a bottle of wine and then went upstairs for a long soak while she sipped a glass of sauvignon blanc in the bath. She then picked out her clothes for the morning and decided that she would wear her classic black Max Mara trouser suit with a plum coloured silk V-necked top underneath. Sitting up in bed she went through the printout of the shop database and began writing out the price for each item onto a roll of stickers by hand. It took ages and Eva eventually dropped off to sleep at around one in the morning.

Saturday morning came and Eva was up at cockcrow. She showered and tried to eat some whole-wheat toast but could only take a few small bites. Her stomach was churning with a mixture of excitement and anxiety. This was it, opening day had arrived. Helen was barely in the door at eight to mind the children for the day before Eva darted out. It was early and traffic was light. *Everyone sleeping in on Saturday morning except for me,* she speculated.

Turning the key in the shop door, Eva unarmed the security alarm and drew her breath as the warm sunshine of the first day of October illuminated her treasures from Paris, Céret, Perpignan, The Bay State and Nantucket Island.

White shelves were laden with blue and white dinnerware, huge white platters, Mediterranean inspired salad bowls and jugs splashed with colours of peppers, chillies and sky blue. Various sized terracotta pots and dinnerware, chunky earthy coloured mugs and storage jars lined the walls. Salt and pepper cellars paired in groups of white, blue and red proudly signalled the flag of their homeland. Intricate copper sculptures stood spaciously on one unit with the light bouncing from one to another in mesmerising patterns. One a ballerina and another a lone fiddler, they seemed to dance and play in choreographed unity guided by golden batons held by the rays of the sun.

The porcelain seagulls with their pebbles and seashells were at home amongst the nautically themed pottery of North America and even the lone blue deck-chair with its emblazoned white red and blue life-buoy setting it off looked fitting in the corner.

Wall hangings filled any spaces between shelves with their delicate fibres intricately woven into abstract patterns and embellished with delicate strips of silk in vibrant indigos, sophisticated teals and understated greys.

Eva set about busily applying the price stickers and carefully putting each piece back in its place until Michelle and Maggie arrived to help her. They were both wearing their plum coloured polo shirts with black denim jeans and looked ready for the day ahead. Opening the door at 9am for the first day of business Eva was delighted to see Daniel bounce into the store and eagerly chose one of the wall hangings that he'd admired the night before.

'Daniel, you don't have to do this,' Eva was half embarrassed and just a little teary.

'Eva, they're beautiful and besides it's a present for Viv so there you go,' Daniel replied, handing over his platinum card.

222

Eva nervously negotiated her first credit-card transaction and then it was done. First sale of the day!

Meanwhile two prospective customers had walked in off the street and Michelle and Maggie had greeted them warmly but didn't approach them. *Remain visible but unobtrusive* Eva had instructed them. Nothing was more off-putting than a salesperson with the demeanour of a swooping eagle. One of the customers browsed for ages and bought nothing and the other one purchased a large Mediterranean salad bowl with a set of cherry wood serving spoons.

By noon things were really getting busy and sales were being rung up at least every ten minutes. There were lots of browsers and plenty of compliments. Michelle and Maggie staggered their lunch-breaks with Eva wolfing down a sandwich in the back-office with a cup of lukewarm coffee. Closing up at half-past-five Eva warmly congratulated the ladies on a great day's work and happily surveyed the gaps in the shelves from where some treasures had departed.

PR Guy had called in during the afternoon and expressed his enthusiasm at how busy the place was for a 'soft-opening' though he seemed much keener to flirt with Michelle than to discuss business with Eva. His job was almost done anyway. He had got the word out quite effectively with the flyers and the well placed ads and now all that remained was for him to plan the official launch for the first of December and to keep up the momentum of the online campaign. He was looking after the Facebook and Instagram accounts for now but Eva knew that she needed to get to grips with these as they would be handed over to her as soon as she had the time to take them on and in the meantime she was paying for that service. In fairness to him he did buy a set of salt and pepper cellars.

Alan's mother had called in and bought an earthenware pot, she was such a genuinely lovely lady but there was no sign of Alan. Not that Eva expected him to come but she felt let-down that he didn't.

With the store closed for the day Eva eagerly tallied the takings and was relieved to be well ahead of target sales. She did the drop off at the bank and headed home with a Chinese takeaway to celebrate her first day of success with the children. Sipping a sauvignon blanc after dinner, Eva curled up on the couch alongside Hannah and Luke to watch a talk show. She let them stay up late and eat ice cream and they seemed to be getting on better than they had been during the week. She kept thinking about the sales of the day and the fact that other people liked her stuff too. The relief was almost overwhelming, it had been such a long day and Eva was looking forward to taking it easier on Sunday. Maggie was going to open up and Eva wanted to make a proper Sunday lunch for the children before she went in later in the afternoon.

She cooked Beef Bourguignon made the way her Dad had taught her. He had been such a great father to her and David. It must have been so heart-breaking for him to see his own wife go from a vibrant active woman full of the joys of life to a shadow of herself as she battled with cancer. He would have been so proud of her now and it was sad not to have someone that close that could really share in the joy of her success. David would be home from California at Christmas time and she had given him a virtual tour of the shop on the ipad but it wasn't the same as having family support nearby. Viv, Fiona and Elaine were the sisters she'd never had and she knew that they were proud of her.

'Beef Bourguignon'

You will need: (Serves 6)
10 small shallots
3 garlic cloves
400g button mushrooms
2 tbsp olive oil
1kg diced shin beef or any stewing beef
5 strips of streaky bacon
1 tbsp tomato puree
750ml bottle red wine
1 bouquet garni (bay, thyme, parsley, rosemary tied together)

224

Sea salt and ground pepper
Fresh chopped parsley to garnish

Method:
Preheat the oven to 150oC/Gas Mark 3.
Peel and finely slice the shallots.
Peel and crush the garlic.
Rinse the mushrooms and cut them in half if they are large.
Heat the olive oil in a large casserole pot on the hob over a medium heat.
Season the beef with salt and pepper, quickly brown it off for a couple of minutes, and then transfer it to a large plate.
Use kitchen scissors to cut the streaky bacon into small pieces into the casserole pot and fry it along with the shallots, mushrooms and garlic for a few minutes.
Add in the tomato purée and cook for 1 minute, stirring it into the mixture. Return the beef and juices to the casserole dish.
Pour over the wine, bring to the boil and stir well.
Add the bouquet garni to the casserole dish and transfer it to the oven to cook slowly in the preheated oven for 2 and a half hours.
Remove the bouquet garni and serve with baby potatoes and garnish with a generous sprinkling of freshly chopped parsley.

[RECIPE ENDS]

Eva got the dinner on good and early on Sunday morning giving the beef plenty of time to yield itself while she headed to the park with the children. The beginnings of fallen leaves crackled underfoot as they walked. Luke had brought his football and raced ahead kicking it as Eva held Hannah's warm hand until they reached the swings and slides. Relaxing on a park bench Eva observed as a couple cautiously guided their toddler on a climbing frame. He was so obviously their first child being minded so

225

preciously like the priceless gift he was. There seemed to be a good few parents on their own too and Eva wondered how many of them were like her, with no one special waiting for them at home.

A couple of hours of fresh air later they returned home with hearty appetites and their dinner was hungrily devoured. She knew that it was one of the kids' favourites, it was comfort on a plate.

Despite Eva's longing to vegetate on the couch with the newspaper for the afternoon she headed into the store with the children in tow. A nice steady flow of customers had been keeping the tills busy all morning and later when it began to ease off Eva let Maggie head home early finishing up the last hour on her own. Hannah and Luke had seemed happy enough to watch a movie in the back office while she worked.

Curling up on the couch at last with the Sunday papers Eva hadn't felt as relaxed in months. The children were tired after the day and went up to bed without any fuss and Eva sipped a large glass of cabernet as she settled in to watch a hospital drama that was more about relationships than patients. The dark good looks of the main doctor were reminiscent of Sébastien. Looking at the character on screen she felt a little lonely and thought how lovely it would be to have Sébastien beside her for company. She missed having someone to cuddle up with.

Her next week set a pattern for the remainder of October, days disappeared with the business going from strength to strength. Mondays were usually very quiet which gave plenty of opportunity to restock the shelves and place new orders, then trade would rise steadily for the remainder of the week with Fridays and Saturdays being the busiest.

With things going so well Eva decided to experiment and set up a section of some speciality foodstuffs. She ordered vacuum packed olives, some jars of olive pastes, and a selection of olive oils in decorative glass bottles from France. She ordered little olive oil dispensers similar to the stainless steel oil canister that she had brought back for herself from Paris. From Nantucket she ordered jars of cranberry relish, cranberry glaze and jam along with a simple cookbook that gave ideas of how to use them with food. She also

226

ordered more candles which were cranberry scented and had dried cranberries pressed into the wax. Everything she ordered she would covet for herself and so far her taste was appealing to plenty of customers. Placing the orders was easy as she did it all online. There was no problem with time differences and she could shop whenever she liked.

Eva worked hard all week and would pick up the kids from Nora by six o'clock each evening. Turning around to cook a meal as soon as she came in the door was the last thing she wanted to do after standing or running around for most of the day but it had to be done. Needless to say her meals were getting simpler by the week with pasta and rice appearing every second evening. School lunch making was a loathed chore, try as she might she often couldn't muster up the energy to make them the night before so she was usually in a rush in the morning to get that done and get the kids out to school on time.

Every second weekend the kids were with Alan and she was getting into a routine of enjoying the time she had to herself now. With Saturdays being so busy at the store she found it hard to stay away from it when Luke and Hannah were on their weekend at home with her but Maggie was more than capable of managing and calling in extra staff when needed.

Eva's first staff crisis had come to a head when trying to arrange rotas for the October bank-holiday weekend and it meant she had to recruit some more part-timers. Maggie had previously asked for that weekend off but Michelle had been looking for it too.

With the kids off school and the child-minder on holidays Eva had no alternative but to ask Alan's mother Mary to come and mind them. It was strange when she stopped to think about it how her relationship with her mother-in-law had actually gotten closer since her separation.

Mary was a pure dote of a woman and arrived with a freshly baked round of brown bread and pots of her blackberry and apple jam. Nothing like a thick slice of the moist loaf thickly spread with butter and smeared with the sweet jam for a lovely homely start to the day.

227

The store had never been busier than that first bank holiday weekend. Where were all these people coming from? It was as if anyone who came to the restaurant next door also took a wander around her shop and sales were through the roof. Eva had made several attempts to get something to eat during the day but all she usually managed was half a sandwich. It was non-stop all day long. They were answering questions, ringing up sales and taking orders for Christmas already.

The ordering was something that had just started to evolve all by itself. People would come in and say that they wanted a number of items wrapped and presented in a basket ready to pick up closer to Christmas and it was still only October. Eva's head was spinning when she closed the door at last and she was on the verge of exhaustion. She'd been on her feet for practically the whole weekend and by the end of business on Monday she knew that she couldn't face another day like it and would have to agree rotas well in advance in future. She would need to have more staff that she could call on and needed to have a contingency in the event of staff members being sick as well. She knew it had been a great day of trade but as the figures totted up she could see that incredibly they'd taken in the equivalent sales of four regular days in one.

Feeling like her head would burst with the list of things that she still had to do she headed home where Mary had a heart-warming stew ready for her supper. It was lovely to come home to some adult company. Mary brewed up some tea after dinner and offered to stay over for the night and Eva gladly accepted and relaxed while Mary sorted the kids for bed and read Hannah her story.

With the children on mid-term break from school Mary offered to take them out to the farm for a few days and Eva jumped at the opportunity. The rest of the week was busier than usual too because of the holidays so it was great to return home in the evening and not have to cook dinner. The children happily stayed with their Gran for three nights and she brought them back in on Friday and minded them at home while Eva worked.

Guilt was getting the better of her and she abandoned the shop for a couple of hours in the afternoon so that she could go home and have lunch with them. Why was it that she was the one who felt guilty when she did her best to be with them as much as she could? Every time she thought of their father now she began to feel more and more resentful towards him and felt it harder to hide whenever he called to pick up Hannah and Luke.

Heading into November with two full-time and five part-time staff, Eva more than needed all of them. The part-timers were students and only interested in a couple of shifts a week. Between days off and rotating staff for working on weekends they were just about covered. Eva was getting more and more competent with using the accounts software on the computer and she was confidently placing and confirming orders online too. She followed Elaine and PR Guy's advice and got a development company to set up an online store for her on her own website and was beginning to see sales coming in from there too.

Eva usually checked her emails first thing in the morning at the shop and had been keeping in touch with Elaine with details of their New York break. They had decided to book a long weekend trip for the last weekend in November and Eva would be taking Thursday until Tuesday off work. Viv wasn't going to be joining them for the break and seemed to be spending most of her free time with Daniel, not that it bothered Eva anymore. She was too busy with the store for going out at the weekends but she would have to regain some sort of social life by the New Year and surely Viv and Daniel would be past the living in each other's pockets phase by then.

The thought of a few consecutive days off was keeping Eva going. Planning was everything to ensure that there would be adequate staff cover in her absence. The timing for the trip wasn't the best with the official store opening set to happen on the first of December she'd only just be back but with the tickets paid for there was no backing out. The kids were so looking forward to it and it was after all to celebrate their birthdays which both fell in November. They had been thrilled at the idea of going on a big trip instead of having a party. Eva was beginning to feel exhausted and having Sundays off wasn't enough to recharge her every week.

229

Even the thought of just sitting on the plane for the six or seven hours appealed to her now, just to do nothing but flick through magazines and relax would be an escape.

On a mid-November Monday Eva arrived at work and was checking the emails when her heart raced to see an email from Sébastien. It read:

'Belle Eva,
I apologise for the long time that I have last written to you. Like you it is a busy time of year getting ready for the ski season to begin and work is crazy. I think of you often and long to see you again. I sincerely ask that you come to visit me at the ski resort in Camurac for a holiday with your children when you can. You will love it.
Love Sébastien.'

It had been weeks since Eva had emailed him and she was sure that her hasty reply had put him off. She had thought of him often and had tried to push romantic notions to the back of her mind. Now here he was just as busy as her and inviting her to come and visit. He had even signed 'Love Sébastien.' Eva read his words over and over until Maggie and Michelle arrived for work. It was the only thing on her mind for the remainder of the day but she was going to give her reply some thought this time and it wasn't until the store closed and things were quiet once more that she replied:

'Dear Sébastien,
You are never far from my mind and I would dearly love to come and see you. My new shop has gone really well so far and we are very busy too. I don't know if it is possible to come to see you soon but I will look at my options and let you know.
Love Eva.'

She knew in her heart that as much as she would love to go to see him there wasn't a hope of arranging a skiing holiday. The store was like a demanding new baby and she was the over-protective mother. It was hard enough to hand over control for her New York trip and things would only get busier coming up to Christmas. She did however browse the Internet for a while checking out flights and dates, indulging a fantasy she knew couldn't be lived out anytime soon.

Work was busy and Eva was delighted with it but because she now had to pay a childminder for after school and holidays she was finding it very difficult to stretch the allowance that Alan gave her to cover all her costs. While her store was doing well she was forgoing paying herself a salary for the first year as her accountant had advised. With no additional income coming in for herself yet she was forking out for the childminding and on the support that she was getting from Alan it was proving very tight. She was having to make cutbacks and was missing out on things that she once would have taken for granted and didn't want to touch any more of her inheritance. Eva approached Alan about the child support agreement and he seemed agreeable enough on the phone but a couple of days later he called her back and said that no he didn't think that was fair and he wouldn't be paying any extra. Eva was furious. What with complaining about the extra weekends she had asked him to mind the children and now not willing to chip in for the minding expenses she was livid. She kept her cool on the phone to him but straight afterwards phoned her own solicitor to make an appointment. He couldn't have it all his own way and Eva wasn't going to let him wash his hands of his responsibilities that easily. So he could have his job and not have to pay anything towards childcare expenses, well that seemed grossly unfair.

Looking back at what she had originally agreed to she felt a little foolish. She had been more than fair when she had gone through the bills and running expenses for the house and had perhaps been too modest. She had even offered that she would begin to cover half the mortgage payments for the house as soon as the store was doing well enough to pay her a salary. But where was she going to be left when the mortgage was paid for? It had been her money that had paid for the deposit on the house in the first place. The support that he was paying was not enough and going forward it wouldn't be enough to see them through college or pay extras for school tours or birthday parties or whatever else came along. As for the custody arrangements he should be available to do more. What were his parental responsibilities? All he was committed to was every other weekend and that gave Eva very little time to herself. Much as she loved her kids she would like to look forward to the odd break or holiday on her own. She knew she was entitled to a lot more and she intended to go after at least what she needed.

Within days she had a meeting with her solicitor and outlined exactly what she now wanted from Alan. Her solicitor advised her that what she was looking for was reasonable and well within her entitlements. However he did warn her that Alan could make things very difficult. She would have to be prepared that if things couldn't be sorted amicably they may have to pursue her demands through some sort of mediation process.

With childminding costs eating into her budget Eva was being frugal with the grocery shopping and hadn't been getting her hair done as frequently as she used to. Why should her standards slip because he was now off living a bachelor lifestyle? There was something really wrong with that. Some of her savings had been used for the shop fitting and initial stock and she wanted to leave the remainder aside for the children, a legacy of her parents that she wanted to pass. The running costs of the business were now being managed with the overdraft and the income that was beginning to come in so she decided to get the accountants to look at the books and see if the business would be in a position to start paying her a salary sooner than scheduled on the plans.

With only a few days to go before the weekend in New York Eva finalised arrangements with PR Guy for the launch party. He was a right little schmoozer and was forever flirting with the girls in the store whenever he called in. But when it came to business he was a smooth operator as well which more than compensated. Again he had placed some well positioned ads in-print and online

232

announcing the upcoming official launch and while he had been putting pressure on Eva to get a celebrity for the opening she had decided against it and would cut the ribbon herself. They had a significant database of customers now built up who would be officially invited to attend along with the staff and some of Eva's neighbours and friends. PR Guy was going to have a professional photographer there on the night to take some snaps for follow-up publicity and he told Eva that she'd have to wear something amazing. They agreed on a caterer and a budget and a few other small details and it was a relief to hand over most of the responsibility to him.

Chapter 18

(BUFFALO WINGS)

Finally the departure date for the trip to New York arrived. Hannah and Luke were beside themselves with excitement as they boarded the plane at Shannon airport on a Thursday morning. The flight took off on schedule with Hannah and Luke excitedly gripping the arm rests as the nose of the plane cut through winter grey skies and rose above the clouds to where the sun always shines.

Eva closed her eyes briefly and let out a deep sigh. She was trying hard to forget about the letter that had been waiting for her at home the previous evening from Alan's solicitor. It was really putting a damper on her spirits. She couldn't believe what she had read. He was being mercenary and it looked like Eva would be in for a bit of a battle. It couldn't all be the doing of his new girlfriend could it? First not wanting to take on any extra childminding weekends when she needed it and now it seemed he was trying to pull the plug from her business as well.

Here she was trying to make a new start for herself embarking on the start-up of a new business with all the pressures that entailed, she was rearing the kids mostly by herself and now having to deal with a husband who was being acrimonious to say the least.

As she thought about it she wondered what was behind it and just couldn't make it out. Was it money? How could it be? She knew that money had always been a motivator for Alan and that he had invested a lot over the years and was continually moving things around with an eye on the next lucrative investment. In recent years he seemed to be even more money conscious and would raise a questioning eyebrow if Eva wore a new outfit. It used to annoy her a bit but only a little as she felt like she was quite entitled to spend their money and she had continued to do so without paying any heed to his sarcastic observations. After all, it had been Alan's idea that she should give up her job and stay at home with the children.

She remembered how happily she had made that choice to stay at home and enjoy Luke's first couple of years and enjoyed it even more when Hannah came along. It made financial sense as child-minding was so expensive and Eva had loved her time with the kids. With both of them at school Eva had been more leisurely in the past couple of years and had a lot more time for herself. Keeping the house, going to the gym and looking after the children with their various activities kept her busy enough but it was too easy going for her and she had always wanted to do more.

She had been mulling over this business idea for at least two years now. Alan had never encouraged her to go for it though and always raised obstacles whenever she mentioned it. He either did that or just said 'yeah, yeah,' and pretended to listen with feigned interest. Looking back it was probably the risk involved in the investment that was his problem not that he thought it wasn't a good idea. It wasn't as if he wanted her to be a stay at home housewife forever, just that he wasn't willing to take a risk on her. He probably would've been quite happy if she wanted to go back to work in an established business with a salary but not to go it alone.

She took the solicitor's letter out of her handbag and reread it. Even though the business was up and running now and was going well he wanted to pull the plug. The house had been used as collateral to secure the overdraft for the business lease and start-up costs and Alan had signed up but now he wanted to renege. It seemed that she must have caught him off-guard in the early days of their split and in his guilt he had agreed to what she had asked for. If the business failed the house could potentially go to the bank if they couldn't clear the business debts. Eva had figured that the house was hers anyway but now it seemed Alan wasn't handing it over so readily. If the business continued to do well the debt would be serviced but why was Alan trying to jeopardise that now? It felt like things were about to get very messy.

The solicitor's letter was requesting a meeting with Eva and her solicitor and it outlined a number of issues that the 'client' wanted to renegotiate. He also wanted to begin legal separation procedures with a view to divorce. Perhaps he felt that if she did lose the house she would pursue him for something else and perhaps she should. Viv was always saying that she should go after what she was entitled to and more but Eva hadn't wanted anything more, until now. She couldn't understand why Alan wanted to take her chance of success away from her though. Eva felt a little bewildered and bitterly disappointed. Disappointed for the man she thought he was and in herself for not seeing through him sooner. He was showing himself to be selfish and now it seemed that he was mean too. There wasn't much point in dwelling on something that was out of her control for now but she vowed that on her return she would play hardball and see what Alan thought of that. He could either go along with what she considered reasonable or she would go after him like the grim reaper with a freshly sharpened scythe.

Eva didn't usually drink when she was flying but on this occasion she made an exception and ordered herself a glass of white wine to try and settle herself down. Travelling with Luke and Hannah to New York was a pleasure. They were so excited and savouring every aspect of their journey. Changing the channels on their headsets and becoming absorbed in one movie after another they sampled their airplane food like critics in a Gordon Ramsay restaurant. Eva sat back and joined in their fun and did her best to put the letter to the back of her mind.

Arriving into bustling JFK airport was a first time experience for Eva. Their hotel transfer was all part and parcel of their 'shopping package' and it made everything so easy. The New York streets were cluttered with yellow taxis and people busily on their way. Elaine had left a message at the hotel reception to say that she was already checked into the room next door to theirs. There was nothing like American service with everyone from the door-staff to the bellboy and receptionist treating them as if they had just arrived from an address in Windsor.

The hotel room was spacious with a view onto the bustling Manhattan streets below. Luke and Hannah stood transfixed as the gigantic advertising hoardings flickered and changed images captivating them as if it was a drive-in movie.

Eva felt like a schoolgirl on tour as she dumped their bags and ran next door to buzz for Elaine. They hugged warmly and returned to Eva's room to meet the children. Elaine was like an Auntie to them and was soon testing the beds with them for bounciness.

The chattering foursome eventually left the room and made their way to their first port of call. It had to be F-A-O Schwarz. Elaine was looking radiant with her tumbling auburn curls bouncing against the shoulders of a vibrant teal velvet winter coat worn over a cream silk shirt and slim fitting dark denims. Eva was also wearing dark denims and was braced for the bite of the New York winter in a cosy black cashmere high-necked sweater worn under a black military style wool coat.

Arriving at the Fifth Avenue entrance they were greeted by 'Bobby the Toy Soldier'. Hannah and Luke hardly breathed a single steady breath from entering to exiting the store. They rushed from one thing to the next with always something more tempting just around the corner. Eva and Elaine joined in the fun as they tried to synchronise playing chopsticks by jumping from one note to the next on the giant floor piano dance mat. Various stations were set up with the latest handheld gadgets to test drive and Luke could have happily stayed there for a week. Hannah was mesmerised by the array of stuffed animals from gigantic giraffes to cute and cuddly soft bears.

It was an effort to get them to leave but with the enticement of ice-skating they just about prised them out the door. By now ravenous with hunger they decided to leave the skating for the next day and to get something to eat instead. It had to be burgers. Nothing else would do for Luke, he was in America and he wanted a cheeseburger.

After their meal Elaine treated them to a horse-drawn carriage ride in Central Park. Over eight hundred acres of paths, lakes and open spaces provided a relatively calm oasis for New Yorkers in search of escape from the city bustle. With jet-lag beginning to set in it was the perfect way to end the evening. Luke and Hannah nestled into Eva drawing the rugs up around them and exaggerating their frosty breaths to see whose fog would blow the farthest as their carriage took them on a tour of the park.

Their second day in New York started with an American breakfast. Basically anything they wanted they could have. Eggs served over-easy or any way you pleased accompanied crispy strips of bacon. Pumpernickel and rye bread arrived in baskets alongside toasted bagels and cream cheese. Freshly squeezed orange juice flowed and stacks of pancakes were high. Bountiful bowls of fresh fruit and strong coffee ensured they were well fortified for their excursions.

The first stop was the postponed ice-skating at the Rockefeller Centre where the kids of course took off like Torvill and Dean reborn, literally skating rings around the grown-ups who were cautiously clinging to the railings and timidly making their way around the rink. Eva got a bit of a feel for it after a while but after an hour she'd had enough. They had to wait for another forty-five minutes for the kids to be persuaded to leave. There was no rush but Eva did want to see as much as she could of what New York had to offer.

Having to nearly drag Luke and Hannah away from the rink they made their way to Bloomingdale's department store. Eva had always wanted to visit and the sight of customers departing with iconic 'Brown Bags' reminded her of the movie 'Splash.' Eva could happily have spent the whole weekend browsing from one department to the next if she had been allowed but the promise of a visit to the toy department would only placate the children for so long. There was some lovely clothing but Eva also wanted to sneak a visit to the homeware department to check it out so she didn't have time to try anything on. There was a Christmas Shop / Holiday section and the kids were happy to browse there for a while as Eva was trying to mentally scan all the stock to get ideas for her own store.

She couldn't resist doing some quick research on her phone to track down suppliers and ordered some exquisite Christmas tree decorations to be shipped home. She's seen nothing like them available at home. She ordered a mixture of baubles, some shaped like pears, in glittering gold and dark plum along with a set of twelve porcelain white figurines hung on gold ribbons depicting the twelve days of Christmas.

The stop-off at the toy department saw Eva and Elaine gladly avail of the seating area while the kids wandered contentedly from one display to the next. They must have been there for at least an hour with no sign of them losing interest.

It was getting dark by the time they left and they decided on an early dinner. This time it was chicken wings that Luke was after and his eyes popped at the high pile of spicy 'buffalo' wings that were placed in front of him. The ice-skating and the jet lag had Eva yawning and they convinced the children that it would be better to leave the trip to the Empire State Building to the following morning when they would have more energy to enjoy it.

Back at the hotel the kids hopped into bed and were allowed to watch TV while Eva went into Elaine's room for a drink from the mini-bar. They'd opened the interconnecting door between the rooms and it was so lovely to have adult company. Relaxing with Elaine it dawned on her that she hadn't been out for a drink since her night out on the town with Viv two months earlier. Elaine on the other hand was having a hectic social life in Boston and the guy she had been seeing in the summertime was still on the scene.

'I'd love to have met him Elaine.'

'Yeah I wish you had too. But you never know you might get to see him at Christmas time.'

'Seriously! Is he going to come home with you for the holidays?'

'Well I'm working on it. My parents have asked me to bring him over so we'll see.'

'It must be serious so?'

'You could say that. Actually I've asked him to move in with me,' Elaine gushed.

'And…'

'And it's happening next weekend!'

'Elaine, that's wonderful. I'm delighted for you. Any chance I get to see a picture of him now?'

Elaine rummaged in her bag for her phone and soon opened up some holiday snaps taken at a log cabin in Vermont. It looked really romantic with one of the pictures being of Elaine living it up and relaxing in an outdoor hot-tub. Eva understood Elaine's previous Ryan Gosling reference as she studied the photograph of Gary with his smouldering eyes. They limited themselves to one glass of wine and Eva hit the sack with Hannah tucked up beside her and Luke sprawled out like a king in a double bed all to himself.

Saturday arrived and it was wonderful to wake after an undisturbed night of just enough sleep. With the kids still slumbering Eva had her shower. The power of it was like an all over exfoliation and it left her glistening and wide awake.

Meeting up with Elaine for breakfast they bartered with the children, agreeing to another go at ice-skating after the trip to the Empire State Building but only if they promised cooperation and patience for two hours of shopping for Elaine and Eva in between.

With terms agreed they hailed a taxi to the Empire State Building at 5th Avenue which was already bustling with visitors. Joining the heaving line they soon realised that Saturday perhaps wasn't the best day of the week to visit.

The queue snailed along until finally, a little over an hour later, they boarded the elevator. Queue induced crankiness was replaced by exhilaration as the elevator sped its way up to the eighty-sixth floor observatory deck. At over a thousand feet above the New York Streets they were not prepared for the view. It was breath-taking. Looking to the West they studied their maps and identified

Madison Square and The Hudson River. To the South lay Wall Street and the Woolworth building and in the Upper New York Bay the Statue of Liberty saluted them from Ellis Island. Using the viewing cameras was great fun and the visit was one that would always be remembered.

The negotiated shopping trip followed and they decided to spend their two hours in Saks Fifth Avenue rather than trek from one boutique to another. Luke played some game on his phone and Hannah tagged along absentmindedly after Elaine and Eva as they salivated in the denim section over Agolde, Mother & 7 for All Mankind jeans.

With names that read more like a concert line-up than clothing designers Eva found it hard to forgo the temptation to purchase these elitely labelled denims but instead opted for a more sensible investment in a couple of Theory sweater dresses. They would be perfect for comfortable yet stylish workwear dressed up with boots. What she was most happy about though was her dress for the shop launch party.

An alice+olivia midi length dress with an asymmetrically draped hemline, it was described as sage in colour though leaned more towards silver or oyster than light green. With delicate spaghetti straps the neckline draped gently and the back was low. It was the epitome of chic glamour.

It was mid-afternoon by the time they lunched and they were all famished. Eva tucked into a fillet steak served with jacket potato and side salad. Hearing the list of salad dressings being rattled off made her almost sorry that she had asked. Luke tucked into a huge pizza while Hannah just picked at some French fries but did justice to a tall ice-cream sundae in the end.

Darkness was falling as they arrived at the Rockefeller Centre for ice-skating again and the lights were beginning to sparkle on the giant Christmas Tree. Everything in New York seemed larger than life. The Christmas Tree stood at over seventy foot tall and forty foot wide. Bedecked with twinkling lights and topped with a Swarovski designed star adorned with thousands of crystals, it made you feel like you were part of some fantastical kaleidoscopic dream sequence to gaze up at it. Hannah and Luke were even more adventurous with the skating this time out and were beginning to skate at speed. Eva and Elaine gave a token effort and fumbled their way around the rink once before retiring for a warm cup of hot chocolate to chat and keep an eye on the skaters from a nearby table.

"What's the latest with Viv's romance anyway?' Elaine enquired.

'She's in her element Elaine and Daniel is so sound. And do you know what? I'd nearly say that she's in love.'

'Really?'

'Yep, she's mad about him and he's mad about her so at least somebody's love life is on track, besides yours that is.'

'Did you mind?'

'Mind what?'

'It being Daniel.'

'No of course I didn't,' and pausing added 'well maybe a little, yes, I did mind a little at the start actually. You obviously thought I might?'

'Naturally. I know that when I heard it was him I was a bit taken back, what with Daniel being so close to you and everything.'

'I'll always have great time for Daniel but there would never have been anything romantic there anyway.'

'And what about your own love life anyway?' Elaine quizzed

'Non-existent.'

'But what about that French fellow, Sébastien?'

'Ah I don't know. We're still in touch by email and I feel like I'm getting to know him, but you can't have a real relationship like that. It's better than nothing though I suppose. Anyway there's no room for a man in my life at the moment.'

'Things are hectic are they?'

'Yes, too busy for men right now, but tell me more about you and Gary anyway.'

'Well I don't know is it the right move, I'm nervous about him moving in Eva. It's such a huge step for me. I'm just so used to my own company and doing what I want for so many years, I nearly think I'm too selfish to settle down with somebody now.'

'Hmmm never say never as they say,' Eva said a little wistfully, wrapping her hands tightly around her hot chocolate. She hated the thought of ending up on her own.

'Sure we'll see.'

Watching her children happily skating, with the bejewelled Christmas tree shimmering in the background, was magical. Eva knew that she was burning a hole in the credit card but for now she didn't care, they deserved to be treated and this was going to be a trip to remember.

Their last day in New York was a lot more subdued than the previous two and they visited the 9/11 memorial and museum. They visited St. Paul's Chapel where they prayed silently and Eva thought of the victims and those who were left behind and what it meant to have the gifts of life and family.

They said their goodbyes to Elaine at the airport and she promised to come and visit when home with Gary at Christmas time. Both Hannah and Luke were quiet on the flight and slept for much of it. Eva hardly slept at all and was planning the week ahead, writing lists of things to be done before the official launch of the shop. And at the back of the mind was that letter.

Arriving back into Shannon airport it was still dark and early as Eva drove back towards Cork. It was a Monday but there wasn't a hope of seeing either the school or the store that morning as jet lag tiredness hit them. They ended up half snoozing and half watching TV on the couch for the day and ordered in pizza and garlic bread for tea. An early night was eagerly embraced and while they had snoozed during the day all three slept soundly through the night.

Eva woke enthusiastically to greet Tuesday morning. Peeling the kids off their beds took some effort but they had to go back to school and routine. Eva was eager to get straight back to work and to find out how they had coped while she had been away. As she might have guessed she needn't have worried at all. Maggie told her that everything had gone smoothly and that their sales were continuing to rise steadily.

Christmas orders from customers were mounting up and one customer had requested one of the wall hangings in a made to

243

measure size and colour scheme and was waiting on a price. When she got in touch, the suppliers informed Eva that there were only two weeks remaining for orders to be placed in time for a Christmas shipment. Maggie made up a notice offering the customisation service and warning of the two weeks order deadline and by close of business they had orders for two more. Because each wall hanging would be unique they were works of art in themselves and Eva felt justified in whacking on a sizeable mark-up. She began thinking about whether she should approach the suppliers and ask if she could be their exclusive stockist in Ireland. She knew that they weren't supplying into Europe yet anyway and there would be no harm in asking.

Studying the database that Maggie was maintaining of items sold, Eva was able to pick out the best sellers and order plenty more of them. She knew exactly what they had in stock, what was on the shop floor and what was on order.

Eva barely had time for a coffee break but when she did she dashed off a quick reply to an email that was waiting for her from Sébastien. The exchanges between them were becoming more casual and she put a lot less thought into her response than the initial ones. She was surprised that he didn't seem to spend much time on the piste at all or his evenings indulging in après ski. At least that's what he led her to believe anyway.

His job seemed to be more on the administration side of things although he did usually ski on the weekends. Eva tried to visualise him in ski gear and conjured up a very dashing image that was probably closer to Pierce Brosnan in a Bond Movie than the real Sébastien on the slopes. She imagined him kitted out all in black and skiing like a professional. With him working in such a sociable arena Eva had no doubt that he would come across plenty of available attractive women and while she knew she held nothing over him she did shudder at the thought of him with someone else. There was no reason that he shouldn't be with other women if he wanted to, but she just hoped that he wouldn't want to.

He had made her feel beautiful and special when she was with him and that was a dimension completely missing from her life at the moment. She worked, took care of the kids and worked some more.

Over the next few days the emails became more frequent. They were casual, very friendly but usually brief. Eva usually wrote hers at work and was always conscious of being disturbed and probably wasn't as free with her choice of words as she might have been otherwise. His emails were welcome distractions from work when they came and in each one he invariably asked her a probing question. His use of phrasing was endearing as he grappled with English grammar like a cute toddler struggling for descriptions. He asked her favourite colour, food, wine, and movie. Each question had her pausing for the answer and replying with her reason as well. Some were easy like purple and steak but others were difficult.

When you're asked to choose your favourite movie you're conscious of how it will define you and the safest bet is to go with a classic. As Eva thought about this she wanted to be honest and thought about the movies that she had watched over and over again. Pretty Woman sprang to mind but no that wasn't her favourite. It had to be the one where an American girl abandons her wedding to seek out the romance forecast to her by a clairvoyant when she was a child. What was the name of that move? She tried to concentrate and think of it but the name just wouldn't come. She could picture the actress and of course the actor Robert Downey Jnr. and the setting. A trip from Rome to somewhere down the coast, where was it again? Was it Sorrento or Amalfi? Maybe it was Positano. Wherever it was it was beautiful and every time Eva watched the movie she promised herself that she would go there someday. It was an unashamed chick flick, pure romance and drama but one that Eva would watch over and over again no problem. The name just wouldn't come until she googled it and then replied to Sébastien that her favourite movie was called 'Only You.'

His questions were fun and it was flattering that he was trying to find out more about her. He asked for her most embarrassing moments and she replied that some were too embarrassing to even mention and he would have to get to know her better first.

Sometimes his emails came across as extremely corny and he'd say something like he hoped that someday she would share everything with him and that he would know her better than anyone else did. Reading that made her giggle and say *what an idiot* to herself but a little bit of her also swallowed it. Even through emails he was a formidable romantic and used powerful language. Eva tried to take this all in a light-hearted way but a tiny bit of her soaked it up and she knew she was falling for it, corny or not. Was it him or just the idea of him? Was she setting herself up for a fall? He told her that he longed to be with her. He said that he missed her and her beautiful body, her scent and her smile. Sure what woman wouldn't fall for that kind of flattery? Eva tried to hold herself back but what was the point really, why shouldn't she indulge her romantic side a little bit? At times she read and reread his emails and questioned whether it was the man or the fantasy of an idyllic romance that she was falling for. The answer was probably somewhere in between. She knew that she could not truly know this man from printed words on a page, words that maybe were as well chosen as her own sometimes. But the real Sébastien was in there somewhere, in between the romantic words and lines he spun. She liked what she was reading and what he was asking and for now it took her mind away from her well extinguished romantic life in Ireland.

Chapter 19

(MULLED WINE)

Within days of returning from New York, Eva found herself on one side of a large mahogany boardroom table sitting directly opposite Alan. Their solicitors were going through the minutiae of their revised agreement and Eva's solicitor was strongly expressing his dissatisfaction with the financial information he had received. When they adjourned they still seemed to be a long way off agreement. There was a divide between them now and Alan was the one who was building the wall.

Eva's solicitor kept calling her and asking her for financial information and it was beginning to take the good out of her break away. The launch of the store should have been at the forefront of her mind but her asshole husband was overshadowing the build-up to that as well. It was the most that Eva could do to bite her tongue and say nothing when Alan came to pick up the kids and take them for the following weekend. She was beginning to despise the sight of him and for the first time in her life knew what it was like to feel hate. The children appeared to have settled into their routine of staying with their Dad every other weekend with relative ease and didn't seem to be aware of the tension.

Eva enjoyed the quiet of the house when they were gone. As much as she loved them she needed the headspace and a bit of 'me' time. Just to have a cup of coffee and sit down with no background noise was bliss. Sometimes Eva would sit too long with her coffee in the quietness and depth of her thoughts until it became an effort to get moving again. But she had plenty to do.

New ideas for her store came to her from the most bizarre sources and she had notebooks stuffed with ideas. To read it would be like trying to decipher KGB secretly coded messages. Who but Eva would know that 'Turkish Delight' or 'Antique Petticoat' had nothing to do with sweets or buying an undergarment but represented the textures, colours and one of a kind finds that she strove to offer in her store.

It was impractical to pursue most of her ideas and collectively they read as her ultimate wish-list with which to furnish her fantasy Georgian mansion.

Losing herself in her lists, magazine clippings and now Instagram pages too she could browse happily undisturbed for hours. Reality beckoned though and right now her reality was busy days ferrying the kids to school, stock-taking, placing orders and doing her best to be out in front in the shop getting to know some of her customers. Maggie had suggested that they ask their customers for their names and email addresses so they could compile a database for preview nights where they would get to buy sale items or new stock before anyone else. Like a V.I.P. list of sorts it was being added to day by day.

Eva enjoyed her work so much that the days just flew by. The one dampener hanging over her was the legal wrangling that Alan had instigated. She tried not to think about it too much but the whole affair seemed to be getting complicated. Her solicitor was asking her for old bank statements, information on stocks, investments, mortgages or loan agreements that she had signed and to list any property or business interest that Alan had ever mentioned.

It was the kind of thing that made her just want to walk away. It was a mess. Vivienne must have had a pain in her middle ear by now from listening to Eva going on about it. But if she did she never showed it. She encouraged Eva to stick it out and to get what she was entitled to. She had brought as much to the marriage as Alan had and so she should leave with an equal share.

The two friends phoned each other all the time and Viv was still in the glow of her blossoming romance. Eva saw Daniel frequently too as he often popped into the store for a quick coffee and to catch up and conversation always came around to Vivienne. The boy was smitten.

The pair of them had been away for several weekends together and Vivienne thought that he was going to ask her to move in with him and this was discussed at length with Eva even though he had yet to ask her.

The discussions would usually take place over the phone or during a hurried coffee break in the restaurant next to the shop or sometimes they'd have lunch in the small office at the back of the shop.

Eva would bring a flask of home-made soup to work whenever she found time to make it. In between spoonfuls of soup or whatever they were having they would discuss the ongoing hypothesis of whether Viv should move in with Daniel.

The day before the official launch they caught up over a quick coffee in the restaurant next to the store.

'He's definitely been hinting strongly about us moving in together Eva. Do you think I should?' Viv asked.

'Hmmm..'

'Yeah, you're right it's too soon.'

'But I didn't say that…'

'But you were going to.'

'No I wasn't.'

'So you think I should then?'

'Well maybe you …'

'Should wait, yeah you're right. It's too soon and I should wait.'

'Viv I never said that. I think you should go with your gut feeling and do what will make you happy for now. Don't think about six months down the line or whether it will work or not, just do what feels right for you.'

'Hmmmm'

'What?'

I'm not sure.'

'Right. So do nothing then, and besides, he hasn't even asked you yet!' and the two of them giggled at the absurdity of the conjured dilemma.

'Anyway enough about you Viv, wait 'til you hear the latest in my love life. Sébastien emailed me again,' Eva confided quietly.

'Again? How many times is that this week?'

'Every day this week.'

'And what did he say today?'

'Well today he said work was busy. He asked how the kids were, was I busy and oh yes, please come to France and he would teach me to ski! And oh he also asked who is my favourite painter!'

'Your favourite painter?'

'Yeah, like an artist.'

'Well I didn't really think it was your decorator's number he was after! So who is it then?

'Haven't decided yet.'

'I'd go for Picasso myself. But Eva what did you say to the skiing question? You have to go, you have to.'

'Viv I can't, and you know full well I can't.'

'Well I know it wouldn't be easy but you would love to go wouldn't you?'

'I'd give my right arm to go Viv, you know that but it's just mission impossible at the moment. I don't know whether I'm coming or going with work and all the legal nonsense, I couldn't just disappear off for a skiing trip.'

'Sure why don't you book something anyway and you could always cancel it if it didn't work out?'

'I couldn't do that. Sure when could I go anyway?' Eva replied despondently.

'What about the New Year, doesn't Alan have the kids for that?'

'Oh don't mention that asshole to me.'

'That bad.'

'I think I'm beginning to despise him now Viv. Sure I told you all about the solicitor stuff.'

'I know, but don't let him stop you from living your life.'

'What do you mean?'

'Well the skiing trip. Sure if he's minding the kids for New Year's couldn't you take off then?'

'He's taking them to some hotel in Rosslare for a few days before they go back to school. I don't know Viv. Wouldn't that come across as very extravagant of me to be off on a skiing trip.'

'But it'd be perfect. Sure you'd only have to pay for the flights, the expensive part of skiing is the gear and lodge and surely Sébastien would look after all that.'

'Ah no Viv I can't.'

'Why not? Sure isn't he always asking you?'

'It's not that. It's just financially. Sure I mightn't have a roof over my head by then.'

'Of course you will. What does the solicitor say?'

'Very little. He just keeps asking me for more and more paperwork and I'm sick to the back teeth of it. It's really getting me down not knowing where I stand. Anyway, forget about it. We'll just have to wait and see. You and Daniel are coming to the launch on Thursday aren't you?'

'Wouldn't miss it for the world girl. Will there be food there?'

'Finger food, little bite-size canapés but it should hit the spot so don't have anything to eat beforehand. Just come straight over after work. I could do with the moral support to help me calm the nerves.'

'What are you wearing?'

'The dress I told you about that I bought in New York with Elaine.'

'Oh yes, that sounds very glam. I'd better dress up for it so. Anyway I'd better head back to work.'

'Text me.'

'Bye hon.'

Eva savoured the last few mouthfuls of soup contemplating their conversation and then sent a quick email to Sébastien.

'Hi Sébastien, I have yet to decide who my favourite painter is and would need to visit a few more galleries to educate

251

myself first! As for learning to ski, perhaps early in the New Year? What do you think?'

A click and it was gone. Vivienne's fault! Yet again she regretted sending an email so hastily but it was out there now and there was no going back.

Another email came in and Eva had no time to ponder the possibilities of a skiing trip any further. It was from the warehouse to let her know that her shipment from New York had just arrived. She emailed back with instructions to send everything that had come in down by courier first thing the following morning.

The day before the launch saw Eva arriving into work at the crack of dawn to get the shop ready. Nora was going to get the kids their breakfast and look after taking them to school so that Eva could make the most of her last day of preparations. She started by taking everything off the shelves and wiping them down with a damp cloth to freshen them up. Next she started to unbox the New York shipment. PR Guy called in mid-morning with some last minute details and they went over the caterer's menu. Flirting again some of the staff noticeably fawned over him whenever he was around. *Lord help the girl that marries him,* thought Eva, *he'll always have one eye on the other side of the room.* Well a wandering eye probably wouldn't cause a problem, it's where his hands and other bits and pieces would be that might. Michelle in particular was so blatantly throwing herself at him that Eva couldn't help but shake her head.

Closing up time came and Eva stayed on late, turning her attention to her newly arrived Christmas decorations from New York. She was pleased with her decision to stick to the shop's theme colours of plums and gold. Baubles and pears, angels and bells, fairies and stars were all unwrapped and glittered and sparkled before her eyes. The white porcelain set for the twelve days of Christmas was delicately wrapped in tissue paper and Eva put them safely to one side in the back office.

She set about filling glass bowls and vases with mixtures of the two different coloured Christmas decorations and sprinkled gold glitter stars onto the white shelves. Damson balloons floated skyward delicately strung with gold ribbon and the place was as ready as it would ever be. Eva slept that night dreaming of powdery white snow slopes littered with gold baubles and porcelain turtle doves weaving patterns through frosty skies.

On the day of the launch party Eva kept busy putting the finishing touches to the store's shelves in between serving the customers but her mind wasn't on the job at all. Her nerves were shattered and she kept going back to the office and making phone calls to remind people to come. She tried to calm herself and reasoned that at least half of those that had been invited had replied to say that they would come. Shutting up the shop an hour early Eva retreated to the back office to change out of her trouser suit and into her dress. It felt even better on than it had in the New York changing room. Accentuating her blue eyes with copper and gold eyeshadows from a Charlotte Tilbury palette she repeated the mantra 'less is more, less is more,' as she added the tiniest hint of gold glitter on top.

Time was pushing on and when the caterers arrived Eva set to work helping to prepare a space on a table for mulled wine, vodka and cranberry juice cocktails and another table for the food. Various tasty bites filled large white serving platters. There were delicate cheese straws, canapés of chicken satay sticks, goats cheese and Parma ham wrapped together in crispy pastry and other savouries that included pork and cranberry patties, fig crostini with melted stilton sitting beside an equally appealing array of bite-size desserts. The caterers had come equipped with a neat little mini oven for the bites that needed warming up. Mini mince-pies, dark chocolate and cranberry biscuit cake and rich chunks of Christmas cake would all be washed down agreeably with mulled wine or whiskey laden Irish coffees.

Opening the doors at seven o'clock with a mixture of trepidation and excitement Eva welcomed a few of her neighbours who had arrived as a group together. They eagerly accepted glasses of mulled wine and wandered around admiring the store and complimenting Eva on the decorations. Vivienne had come earlier

253

to help out and now stood sipping a glass of mulled wine wearing a chocolate brown midi length Fendi dress with a deep V back teamed with three inch heels. Admiring Viv's style Eva was glad that she had glammed up as the room filled up with even more well dressed women. Christmas carols played subtly in the background and Eva did her best to greet everyone as they arrived. PR Guy was earning his salt big-time and arrived with a journalist and photographer in tow from a well-known fashion magazine that also had an interiors section. With a glass of mulled wine and a room full of friends, neighbours and customers from her V.I.P. list Eva felt relaxed and confident as she spoke her few well-rehearsed words and then proudly cut the plum coloured ribbon emblazoned with the words 'Living & Dining etc.' in delicate gold letters to officially open her new store. She was warmly congratulated by her accountant, her solicitor and even by a representative from her bank. Mary, her mother-in-law, had arrived with two of her friends and oohed and aahed at every turn, promising to be in before Christmas to pick out some gifts. The photographer seemed to be flashing every few minutes and the journalist quizzed Eva about the sourcing of many of her items on display. The mulled wine and hot whiskeys flowed and the food gradually disappeared until the crowd began to dissipate and the caterers wrapped up for the evening leaving behind a couple of bottles of unopened red wine. Eva felt euphoric and went in search of a bottle opener for a quiet celebration now that things had wound down. She nearly lost her life when she opened the back office door and briskly closed it again scurrying back to tell Viv what she had just witnessed as she tried to stifle her laughter. She whispered to Viv that she had just seen Michelle and PR Guy shagging in the office. The pair emerged within minutes oblivious that Eva had witnessed their antics. It was hilarious to observe their attempts to behave normally, carefully avoiding each other as they gathered their belongings and said goodnight. Eva had no doubt that they would be meeting up around the corner and that Michelle would be in for a repeat performance. While it was totally inappropriate behaviour from a professional, Eva decided to say nothing and to just let it go. PR Guy had after all done a great job and all going well he had probably scored her some great publicity. Eva didn't think it was worth bothering to reprimand Michelle either but she certainly wouldn't be leaving her in charge of the store on her own anytime soon.

The second day of December saw Eva in early to work again. This time she had a vicious hangover, a pair of rubber gloves and a mop and bucket. While the caterers had done their best to clear away most of the evidence from the night before, there were a few carelessly strewn half glasses and cups around the place and the floor was absolutely filthy.

Viv had stayed with her well into the small hours toasting the success of the evening and they must have finished almost two bottles of red between them. Eva set to work fastidiously mopping the floor with soapy wood cleaner and a throbbing head until the old wooden boards gleamed again.

That morning was ferociously busy with one sale after another and Eva popped a couple of paracetamol to help her through. She was just about to go on a lunch break when she got a call from her solicitor.

'Hi Eva. It's John. Well done last night, the party was fantastic.'

'Thanks John, I'm so glad you enjoyed it. What can I do for you?' Eva knew fine well that a telephone call from him was never a social one.

'Yes Eva I'd like you to come into the office today sometime if you can manage it.'

'Well I was just about to go to lunch.'

'Perfect. Come straight over and I'll order in some sandwiches,' he said, hanging up.

'Perfect my eye,' muttered Eva. The last thing she needed to go with her hangover was some more legal shenanigans. Being in possession of every bit of banking and financial detail that Eva could lay her hands on she couldn't imagine what more he could possibly want. Some of the records went back ten years or more. So now what?

Well she didn't have to wait long to find out and after a five minute drive in her jeep she was sitting across the desk from John. She accepted a coffee and took a bite from a spicy Cajun chicken and salad sandwich as John began.

'Well Eva, I've a draft agreement here in front of me that has been thrashed out between ourselves and Alan's solicitor. So just take a few minutes to go over it and to see what you think. I should warn you however that you may not be quite ready for everything you're about to read.'

His tone and words were ominous and Eva drew her breath as John pushed the document torturously slowly in her direction. Eva looked at one of the pages in front of her and then the next. At first all she could see was numbers. There were different currencies and symbols and they all mingled on the page merging into a cacophony of confusion. There were plus and minus figures in red and in black and then a bottom line figure. Eva frowned, shaking her head in disbelief.

'Does this mean what I think it does?'

'Yes Eva,' John replied soberly.

'Do you mean to tell me that Alan is broke?'

'Well I wouldn't go as far as to say that he is broke Eva.'

'But this can't be right. What about the properties? All the money that he was investing?'

'I'm afraid it's gone Eva.'

'Gone? What do you mean gone?'

'If you take the document home with you Eva you'll see it's quite complex but the bottom line is that Alan switched from investing in property to investing in e-commerce stocks and shares and it didn't pay off.'

'What do you mean e-commerce?' Eva was genuinely baffled.

'I mean shares in up and coming technology companies that looked prime to boom but then crashed.'

'What? But what about the properties?'

'Eva it's all in the report and you'll need to take your time to read it. But you'll see that besides your home and the city centre apartment there isn't any.'

'So what are we actually looking at?' Eva asked grimly.

'Eva, it's not all bad news. If you read on you'll see that we've drafted an agreement whereby eventually Alan will sign the house over to you and you will sign the apartment over to him. He will continue to pay the mortgage on your house for now and the child support has been increased as we discussed, this maintenance payment continues until the children are finished college. He no longer wants to withdraw his support for your business loan, that demand is being dropped and it wouldn't have been possible for him to do that anyway as he'd already signed with the bank for that and he is staking no claim in it either. And your inheritance savings are yours to keep.'

'Oh thank goodness.' Eva sat quietly for a couple of minutes trying to take it all in.

'So let me get this straight, he will sign the house over to me and pay the mortgage and pay increased child support until the children are finished college?'

'That's what we're heading towards now Eva. He's on a very good salary with bonuses and can well afford to do that so if you want to ask for more now is the time to do it. So read it through carefully Eva. He also wants to pursue a judicial separation.'

'You mean divorce?'

'Yes Eva, eventually in time he wants to divorce but for now a legally agreed separation. You have to be two years living apart before you can divorce.'

'Oh,' Eva felt floored. It felt like Alan was calling all the shots again and she had no control.

She left the solicitor's office with a spinning head and couldn't face returning to work. Instead she drove out of Douglas in the direction of Rochestown and onwards along the water's edge until she arrived at Monkstown. She parked her jeep and sat on a bench trying to make sense of her situation. She must have sat there for an hour before Viv arrived.

The friends found a table in the Bosun restaurant across the street, which was one of Eva's favourite lunchtime haunts. But today she didn't taste the food at all as she filled Viv in on the details of her meeting with the solicitor.

'Is he sure that's all there is? I mean could Alan have property hidden or invested money abroad or something?'

'Maybe, I don't know Viv, but the solicitor seems to think it's all above board. I signed so many papers over the years without looking at them but still this all now makes sense somehow. When I look back at how cautious Alan used to be about money in recent years I'm thinking that he wasn't being miserly at all; he was probably just worried.'

'Well I hope you're not feeling sorry for him Eva.'

'I don't know what to feel to be honest. I'm shocked. But I have misjudged him though Viv. I had him painted as a right scrooge in my head and in reality he was just being careful.'

'He could have told you though Eva.'

'Maybe he thought I wouldn't want to know. I mean there was me living like we were loaded splashing out on expensive clothes and lavish weekends away. He must have been having regular mini strokes with the way I used to be blowing it.'

'You were not Eva, you were never extravagant with your spending! So now what happens?'

'Well he's no longer trying to pull his support for the business and it's too late to do that anyway as it's all signed up with the bank. But now having the house as collateral for the business puts a whole new perspective on things.'

'In what way?'

'Well if the business goes under I could lose the house and there won't be anything else to fall back on.'

'Right. But Eva the business is flying I'd say isn't it?'

'It is Viv, I can't believe how well it's going. Just as long as it keeps going I should be alright. It feels like I've taken a huge gamble though Viv.'

'Eva it's working though you know it is. Sure the place is thriving. And say worst case scenario, you'd never end up owing that much through your business, your house is worth a lot of money you know Eva. If worse came to worst you could remortgage to pay off any debts. You'll be fine.'

'Well I can't back out now anyway. But still Viv I really have to give it everything. Do you know what though? I am really peeved that I had to learn about this through the solicitor. I mean Alan must have known that all this was about to come out. Why didn't he tell me?'

'Pride I suppose Eva.'

'Would it have been that hard to tell me that he had tried investing for our future with all good intentions and that it didn't work out? I wouldn't have thought any less of him. I mean things could have been so different if he had just told me.'

'But he didn't Eva.'

'Do you think I should call him?'

'No Eva, I don't, as the saying goes he's made his bed and I think you're forgetting the bigger picture here, he wrecked your life and not the other way around.'

Eva returned to work with renewed purpose. The doubts about having to give up the business because of Alan relinquishing his support were now lifted. Her home would be her own in time and all that she had to do was to keep the business going. Her destiny lay in her own hands now.

Her next appointment would have to be at her accountant's office. Coming up to Christmas she knew that this was the time to make money and she wanted to make sure that she was maximising all opportunities to do so. They would have to open longer hours and there would be no alternative but to open early on Sundays as well which would mean more part-time staff but the income would far outweigh those costs. She thought of Hannah and Luke and what this was going to mean for them. She would have to work longer hours but there was no alternative. As someone had once told her, guilt is a useless emotion.

Chapter 20

(APPLE CRUMBLE)

The first week of December had begun and the shoppers were out with a vengeance. Eva had been in touch with the suppliers of the silk wall hangings in the U.S. and her solicitors were drawing up an agreement with them so that she would be the exclusive stockist in Ireland. The wall hangings were proving to be extremely popular and she wanted to make sure that she remained the sole supplier.

Maggie had persuaded her to order some wicker baskets lined with linen in a variety of sizes to make up gift baskets and they were also selling well. Eva had made up baskets with some of the cranberry encrusted scented candles and jars of cranberry sauce from Nantucket alongside olive tapenades, jars of black cherries in kirsch and spiced shortbread that Fiona had sourced in France. Adding a couple of sparkling baubles in gold and plum was the finishing touch to the gourmet baskets. They were selling quickly with some customers choosing to make up their own gift baskets. It was yet another gem of an idea from Maggie.

The shop's reputation was building and the shoppers that came in seemed to have plenty to spend. Working long and hard to keep the shelves stocked and the customers served, the first week of December wrapped up with sales more than doubling Eva's projections.

Her accountant was more than impressed with her trading figures. He advised her to tighten up on her shipments planning and after a few other suggestions he also advised that she could begin to take a salary from the business herself. It would be the difference between dreading and enjoying Christmas and she'd be well able to splash out on the kids.

Eva's next encounter with Alan when he came to pick up the children for the weekend was significantly different than the previous one. Instead of boiling with rage she pitied him. She could see that he was uncomfortable with her now knowing everything about their finances. He asked to speak with her alone for a few minutes before heading off with the children and said that he was hoping to eventually sell the apartment in the city and to buy a house in Ballincollig if that was okay with her. How things had changed that he now had to ask for her approval. Eva agreed without hesitation before hugging the children goodbye for the weekend.

She was beginning to have a bit of a ritual on the Friday nights that they weren't around. It would start with a long soak in a warm bubble bath. She'd moisturise and top up her fake tan afterwards and then either watch a chat show or stream a movie enjoyed with either a couple of glasses of wine or maybe half a tub of chocolate ice-cream or sometimes both. She'd work all day Saturday and have an early night and then work all day Sunday. She wasn't going to take a day off again until after Christmas and there was only three weeks left to go.

With all the hours she was working she wasn't sure whether she should have committed to an Interior Design project that Daniel had offered her a couple of days after the launch but it was too late to change her mind now. The project was small but lucrative enough to be tempting and involved accessorising the penthouse apartment in the complex above her store.

As far as Eva was aware most of the apartments were sold and occupied already however the penthouse was yet to be sold. Daniel asked her not to mention it to anyone but to let him know as soon as possible if she'd take it on. After mulling it over for about thirty seconds she saw dollar signs in her head and agreed to take it on. She still wasn't to mention that she had gotten the project to

261

anyone until after the occupants had moved in and while Eva thought it an odd request she agreed. It was to be ready by Christmas Eve and although under enough pressure already Eva was determined to get it finished on time.

Daniel had given her carte blanche with the project and trusted her taste completely just requesting that it would be elegant while still being modern. The penthouse was already painted and furnished in a neutral palette of creams and soft taupes that needed to be brought to life. Eva often felt like she was on a covert mission as she'd wait for the staff to leave the store in the evening and then select some pieces from the shop floor before sneaking upstairs to decorate the penthouse. It might be a couple of glass vases one evening or a wall hanging or rug the next. She sourced some tall floor lamps and additional end-tables locally along with an array of exotic potted house plants. Her terracotta range of storage jars warmed up the stark white kitchen.

When Eva checked her emails at home one evening later in the week there was one from Sébastien. As usual her tummy fluttered as she opened it in anticipation. However she read this one with dismay. He was giving her details of what airport she should fly into for her New Year's trip to Camurac and she read his words of enthusiasm with regret. She just couldn't commit to it now and was so sorry that she had suggested that she would. Perplexed as to how she could explain without going into all the details she was glad she had opened it at home. After taking some time to mull it over a tear fell as she replied :

'Dear Sébastien,
I am so sorry but I will have to postpone this trip. It is just the wrong time to leave the business and I have to give it my full commitment for now. There are some complications that need to be sorted out but please be assured that I would love more than anything to visit you but now is not the right time.
I hope that you will understand.
x Eva.'

262

Reluctantly sending her on their digital journey Eva switched off her laptop and went to the kitchen to indulge in some therapeutic home- baking with Hannah. Together they made some sausage rolls and an Apple Crumble.

'Apple Crumble'

You will need:
2kgs of cooking apples
50g caster sugar (for cooking the fruit)
100g plain flour
50g wholemeal flour
50g porridge oats
100g unsalted butter
200g light golden brown sugar
Butter to grease baking dish

Method:
Preheat the oven to 170°C/Gas Mark 5.
Core, peel and chop the apples into smallish chunks and cook in a saucepan with a splash of water and the caster sugar over a medium heat until softening (still with a bit of bite and not a pulp). This takes about 5 minutes.
Put the plain and wholemeal flours and the oats into a mixing bowl and chop in the butter.
Use your fingertips to crumble the flour, oats and butter together until it starts to resemble breadcrumbs.
Add the brown sugar and mix well with a fork.
Place the cooked apples in a large greased baking dish and scatter the crumble mixture on top – press it down lightly but do not over-compact it.
Bake for 35–40 minutes.
Delicious on its own, even better with custard or vanilla ice-cream.

[RECIPE ENDS]

After eating a couple of the freshly baked sausage rolls for tea, Eva tucked into a portion of the crumble. Adorned with a scoop of vanilla ice-cream it was delicious.

Another busy week was flying by and it really didn't make a difference if it was the beginning or end of the week as no matter what day it was Eva was working. Time with the children now revolved around dinner time which she kept sacred as a time when she would cook for them and sit down with them for an hour before heading back to work and creeping in later to kiss them goodnight. Eva's child-minder Nora was heaven sent with her daughter Helen filling in for her at times. It was a hectic few weeks and Eva's normally well-kept home was gathering dust and the pile of un-ironed laundry continued to grow in size.

With mid-December upon her, Eva snuck into work at five o'clock one morning armed with a calligraphy stencil set, some gold paint, an artist's easel and a very small Christmas Tree. She worked excitedly without stopping until just before nine o'clock Maggie arrived as Eva put the finishing touches to the tree. Maggie stood outside the window with her mouth open and eyes wide while Eva flicked the switch for the lights and joined her to admire her new window arrangement.

It was an enchantment brought to life. The tree was decorated with baubles of frosted plums and golden pears that magically sparkled in the twinkle of the soft white fairy lights. The once wooden artist's easel was now spray painted in sparkling gold and stood alongside the tree displaying a big plum coloured card with the words :

'On the first day of Christmas, my true love gave to me, A partridge in a pear tree'

in beautifully scripted gold lettering against the plum background. To complete the display there hung on the middle branches of the tree a carefully placed white porcelain partridge dangling from a gold string.

'Oh Eva it's beautiful,' gushed Maggie.

'Do you think so, really?'

'Do I what? I've never seen anything like it. It's so pretty and simple it just takes your breath away. It's magic Eva. Pure magic.'

'Come in and I'll show you the rest of the set,' and Maggie followed her inside to where she delicately unwrapped another piece of the white porcelain set that she had bought in New York.

With each passing day Eva arrived early and would add the next line of the song to the board and the next piece of white porcelain to the tree until she had two turtle doves, three French hens and four calling birds all proudly on display alongside the lone partridge.

With only a week left until Christmas Eva took a couple of hours off to do her Christmas shopping for the children. She drove over to Mahon Point so she could get it all done under one roof in the shopping centre. Racking her brains as she scoured for what to get for Luke, she knew Hannah would be easy and happy with anything. Eva's fee for the Interior Design project was going to pay for Christmas and she was going to splurge on a new outfit for herself and with a salary coming in on top of that she knew she could afford to really splash out. She picked out a gorgeous pink silk pair of pyjamas for Hannah that were embroidered with little butterflies and came with a matching eye mask. As if a nine year old had any need for an eye mask, maybe she could wear it herself. Settling on a smart watch for Luke's main present and a handheld game console for Hannah she was satisfied they would be happy.

Next up was the present shopping for Viv and Daniel, Elaine, her mother-in law, her brother David, the child-minder and babysitter and a few small gifts for neighbours and the staff. She spent a small fortune on perfume and aftershave and splashed out on Maggie and bought her a jar of 'Crème de la Mer' and a hand painted silk scarf.

After paying she turned to go and quite literally bumped into Alan. Both of them were completely taken by surprise and it took a minute to realise that someone was standing alongside him.

'Eva, how… how are you?' Alan enquired, as the colour rose in his cheeks.

'Not too bad and you?' Eva replied, managing to keep her tone cool and steady.

'I I I… I'd like you to meet Sophie. Sophie this is Eva,' Alan stuttered awkwardly.

'Nice to meet you,' Eva said, politely offering a hand which was shaken warmly. Her words had fallen out automatically. As Eva met Sophie's gaze she didn't feel anything at all towards the woman and was surprised at how easy she found it to be pleasant. Where once she thought she would have punched her if their paths had ever crossed, here she was calmly saying goodbye and just walking away.

She couldn't help but look back after a few paces and observe Alan with his arm around his new partner's shoulder. She watched as he walked in the other direction with another woman beside him and wondered why her heart wasn't breaking. Was it because Sophie had turned out to be a much plainer version of the glamorous counterpart that Eva had always envisaged, could she be that shallow? Maybe. Or was it because she didn't love Alan anymore and she now felt more fulfilled on her own than she had ever been in all her years with him? Her life was her own and she controlled every aspect of it. That felt really good.

Parking outside her shop she headed back in to work with her bags of shopping stored in the boot of her car. She stopped to look at the window display and hoped that she hadn't forgotten anyone while her breath formed a gentle fog in the cold winter air. Admiring the tree she entered the bustling shop and felt the glow of Christmas cheer wrap her up warmly as carols played softly in the background.

With the deadline for finishing the Penthouse rapidly approaching she was receiving check-up calls from Daniel every second day. As much as she assured him that it was all on target and it would be perfect, he was uncharacteristically apprehensive about it.

Each morning she'd get up early and shower before calling the children for school and making the dreaded school lunches. With the kids at school she relished her first chore at work each morning

266

in the final countdown to the holidays. She would carefully script a new line of the twelve days of Christmas song in gold lettering onto the plum card and add another delicate white porcelain decoration to the tree. The days were passing by and now five golden rings, six geese a-laying, seven swans a-swimming, eight maids a milking and nine ladies dancing were creating a busy looking scene on the Christmas tree in her shop window.

Her second chore of the day was to check emails from suppliers and the warehouse to see whether orders were on the way or had come in. Emails from Sébastien were now less frequent. Whether it was because he was busy as he said or that he was losing interest now that she wasn't going to be visiting him Eva wasn't quite sure.

He had asked her to change her mind but she just couldn't. She thoroughly enjoyed their email exchanges though and receiving one made her day. She felt like they had been really getting to know one another, what the other liked and didn't like and they shared an optimistic outlook and enthusiasm for many things.

Invariably after an email from Sébastien, Eva would be a bit distracted and stay online browsing the net for a bit. She loved checking out the latest stock on the department store websites, especially the homeware. Tactile fabrics and materials usually featured such as leathers and suedes. Browsing through the clothes section Eva would bemoan her wardrobe or rather the lack of it this season. She had bought herself a new outfit for Christmas but her work clothes were largely from old stuff in her wardrobe and she was badly in need of new footwear. She'd usually wear her black trouser suit to work with a silky camisole underneath it or a DVF wrap dress or one of the sweater dresses she'd bought in New York but she felt that she could badly do with a shopping splurge.

Sometimes her browsing would wander to Camurac, the ski resort where Sébastien was working. She even went so far as to check out flights and knew the best route was through London and that the cost needn't be that outrageous. She would indulge herself in brief reunion fantasies until invariably Maggie or someone would interrupt her imaginary liaisons.

After checking on emails she'd have a coffee with Maggie and decide on the staff breaks for the day. With only three days remaining until Christmas Eve, Eva was beginning to feel burned out. She would be taking Christmas Day and Stephen's Day off but after that it would be bedlam again with the sale season looming. She asked Maggie to cover for her for the start of the New Year so she could take a few days off and recharge the batteries when Alan would be away with the kids.

The Penthouse project was finished and now included a decorated Christmas tree as part of her accessorising. Daniel had yet to see it so she hoped that he and his client would be pleased with the end result.

The last day of school arrived and Eva collected the children after a half-day and brought them to the store. Luke happily browsed online in the office while Hannah stood in the shop window pretty as a picture playing with the decorations on the tree.

The ten lords a-leaping had been added to the tree that morning and as Hannah played distractedly moving figurines around a young freelance photographer entered the store. He asked Eva if he could take Hannah's picture outside unbeknownst to her. Eva hesitated but then agreed when he promised to send it to her for approval before attempting to get it published.

Eva stood watching in the distance while Hannah played innocently, the sparkle of the fairy lights casting a glow on her sweet face and white blonde curls. She looked like a little Christmas Angel herself as she played. Eva felt a lump in her throat and thought back to a year ago. She had so much time with them then. This time last year they would probably have been adding pieces to their crib and making star-shaped Christmas cookies for their Dad coming home from work. The photographer's bulb flashed in the window jolting Eva back to the present.

The shop was busy but Eva took Hannah and Luke out for an hour on the pretence of a late lunch break. She stole up to the penthouse with them and they helped her to put the star on the top of the tree. It was four o'clock in the afternoon by the time they returned and they bought some sandwiches to eat in the office. It was Eva's first bite since breakfast and she was famished.

The day before Christmas Eve was a Friday and the panic buying was setting in apace. Some people seemed to be buying all of their Christmas presents in her shop and one customer had left with ten individually wrapped parcels. The pre-ordered gift baskets were being picked up and new ones were constantly being made up as well. Viv called in briefly and in the midst of the mayhem Eva found it hard to follow what she was saying above the noise but it seemed she'd gotten it into her head that Daniel was definitely going to be asking her to move in with him. Elaine was also home with her new man Gary and Eva felt bad that she hadn't met up with them yet but they were going to call over on Christmas Eve for a drink.

Well if she had thought she'd been busy so far, nothing could have prepared her for Christmas Eve. The morning had arrived with a flurry of powder white snow which continued to fall as if in slow motion. The Eleven pipers piping were finally joined by the Twelve drummers drumming on the Christmas tree. When Eva opened the door of the shop at nine o'clock there was a queue of people already outside. Eva was speechless, where were they all coming from? Maggie arrived in a bustle of excitement and could hardly speak as she showed Eva the back page of the newspaper. There, taking up half of the back page of the newspaper was a colour photograph of Hannah as she played with the decorations on the tree and the caption below it read:

'While visions of sugar plums danced in her head.'

Eva couldn't hold back her tears, mixed emotions of happiness and guilt merged as she looked at the picture of Christmas innocence. Maggie pretended not to notice the tears and excused herself to make coffee while Eva did her best to regain her composure. She didn't have time to indulge herself as one of the customers who had queued asked her to make up five gift baskets for her. One after another they thronged in until mid-morning saw PR Guy arriving in. He had to literally jostle his way through customers to reach Eva.

269

'How did you manage that?' He asked, gesturing towards something on his phone that Eva couldn't see.

'Manage what?' she replied.

'The publicity.'

'Publicity?' she responded and the penny dropped as she caught a glimpse of the picture from the newspaper on his phone. Apparently the picture was online as well and getting lots of 'likes.'

'Eva the picture's gone viral! If I'd scored a client that kind of coverage I'd be charging megabucks,' he joked. 'You do know that the twelve days of Christmas don't start until tomorrow though right?' and not waiting for an answer he went off to find Michelle who advised him on a gift for his mother!

Eva looked around and felt almost claustrophobic. The place was so crowded. She'd had to get the courier to bring down more stock from the warehouse twice and two more part-timers in to cope. The phone was ringing off the hook. One person was permanently on wrapping duties, another was stocking shelves, two people were on the tills while two more were helping customers and filling in when breaks were taken. It was Hannah's picture that was drawing them in and Eva eventually shut up shop having done three weeks' trade one day. They closed up at six o'clock so that everyone could get home in time for Christmas. It had been phenomenal all day long and now it was quiet but there was still one more thing that Eva had to take care of before going home.

She locked up the shop and then went upstairs to the penthouse to wait. She made some fresh coffee in the carefully chosen Italian coffee maker and waited for Daniel to arrive. He turned the key, entered and his eyes lit up as he surveyed the living room.

'Perfect. Eva. Perfect. I knew you wouldn't let me down.'

She gave him a tour and he enthused at every finishing touch. The designer glass vases filled with fresh cut lilies flickered in the light reflected from glass bowls dripping with sparkling fairy lights. She had grouped scented candles together of different sizes in front of a mirror in the bathroom and had a glass bowl full of lemons studded with cloves on the kitchen counter. The scattered cushions some of which were faux fur and others embroidered silk looked more than inviting on the cream leather couches. Sumptuous rugs and delicate wall hangings added splashes of colour in rich tones of mulberry and ruby red. The windows were delicately embraced with swathes of transparent muslin and a telescope faced towards the constellations stood ready for a viewing. With the smell of freshly brewed coffee, cinnamon candles and the decorated Christmas tree the place was more than ready to move into.

'So why all the secrecy anyway Daniel? Who's the client?' she quizzed him.

'Can you keep a secret?

'You know I can.'

'It's for me.'

'You, you're joking me. I never thought you'd ever move in from the countryside.'

'Well I will if Viv joins me. What do you think?' he asked cautiously in a half whisper.

'Have you asked her yet?'

'You know full well I haven't. Sure the two of you are as thick as thieves and you'd be the first she would have told. No, I'm going to ask her tonight.'

'Well I'll wish you good luck Daniel though I'd say you'll hardly need it.' She hugged her good friend tightly and wished him a Happy Christmas before heading for home.

She was home by eight and had plenty of time to shower and change for Elaine calling over. She wore her alice + olivia dress from the launch party. Well if Ryan Gosling's half-twin was going to be in the house she would at least make an effort. Her brother David was home and staying for the holidays. He was helping to decorate by blowing up balloons while the children who were hyper and had Christmas carols playing full blast kicked the balloons around the place. Eva left them to it and put some delicate filo wrapped parcels of cranberries and brie to heat in the oven and then Elaine and Gary arrived.

271

Luke, the man of the house, let them in and Elaine was full of admiration for everything. Gary was as good looking as he was in the photograph that Elaine had shown her and even Hannah seemed smitten. They'd a lovely evening with Helen and Nora calling over to join them in a glass of champagne and Viv texted to say that they'd call over too. The children's pile of presents was growing larger with every ring of the doorbell and soon Daniel and Viv arrived. Daniel presented Hannah and Luke with a chocolate Santa each. Eva could see by Viv that Daniel must have asked her to move in with him as she was beaming from ear to ear.

Eva offered them both a glass of champagne and when Daniel took his he said he wanted to propose a toast.

'To Eva and to the future, may your success grow and grow.'

'Here, here,' was echoed all around until Daniel added

'and I'd also like you all to join me in a toast to my future bride. The beautiful Vivienne.'

Eva joined her friends with enthusiastic exchanges as Viv displayed her ring. 'Oh My Gods,' were interspersed with oohing and aahing as another cork popped and champagne flowed.

'Eva that apartment!' Viv exclaimed. 'I knew you had a flair for interiors but it's just something else.'

'Thanks Viv but don't you mean penthouse darling!'

'What are ye on about?' Elaine quizzed looking thoroughly lost.

'Ah Elaine this girl is moving above her station now you know,' Eva began as she filled Elaine in on the 'mysterious' project that Daniel had her doing over the past number of weeks. The evening wore on and Eva chatted to her friends who were getting carried away with talk of wedding dresses, flower-girls and Caribbean honeymoons until it was time for them to go home and for Santa to visit.

At almost midnight David carried Luke up to bed and Eva changed a sleepy Hannah into her new pink pyjamas before settling her for bed. Hannah was chuffed that Viv wanted her to be a flower-girl and went to sleep happy.

Returning downstairs Eva sipped another glass of champagne as she cleared up and then set the table for Christmas dinner. This year her brother would take Alan's place at the table. She covered it with a deep red tablecloth and then polished up the silver Newbridge cutlery before laying the table. The dinnerware was Vera Wang for Wedgwood lace gold collection, white dinner plates with a beautiful gold trim. Each carefully placed napkin was starched white and secured with a gold napkin ring. Gold and deep red baubles were scattered on the table onto which she sprinkled a scattering of tiny gold stars. A large polished silver candelabra with five deep red candles was the centre-piece and with crystal glasses at each place it was the picture of luxury. A delicate silver reindeer proudly held a white place card in its antlers with each of their names carefully scripted in gold.

Santa came while the children slept and Eva was woken by their enthusiastic yelps at seven in the morning. Hannah came up and got into bed beside her while Eva tried to set up her toy and figuring out how to charge it. There was no point in trying to get to sleep again so Eva went downstairs in her cream silk slip nightdress with matching dressing gown and soft slippers. She brewed a pot of fresh coffee and had it with a toasted bagel spread with cream cheese and topped with crispy bacon – David's speciality. He was still on a different time-zone and up before them all. The children were eating bars from selection boxes and Eva began to prepare the bread-stuffing for their dinner later. She chopped onions, fresh parsley and thyme and melted real butter to soak into the breadcrumbs. Making double the quantity that they would actually need, it was one of Eva's favourite foods and she knew that she would be eating it cold out of the fridge for days to come. She left the stuffing to cool down and went to open her own presents that were under the tree.

A tall strangely shaped present from her childminder Nora turned out to be a beautiful white luxury orchid plant set in a white ceramic pot. Daniel had bought her a cocktail set in chrome with an ice bucket, cocktail shaker and the requisite tools and Viv had given her a gift voucher for a day spa in town. There was an Italian risotto gift-set from Elaine who obviously knew how much she liked to cook and from Mary she had received a beautiful baroque

273

style gold photo frame. David had ordered an amazing hamper stuffed with gourmet goodies from Ardkeen Quality Food Store. But the ones that meant the most to her were the presents from her children and she knew they had taken ages to pick them out. Luke had selected a pedicure set and Hannah a new pair of fluffy slippers. Feeling rather special she put on the slippers and went to put the turkey in the oven before they all changed into their new Christmas clothes and headed off to church.

Christmas Day and St Stephen's Day seemed to merge into one another and Eva absolutely dreaded the thought of going back to work. There was no choice though and she had to be in early to get ready for the sales.

Once again Mary was helping her out and it was lovely for the kids to stay at home and in their pyjamas with their Grandmother looking after them for the day. Keeping the shop closed another day was not an option and like most things once she was there it wasn't quite as bad as the thought of it had seemed. She would have loved to spend some more time snuggled on the couch with the kids over the holidays but it wouldn't happen this year. The frenzy of the sale shoppers almost surpassed the panic buying of Christmas Eve. She had marked down all the Christmas related stock quite substantially but still with margin enough to clear a good profit with only a slight discount off the other stock. New Year's Eve was looming and people were still buying dinnerware for parties, champagne glasses for celebrations and decorations for the next year.

Nora was ready to look after the kids again for the few days that remained before Alan collected them on the morning of New-Year's Eve. They were going away with him to a hotel in Rosslare for a full week and had their bags packed and seemed to be looking forward to the adventure. Eva said goodbye to them with a lump in her throat and didn't like the thought of ringing in the New Year without them. Viv and Daniel's engagement party proved a huge distraction however and Eva saw in the New Year celebrating with them and their family and friends at their new apartment.

Eva felt a little awkward when Daniel drew her aside to introduce her to some guy at the party. Groaning inwardly at the thought of being so obviously set-up and having to make small talk with a complete stranger she smiled as politely as she could and launched into the usual small-talk. But as their discussion unfolded it turned out that it wasn't Eva's body but her style that this guy was interested in. In fact he had a business proposition for her. Eva couldn't believe her ears. He was so impressed with the penthouse that he wanted to contract her to do the interior for a new eighty bedroom hotel he was developing on the outskirts of the city. And it wasn't just the bedrooms, he wanted her input on everything from bedroom fittings to the lounge and bar, dining and foyer area. He particularly liked the original wall hangings and when she suggested that something could be commissioned on a larger scale if he wanted, it was music to his ears. He kept specifying how he wanted originality and quality first and foremost and that he had been very impressed with the stock in her store and how far she had travelled to source things. Eva couldn't help beaming from ear to ear and as she did the mental arithmetic she knew there was no going back now.

Leaving the party with Mr. Edward's business card and an appointment for a week's time Eva returned to her empty house just before midnight on New Year's Eve. She had embraced Viv and Daniel warmly before leaving and despite their protests to stay and ring in the New Year they understood when she just wanted to go. The previous New Year's celebrations had been with Alan celebrated quietly at home but this year she was on her own. David had returned to California and invited them over for summer holidays and maybe she would make that happen.

With a New Year just beginning there was plenty of life to be living and the hard graft of the past nine months was now paying off. She knew that the new proposal from Mr. Edward's would add another dimension to her business and it was going to go from strength to strength and that pretty soon she would be revising her business plan. Opportunities were there for the taking and she began to scribble into her bulging notebook as she sipped a glass or red wine. 'Time for the East,' she wrote and looking at it, it struck her as maybe a name for a new shop. Places like India and Turkey remained unexplored by her. There was so much that she still wanted to do. The 'online' catalogue would have to be widened and she also toyed with the idea of introducing a coffee dock for customers in the store.

With the lights flickering on her Christmas tree Eva closed her notebook, put on some Christmas carols and treated herself to a large Bailey's on ice. She hadn't noticed the missed calls on her phone which had been on silent and when she checked there was a message from the children wishing her a Happy New Year. There was another message too and she listened to Sébastien's husky tones wishing her a Happy New Year in French saying how sorry he was that he didn't get to talk to her.

Looking at Mr. Edward's business card on the coffee table and listening to Sébastien's voice as she replayed the message for a third time, Eva felt excitement wash over her and tingled inside like a giddy school girl as she took her drink of Bailey's with her and bounded upstairs to her laptop. Thirty minutes of googling later was all it took. '*Am I nuts or what?*' she asked herself. But it was done now and all that was left to do was some frantic packing.

Touching down in Stansted on an early morning flight Eva had two hours to kill before being called to board the flight to Carcassonne in France. Had Sébastien received her email and messages by now she wondered? It was only ten in the morning. What if he wasn't there? Maybe she should have waited to call him first and checked that it was okay. Should she call him now? 'Stop it.' she scolded herself trying to vanish any possibility of a negative outcome to her fitful expedition. There was no turning back now.

The magazine and newspaper that she had bought at Cork airport had remained in her bag until the flight to France. Flicking through the pages of the magazine she tried to take in the content. Turning instinctively to the interiors section she gasped. There looking back at her was her own picture at the launch of the store above a glowing review of the shop. How could she have forgotten? Fair play to PR Guy he had said he would get her in there and he had. The write up was glowing and quite detailed and she was delighted when they mentioned the exclusivity of some of her ranges. Eva felt that at last she was beginning to shine at something and it felt good.

Arriving into Carcassonne airport the luggage belt colourfully chugged along displaying an array of skis, ski boots and bags of all shapes and sizes. Finally Eva's own luggage arrived and she took a minute or two to pull up the handle until she emerged through the arrivals door wheeling it behind her. Her name stood out written in large letters on a white card held aloft by a suited gentleman. He was in fact a chauffeur and he informed her in perfect English that Monsieur Beauvais sent his apologies as he was unable to come himself because he had an engagement but his jet would return soon and he would meet her at the lodge.

Jet, Eva said to herself, *what was he talking about?* She happily followed him as he took her bags and guided her outside to where a black Mercedes was waiting. The drive took just over an hour as they drove further inland and arrived at the mountain village of Camurac white with snow.

The lodge as it turned out was no ordinary ski lodge and from the way the chauffeur spoke of Monsieur Beauvais, Eva's hitherto formed impression of Sébastien as working in some back office taking ski holiday bookings was turning out to be somewhat misguided. The chauffeur brought in her bags and handing over the key instructed her that she should make herself at home.

A huge bunch of red roses was the first thing that greeted her and was accompanied by a note in Sébastien's typically lavish romantic style.

'Ma cherie tu es enfin arrivé. I count the minutes to be with you. x Sébastien.'

Eva took off her faux fur coat and took three steps down to a seating area of sumptuously soft leather couches that just begged to be sprawled on. She helped herself to a piece of dark chocolate and let it melt in her mouth as she then explored the room. On the coffee table there was a large silver dish filled with bright green apples and even though she wasn't hungry Eva took one and bit into it. It was crunchy and juicy and almost bitter but it was delicious as it mingled with the taste of dark chocolate still in her mouth.

Looking out the windows she could see skiers weaving their way down the slopes. Sébastien's bedroom was carpeted in thick cream and the large bed was made up with a crisp white duvet scattered with crimson cushions. The bathroom was like something out of a five star hotel, all blacks and gold and it even had a Jacuzzi bathtub.

Returning to the kitchen she checked out the contents of his fridge and even though she was starving she didn't feel like she could eat much yet. Instead she made herself a Nespresso coffee and sat at the kitchen counter and tried to read her newspaper.

She couldn't concentrate so instead she flicked through some of Sébastien's magazines. She struggled to take any meaning from the French words and turned to what looked like a brochure for the ski resort. As she opened the front page of the brochure she attempted to read the introduction in French and then noticed that it was translated into English as well. The patron was pleased to extend a welcome to all guests at this state of the art skiing facility that offered accommodation either in the luxurious main hotel or in one of the thirty exclusive modern ski lodges. It went on to detail the number of slopes available and Eva read through it with vague interest until something caught her eye. The signature of the owner was at the bottom of the page and it was signed by Monsieur Sébastien Beauvais. Well if she hadn't felt out of her league before then she certainly did now. Her nerves were getting the better of her now and she tried to relax by turning on some music for a while. Would he still fancy her? Was she good enough for him? Was he ever going to arrive? She went to the bathroom and touched up her make-up and tried to calm herself. Figuring out a digital device and somehow managing to put on some music that then emanated from hidden speakers somewhere occupied a few more giddy minutes.

278

Removing her shoes she sat on a plush couch in the living room, sinking into it as she curled up in front of the crackling fire. Eva didn't have to wait long more until she heard a key turn in the door and Sébastien let himself in. He looked even taller than she remembered and she said nothing as she drew her breath and he walked slowly towards her. He wasn't smiling exactly but had this look, sombre and brooding at the same time, looking straight into her eyes. She breathed deep and rose to embrace him as he pulled her close burying his face in her neck and hair as he then began to gently kiss her. Inhaling his musky scent, feeling the light stubble on the face of this beautiful rugged man Eva knew she was exactly where she wanted to be and all doubts disappeared. Sinking together onto deep pile rugs in front of a roaring fire where they would later drink champagne straight from the bottle and toast to a New Year, who knew where it would lead and who cared?

For right now it was so much more than good enough, it was perfect.